KRISTINE SMITH

ENDGAME

An Imprint of HarperCollinsPublishers

This is a work of fiction. Names, characters, places, and incidents are drawn from the author's imagination or are used fictitiously and are not to be construed as real. Any resemblance to actual events, locales, organizations, or persons, living or dead, is entirely coincidental.

EOS
An Imprint of HarperCollins*Publishers*
10 East 53rd Street
New York, New York 10022-5299

Copyright © 2007 by Kristine Smith
ISBN: 978-0-06-050359-8
ISBN-10: 0-06-050359-9
www.eosbooks.com

First Eos paperback printing: November 2007

HarperCollins® and Eos® are registered trademarks of HarperCollins Publishers.

Printed in the U. S. A.

10 9 8 7 6 5 4 3 2 1

PRAISE FOR THE JANI KILIAN NOV
KRISTINE SMITH

"A fine new voice in the field of science fiction."
Nebula Award-winning author Catherine Asaro

"Perilously fascinating . . . impressive and entertaining."
Locus

"A taut, suspenseful, believable exploration of what
happens when alien and human passions collide,
seen through the lens of one of science fiction's most
remarkable protagonists."
Julie Czerneda, author of *Hidden in Sight*

"Smith balances . . . taut mystery with vivid characters and a complex, ever-evolving plot. . . . Sure to appeal to readers who appreciate well-drawn characters
and sophisticated milieus."
Publishers Weekly

"Remarkable . . . extraordinarily solid . . . complex
and deftly shaded . . . with vivid, memorable characters—a universe of power politics, commercial and
political espionage, and personal and interpersonal
relationships."
Elizabeth Moon

"Deep intrigue, richly diverse characters, and a plot
entangled enough to delight—Kristine Smith super-
cedes herself with each new book."
Janny Wurts

By **Kristine Smith**

For my Mom and Dad

Acknowledgments

The list of people who have helped me over the course of this book, and this series, began long and over the years has grown ever longer. In particular, many thanks are due Katharine Eliska Kimbriel, who started as a teacher and became a friend. Elizabeth Moon, who took me under her wing at my very first science fiction convention—Intersection '95 Glasgow (yes, I know—first con was a Worldcon—what was I thinking?)—and made me feel welcome. Joshua Bilmes, who believed in the series and sold it. First readers Dave Godwin and Dave Klecha, for their input and expertise. Berry Kercheval, Melanie Miller Fletcher, Julia Blackshear Kosatka, Tom Hise, and Doranna Durgin, and the rest of my online gang, for support online and in emails, for listening to my wails. Julie Czerneda, for reading the *Endgame* draft and for that one phone call that helped so much. Diana Gill, my editor since the beginning, for her patience, and because she always asked the deceptively simple question that turned the tale on its ear and helped make it better.

And finally, to Mom and Dad, who I know are watching.

ENDGAME

CHAPTER 1

The altar room in the Haárin transept of Elyas Station proved much more suitable than Imea nìaRauta Rilas had feared, warm and quiet as any in Rauta Shèràa. A place of clean, white stone, dark woods, and polished silver metal. A place of preparation, and acceptance of the will of the gods.

She had spent half the station-morning in prayer, as was proper for a godly bornsect. She had stood with her back straight, arms raised above her head, and intoned supplications to her favored goddess until the dry air rasped her throat and she grew light-headed from having stood so still for so long. Now, she lowered her arms in a smooth downward sweep, the cramps in her muscles and pain in her joints blending to form yet another prayer.

As her hands fell to her sides, Rilas felt the cuffs of her shirt tumble over her wrists. How she hated this shirt, its blue as blinding as that of an alarm illumin. How she hated her trousers, as purple as her shirt was blue. She thought of her usual clothing, her flowing trousers and overrobe in subtle shades of sand and stone. Her soft tan boots, so much more appropriate than the stiff black things she wore now. She imagined her hair as it should have been, arranged in the braided fringe of a breeder instead of as it was now, loose as a mane, its only binding a leather coil. *A horsetail.* Such was what the Haárin called the style, in imitation of the humanish. *Anathema.*

Rilas turned and walked to the narrow bench next to the entry, where she had set her slingbag. She hoisted it to her shoulder, felt its comforting heft bump her hip. So many things did it contain. And still a few more did she need to add. *Such I must do, and quickly.* Before it came time for her to board her shuttle to the city of Karistos.

Yet as much as she wished to depart, still she hesitated. She felt agitated, angered, as she had so often over the course of her journey from her blessed homeworld of Shèrá to this most ungodly of destinations. So much planning and preparation. *And now I am here.* At that point where planning and preparation transmuted into action and realization. Completion. Triumph.

And yet . . .

Rilas let the bag slide down her shoulder onto the top of the bench. She opened the flap and hunted, through the clothes and the tile samples and all those other objects of no importance. Once she reached the bottom support panel, she touched first one corner, then the one diagonally opposite. The panel separated from the bag frame with a soft *click.* She pushed it to one side and reached into the shielded compartment beneath, felt the tension leave her as soon as she put her hand on the shooter.

She lifted the weapon from its hiding place, confirmed its standby setting by pure reflex, then turned to a bare wall and sighted down. The case fit the curve of her hand, the weight filling an emptiness she had not realized she felt until now. Yet she knew she should not have felt surprise, for such was as it had always been. She possessed metal in her soul, nìRau Cèel had once told her, and as always he spoke truth.

Rilas bared her teeth. *Such is as I am.* Joy filled her as the air she breathed. Even her godless apparel no longer angered her. She always felt most as herself when she held a weapon in her hand.

She stood for some moments, arm extended, imagining targets past, targets yet to come. Then she lowered her arm, this time more slowly. Turned back to her slingbag and returned the shooter to its hiding place. Refastened the bag, raised it again to her shoulder, and departed.

The Elyas Station passenger concourse battered Rilas to the pit of her soul. Voices, humanish and Haárin, combined to a cacophony that pierced the brain. Corridors as long tunnels, walls colored red and blue and purple, lined with darkened rooms—the interiors of which she could not see, marked by signs she did not understand. Smells, ungodly and sickening, a mingling of hot foods and brewed drinks and bodies that had not entered a laving room for days. Tension, as those stenches enveloped her and those bodies passed close enough to touch.

She glanced at an idomeni timeform that hung from a purple-tinged wall, and her step slowed. Her shuttle had not yet arrived at its dock. Once more she had miscalculated, rushed when she did not need to do so. Once more she had time.

More time than I need. Her usual problem, and also, she knew, the cause of her anger. For that time needed to be spent somewhere, and as she traveled on public spacecraft, that meant she spent it in places such as these. Mongrel places, tainted by humanish, and by Haárin who had lost their Way. She watched them walk with one another, converse with one another, these misbegottens. Humanish, their hair braided in breeder's fringes whether they had bred or not, their clothes the flowing overrobes of the most strict bornsect. Haárin, hair clipped skull-close or left unbound, the females in wraps of cloth that clasped their forms or fluttered about them as though torn by winds, the females and males both in blinding patterns and colors avoided by even the most unruly outcast.

Yet I appear as one with them. Rilas pressed a hand to her stomach, and felt her soul rumble. *Elyas is a godless place,*

Cèel had warned her, *more so than any of the others you have visited. There, you will witness such as you never imagined possible.* She remembered the weariness in his posture as he spoke, the anger in his bowed shoulders and the turn of his head.

"Soon, nìRau," Rilas whispered to herself. "Soon it will be as it was." As the gods meant it to be, before all had been sundered and defiled. Before the ungodly had put it wrong. "I shall put it most right, and truly." She lowered her hand from her stomach and clenched it. "Soon."

She stood in place and uttered another prayer to her favored goddess, and felt herself calm. So often had she called upon Caith in her times of uncertainty, and just as often had Caith heard her pleas and brought her peace. *In your blessed chaos, goddess, allow me to find my Way.* She kept her head bowed as she prayed, and pretended to read the covers of an array of newssheets displayed in a shop window. In a godly place, she would stand most straight, as she had in the altar room. Then she would raise her hands above her head and plead to Caith in the keening voice of an abject suborn. *But such would call attention, and I am about on secret business.* Business such as that which she had performed on Amsun, and before that on Padishah and so many other humanish places. She bared her teeth for a moment only, savoring the pleasure of her task. *I perform as I must in the midst of my enemies, and it is their methods that I use.* From her names, to her clothes, to the information in the documents she carried, she was as a liar, and when she lied, she became as one with her goddess. *I am of Caith now.* She raised her head to stare at her blurred reflection in the glass, and the warmth of peace filled her. *I am as chaos—*

She sensed a shape out of the corner of her eye, a shadow she had not detected before. Her heart slowed, its beat strengthening. She turned, her hands raised to chest level. Made ready to strike, as she had so many times before—

—but saw no enemy, only a misshapen thing perched atop a pedestal, grey as old stone, tongue lolling and teeth bared. She stepped closer and examined a face as long as a beast's. Then she moved on to its clawed hands, reaching out and touching the cold, smooth surface.

"It's called a gargoyle."

Rilas turned to find a humanish standing at her shoulder. A male, dark-skinned as a Pathen. He wore his black hair clipped short, as was proper for his kind. But he dressed in a most outrageous Haárin style, his shirt and trousers assaulting the eye in clashing shades of green and orange. He looked her in the eye as he spoke, as was the humanish way. A most unseemly familiarity.

"They're the guardians of this place. They watch over the pilots, the mechanics." He edged closer to Rilas, until his shoulder grazed hers. "We've never had an accident with fatalities at this port. We're the only station in the Commonwealth that can make that claim."

Rilas took a full step back, as she had been taught. *You must be most direct and obvious when you repel humanish males*, one instructor had told her most long ago, *otherwise they do not understand.* Many found the long limbs and gold-toned skins of idomeni females attractive, and the efforts of some of them to convince the idomeni females of such had led to unseemly incidents. *I can allow no unseemly incidents now.* Thus would her trained hands remain at her sides, and her yen for the shedding of blood remain unsatisfied.

"I have never seen one of these gargoyles before." Rilas kept all inflection from her voice, and did not look the male in the face. His sort found idomeni eyes most attractive as well, a fact beyond understanding. *Cat eyes*, they called them. *Fool*, Rilas thought, *and blind besides*. She had studied many images of cats, and none of their eyes appeared as hers. Her pupils were as round, not slitted, her iris and sclera dark and pale gold, not a single color. Not as a cat's at all.

"You've never visited our famous station before?" The male bared his teeth. "The architect wanted to construct a Gothic cathedral in the outer reaches of the Commonwealth. There were plenty who said we should have stopped her, but scratch an Elyan and you'll find two things—a unique sense of humor, and bred-in-the-bone pissiness about being told what to do." He pointed toward the wall at the far end of the tunnel-like concourse. "We're particularly proud of our Rose Window."

Rilas looked to the immense circle of glass that filled the space, whorls of blue and yellow separated by translucent red. Blessed red. The holiest of colors. The privilege of priests, used to tint an artificial window that spread artificial light over this most blasted and soulless of places. "A godless thing, and truly," she said, turning away from the sight that even her love of chaos could not make as right.

The male tilted his head and tried to draw her gaze. "I admit this place isn't to everyone's taste." He waited, as though expecting Rilas to respond. When she did not do so, he backed away from her. "There is an area in the east corridor set aside for the more orthodox idomeni." He jerked his head downward, a rough humanish bow. "My apologies for bothering you."

Rilas watched him go, remaining still until his garish form disappeared among the crowd and she felt sure that he would not return. Only then did she walk across the concourse and enter the locker area where Haárin passengers stored their belongings between flights. She encountered several as she made her way down the narrow corridor, and noted that she appeared most as they did. She looked as her name now, ná Nahin Sela, the oddity with which nìRau Cèel had christened her before she left behind the warmth of her native Rauta Shèràa and departed her blessed homeworld of Shèrá. Her dominant had never before chosen the name under which she would perform her assigned tasks, but in this instance they had both felt it appropriate. Most seemly, and truly.

"Nahin." She walked the narrow aisles separating the rows of lockers, repeating her name as some did their gate numbers and departure times. When she came to her locker, she acted the tired traveler in case she encountered any other

Haárin, fumbling with the touchlock and struggling to remove the bags as she had seen others do. This was not difficult, as the handle of one bag was not long enough to loop over her shoulder and the other felt as though it had been filled with bricks.

Fools! When next she spoke with those who had rented this locker and left the bags for her, she would berate them. Her travel documents listed her vocation as "tile broker." Did those who assembled that which she needed think she meant to carry tiles on her person! She hefted her clumsy burden of purchases and baggage and hunted for a laving room.

By the time she found an empty laving cubicle, the first call for her shuttle sounded throughout the locker area. She opened the cubicle door with a vend token and edged inside, the weighty bags banging against her shins. She hefted them atop the narrow counter, then began her preparations.

First, she removed cleansing materials and washed her face and hands, tucking strands of hair behind her ears and studying herself in the small mirror. *Most as humanish, and truly.* She wrote a symbol in the air as a gesture against demons, then resumed her search through the smaller of her bags, rooting past shoes and a tightly folded weatherall until she came to the thing she sought.

The small case looked as something that would hold earrings or hair ornaments. Indeed, when she opened it, such was what she found. She fingered past the fine gold loops and tangles of braided cord and beads until she found that for which she searched. A ring, alternating bands of gold and silver set with a scattering of small stones.

Using her thumbnail, Rilas worked one of the stones loose from its setting. The colorless disc appeared smooth and featureless to her eye. She held it to the cubicle light and tilted it back and forth, in search of any scratch or crack. Satisfied that none existed, she held the disc under the faucet and rinsed it under a stream of warm water, working it between her fingers as she did. Just as it flexed and began to soften, she positioned it on the tip of her index finger and bent low over the sink, using the thumb and index finger of her free hand to hold open her right eye.

She flinched as the warmed plastic touched the surface of her eye. The disc adhered and spread, squeezing her cornea—tears dripped into the sink as she fought the urge to sneeze, forced herself still, and quiet. She had performed the same action on Amsun, on Padishah, and numerous other places, yet every time, it felt as a surprise. She blinked once, slowly, and felt the lens settle into place. Blinked again. Then she raised her head and looked into the mirror.

Her right eye looked much as it always did. Shinier due to the tears, but not injured. She leaned toward the mirror and looked more closely, until she was satisfied that the edges of the lens were as invisible. She waited until it absorbed its weight in water and the squeezing feeling subsided, then picked up the small case once more and resumed her exploration.

The second thing for which she searched, she found stuck to the end of a hair clasp. She pried this clear disc from its setting as she had the lens, then warmed it under running water, massaging it until it, too, softened. Then she held it to the opening of her right ear, shivering as she felt it adhere and spread. "Fourteen," she whispered, knowing from experience that the sensor that had attached itself within her ear canal would replay her voice as though she spoke aloud. "Fourteen times have I performed these acts as my dominant has bidden me." She would speak her thoughts aloud from now on, and use exact numbers, dates, hours. The time had come to be precise in all things.

"I am Imea nìaRauta Rilas, and this is my book." She spoke to the mirror, and imagined the lens recording her reflection, her expression, as she knew it did. "I speak from laving cubicle number ten, locker area seven-oh-four, level fourteen, east transept, Elyas Station." She paused, then uttered the date, the time. "My purpose in coming here is to kill ní Tsecha Egri, at the bidding of my most godly dominant, Morden nìRau Cèel."

Rilas tensed as the second call for her shuttle echoed. Outside her cubicle door, up and down the aisle, voices rose. Doors clicked open. Footsteps sounded. She closed the jewelry case, returned it to the small bag, and resumed her search. *If I miss this shuttle, I will forfeit my billet.* Purchasing another would be simple enough, but it would be best, she decided, if she left this mongrel place as quickly as she could. Too many dangers awaited out in the concourse. Too many friendly humanish males. Too many chances to be remembered.

She paused, and willed herself calm. There was still one more thing she needed to find, and if she could not do so, there would be no point in continuing. She set aside the small bag and opened the larger one. The things she had thought felt like bricks proved to be embossed metal cases of the type that opened to form displays. "Displays for ná Nahin, a broker in tile." She opened one case, then another, feeling her calm ebb as the seconds passed and she flipped open cases then slammed them shut as prayers turned to curses and her temper rose—

She found it in the last case, on the bottom of the bag, as was usual. A flat container the size of her hand, greyed blue in color and cold to the touch. She scraped a fingernail over the surface and watched as a thin layer of frost curled, then evaporated. She held the container gingerly, using her fingertips only, so as not to warm it too much, and opened the lid.

The cold that emerged caused condensate to form in the air above—Rilas waved it away with one hand to prevent the moisture from settling on the most special objects within. Her prizes, so carefully designed and produced.

The projectiles filled both sides of the container, arranged lengthwise and nestled in molded depressions in the inner liner. Three on each side for a total of six—two less than she had wanted, but those who made them had told her that she was lucky to get as many as this. *So they said. So they claimed.* She never knew when to believe scientists. They shied away from her, and avoided telling her all they knew unless ordered by nìRau Cèel. *And even then . . .* She wondered about them, even as she knew that they had no choice but to aid her.

She lifted one of the projectiles from its niche and held it up as she had the lens. Muted silver—as long as her small finger, tapered at one end and flattened on the other—the small missile caught the cubicle light and split it as a prism would, sending a shard of rainbow shimmering across the ceiling. Rilas tilted it one way, then the other, looking for seaming or an opening, an inner darkness or shape that revealed that which it contained. Then she returned it to its place and closed the case. Tucked the case back in the bag and closed that as well. Tossed shop wrappings in the trash bin and gathered her baggage. She had all she needed now. It was well and truly time to leave.

The rasp of her boot soles against the bare floor filled the cubicle area. She met no one until she made her way through the narrow, winding aisles and reentered the concourse. The racket of voices battered her for an instant only, receding to nothing as the calm overtook her. Such was a familiar sensation, one she esteemed as she did her dominant and her goddess. She and her task had become one, and would remain as such until she discharged it.

As Rilas approached her gate, she passed a news kiosk. It was a humanish-looking thing, rounded as a hive, covered from floor to top with signs advertising concourse shops and with bright images from the covers of magazines. She quickened her step as she approached the garish thing—such subject matter held no interest for her.

Then one image among the many caught her eye. Her step slowed, then stopped. She approached the kiosk and with a cautious hand removed the latest copy of an Elyan publication from its rack.

The face that stared back at her, she had seen too many times before. In reports from her dominant, compiled by his spies who labored throughout the humanish Commonwealth. In holoVee displays, when important events of the past months replayed. In her mind's eye, as she considered her task and all that might prevent its completion. The face, brown-gold as some Pathen. The eyes, green as Sìah. The hair, black and clipped as short as that of the most ungodly Haárin.

Kilian. The name choked Rilas. Jani Kilian. The Kièrshia. The Toxin. The bringer of pain and change. Rilas felt her calm depart as she thought of her, living a damned life in a damned place on the world around which Elyas Station orbited. Once, Kilian had worn the uniform of her soldierly Service and committed crimes that it pained any godly idomeni to recall. Now, twenty humanish years later, she served as a priest at the bidding of godless Tsecha, a mockery of all in which any godly idomeni believed. Ruled over a mongrel enclave that had no right to exist, a place of infamy and broken faith, of false teachers and the lies they spread to promote their own power.

"Toxin." Rilas touched a finger to the middle of Jani Kilian's forehead and traced a small circle once, then again. As the final call for her shuttle sounded, she paid for the magazine with a vend token. Then she rolled it so as to hide Kilian's face and hurried to her gate.

CHAPTER 2

... for these reasons, the wholeness of a soul is not
dependent upon the health or condition of the physical
body in which it resides, and those who espouse such
are ignorant of the will of the gods. Therefore, to allow
the death of a body for the stated purpose of preserving
the integrity of its soul is as sacrilege, and those who
defend and perform such acts are as anathema ...

Jani Kilian read the passage once, then again. Then she
closed the leather-bound scroll and backed away from the
pedestal on which it rested for the first few steps, reluctant to
turn around. *It won't bite.* Well, not yet anyway. "When will
you publish it?"

Ní Tsecha Egri stood in front of the workroom's narrow
window and looked out over the Bay of Siros. His orange
shirt rivaled the rising Elyan sun in brilliance, his bright blue
trousers sedate by comparison. He wore his hair in the idomeni equivalent of a Service burr, and the blaze of backlight
through the glass rendered the short, pale brown strands
nearly invisible, accentuating the outline of his skull.

He cracked open the pane seals, allowing the smells of
sea and sun into the workroom. "I already have, nìa." He
didn't look at her as he spoke. "Ná Meva sent the transmission to Rauta Shèràa Temple yesterday evening."

Ná Meva. Jani imagined the elder female bearing down
on the enclave com room, the wafer containing Tsecha's
treatise gripped like a ward against demons, grey-streaked

horsetail flicking with each stride. *Yet another exiled propitiator.* At the Elyan enclave only a few weeks, and already Tsecha's invaluable sounding board in matters of theology. *They're two peas in a pod.* Meva as eager to disseminate her dominant's seditious essays as he was to write them.

Unlike some of us. Jani slumped against the wall and tugged at the front of her grey wrapshirt, a near perfect match for her grey trousers. She never felt comfortable in the clashing bright colors that most Haárin and Thalassans wore, preferring to stay with drab and somber despite the ribbing she occasionally took. "If you already sent it, why pretend to ask my advice?"

"I do not *pretend*, nìa." Tsecha's shoulders rounded in anger. "I esteem your advice." He straightened slowly. "I did consider my arguments with care. I spent much time reevaluating bornsect histories. I could find no flaw. I then gave a draft to ná Meva, and she could find nothing to dispute."

"You showed it to her before you sent it." Jani heard her own voice, soft and steady, and wondered at her calm. "But not to your religious suborn. Not to the one you're training to take your place. Not to me."

Tsecha stilled, his hesitation obvious. Weighing his words—another humanish habit he had adopted. "You have learned much these past months, but not enough to contribute to this level of discourse." He looked across the room at Jani, the backlight casting his face in shadow, obscuring his expression. "Not yet. In time, yes, I will discuss these matters with you in the same depth as I do with Meva, but until that time . . . " His voice had grown quieter, the usual booming baritone thinned and drained. "I must be sure of the logic of my arguments. Rauta Shèràa Temple will take any error and use it to render the entire treatise as nothing, and I cannot allow that to occur."

Jani pushed away from the wall and paced the workroom. It was the largest and most well-appointed space in the small house, which was located in the heart of the Thalassan enclave. Tsecha had claimed it as his own despite the objections of ná Feyó Tal, the dominant of the Elyan Haárin and his nominal superior, who felt he should reside within her enclave. But bowing to authority had never been one of Tsecha's traits. *Neither is listening, come to that.* "You've called the entire concept of Wholeness of Soul into question. One of the cornerstones of Vynshàrau faith."

"Most other bornsects believe in the concept as well, to their great detriment." Tsecha once more turned his face to the window. "It is an argument that needs to be made."

But do you have to make it now? Jani kept her comment to herself. She'd never held back her own actions for the sake of anyone, family or lover or friend. Maybe this was just life's way of paying back with interest. "The new meeting room's not ready. Dathim told me he'll have to work through the night."

"You change the subject, nìa. Have I angered you that much?" Tsecha shut the pane, then turned and walked to his worktable, a V-shaped stone slab that took up almost a quarter of the room. "So he will work. So he will complain. And still the room will be completed on schedule, and the visit will take place tomorrow, as is planned." He fussed with a stack of wafer folders. "It is a social visit, nìa. So Governor Markos has told us. A courtesy call. I do not know why you worry so."

Jani stopped in front of the table and studied her old teacher. Read their shared history in his stark, high-boned face, the mutiny, and the subterfuge, and the lies. "Governor Stanislaw Markos of the Commonwealth colony of Elyas is coming here to ask you to act as go-between for him with Wuntoi and the other anti-Cèel bornsect dominants. He's bringing with him the governors of Amsun and Hortensia."

Tsecha rolled his eyes, but the gold on gold shading of his sclera and irises blunted his attempted display of humanish irritation. "I know all this, nìa. I do not know why you are telling—"

"Secession. Elyas wants to secede from the Commonwealth, and Amsun and Hortensia and the rest of the Outer

Circle want to go with her. They believe Cèel is on the way out, and the Vynshàrau with him, and they want to make nice with Wuntoi and his Pathen because they're the likeliest successors. That's why they need you. They know they'll need the support of the Outer Circle Haárin to have any hope of pulling this off, and the Haárin support Wuntoi as the next Oligarch." Jani planted her hands atop the table, spread her fingers, pondered her gold-brown skin. "This could blow up fast. You should be keeping your head down now, for the sake of Markos and the others, if not for your own, and instead you're attracting attention—"

"The danger is the governors', nìa. They are the ones who wish to secede." Tsecha leaned against the table, his voice deceptively light. "If their attempt fails, it does not affect the Elyan Haárin."

Jani fought the urge to grab Tsecha by the shoulders and shake him. "Thalassa, in case you've forgotten, is in a different situation than the Haárin enclave. You'll dodge the spray when it hits the fan. You'll be able to leave. You'll have a place to go. But what the hell do you think will happen to Thalassa? We're hybrids, in a diplomatic no-man's-land—" She stopped when she heard her voice ring in her ears and saw Tsecha's shoulders start to curve. "You could have waited," she said after her heart slowed and her hands unclenched. "Your treatises. You could have published them some other time."

"They are necessary now, nìa." Tsecha averted his gaze as he spoke, something he seldom did when they stood so close together. "To alter thinking. To persuade, and enrage."

"I think you have the 'enrage' part covered." Jani turned and walked to the other side of the room. "I'm not too sure about 'alter' and 'persuade.'" She stopped in front of a display niche and plucked a small stone ovoid from its base. "It's hard to get anyone to listen once tempers overheat," she said as she hefted the stone. "I should know."

"I must speak. I must protest—"

"But why now?"

"You do not—"

"I don't mean to interrupt."

Jani and Tsecha both fell silent and looked toward the entryway.

"Ní Tsecha. Jan." Colonel Niall Pierce doffed his brimmed white lid and stepped just inside the room. "Just came from the new meeting house. Checking on preparations for tomorrow." He wore semiformal kit of dress desertweights, the white tunic and gold-trimmed headgear startling against his tan trousers and sun-baked face. "Dodging flying tile shards." He grinned, the scar that cut his face from his nose to the corner of his mouth twisting the expression into something sinister. "Ní Dathim Naré is not happy."

"Dathim is never happy." Tsecha gestured impatience, the edge of his hand cutting through the air like a blade. "Always he complains of schedules, of lack of supplies, of . . . "

Jani watched Niall, who seemed transfixed by Tsecha's rant. *He knows we're meeting the governors, but he can't figure out why.* She had tried to keep him from getting involved in the security arrangements for the get-together, but he was Admiral General Hiroshi Mako's man on the spot, and the presence of three high-level colonial officials dictated his participation. *He'll escort them here and wait outside while we talk to them. He won't be able to find out a thing.* She hoped. She prayed.

" . . . and still, he is not satisfied!" Tsecha stepped around the table and strode to the door. "I will go and speak with him." He brushed past Niall, barreling through the foyer and into the street. "Ridiculous, and truly . . . "

Jani stepped outside in time to see the brightly garbed figure vanish down an alley between two houses. Sensed Niall draw alongside, and felt his stare etch the side of her face. "Go ahead and say it."

"I never thought I'd see Tsecha grasping for an excuse to get the hell away from you." Niall set his lid back atop his head, then squared it by running the thumbs and forefingers of both hands back and forth along the brim. "I debated whether to go in. Then your voices began carrying and folks stuck their heads out to listen. Decided I had better throw myself on the grenade before they started selling tickets."

Jani glanced toward a nearby house in time to see a head duck back inside a doorway. "We weren't that loud."

"The sound-shielding doesn't exist that can filter out ní Tsecha Egri once he boils over." Niall stared up at a seabird that swooped overhead. "Anything you can talk about?"

Jani gauged the man out of the corner of her eye. With his skin, uniform, and bronze Service burr, he appeared as grave as she, a study in brown and white. He stood a little shorter than she did, his frame lean and muscled, his narrow, wolfish face hardened further by the cheek-cleaving scar. Only his eyes, honey brown and long-lashed, offered a sense of his humor, his well-schooled intellect, his warmth.

His nosiness. Jani pretended interest in the blooms that filled a streetside planter. "What's the word?"

Niall studied her for a moment, then shrugged. "Avelos and the Amsun gang just arrived and are currently ensconced in Markos's villa. Wallach and the Hortensian contingent won't arrive until dawn. Cutting it close, in my opinion, but they didn't ask my advice regarding travel arrangements." He drew closer and lowered his voice as a trio of Thalassans emerged from a house across the way. "Jan? We may be on different sides of the fence, but I can still listen to whatever you can afford to tell me."

It's your skill at filling in blanks that worries me, Colonel. Jani watched as more Thalassans wandered into the street. "Do you want to take a walk?"

Niall exhaled with a grumble. "You want to walk, we'll walk."

They set off along the narrow lane, past the low, white houses with their arched doorways and passages and domed roofs in shades of blue and yellow. While a few Thalassans had brought plants from their home colonies to display in window boxes and planters, native flora dominated the landscaping. Instead of hybrid lawn, creepers in blue and red-dappled green carpeted the spaces between houses, their low tangle broken up with clusters of the same brilliantly flowered shrubs that dotted the hillsides. Like Karistos, Thalassa hugged the cliff line, and the creepers had been trained to stream over the edge, fringing the rock face with variegated ropes of leaves. Views of the Bay of Siros filled the eye from three directions, and the buildings closest to the brink had been trimmed with terraces so Thalassans could enjoy them whenever they wished.

"I still can't get used to this scenery. Been here six months Common and it still takes my breath away." Niall leaned against a guardrail and pulled his nicstick case from his trouser pocket. "So." He removed a silvery cylinder and crunched the ignition tip, then stuck the filter end in his mouth and took a pull. "You two having another difference of opinion?"

Now it was Jani's turn to shrug. "It happens."

"More and more, seems like. What was it this time?"

Jani rolled up her shirtsleeves and held out her arms so the sun could warm them. "I thought that Thalassa would take the place of Rauta Shèràa for him, that he'd come to consider it home. Now I think it reminds him of what he lost. He spent his entire adult life up to his chin in worldskein politics. He was one of the most influential idomeni who ever lived."

"He still is, gel." Niall tugged at his tunic's banded collar, then wiped a few beads of sweat from his brow. Even with cooling cell-equipped clothing, Elyan heat battered non-native humanish with ovenlike intensity. "Just because Cèel stripped him of a title and made him Haárin? Doesn't mean a damned thing to anyone I talk to. Call him by his bornsect name, Avrèl nìRau Nema. Or call him Egri nìRau Tsecha or ní Tsecha Egri or a sack of laundry. He's still a power to be reckoned with." He stepped back from the rail until the shade of one of the Karistos region's weird palm trees fell across him. "Cèel thought that if he made him Haárin, he'd neuter him. All it did was give him the freedom to rebuild his power base, surround himself with like minds." He took a last drag on his 'stick, then flicked the spent cylinder into a trash bin.

"He never needed moral support, or an audience." Jani pushed down her sleeves and refastened the cuffs. "He believes that which he believes. Fine. It's not just duty that compels him to speak out, it's something more. It's in his blood and bone, the air he breathes. He could no more keep quiet about what he feels is wrong with Vynshàrau religious doctrine than I could flap my arms and fly across the bay."

She paced along the rail. "But what he doesn't realize, or *want* to realize, is that every time he shoots off his mouth, I'm the one who gets hit with the flak. Questions about where *I* stand. Rumors that Thalassa is a training ground for anti-Commonwealth extremists. And when I try to tell him that Thalassa doesn't have a diplomatic leg to stand on, that Chicago is afraid of us and *his* radicalism is assumed to be *our* radicalism, he tells me that I do not know of that which I speak." She stopped and glared out at the sun-seared water until her eyes teared from the brightness. "So on he flames. I put out one fire, and a week or two later another pops up to take its place." She turned to Niall to find him leaning on the rail and watching her, his head cocked. "What?" She caught the bare twitch of his lip, and felt her face heat. "Shut up."

"I'm not saying a word." Niall straightened, then pulled a linen square from his trouser pocket. "And I'm not taking one iota of cold pleasure in this at all, even though any sort of chill would feel like heaven at the moment." He ran the cloth over his face, then folded it into a tight square and tucked it up his sleeve. "'How does it feel?' will never cross my—"

"Niall."

Niall raised his hands in mock surrender. Let them fall, and walked toward the stand of weird palms. "You and I . . ." He lowered onto a rickety chair someone had left beneath. Braced his hands on his knees and looked out at nothing. "We had to build walls around parts of our lives. It's not always easy. I know you well enough to pick up when you're holding back, and I'd guess you could say the same about me. It's difficult, dealing with the conflicts and the suspicion. But when you've a friend . . . " He switched his gaze to the flagstone at his feet. "It's worth it." He sat still and silent for a time, then shook his head as though awakening from a daze. "Tsecha's a strategist, a thinker. You're more a tactician, a field man. I always thought you complimented one another well."

"That depends on whether we're fighting the same battle, doesn't it?" Jani kicked at a loose flake of flagstone, sending it skittering across the terrace. "If we start to fight one another, who do you think has the advantage?"

Niall sat back and folded his arms. "The strategist. They would take the long view, have backup plans in place. But sometimes they get wrapped up in theory and miss details . . . " Again, a shake of the head. Harder, this time. "Tsecha would sooner die than fall out with you. I think it would break his heart." His eyes widened. "*Christ, Jan.*" A scrabble for another nicstick. The sharp *crunch*, followed by the cloud of smoke. "Growing pains. This place has exploded since you arrived here a year ago, and you're still shaking things out. He's adjusting to life in the enclave. You're adjusting to duties as a priest-in-training and the dominance of Thalassa. Stands to reason you'd fight. If you didn't, I'd ask John to check your vitals."

Jani looked toward the settlement, the newest homes that stood on what a month ago had been open land. "There are those here who have no place else to go. Their families disowned them when they hybridized, and their governments don't trust them because they don't know whose side they're on. If Chicago decides that there's some sort of militant hotbed developing here, what action do you think they'll take? Hell, Niall, you get the memos. You have the list of who to pick up first." *And I bet I know whose name is at the top.*

Niall looked everywhere but at her. "I take from this that we have another theological essay to look forward to." He glanced at her sidelong, then turned his attention to his nic-stick, working his thumbnail between the filter and the body and prying them apart. "I've read the previous offerings, in translation, of course. He does tend toward the carpet bomb approach when it comes to stating his case."

"He's idomeni. Carpet bombing is standard operating procedure." Jani tapped a beat atop the rail. "He will make his point, regardless of the cost to himself. Or anyone else."

"And you won't?" Niall stared at the dismembered 'stick as though he'd never seen it before, then tossed it into the trash bin. "Parts of Chicago still bear the scorch marks, Jan. You're as radical as he is."

"Would you believe I'm learning circumspection?"

"Not without witnesses."

Jani grinned, but the expression soon faded. "We're here on sufferance, we Thalassans. Beggars, being allowed a place to squat because we're quiet and don't bother any-one." She motioned to Niall, then started walking across the terrace back to the house-lined street. "That can change so quickly, and then what?"

"You're worried that Stash Markos will kick you off Elyas. *You?*" Niall rose and fell in beside her. "He never struck me as the type to harbor a death wish. You're talking nonsense, gel." He glanced overhead and sighed. "I blame this damned sun." He fell silent, fixed on the uphill climb. Then he drew a deep breath. "So, I expect that Markos and the others are coming here to consult with Tsecha about that bombing at the Haárin docks on Amsun."

Not up to your usual standard, Colonel. Jani struggled to keep her face blank. *You're usually so much more subtle when you pry.* "Yes. They want to make sure the word gets out that they support the Amsun Haárin, and that they'll not rest until they apprehend the parties responsible." And there was her reply, just as stilted. But as good a tale as any, and even more so for being partly true.

Niall studied her, the brim of his lid shading his eyes, hiding them from her gaze. Then he gripped her elbow and pulled her to a stop. "Whatever happens, whatever—" He looked up the street, now filled with hybrids working, talking, and lowered his voice to a rough whisper. "You'll get some warning. I know people. I'll get you out."

"What about John and the others?" Jani nodded toward the bustle. "I wouldn't leave without them." She watched Niall look up the street again. Saw his shoulders sag, and knew his thoughts as though he spoke them aloud. *It's a town now, Niall, with schools and shops, a Net station and a shuttleport. How do you evacuate it without anyone knowing?* She resumed walking, then paused until Niall caught her up. "Mako still give you a hard time about hanging around with me?"

Niall shook his head. "Not as much as he used to."

Meaning he's happy to have a spy in the midst of this brew. Jani pressed a hand to the back of her neck and tried to massage away the growing tightness. "Did you want to check out the meeting house again? Maybe the shards have stopped fly—"

The siren cut the air like a scream, stopping everyone in mid-word, mid-stride. Blessed silence fell for an instant, then another howl. A youngster cried for her home-parent. A few hybrids headed for doorways.

"Shuttle's coming!" a male shouted as he started trotting up the street. "That's the new signal."

Jani looked at Niall, to find that he had pulled his shooter, his knuckles blanched against tanned skin.

"*Jesus.* Maybe you could tell your crew to lower the pitch a little." He powered down the weapon and holstered it. "Damned thing sounds like a shatterbox just before it hits. Bloody banshee wail—"

"I'll tell them." Jani pulled in a deep breath in a futile bid to slow her fluttering heart. "Looks like we have a visitor." She started to walk, one slow step after another. *Breathe. Breathe.*

"Wallach? His crew is scheduled to touch down at Karistos. That's where my team is." Niall quickened his pace and brushed past her, funneling his panic into motion and anger. "Flying fuck governors with their flying fuck timelines and their flying fuck—" He touched his ear, activating the com-link to whichever subordinate was unlucky enough to be first in the queue. "Beck! What the hell—"

Jani held back until Niall had moved well out of earshot. Inhaled, and felt her heart trip, then slow. Continued to walk up the road, lined with low white houses . . . felt the sun . . . the heat . . .

. . . the slip of sand beneath her boots . . . a sensation of sliding. . .

. . . the hum of a shooter, the pound of her heart . . .

. . . the line of tents.

She closed her eyes. *Please, Lord. Not now,* she prayed. *Not now.*

CHAPTER 3

By the time Jani reached the landing field, the rest of the enclave had already gathered along the runway. She scanned the crowd and spotted a cluster of medcoat-clad Thalassans crowded around a tall, slim figure, like children around a parent.

John Shroud surveyed the scene like a landowner regarding his domain. He smiled when he spotted Jani, and freed himself from the confines of his laboratory tribe. As always, he wore formal clothes beneath his medcoat, a daysuit in palest grey undertoned with blue. His wheat-blond hair had been freshly clipped into a Caesar fringe, which framed and accentuated his monkish visage.

Hello, Doctor. Jani held out her hand, felt her disquiet ease as John's long, strong fingers encircled her own.

"I just spoke with Niall. He's trying to find out who it is." John put his arm around her shoulders and pulled her close. "Governor Wallach's shuttle just touched down at Karistos, so that's off the list. No one's requested permission to make an emergency landing." He looked toward the runway and shrugged. "It's a mystery." He rested his chin atop her head. "Niall seemed a little shaken."

"It was the new approach alarm. It took us both by surprise." Jani backed away so she could look John in the face. "Maybe they could ramp it down just a little bit."

"You're the boss. Tell them. It will be done." John shrugged lightly, a problem easily solved. Then he looked at her, and his gaze altered from affection to professional assessment. "Are you all right?" He moved back so he could see her face more easily. "Niall's not the only one who looks like he's seen a ghost."

"I'm fine." Jani pressed her face against his medcoat, in part so she could take in his scent, but mostly to keep him from questioning her anymore. "There's too much going on is all."

"That's news." John gave her shoulders a squeeze. "I wish Niall would get a move on. Some of us have work to do."

"I see it!" someone shouted. "They're coming in over the bay!"

Conversation ceased. Everyone turned toward the water just as a black dot broke through the clouds. It grew rapidly, wings becoming visible, sunlight flashing off the metallo-ceramic skin.

Jani raised her head and squinted at the approaching shuttle. The underside looked dark, as though the craft had made a bad landing and scraped the hell out of the thermal coating. Then the mess of lines and shading resolved into an all too familiar pattern, two snakes twining around a winged staff. Her stomach tightened. "John? Is that what I think it is?"

"It's a caduceus." John's voice emerged a puzzled rumble. "What the . . . ?"

"It's a Neoclona shuttle, Doctor." Niall shouldered through the crowd to join them. "Expecting any visitors?"

"No." John released Jani and moved closer to the runway's edge as the shuttle passed overhead, then banked for the last time and settled into its final approach, wings flexing and reshaping to compensate for the crosswinds. Then it touched down, dust billowing behind it like a windblown veil, its engines cut back to near silence.

Jani moved in beside John. Took his hand in hers, and felt the barest hint of sweat on his palm.

The shuttle slowed until it drew even with them. As soon as it stopped, the door to the passenger cabin swept upward while the exit stairway emerged and unfolded to the ground.

Valentin Parini stepped up to the threshold before the stairway extended completely. He wore a daysuit in somber greyed green, the severe lines disturbed by the briefbag that hung from one shoulder.

John shook loose Jani's hand, then straightened the already flawless lines of his medcoat.

"I thought he was never supposed to embark on a long haul unless he told you?" Jani watched Val as he let his foot dangle over the first step, waiting for the stairway to stabilize.

"He's not." John's voice sounded like the rumble from the depths of a cave. "It was an agreement he, Eamon, and I made at the beginning, that we would each know where the others were at all times."

"Eamon broke that rule." Jani waited for an answer, and looked over at John to find him watching Val with narrowed eyes.

"Val and I never did." He fell silent, his face a professional mask.

Val collected himself as he started down the stair, disdaining the handholds that ran along both sides. As soon as he hit the ground, he hit his stride, a saunter that had over the years made fists itch and teeth grind from one end of the Commonwealth to the other.

John waited until Val had crossed the invisible halfway point before walking out to meet him. His step was weightier, but just as fluid, with the deceptive quickness of molten metal flow.

Then came the hitch in Val's step, the slowdown as he drew nearer to John. When no more than a couple of meters separated them, he stopped, the shock that filled his eyes at war with the unperturbed attitude he struggled to convey. He shifted his weight from one foot to the other, glancing at Jani without seeing her before returning to John.

It's the first time he's seen John in person since he hybridized. Jani looked at her lover and tried to see him as his best friend did, comparing the albino presence that Val had known so well with the pale blond, gold-skinned figure that stood before him now. *And let's not forget the eyes.* The same silvered blue as John's daysuit, as glittery as jewels when he smiled.

Val fought to appear detached, but his face kept betraying him, dismay and shock and affection jockeying for the lead, with professional curiosity bringing up the rear. His jaw slackened as his eyes widened, the only sound emerging from his mouth a strangled, "I—"

John smiled, stopping just short of a full-blown idomeni teeth-baring. "It really is me, Val."

"Your voice hasn't changed. It still"—Val gestured at waist height—"sounds like it's coming up through the ground." His pronounced widow's peak and arched brows giving his high-boned face a catlike cast. "The Mistys you sent didn't do the transformation justice. My God." He held out his hand. John took it, and they shook. Then the grins broke through and John pulled Val close.

"Any idea what he's doing here?" Niall muttered.

"None." Jani watched man and male hug, Val thumping John's shoulder while John mumbled something that made them both laugh. "I'd like to believe that it's purely a social call, but somehow I doubt it."

Val broke away, wiping his eyes with his sleeve. Then he turned to Jani. "You, my pensive beauty. My one and only girl." He moved in and embraced her, wrapping her in an odd combination of herbal cologne and the ozone sharpness of freshly cleaned cloth. After a moment, he released her and stepped back, lips twitching as though he wanted to say something else but couldn't find the words. His eyes were bloodshot, their deep hazel dulled by spent nerve. He raked a hand through his ash-brown hair, disturbing its structured style and looking even more as though he'd just awakened from restless sleep.

Jani struggled with her own conflicting emotions, relishing the sight of her old friend while at the same time wondering why he'd come. "You look tired."

Val shrugged. "Long hauls always wear me down. If the cabin fever doesn't get you, the monotony will." He started to say more, then stopped and hung his head. "There's something else—something I—oh, *hell*." He turned back to the shuttle, one hand pressed to his forehead as though a headache had come to call.

Jani followed his pained gaze, and saw that the passenger cabin door still gaped open, as though someone else still needed to disembark. Then the name formed in her mind just as the all-too-familiar figure stepped into the doorway, white-blond Service burr shining in the sun.

"What in bloody hell . . . ?" Niall's hand went to his sidearm.

Captain Lucien Pascal paused at the top of the stair, looking first toward the bay and the cliffs beyond, then scanning the crowd. He wore desertweights, the sand-toned short-sleeve shirt highlighting his pale hair and tanned skin. As soon as he spotted Jani, he pulled his garrison cap out of his waistband and set it atop his head, then started down the stairs at an easy lope.

"Val?" John's voice was tight, his relaxed air vanished.

"I can explain." Val licked his lips. "It's a *long* story, though."

"I have all the time you need." John drew closer when he realized they stood surrounded by perked ears and curious glances. "*Dammit.* Of all the people you could have carted here—"

"Pascal." Niall stepped in front of Jani just as Lucien drew near, blocking him as well as any wall.

"Colonel Pierce, *sir*." Lucien came to attention and snapped a salute, then removed a documents slipcase from his trouser pocket and held it out to Niall. "Captain Lucien Pascal reporting for duty as ordered."

"*What?*" Niall took the slipcase, ripping open the seals

and yanking out the contents, while off to one side John and Val argued in low tones.

Lucien, meanwhile, offered nods and the occasional smile to the Thalassans who had crowded closer. He looked as always like a Service recruitment poster, desertweights fresh, shoes polished to mirror brightness. His orange rank tabs, ribbons, and designators had been perfectly aligned, and his garrison cap set at the optimum angle to imply just enough jaunt with a minimum of cocky. Add to that a frame graced with just the right amount of muscle to flesh out his ranginess, the face of a fallen angel, and chocolate brown eyes that reflected soulless depths, and what you had was the stuff of dreams.

Or in my case, the odd nightmare. Jani surveyed the Thalassans who crowded around them, and to her surprise noted that it was Lucien's forearms and not his looks that attracted the bulk of the attention. Crosshatched by raised scars that had healed white, they served as souvenirs of, judging from the mutterings, one of the more famous battles ever fought by a member of the Commonwealth Service.

"He fought one of Cèel's security dominants within the challenge circle—"

"He killed him."

"He had no choice—"

As usual, Lucien seemed oblivious to the upset he'd caused. He leaned as close to Jani as he dared while Niall continued to pore over his orders. *"Speaking of taking my breath away,"* he whispered in French.

"And he shall spread discord wherever he goes," Jani replied in English. "What the hell are you doing here?"

"Now, is that any way to—"

"Pascal."

Lucien shot Jani a pointed look before drawing up straight and turning to Niall. "Sir."

"I haven't had a chance to check my inbox for my copy of these orders." Niall flicked a corner of the documents sheaf with his fingernail. "Signed by Supreme Command, as I'd have expected." He chose his words with care, loath to even hint at the fact that his revered commander might have inflicted Pascal on him without so much as a "Do you mind?"

"Yessir. Arrangements were made in haste." Lucien's voice came light, imbued with innocence and a sincere desire to help. "Due to the scheduling, I needed to impose upon Doctor Parini and invoke billet privileges in order to arrive in good time." He turned to John. "Please let me know, Doctor Shroud, if Neoclona wishes to pursue remunerations."

"I intend to." John shot another glare at Val, who swallowed hard and fixed on his shoes.

Jani glanced at Niall, who looked ready to smoke the entire contents of his nicstick case at one go.

"We should get inside." Niall folded Lucien's orders and stuffed them back in the slipcase, then turned to Jani. "I would like to use your comroom, if I could."

"Going to shoot Mako a missive?" Jani turned and followed John, who must have decided that they had provided the rest of the enclave with enough gossip fodder for one day and started the uphill trudge to the Main House.

"You could say that," Niall spoke in a rough whisper, mindful that Lucien had fallen in just a few paces behind. "Assigning that sonofa—to *my* staff." His face flared. "What the *fuck* is he thinking?"

"Are you sure the orders aren't forged?"

"Could you check?" Niall's face lightened for an instant, then the storm clouds gathered anew. "Don't bother. That professional piece of ass knows damn well that if he took Roshi's name in vain, he'd take up permanent residence in the brig within a week. Even he's not that reckless." He smacked the slipcase against his thigh. "God*damn* it."

"Why?" Jani tried to catch Val's eye, but he avoided hers, feigning interest in every stone and shrub he passed. She stared at the top of his head, willing him to look at her, but he remained fixated on the rocks and scrub as though they were the most fascinating things he'd ever seen.

"Tell me and we'll both bloody know." Niall jerked a thumb back over his shoulder at Lucien. "Go collect your gear, Captain. And hang onto it. You may need to move at a moment's notice." He exhaled with a growl. "Right back to Earth, if I have anything to say about it."

Jani glanced back at Lucien, who gave her a smile that might have counted as ingenuous as long as she didn't look at his eyes. They shone, alight with the simple joy he always derived from making a difficult situation even worse. He pursed his lips and mimed a kiss, then turned and trotted back to the shuttle. "I don't like this."

"*You* don't like it?" Niall glared at the slipcase as though it held his death warrant. "It's Roshi's signature—I'd know that anywhere. His personal parchment." He folded the case in half and shoved it in his trouser pocket. "Bloody fucking hell."

They continued the hike to the House. The wind picked up, blowing sand with abrasive force, as though hurrying them on their way.

The sand around Knevçet Shèràa is darker. The sands of light's weeping, that holiest of idomeni shrines. *Until I desecrated it.* Jani quickened her pace as grains struck her face and neck, a stinging cloud, as though she walked through an insect swarm. *The sand stains.* She remembered the smears on boots and fatigues. *Rust red, like clay.* Not like the color of blood. Not like that at all.

"You all right, gel?" Niall trotted up to meet her. "You took off like a rocket back there."

"Fine. I'm fine." Jani walked on up the hill, holding her head up despite the stinging, so she wouldn't have to look at the sand.

A hasty lunch was assembled from the remains of Thalassa's communal mid-morning sacrament and set up in one of the Main House's private dining rooms that overlooked the bay. Niall demurred, claiming prep for the next day's meeting as an excuse, then headed for the basement comroom, Jani's access codes in hand. Lucien arrived a few minutes after his new commander departed, and was about to be sent to the kitchen by John to scrounge what he could until Val intervened. The meal proceeded in awkward fits and starts until Val delved into the contents of the liquor cabinet and settled into his oft-assumed role as the unofficial entertainment.

" . . . and so Eamon stands up before the entire banquet hall and holds up the biggest brassiere I have ever seen." Val paused to take a sip of port, then eased back, glass in hand. " 'A contest,' he announces, in that overwrought burr of his. 'To the woman who can fill this goes the honor of spending the night with me.' So I dig into the centerpiece, pull out two huge cantaloupes, and toss them across the table to him. 'Eamon,' I said, 'just fill it with these. You'll never know the difference, and you can name the first little blossom after me!' "

Jani laughed while eyeing John, who grinned sheepishly.

"Our annual conferences were once the stuff of legend." His grin twitched. "They grew more sedate as we aged."

"Yeah, like the time you tr—" Val stopped, his mouth hanging open in mid-word. He closed it slowly, then silently dropped the subject by taking another sip of wine before turning his attention to the cheese platter.

"Someone's been holding out on me." Jani smiled at John, who winked in reply. That elicited a restive grumble from Lucien, who had spent the entire meal listening to such reminiscences and had grown more irritated with each passing tale.

All this shared history, and you're not part of any of it. Jani glanced at Lucien to find him sitting slumped, fingers interlaced around the base of his brandy snifter, eyes fixed on Val.

Val looked at him once, then again. Then, with a sigh, he set his glass on the table and slid back his chair. "This luncheon was extraordinary." He patted his board-flat stomach. "And filling. If I don't move around, I'll fall right asleep." He wadded his napkin and tossed it atop his plate. "I've been dying to see this place. Mind giving me the grand tour?"

John looked at Jani, then at Lucien. Then he shrugged, placed his own napkin atop the table, and stood. "Why not?" He turned to Jani. "Just give a shout." He shot a glare in Lucien's direction, his jaw working, then nodded to Val. "Let's go."

Jani watched them walk to the French doors, then bobble the "Who leaves first?" with the overwrought courtesy of new acquaintances. They sorted it out after a few moments, John standing on ceremony as host by stepping aside until Val exited ahead of him with a tight smile. She waited until the doors closed and the two had disappeared from view. "What did you do to Val?"

"Nothing he didn't ask me to." Lucien swirled the scant remains of his brandy. "God, talk about beyond the call of duty. Eamon and the melons—how many times did I hear *that* story? Five. Six." His lip curled. "They all sounded the same after the first week. And everyone calls Val Parini a raconteur. It was enough to make me look forward to Pierce's babbling about opera." He raised his snifter toward the door in a solitary toast. "Thanks for the lift, Doc." He lowered the glass and drained it, tilting his head back in order to extract every drop.

"You poor, tortured creature." Jani plucked a lemon wedge from her leftover garnish and bit into it, taking what pleasure she could in Lucien's wince. "You didn't answer my question."

"Mako wanted someone familiar with all the players to look over Pierce's shoulder." Lucien regarded his empty snifter for a time, then hefted the brandy decanter from the trolley alongside the table. "I mean, Pierce is his dog and all, but sometimes he wonders whether he's as forthcoming as he should be, seeing as you're involved."

Jani watched as he filled the snifter halfway, then added another splash for good measure. "I didn't realize he trusted you that far."

"Some people appreciate my capabilities."

"No accounting for taste, I guess." Jani stood and circled the table. The temperature of the room had been lowered in deference to humanish comfort levels, and the jacket she had donned failed to keep out the chill. "I need some air." She pushed through the doors that led out to the balcony, felt the heat welcome her like an old friend, the bay breeze ruffle her hair. She leaned against the stone railing and spent a few quiet minutes watching bayskimmers from the Karistos Yacht Club fast-float across the water.

When she heard the doors open again, she clenched her fists.

"The scenery reminds me of the Greek Islands." Lucien drew alongside, snifter still in hand, the fill level depleted by half. "Anais took me on a cruise to celebrate my appointment to East Point." He leaned against the railing, and smiled for the first time since lunch began and the stories started. "And a good time was had by all, including a few she never knew about." He paused to take yet another swallow of brandy, glanced at Jani over the rim of the snifter and stopped. "What?"

"I'm not used to seeing you toss down the liquor." Jani slowly opened her hands and pressed them to the warm stone. "Alcohol dulls the senses, you always said, and you needed to keep yours sharp."

Lucien lowered his drink, then set it atop the railing. "Chicago's not the same since you left."

"Lucien, this is me you're talking to, remember?"

"I haven't forgotten." He stared at the snifter. Then he grabbed it, drained it in a single swallow, turned and flung it at the stone arch bordering the doorway. The glass shattered with a sound like a shooter crack, the shards flashing back sunlight as they flew apart and scattered across the tiled floor.

One piece skittered in front of Lucien's foot. He stepped on it, twisting his shoe into it, then pulled back and looked at the powder he'd left behind. His breathing came rough, as though he'd been running. "I haven't forgotten a thing."

Jani remained silent. Every so often a fissure developed in Lucien's carefully maintained veneer, a hint of what he could do if he ever threw off the restraints he'd imposed upon himself, ever said "Hell with it" and let fly. *And he feels that way now.* Which meant she had something else to worry about in addition to the reason for Val's visit and tomorrow's meeting with the governors.

"You were always willing to believe anything about me." Lucien paced along the railing, back and forth, like a caged animal. "Anything but the truth." He stopped, eyes fixed on the water. "I had to see you. I was going crazy in Chicago—I would have said or done anything to pull an assignment here. So, I went to see Mako. I had done a few favors for him in the past. He owed me."

"You're trying to drive a wedge between Roshi Mako and his colonel." Jani stepped away from the railing and pretended to examine blooms on a potted shrub. "Don't think Niall will forget that."

Lucien turned slowly. "I know what Pierce thinks of me. I know what he'll put me through. I'm willing to deal with it." His eyes met hers, bottomless wells of brown. "I love you."

Oh Lord—anything but this. Jani pressed her hands to her temples and squeezed. *"Lucien."*

"I mean it."

"Lucien, it's a one hundred twenty-five meter drop into the bay from this balcony. Don't bloody tempt me."

Lucien stared at her, his expression blank. Then, as though some internal valve finally released, he smiled and sagged back against the railing. "We both just need to relax." He patted his trouser pocket, then reached into it. Pulled out something, and held it out for Jani to see. "Remember this?"

She caught a glimpse of dull coral shine, the color silvered by the sunlight. A small sphere, a centimeter or so in diameter. *Oh. Hell.* Her face burned.

"I showed it to Val on the way here. He offered to buy it. How's that for tacky?" Lucien rolled the pearl between his

fingers. "He kept commenting on the color. Pink or peach—
he couldn't make up his mind. What would you call it?"
When Jani failed to reply, he shrugged, his smile altering
from simple and open to something with an edge. "I didn't
tell him how I came to acquire it, of course. Did you even
realize that the string had broken? I know I was focused on
other matters." He held the pearl up to the light. Then he
raised his other hand, pressed the tip of the index finger to
the bottom of the pearl and massaged it. "Do you know what
this reminds me of?" He watched her face as he slid his finger against the pearl from tip to base once, then again, and
again. "It's just like—"

"Please keep it to yourself." Jani looked down and found
she held the crumpled remains of a half-opened bloom, its
stem snapped at the neck. "You're never this coarse. You are
drunk, aren't you?"

Lucien pouted. "I keep souvenirs. You know that. I've got
one of Val's—"

"What is the real reason you came here?"

Lucien took a deep breath. Pocketed the pearl and stood,
brow furrowed, as though trying to recall something. An Angel of Death, at a loss as to what to destroy next. "The usual.
Spread wrack and ruin. Doom, death, disease, and despair."

"Mission accomplished." Jani tossed the remains of
the flower over the railing. "Does that mean you can go
home?"

"Mako sent me to observe the general situation and report
back. A second pair of eyes. Sometimes I do tell the truth
the first time." Lucien passed a hand over his face. "I have
missed you, you know, disinclined as you are to believe it.
I won't ask if you missed me. Judging by the expression on
your face, I know your answer." He glanced over the railing.
"Hundred twenty-five meters. I'll have to remember that."
He turned and headed for the doors. "If you'll excuse me, I
really need to find a bathroom."

"Lucien?" Jani waited until he stopped. "Whatever shit
you're thinking of pulling, reconsider."

Lucien tried to turn, but caught the side of one shoe on the edge of a tile and stumbled. "God, I am drunk, aren't I?" He righted himself slowly, shaking his head at the wonder of it all. "You have enough to worry about without looking for trouble from me. Val's visit is not social, in case you haven't guessed. The PM ordered him to buy out Shroud's share of Neoclona. A single digit percentage of what that share is worth, and that number's a hell of a lot closer to zero than it is to ten. No more research. No more consulting. He's to find other things to do."

What lunch Jani had managed to eat congealed in her gut. "Why?"

"As a warning to other bad little captains of Commonwealth industry who might consider hybridizing. Or working so closely with the Haárin." Lucien paused to breathe. The alcohol had him by the throat now. "Things are tense, in case you haven't noticed. Human separatists are bombing Haárin docks, Cèel wants to sever diplomatic relations with the Commonwealth, and—the first shots—in any war would likely be fired—in a place like Elyas." Sweat soaked his shirt and slicked his face, making him look as though he'd been caught in the rain. "Now, two percent of Neoclona is still more money than any normal person might expect to see in a lifetime, but it isn't just the money. It's the power, and the influence, and let's not forget the medical research capabilities." He pulled a linen square from his pocket and wiped his face, his neck. "With your principal means of support gutted, where does that leave Thalassa? Where does that—leave you?" He grimaced. "I need— Excuse me." He turned and double-timed through the dining room and out the door.

Jani leaned against the railing as soon as Lucien disappeared from sight. Her gut ached. Her legs felt weak.

Two percent. She imagined John's expression as Val broke the news. The sun still warmed, but she couldn't feel it. The bayskimmers still floated, but she didn't see them.

CHAPTER 4

Rilas steered the skimmer as close to the cliff edge as the directionals allowed. The vehicle's wake sent dried brush tumbling over the rocks, while its high-pitched hum and the shadow it cast as it coursed over the ground drove small animals to the shelter of shrubs and burrows.

In the rearview, she watched the domes and painted rooftops of Karistos recede, replaced by rocky summits that jutted into the cloudless sky. After driving for a time, she stopped the skimmer beside a tumbled mass of stone, hoisted her slingbag from behind her seat, and disembarked. She walked to the edge of the cliff, then along it, looking out to the bay every few strides.

In the short time she spent walking, three skimmers passed her. All carried humanish, who drove too slowly and watched her as though they had never before seen an Haárin. The cliffs of Karistos and the Bay of Siros had become popular places for tourists, and Rilas knew the traffic would grow as the day proceeded. "Most unfortunate. This would have been a good place." She drew a small scope from one of the slingbag's many pockets, held it to her eye, looked toward the bay and the line of cliffs beyond. In the scope's viewer, she at last caught sight of Thalassa, a scatter of glistening rooftops, blue and yellow in the sun.

Rilas touched a pad on the side of the scope, activating the device so it could read and measure. Distances. Heights. Angles. Depths of rooms and thicknesses of walls. After completing the task, she returned the device to her bag and strode back to her skimmer. Already half the day had been spent searching, as had the entire day before. She did not like to take so long to make preparations, but Karistos had proved a strange place, much worse than nìRau Cèel had described.

She stood beside the skimmer, one hand on the door control, until a humanish male driving alone slowed and asked if she required assistance. She gestured that she could not understand him, then entered her vehicle and drove away. Too quickly— she knew she moved too quickly. She could see the male in her rearview, watching her. Would he remember her? Or did all female idomeni look alike to him, as nìRau Cèel said?

Damned godless place. Never again would she act as a tile broker. As ná Nahin Sela, she had wasted hours at the Trade Board displaying samples and discussing colors and glazes, meeting with prospective customers. *NìRau Cèel told me that I must act as that which I am supposed to be.* Such was the nature of cover. *If I did not act as a merchant among the Elyan Haárin, I would be noticed.* But the training she had received in Rauta Shèràa had not prepared her for these Haárin, who ate and drank in the streets as animals, who looked her in the eye even though they were unknown to her.

Then there were . . . those other. The anathema. The hybrids. She had seen two of them at the Trade Board, a male and female, so much as demons in their misshapen strangeness. Thick limbs. Pale eyes and skin. They had once been as humanish. As humanish, they should have remained.

Rilas drove and studied each passage, each summit. Prayed to her goddess for guidance, and for strength. *This place is of your doing, Tsecha.* Soon, he would pay the cost of his sacrilege.

* * *

The sun passed prime. As it began its downward arc, Rilas passed a rocky slope crowded at its base with rubble and dying scrub. She drove past it as she had so many others, and had traveled quite far along the cliff road before she realized what she had seen.

She turned around and drove back to the place, alert to humanish tourists, or shuttles making their final approach to the distant Karistos port or the Service field. Alert to any sign that someone, somewhere, might see her. She fought the desire to reach into the slingbag and remove and activate the devices that could scan the skies as she could not. Monitor the roads. Watch her back, as a humanish would say.

But she dare not. All around Karistos, craft from the humanish Service traveled, scanned, searched. Her devices, while most useful, were also most illegal, and she could not risk their detection now, while she still prepared. In a day or two, when she completed her task and had gone, let the Service find what they would. *Some of it will look most as familiar, as we stole it from them.* Rilas bared her teeth at the thought. Humanish did not believe Haárin capable of stealing, just as they did not believe them capable of subterfuge or sabotage. Most foolish of them, and truly.

She approached the pile of rubble, her joy fading. She slowed the skimmer, hunting for the signs that had attracted her attention and compelled her return. At first she could not detect them, and wondered if she had erred.

Then, finally, one by one, she saw them. A glimpse of masonry colored the same browns and whites as the surrounding stone, barely visible through tangled branches. Straight lines where none should exist, the broken edges of a wall smashed to ruins by the rockslide.

She steered her skimmer behind the rockslide so it was hidden from the road. This time, she activated her shooter. Then she powered down the vehicle, hoisted her slingbag, and disembarked.

Rilas savored the heat, the one welcome surprise that

Elyas offered. Wondered at the stone, the sparse vegetation, so much as Rauta Shèràa that she felt as though she tracked quarry on her homeworld. The thought upset her, and she struggled to push it from her mind. When nìRau Cèel counseled her, he had been adamant. Assassination or sabotage, what acts she performed could not be committed on Shèrá. Too much risk of discovery, he had told her. Too much danger, for both of them.

She held her shooter at the ready as she approached the house, circling the place once before pushing a rock aside with her foot and passing through the partly collapsed doorway. She stepped around a pile of rubble and into what had once been a room. Remains of furniture, sticks of polywood and scraps of weave, littered the space. Some lay scattered across the floor, the rest wadded in corners, where it served as bedding for the animals whose claws Rilas heard skittering against the cracked and stained tile. She sniffed the air, grimacing at the tang of waste and rotted flesh, the stench of the things which lived in this place mingled with that of the things which had died. An unseemly place, and truly. None would look for even the lowest Haárin in such as this.

Only when her eyes had better adjusted to the half-dark did Rilas explore further. Grit and dried leaves crunched beneath her feet. Sunlight streamed in through a lone window, highlighting dust motes that leapt and fell like sparks from a fire, disturbed by her passage.

She set her slingbag on the floor. A short time spent pushing aside rock and clutter left her with a space through which she could maneuver as well as a path to the window. She hoped that it would look out over the bay, and was pleased to find that it did. "I can just see the water." And beyond that, the curve of land that held her target.

Rilas recovered her bag from its resting place and carried it to the window, set it on the dusty floor and opened it. She removed wrapped tubes, a small box, a roll of heavy cloth. First she removed the wrapping from the tubes, then laid out the smooth plastic on the floor to serve as a barrier. Lay the tubes atop it, followed by the box and the cloth roll.

She knelt. Picked up the tubes, one short and one long, fitted them together, then set them aside. Unrolled the cloth and removed three items. First, two curves of metal, one large and one much smaller, the stock and the discharge mech. Last, her prize, her most valued thing. A clear glassy cylinder shot through with lines and discs of color. Her sight mech.

She worked with a speed born of practice. Attached barrel to stock. Fastened discharge mech to the underside of barrel, sight mech to the top. Removed the sighting device from her pocket, attached it to the sight mech, and activated data transfer.

Rilas watched the colors in the sight mech brighten and dull, flash and fade. As the last burst of color faded, she detached the sighting device and tucked it back in her pocket. Only then did she rise, turn to the window and raise the rifle. Bracing the stock against her shoulder, she poked the barrel through a gap in the shattered pane and lowered her eye to the sight mech.

Fully assembled, the rifle felt weighty, but balanced, like a finely crafted shooter. She paused to run her hand over the barrel, savoring the smooth chill of the dull black metallo-ceramic. She then resumed her check, studying the bay and the cliffs beyond through the sight mech.

It is as though I stand there. After all this time, after completing so many such tasks for nìRau Cèel, she still marveled at how the mech magnified the distant view, how the micro-lenses moved in concert to sharpen, brighten, provide contrast, expose detail no idomeni eye could detect unaided.

Rilas scanned a road that diagonaled along the cliff face and wound past structures before vanishing at the summit. She moved on to a larger structure, one of the largest she had seen on Elyas, which jutted from the cliff face as though part of the stone. Through windows, she could see figures. The accursed hybrids whose existence pained nìRau Cèel so.

Click—click—click. Her finger twitched on the discharge mech—with each faint *whirr* of the mechs, she imagined bodies falling, souls destroyed, lives extinguished. She scanned other areas of the enclave—

Click.

Walkways. Verandas. Open spaces.

Click.

Killing, killing. Taking life that had no right to exist.

Click. Click. Click.

A small balcony.

Rilas stilled. Eased the pressure on the discharge mech. Watched.

Jani Kilian. The Kièrshia. The cursed thing. Standing, alone on the balcony. She wore a wrapshirt and trousers in grey, plain and free of adornment save for a thick cording of silver woven into the shirt cuffs.

Rilas released the charge-through and looked away from the scope. Her heart beat strongly—she could feel it pound. Her hands were as dry, her mind, as clear. Such was as they were during the best of times, when Caith blessed her and bade her act as her talents demanded.

She set aside the rifle, then knelt upon the rubble-strewn floor and rummaged through her bag. Small stones dug into her knees; she used the pain as a spur, a sign of favor from Caith that it was right for her to act. She removed the frosty flat container. Opened it. Took out one of the chilled projectiles, inserted it into the rifle magazine, clicked the chamber closed. Heard the cylinder slide into place, the rifle hum in activation.

The payload is typed to Tsecha. Even as the technician's words echoed in her head, Rilas lifted the rifle to her shoulder and sighted down, capturing the dark head. Edged the weapon one way, then the other, until the scope signaled TARGET CENTERED with a single yellow flash, and she fixed on the face. Skin dark as Pathen, eyes green as Sìah, combined with weak human bones. The face of an overgrown youngish, a mutant, a made thing.

The payload is typed to Tsecha.

"But it might work with her. The idomeni part of her is of Vynshàrau. There could be enough—"

The payload is typed to Tsecha.

Rilas forced herself to breathe. The Kièrshia stood, unmoving as stone, eyes fixed. A target as she had never had, still and quiet and alone. If this one fell, no one would know for hours.

Then Kièrshia shifted her stare until it seemed to Rilas as though she saw her and studied her in turn.

You should die. Rilas's finger tightened on the charge-through. *You must—*

Tsecha.

Rilas stilled. Cursed the name that filled her head even as she knew it had been sent by her goddess. Relaxed, drawing in one slow inhalation of stagnant air, followed by another. Another.

"Fool." Rilas stood still until she calmed, until she could no longer see the strange green eyes in her mind. Then she broke down the rifle and repacked the components.

I will return to Karistos. I will make sacrifice, and pray, and prepare. Then tomorrow she would return to the ruin and kill the one for whom the weapon had been designed. Avrèl nìRau Nema. A name that had once been and was now no more. Ní Tsecha Egri. A life that was now, and would soon not be.

Rilas shouldered her bag and, with careful steps, departed the ruin. No humanish males lurked in wait outside. No tourists. No movement but branches and leaves in the wind, no sound but animals.

CHAPTER 5

Jani heard the French doors open, but didn't turn to see who her visitor was. She already knew. "It's so nice and quiet out here."

Footsteps from behind, soft on the tile. "Ní Tsecha's over at the never-ending project that is the new meeting house." Dieter Brondt, her secular suborn and resident spy, drew up next to her. "He's arguing with ní Dathim about the tile-work."

"Again? And what does he want me to do about that?"

"Make ní Dathim see things his way." Dieter grinned, the expression lighting his round face. "Because we all know how well ní Dathim listens to you."

"About as well as he listens to anyone." Jani paused to rub her eyes. Her head ached from the brightness of the sun off the water, yet the last thing she wanted to do was leave the balcony.

Dieter bent and picked up one of the crystal shards. "I ran into Captain Pascal on the walkway, and immediately directed him to a bathroom." He examined the fragment, then looked around at the other pieces scattered across the balcony floor. "It didn't sound as though lunch agreed with him."

"Heat and brandy."

Dieter winced. "He's on his way to Fort Karistos. Got a com from Pierce to report immediately. 'Scarface blinked,' was how he put it." He gave the shard a last look, then tossed it aside. "Is everything all right?"

"John and Val." Jani beat a cadence on the railing with her fists. "Where are they?"

"The clinic." Dieter planted his feet and folded his arms. He wore a wrapshirt and loose trousers in patterned orange and white. Hybridization had claimed him late and done little to lengthen his bones or slim his stocky frame, leaving him resembling a fitter than average Buddha with cat-yellow eyes. "Doctor Shroud took Doctor Parini on a tour." He cocked his head. Concerned Buddha. "Is something wrong?"

"Captain Pascal gave me some news before he went to lose his lunch. I don't know whether to believe it or not."

"Would the fact that the good doctors have been holed up in Doctor Shroud's office for the whole of their tour help you decide?"

Jani shot the male a hard look. "Does anything happen around here that you don't know about?" She fielded his blank stare and shook her head. "Val's been sent here to cut John's heart out." She stopped, as though speaking the words would give them a reality they didn't otherwise possess. *But they are real, dammit.* When it came to digging out the nasty, Lucien gave Dieter a run for anyone's money. "He's to buy out John's share of Neoclona. At two cents on the Common dollar."

Dieter's brows twitched skyward. "That's . . . a kick in the teeth." He stroked his chin. "But is it a surprise?"

"Maybe not. Cut off the money, and the Thalassan beast will sicken and die." Jani turned her back to the water and studied the stark white facade of the Main House. "Maybe the surprise is that they waited this long to do it." She pushed off the railing and started for the dining room. "I'm going to stop off at John's office before I go to the meeting house."

"Jani?" Dieter hurried after her, soles crunching on bits of scattered glass. "There are solutions, surely?"

"They should've been put in place already. Assets transfers take time. So do setups of dummy corporations." Jani stepped out onto the walkway that ringed the third floor of the office-laboratory-apartment complex that was the administrative, social, and medical focus of the Thalassan enclave. "That's why Val didn't let John know he was coming. Whoever sent him didn't want to give John the time to adjust." She looked over the railing and down to the ground level central courtyard, where the kitchen crew were setting up for mid-afternoon sacrament, jamming and angling mess tables as best they could amid the planters and fountains. "First rule of auditing. Never call ahead."

"I wouldn't have." A little of the old Colonel Brondt, Elyas Station Service liaison and spotter of smugglers and other illicit life-forms, flashed in Dieter's eyes. "Neither would you."

"Maybe." Jani caught a whiff of curry from the dining area below. She'd have savored the aroma normally, but nerves had claimed her gut as their own and she felt the acid rise in her throat instead. "Bit different when you're on the other end, though." She headed around the walkway to the lift, nodding to the hybrids she passed along the way while at the same time keeping an eye out for any sign of Lucien.

"Doctor Parini can be made to listen?" Dieter followed after her, a misshapen shadow. "He and Doctor Shroud have been friends for so long."

"Depends who has Val by the short hairs." Jani thumped the lift call pad with her fist. The cabin opened—she stepped inside, then turned to face her suborn. "He didn't come here because he wanted to, he came because he was forced, and by someone who knew just how hard to yank. Pretty select list, don't you think?" She raised a hand in farewell as the lift door closed in Dieter's worried face.

The basement laboratory-clinic proved the same low-key madhouse as always, technicians and medicos bustling along the maze of corridors like the white-coated ants they were. Jani negotiated the twisty trail to John's office, then paused and pressed her ear to the door to check if any yelling could be detected through the combination of sound-shielding and the vibration-dampening door panel. She sensed nothing. Took a deep breath and hit the door pad.

John and Val fell silent as she entered, just-spoken words charging the air like static. John sat at his desk, working a small exercise ball with one hand, rolling it over and over again between his long fingers. Val sat on a short couch set against the wall, arms folded and shoulders hunched.

"Jani." John glanced at Val, then away. "We've just been catching up on old—"

"Two percent." Jani dragged a visitors' chair to the side of the desk opposite John and sat. "No more practicing medicine. No more research."

Val's mouth dropped open. "How . . . ?" Then his face flamed and he covered his eyes with one hand.

Yes, Lucien ratted you out. What the hell did you expect? Jani looked across the polished ebony desk at John, who stared back as though she'd just plucked a rabbit out of thin air. "I have my sources."

"Without a doubt." John shook his head, then bounced the ball atop the desk, caught it, and bounced it again. "Val is here at the PM's request. Given the deteriorating relationship between the humanish and idomeni, Li Cao feels that a hybrid at the head of one of the largest commercial entities in the Commonwealth is too great a security risk to tolerate." He gave the ball one final bounce, then stashed it in a drawer and stood. "Anyone want coffee?" Without waiting to see whether anyone actually did, he walked to a lowboy at the far end of the room and started assembling the brewer.

"I'm just the messenger." Val glanced at Jani sidelong, as though reluctant to meet her eye. "The real negotiations will go on in Karistos between lawyers from the Justice Ministry and our—" He shot a look at John, then concentrated on his hands. "—and Neoclona's legal team." He shrugged. "And whoever John hires to represent his interests."

"These negotiations began last week, apparently." John

offered Jani a chill smile. "I'm left to scramble. I've already contacted a firm in Karistos that I believe can hold its own." He set out cups, cream, and sugar on a tray while the weighty aroma of his coffee filled the office.

"Why now?" Jani edged away from the desk so John could set down the tray. "John's been here a year. It took Cao that long to decide he was a threat to Commonwealth security?"

Val rose and walked to the desk. "She called me in one day, about two months ago. Oh, it had been busy. Tsecha had just let loose one of his theological broadsides, a story about you had appeared in a scandal sheet, and one of the more conservative ministers questioned John's loyalty during public debate." He spooned sugar into a cup, then waited while John filled it to the brim. "That's when I screwed up." He paused to sip. "She asked if I felt whether the idomeni could win John's loyalty." He looked at John and shook his head. "I told her that the only two things that had won John Shroud's loyalty were his work"—he closed his eyes—"and Jani Kilian."

John set down the carafe. "Very dramatic, Val, but not the wisest choice of words." He hoisted his own cup, then set it down with a clatter, sending scalding brew in all directions. "*Dammit!*" He grabbed a dispo tissue from the dispenser on his desk and wiped hot coffee off his hand. "What is she afraid of, that I'll start working for Rauta Shèràa? Even if I wanted to, Cèel wouldn't take my help on a plate—it would be a repudiation of everything he believes. Or does she think I'll infect the entire Commonwealth with a hybridization bug?" He crumpled the dispo into a tight ball and hurled it into a deskside trash bin. "It doesn't work that way, Val—didn't you tell her? Hybridization is still a slow, labor-intensive process tailored to the individual, and that's not likely to change anytime soon. If she's worried about hybrids by the millions overrunning her government, she's an idiot!"

"She wants to take out the financial underpinnings of this place." Jani gripped her cup in both hands. John had lowered the office temperature in deference to Val, leaving it much too cold for her comfort. "Something happened, and she thinks shutting down Thalassa will help solve the problem." *Something to do with secession. Cao must have heard the rumors.* She picked over one possibility in her mind, then another, until she sensed the stares. Val's unspoken prayer that something she'd say could get him off the hook. John's, that she could give him something to pry Cao's grip from his throat. "I don't know what that could be."

"Well, so much for that." John doffed his medcoat and draped it over the back of his chair. "I have an appointment with my new legal team in an hour. I need to get ready." He looked at Jani. "I'd like you to be there. I know they'll have questions for you. I'm hoping you can at least answer those." He brushed past her and out the door without waiting for a reply.

The door closed. Silence settled. Jani touched her cheek. The sense of having been struck, but without the blow.

Val walked to the wall opposite and focused on one of the framed hangings. "He still has that one." A shade of a smile, soon vanished. "It's hitting him now. It takes a while, with the big things. He got angry when I told him, yeah, but now it's sinking its roots." He hung his head. "I'm just letting you know. I don't think you've seen it. It can get rough."

"Thanks for the warning." Jani turned to look at the image. It must have dated from Val's and John's medical school days. Two gangly young men with toothy grins standing on the steps of a building. Val's hair flopped over his forehead, while John wore a wide-brimmed hat that he'd angled to shade his eyes from the sun. "Is there anything you can do?"

"My influence with Li Cao doesn't extend beyond the tip of my nose." Val's shoulder twitched. "She's declared this a matter of Commonwealth security. If I fight her, she'll take away both our shares and hand them over to Eamon, which would be pretty much the same as her taking over the company." He walked back to the desk and set down his cup. "But there's the election in three months. Yevgeny Scriabin is standing against her, and he's a reasonable man. Most of the pundits are predicting he'll beat her."

"That's three months. A hell of a lot can happen between now and then." Jani swallowed hard as John's coffee took up where the aroma of the curry had left off. She set down her cup, then rose and headed for the door. "I need to see Tsecha before I meet with John's lawyers."

"I'll go with you." Val hurried after her. "At least part of the way. I need to walk. Cooped up on a ship for six weeks with—" He stood aside so Jani could precede him through the door, then hesitated. "This isn't like I thought it would be, to say the least." He stepped out into the corridor, glancing up as though he feared the ceiling might fall on him. "I envisioned a nice, relaxed visit. Dinners in little out-of-the-way places, capped off by dancing and plate smashing. Maybe some sailracing during the day. Then one day, Li Cao calls me, and it all falls apart, bit by bit." He quieted until they entered the lift and the door closed. "I have . . . some explaining to do." He tried for a weak grin, but managed only a wince. "I tried to work up the nerve after lunch, but His Highness sent me out of the room."

Jani shook her head. "Not now, Val."

"If I don't tell you now, I'll lose my nerve." He stepped aside so she could exit the lift first, then fell behind her as they cut across the central courtyard and through a series of demirooms separated by aquaria and low screens.

Jani waited until they departed the Main House and rounded the vast rear yard. "Val?"

"I think I'm losing it. My nerve." He dragged off his suit jacket and slung it over his shoulder. "Dammit." He stopped at the top of the cliff road and looked out over the water. "It's so beautiful here. Hotter than fucking hell, but—" He ran a hand across his brow, already dotted with sweat. "But everything beautiful has a price, doesn't it?" His eyes brimmed. "I'm sorry."

Jani waited until Val cleared his throat and wiped his eyes. "Want me to tell you what happened? You can nod or shake your head at suitable intervals, and it will be like you never really said anything at all."

"You think you know all the words to this one, do you?" Val started down the road, his step slowing as the soles of his dress shoes slid on the gravel.

"In several languages." Jani tried to study him without seeming to. He kept his eyes fixed on the road, braced for the words he didn't want to hear. "First verse—Lucien started hanging around your flat after I left Chicago to return to John. His pretexts were feeble at best. Some bit of news from one of the ministries, or a rumor he'd heard at Sheridan. Being a man of the world, you saw through his act immediately, even felt irritated by his lack of subtlety. But even though you knew he was trying to play you, you just couldn't make yourself send him on his way. He had a connection to me, and he offered all the right responses when you railed against John, which I'm sure you did at least a few times or you wouldn't count as a living, breathing being." She looked away as Val's face reddened, allowing him an illusion of privacy. "Besides, he's just so damned decorative. You did once tell me that you could watch him all day."

Val snorted, denying the inevitable even as he worked closer to admitting to it. "He's not the first good-looking boy to stake me out."

"No, but he's the best-trained. He's an assassin, Val. Gauging the victim is what he does." Jani held up two fingers. "Second verse—after you got used to his coming around regularly, he pulled back. Stayed away for a week or two at a time, then turned up with weak excuses. Just to see how hooked you were." They came upon a small sitting area wedged between two houses, and she stopped and sat on a stone bench.

"I passed that test." Val unfastened his shirt collar, then bent over a tiny fountain and let the water spray over his face. "I wasn't a complete idiot."

Jani nodded. "He figured that out. So when you told him that you were leaving to visit John, his request to accompany you was completely businesslike. Being under orders from

Mako himself, he claimed billet privileges, then left you to mull it over. He knew he had you backed in a corner—what could you do but agree? You already suspected that Cao didn't trust you, that her summons was a warning to you as well as to John. It worried you what might happen if you added to your troubles by tossing out Mako's chosen rep on his perfectly formed ear."

Val dragged a linen square out of his trouser pocket and wiped his face. Then he sat beside her and sighed. "Jani—"

"Pressure points, Val. Weakness. Like I said before, he has a talent for spotting them."

"He's not the only one," Val said through his teeth.

Jani hesitated. "Now, the chorus. He had set you up so you had to cart him here or risk appearing disloyal. So, cart him here you did. He should have been content, you'd think, but this is Lucien we're talking about. You had rejected his advances up to that point, and that was a situation that could not be allowed to continue. Even engineered sociopaths have their pride."

"There are only so many places to hide on a ship, and none of them works for long." Val spoke low, as though to himself. "Every damned time I turned around, there he was. His favorite trick was to catch me in the gym locker room or sauna, wander in stark naked and pretend to be surprised to see me. 'I'm *so* sorry, Doctor Parini—I didn't realize you were here.' Yeah, right."

Jani grinned in remembrance. "A bit obvious, but a tried and true method with some history of success."

Val returned her grin, but the expression withered. "After a few quiet days, I thought he had finally gotten the message. Then one ship-morning, about three weeks out, he showed up at my cabin door with a copy of whatever newssheet had been transmitted that day. He was fully clothed, believe it or not. A little rough around the edges, actually. Tired. Distracted. As though he'd given up." He paused, his eyes clouding.

"He handed me the newssheet," he said after a time. "I took it. I said 'Thank you, Captain Pascal,' and he replied,

'You're welcome, Doctor Parini.' We—" He stopped again, inhaling with a shudder. "We just stared at one another. Might have been for a minute or so. Might have been an hour for all I could tell. Neither of us said a word, we just . . . " He swallowed hard. "Then he stepped inside, let the door close behind him. Took the newssheet from my hand, folded it, and set it atop a nearby table. Then he—" He closed his eyes, lips parting ever so slightly. His breathing quickened as his hands clenched and flexed, twisted the linen until it tore.

Then his eyes snapped open. He shook his head as though emerging from a daze and sat forward, elbows on knees, hands dangling between. "You're going to tell me it was an act." He examined the damage he'd wrought upon the linen square, then wadded it and shoved it in his trouser pocket.

"It's *all* an act." Jani put a hand on his shoulder. "Trust me, it's better when you accept it. It makes him a known quantity, with no surprises. A certain brand of simple comfort when the real world becomes too complex to deal with."

Val's lip curled. "Aren't you the understanding one?" He fell silent for a few moments, then sat up and eyed her expectantly. "Your turn."

Jani considered a display of innocence, but decided confusion more believable. "My turn for what?"

"I'm not the only one laying bare my soul here, am I? Be fair."

"What do you want to know?"

"The story behind that pearl. He showed it to me on the way here. Told me he bought it, but we both know that's a joke. He never paid for anything in his life." Val straightened his legs and examined his dust-covered shoes. "I read his MedRec once, remember? I know he keeps souvenirs of events in his life he considers memorable."

Crap. Now it was her turn to shudder, to hem and haw. "What makes you think the pearl's mine?"

"I have my reasons, which I will explain after you tell me the story behind it."

Jani felt the heat creep up her neck. "It's from my dowry."

She fielded Val's surprised look. "My parents turned over my dowry to me when they first came to Chicago, and one of the pieces was a pearl necklace." She paused. "One . . . night, I wore it during . . . "

"During . . . ?" Val leaned toward her. "During a fire drill? During charades? What?"

Jani tried closing her eyes, but images flashed that she didn't want to see at that moment. Instead, she concentrated on a scatter of stones at her feet. "I wore it to bed. I had worn it that evening, and didn't take it off. During a particularly active moment, Lucien . . . yanked on it, and the string broke. Pearls everywhere. If I'd known they hadn't been tied properly, I never would have worn them. Those damned things turned up under the furniture for months." She shrugged, forced herself to look Val in the face. "See? No big revelatory episode. Just something I'm sure he saved to embarrass me."

"Probably." Val sighed. His mood seemed lighter, as though her confession had bought him some degree of dispensation. "Why did we let him get under our skin? We're grown-ups. We should have known better."

"They tell you everything you want to hear, and they know how to show you the face you want to see. Even when you know in your bones that you can't trust them, you still try, because you can't accept the fact that they can't feel and that there's nothing they won't do to ensure their survival." Jani rocked to the side until she bumped against him. "Guess who told me that?"

"Dirty pool, Jan."

"I'd just let him into my home when I knew he had set me up to be killed. You tried to warn me."

"But I was wrong. You figured out later that he had blocked the attempt. He pushed you out of the way, took the shot himself. He saved your life." Val frowned. "Granted, he was the one who got you into trouble in the first place." He raked a hand through his hair, then sat forward and buried his face in his hands. "Oh, *crap*."

"He leaves behind wreckage wherever he goes—compared to some, you got off easy. You're here, in one piece. No one shot at you. You're a bit chastened, but you'll get over it." Jani held out her hand. "You survived. Congratulations and welcome to the club."

"Hip, hip, hooray." Val sat up. "Remember when I said that I knew the pearl had to have belonged to you?" He took her hand and squeezed it, then continued to hold it. "About four days out, he started pulling away. Moved his things out of my cabin. He said that he needed to prepare for Niall, but I knew that was bullshit. As if any amount of prep in that regard would do him any good."

Jani tried to reclaim her hand, but Val had it locked up tight. "I wonder how Mako was able to shove him down Niall's throat considering—"

"Don't change the subject." Val glowered a warning. "By the time we were two days out, *he'd* started avoiding *me*. Last night, as we were getting ready to dock at Elyas, I lay in bed, *alone*, stewing in my own juice, when it hit me how much of our time together had been spent talking about you. Your accomplishments. Your background. Things you and he had done together. I even recalled a rather spirited discussion concerning the exact color of your eyes." He regarded her with something akin to pity, mixed with something else that looked a lot like fear. "I'm not very happy being me at the moment, but the one thing I can take comfort in is the fact that I'm not you. I was just something to help pass the time, I know that now. But you, you're his obsession." He smiled sadly, then held her hand to his lips and kissed it. "I need to get back. I want to talk to John before he meets with his lawyers." He released her hand and stood, then circled around the bench and headed back up the road to the Main House.

Jani massaged the spot on her hand that Val had kissed. "Welcome to the club." Problem was, after you paid the initiation fee, you kept paying and paying and paying . . .

I should have guessed that Lucien would keep a souvenir of that night. Like most of their eventful evenings, it hadn't been planned. Lucien had finessed them an invitation to a dinner at one of the ministries, but she hadn't wanted to attend. When she tried to beg off, however, he listed the reasons why she needed to go, all sound business-related incentives of the sort he could recite in his sleep. The issue settled, he had arrived to collect her, passing the time in her sitting room while she finished dressing.

What the hell got into me? She had donned the requisite undergarments and ridiculous shoes. A conservative gown in dark blue. Removed the jewelry satchel from her armoire and opened it, revealing her dowry, the trays filled with gems, gold, and platinum. Picked through the necklaces, bracelets, and earrings.

Then she removed the gown, the ridiculous shoes and undergarments, and dressed herself in as much of the glittery stuff as she could hang from her neck, loop around her waist, hips, and ankles, and wrap around her arms. Out of fifteen kilos of chains, links, and set gems her parents had brought her from Acadia, she managed to don at least five. Gold, topaz, and emerald. Strings of diamond beads. And the pearls.

Lucien had turned as soon as the bedroom door opened. Started to say something, then stopped and stared as she posed in the bedroom entry, still and stylized as one of her mother's statues. She didn't speak and neither did he—adaptable animal that he was, he never asked a single question. He simply walked toward her, peeling off his dress uniform along the way until, by the time he reached her, he was as naked as she was.

He called me a goddess. Among other things he murmured. Whispered. Shouted. So enraptured had they been with one another that they hadn't even noticed the necklace had broken until the morning.

"That was some night." And now the time had come to pay the price for it. "What have you come to collect, Lucien?" She stood and continued on her way to the meeting house. "And who have you come to collect it for?"

CHAPTER 6

"It does not make sense." Tsecha pointed to the half-tiled wall, a mélange of delicate colorings and sketched detail. "What is this? I have never seen anything such as this before."

Ní Dathim Naré, Tsecha's secular suborn, stood beside his dominant with the ill-concealed irritation of an artist coping with the criticism of a wealthy but tasteless client. "Through the middle is the line of the cliffs. Drawn there are the houses of Thalassa. If you stood on a craft, out on the bay, you would see this place as such." Judging from the increasing curve of his shoulders and the stiff set of his jaw, aboard a craft out on the bay was exactly where he wished Tsecha was at that moment.

Tsecha stepped close to the wall. "It does not look like a cliff."

"It does from here." Jani leaned against the wall directly across from the mural. "I think you need to stand at least five or six meters away for it to all fall into place."

Dathim nodded. "At least five or six meters."

Tsecha took a single step back from the work, shoulders curving in irritation. "It does not help."

"Five or six meters." Jani and Dathim spoke in unison.

Then Dathim took the bull by the horns, or in this case the propitiator by the elbow, and dragged him backward, marking off the distance with measured strides.

"Here." Dathim released his dominant, then stepped back and waited, arms folded, feet planted shoulders' length apart, like a djinn from one of Niall's operas. Tall and broad, dressed in dusty white workclothes that contrasted sharply with his gold-brown Vynshàrau coloring, he seemed a construct of wood and stone, as one with the buildings surrounding them. "Do you see it now?" His voice, a deadpan rival of John's, rumbled like a seismic shift.

Tsecha stared at the wall, tilting his head to one side, then the other. "I am not sure. Perhaps, nìa, we should request Doctor Parini's assistance?"

Jani shrugged. "John's the art collector. He knows more."

"But John has already seen this wall many times. Doctor Parini provides a fresh eye." Tsecha looked back over his shoulder at Jani and bared his teeth.

Fresh eye, my . . . Jani had to smile back. "You didn't ask me here to talk about the wall. I should have guessed."

"It will not be completed in time for tomorrow's meeting. Such is as it is." Dathim picked up a square of tile with a glaze like the clear aquamarine of shallow water and walked to his worktable. "I thus have time to seek out the opinions of others." He inserted the square into one of his array of tile cutters, then bent low over the device and adjusted the settings. "Others, who know more," he added, not quite under his breath.

Tsecha ignored his suborn's mutterings. He clasped his hands behind his back and walked over to Jani, light mood dissipating with each step. "Of what did Doctor Parini speak? The damned cold of Chicago? His boredom now that his friends have left him?" He paced back and forth in front of her, an older, wiser, more patient djinn.

"Li Cao sent Val here to inform John that he's being bought out. John's opinion on the subject is not being considered. He'll be paid two percent of what his share in Neo-clona is worth." Jani remembered Lucien as he broke the news. Drunk, angry, the information he imparted a payback for her rejection. "Val made matters that much worse by bringing Lucien with him." *And I hope he heaved his guts out.*

"Ah, Captain Pascal." Tsecha walked a tight circle. "He grew bored in Chicago as well, without you to torment."

Jani kicked a tile shard across the floor as another scene from the balcony flitted through her brain. *I love you.* Oh, for the days of myth, when djinn walked the land and gods smote liars with thunderbolts. "He says he's here to act as a fresh eye for Admiral General Mako. I don't believe that."

"Nor would I." Tsecha touched Jani's arm, then gestured toward the patio located in the rear of the meeting house. "For Mako despises him. This we know, and truly."

As they entered the patio, the heat hit them full force, untempered by the breeze off the bay. Tsecha inhaled deeply as soon as the sun fell on him, as though he could breathe in the light. "Cao fears John will become an Haárin, and will use his money to support Haárin enclaves, and Haárin companies. That he will rebuild Haárin docks destroyed by humanish bombs. This, I most believe." He sat atop a pallet of floor tile. "Such shows her lack of understanding. John would never be accepted as Haárin. It would be an impossibility."

"Haárin would take his money, though. If he offered it. Which he hasn't." Jani leaned against a stone wall, then slid down to the patio floor. *And so it begins.* The back and forth. The sifting of data until a conclusion could be reached. The hardest process, but in the end, the most educational. *Politics.* The glib, inadequate word that described the many faceted relationship between Commonwealth and worldskein. "Lucien said that John was being made an example. 'If we can destroy one of the most powerful men in the Commonwealth, what could we do to you?'" She slipped off the jacket that she'd donned back at the Main House, then leaned back against the wall and let the heat absorbed by the stone seep into her shoulders. "My concern is that she's heard rumblings about Elyas' desire to secede."

Tsecha shifted as though he sat on a sharp edge of tile. "Talk of colonial secession. I heard such even when I served as ambassador in damned cold Chicago."

"But here we have an actual plot, with names attached." Jani picked at a jacket seam, stopping when she yanked too hard and the material split. "John is so far removed from all that. All he's done since he arrived here is perform research and hybridize the willing." She imagined faces seen every day at the Main House, on the cliff road and the other enclave streets. Eager, hopeful faces. "Some of them will die if he can't treat them anymore, if he can only use the technology he's already developed. We're all moving targets, constantly changing. A treatment that will work on us one day could kill us the next."

Tsecha nodded, an exaggerated up-and-down. "So, he is needed to keep Thalassans alive. Such is an ethical issue. If Li Cao destroys him, she destroys others as well. Innocents." He brightened. "Would you like me to write a treatise on the subject, nìa?"

Jani ignored the question, and instead dreamt of thunderbolts striking far-off prime ministers. "How can she do this? We aren't Commonwealth citizens anymore. We can't vote. Half of us started life as idomeni. It's not—"

"You have not answered my question about the treatise, nìa."

"Let's not do that right away. Your treatises tend to shear off the tops of heads. It's bad enough when you take on idomeni. Your style may backfire with humanish."

"Ah." Tsecha ran his finger across his forehead and bared his teeth. Then he stood and strolled across the patio, eyes fixed on the sunburst murals with which Dathim had covered the floor. "So. John will no longer be able to treat hybrids. The hybrids of Thalassa, whom I esteem greatly, even when my nìa claims I do not." He glanced across at

Jani. "My nìa, whom I also esteem greatly." He stopped and raised a hand, index finger pointing upward. "Li Cao deems this. Tomorrow, we meet with those who work against her. It is most simple. If Markos and his other secessionists wish my support, they will see that John can continue to do that which he does. Even now, they will support him by telling Cao that she cannot do that which she plans."

Jani worked to her feet. "They'd be taking a risk."

"They take risks now." Tsecha shrugged. "One more will not make their chance of death any greater. They must agree to support Thalassa, which means that they must work now to help John. Or they may swing."

"Swing?"

Tsecha mimed looping a rope and putting it around his neck. "Swing." He yanked his arm upward and stuck out his tongue.

"Thank you for that visual." Jani managed a laugh. "Can you give John your support even if Markos and the others can't? Can the Elyan Haárin do anything to compel Li Cao to back down?"

Tsecha raised a hand to chest level, then curved it in question. "She would demand, I think, that the Haárin leave the Outer Circle, which is something that would most please Cèel as well. He starves his colonies, allows them no supply or repair. Samvasta, Nèae, Zela, with their broken Gate-Ways and half-empty enclaves. He drives the Haárin who live there to the humanish, and now Li Cao would drive them back to him."

"What if you pledged to sink your teeth deeper? Take over more businesses, more docks?" Jani sighed. "That might scare her, which will cause more problems than it solves." She tied the sleeves of the jacket around her waist, then walked to the entry that led back into the house proper, boots scuffing against the inlay with a sound like sandpaper. "God, this is a mess."

"We will think of something, nìa." Tsecha moved in beside her, his soft boots silent on the stone.

"Why do we have to?" Jani paused at the entry. "Ná Feyó is your secular dominant. Ná Gisa is mine. Technically. When she sticks her head out of whichever greenhouse she's working in long enough to give me the time of day."

Tsecha regarded her calmly, as though they discussed the weather, not political subterfuge and rebellion. "I most esteem Feyó, but she worries too much of authority, and the opinions of the other enclaves. Power has made her cautious, and this is, I most believe, a time to be daring."

Jani leaned against the entry so that she stood half in and half out of the house, one side in shade, the other in sun. "You want daring, you should bring Gisa with you to tomorrow's meeting."

"Nìa."

"OK, she's irritating, but she merits some regard. She helped create Thalassa."

"She did that of which she was capable. Now her time is past." Tsecha stood in the comparative darkness of the entry. "Rebellion requires focus if it is to be worth anything, and Gisa lacks focus." He leaned forward, the edges of sunlight striking him, highlighting the lines on his face. "If you say black, she will argue white simply to argue. Such is not an attitude that is needed. Not now."

"So you and I can continue to do all the diplomatic dirty work, then hand off all the pretty decisions to our dominants, wrapped up and ready to go."

Tsecha nodded. "Yes. Such is what we do." He reached out and tapped the top of her hand with his fingertips. "As we did in Rauta Shèràa, and in Chicago. As we will always do."

"Something to look forward to." Jani reached up and struck her fist against the top of the doorway as she passed through into the cool of the entry. "Any feedback yet on your latest broadside?"

Tsecha hesitated, hand once more curving in question. Then he bared his teeth. "Wholeness of Soul." He walked farther into the meeting room, stopping to study the floor, a room-spanning blue and white whirlpool. "It is too soon. I would not expect even an acknowledgment of receipt until tomorrow or even the next day." He dragged the toe of his boot along one of the blue-white borders. "Does it still worry you?"

"Everything worries me." Jani lowered her voice as two coverall-clad hybrids entered the house and began carrying stacks of tile to the table where Dathim worked. "Niall doesn't think it will be a problem."

"Colonel Pierce." Tsecha offered a more humanish-looking, close-lipped smile. "To whom you tell everything."

"Not really." Jani felt the heat rise up her neck as she thought of all the things she would never think of telling Niall. "I tell you more than I do anyone. Including some things I hope you don't understand."

Tsecha did a decent imitation of a humanish throat-clearing. "I understand more than you believe, nìa."

"Great." Jani covered her eyes, then let her hands fall. "All my idiocies exposed." She felt more welcome laughter bubble up, until an all-too-familiar figure entered the room and stopped it dead. "Ná Meva."

"Ná Kièrshia. Glories of the day." Ná Meva Tan bustled in, a headmistress on a mission, the long tail of her bright green wrapshirt flaring in her wake. "Ní Tsecha. Glories of the day to you as well." Her grey-streaked horsetail swung out as she spun around to survey the entry. "More than yesterday, but not yet complete, ní Dathim!"

"Everyone is a critic." Dathim turned to face them. "But I see no one picking up a cutter." Tile dust streaked his face like paint. "Until they do, they can shut up." He gestured to one of his hybrid helpers to bring another stack of tile, then turned back to his table.

"Hah." Meva bared her teeth as the hum of the tile cutter filled the room. "Ní Dathim is as he always is."

Aren't we all? Jani stepped back as Meva and Tsecha fell into a discussion of the patterns Dathim had chosen for the meeting house floors. Meva stood as tall as her religious dominant, her face as stark, her eyes as gold. Like Tsecha, she projected implacability, the inevitable progression of a wave. Rauta Shèràa Temple had cast her out just before Morden nìRau Cèel locked her up, and Tsecha had offered her a place without first confirming with ná Feyó that such would be acceptable. *Meva treads on toes.* Such was her way. *I do like her . . . for the most part.* But she provided Tsecha the opportunity for theological debate that he had lacked for years, and like a desert plant after the first rain of the season, he had flourished.

Then came the first treatise. The second. *And now this one.* The rhetoric escalating as the subject matter cut closer and closer to the heart of what it meant to be idomeni.

"The significance of this—" Meva gestured toward the spiraling whirlpool, then turned to Jani. "You recall such, from your instruction?"

Damn. Jani left the refuge of her corner and joined the two elders near the middle of the floor. "The twinned spiral." She racked her brain. "Blue for water, white for air. The connectedness of life elements, separate yet united, traveling in the same direction until oneness is achieved." She glanced at Tsecha, who continued to study the floor. At Rauta Shèràa Academy, students could find themselves subjected to testing at any time, and as one of the past masters of that particular art, he would see no reason to interrupt what he saw as valid examination.

Meva nodded. "Shiou oversees this progression, of course, for she is of order."

"No." Jani bit back the word *inshah.* Teacher. That title, she reserved for one and one only. "The progression is overseen by Anèth, the guardian of passage, migration, transition—"

"He is body-son of Caith."

"No, he—" Jani caught Tsecha's flinch, and knew she'd failed this particular test the instant before Meva bared her teeth and let out a derisive bark of laughter.

"Anèth *is* body-son of Caith, for chaos and transition are

also separate but united. In any transition is the potential for chaotic progression." Meva stepped out to the whirlpool's center and paced around it. "This is a representation of Anèth's guardianship, for the elements remain united to the end. If such represented his relation with Caith, the whorls would diverge along the way, and form eddies, and curve back on themselves. Such as the representation on the secondary floor of Rauta Shèràa Temple—Tsecha, do you recall such?"

"Yes, ná Meva, I recall it most well." Tsecha finally turned to look at Jani, his hands clasped behind his back, his gaze fixed at a point over her left shoulder. The formality of the Academy returned. "The colors of divergence are more similar. Darker gold and lighter, in depiction of the relation of body-mother and body-child. The game of pattern stones evolved from this. The changing patterns represent the interruption of the journey as chaos enters, for the pattern change is unexpected, unbidden." His Vynshàrau Haárin acquired High Vynshàrau inflections as his manner grew more detached. "You should study more, Jani Kilian. You should know this by now."

Words from the past, driven home with the softest yet most direct of blows. "Yes, *inshah*. I will do so." *I will add it to my goddamned list.* She stood up straight, left arm crossed over her chest, a student's posture of respect. Tsecha raised his left hand in dismissal, the barest flick of a finger, before falling in behind Meva and following her into the adjoining room.

So much for that. Jani walked to the door, face aflame. *At least the hybrids are outside.* Otherwise the news of Tsecha's reprimand would have coursed through the enclave by the time she reached the top of the street.

"Ná Meva speaks of you to ní Tsecha."

Jani stopped and turned back to the worktable, where Dathim smoothed the edge of a tile triangle.

"She does not believe you should act as a propitiator." The Haárin's attention remained focused on the cutter, his fingers flicking over the controller. "She does not believe it is that which you are."

Jani shivered as chill anger drove out the heat of embarrassment. *I never spoke against her to him. I knew he esteemed her, and I kept my mouth shut.* Proof once again that no good deed ever went unpunished. "And what does she think I am?"

Dathim shrugged. "She never says." He glanced at her through a haze of white powder. "Ní Tsecha defends you."

Then he stands back and lets Meva test me. And has the doubt she instilled confirmed. "I have to get back to the Main House." Jani hurried into the street, where the sun shone and the air tasted of the sea instead of the chalk of tile dust, the gall of softly spoken words.

The first dream had been simple enough. Half walking, half sliding down a dune in her drop-dead whites, the most formal of the Service dress uniforms, trying to reach the tents, just visible in the distance. The Laumrau tents.

But she never reached them. The slide down the dune never ended, and the tents never drew closer.

"That one's not bad." Jani had heard worse. From Niall. From others, over the years. Seen worse, during a time when her unmonitored hybridization warred with her Service augmentation, and old friends and enemies returned from the dead to say hello.

But she had never dreamed of Knevçet Shèràa. Until these last few weeks . . .

"Stress." Jani perched on the rock formation just outside the Main House's rear entry. "Fear." Worry about Thalassa. *And now this.* She tried to work up the nerve to get up, to go inside and meet John's lawyers. What if she hurt John's case? What if she said the wrong thing?

Hello, my name is Jani Kilian, and I have blood on my hands.

Twenty-six Laumrau, taking sacrament in their tents.

Twenty-six faces. Each so different, yet wearing the same

look of surprise when she raised her shooter and fired.

"I did what I had to." Jani picked up a stone and skipped it across the scrubby ground. "I'd do it again."

She had just gotten used to the everlasting slide down the dune when, last night, a new dream took its place. She wore desertweights this time. Stood at the opening of the first tent. Tried to rip open the flap, only to find that there wasn't one. Kept trying, and kept trying, grabbing for something that wasn't there—

—until she heard the noise behind her, the hum of a shooter in active mode, and knew if she moved, she would die . . .

. . . but that if she stood still, she would die anyway.

"Decisions, decisions." Jani forced a laugh, then fell silent. Then she eased to her feet, walked to the door, and keyed inside.

CHAPTER 7

Jani heard the raised voices as soon as she entered the court-yard. Two daysuited men stood nose-to-nose in the middle of the largest demiroom, while around them other daysuits watched in grim silence. Meanwhile, another group stood in the foyer, three men and two women with handcarts, their attention fixed as well on the escalating argument.

Then a familiar figure moved from the shadow of a planter and hurried toward her.

"Where the hell have you been?" John's voice shook.

"I was with Tsecha." Jani looked past John to the arguing men. "What happened?"

"Officials from Justice arrived fifteen minutes ago with a warrant." John led her back across the courtyard toward the demiroom. "They want everything—records, data. Anything related to research and treatment."

Jani looked toward the group with the handcarts. The *empty* handcarts. "What have they taken?"

"Nothing. Yet." John stuck his clenched fist against his thigh with every stride. "If Quino thinks—"

Quino? As Jani approached, the arguing men fell silent. Then the shorter of the two turned and planted himself in her path.

"Ms. Kilian." He was a small-boned hawk of a man, attired in darkest blue. "I will have to ask you to—"

Quino. "We've met." Jani pressed close, crowding him, forcing him back. "Joaquin Loiaza. You once stood between me and a ComPol arrest warrant. At John's behest, if I recall."

Loiaza stiffened. "Yes, I do remember." He recovered smoothly, his smile a cool, social curve of lip. "Such a long time ago—"

"Less than two years, but I can understand why you might prefer to forget it considering you're now playing for the other team." It was Jani's turn to smile as Loiaza's face darkened. "Explain your presence here."

Loiaza's eyes widened as he took in the full-bore hybrid turnout—the gold-toned skin, the green-on-green eyes. The top of his head barely reached Jani's shoulder, and like most every other man faced with that height difference, he countered by standing as tall as his spinal column would allow and raising his voice. "We are here by the authority of the Commonwealth—"

"Which means nothing to me." Jani paused to breathe, then let the words flow. "This is not an Elyan settlement, Mister Loiaza. This is Thalassa, an autonomous enclave. The Commonwealth has no jurisdiction here." Out of the corner of her eye Jani saw the man with whom Loiaza had argued scrabble in his jacket pocket. He removed a handheld, then turned and started whispering to another man who stood nearby. "As secular suborn to the enclave dominant, ná Gisa Pilon, I am the authority here—"

"Indeed?" Loiaza glanced back at the group behind him, who had broken out the handhelds as well. "I do not recall Thalassa ever having been recognized by the Commonwealth government."

"His Excellency, Stanislaw Markos, Governor of Elyas, has seen fit to recognize our autonomy by treating the Thalassan boundaries as borders, and in other ways. I will leave it to you to explain to him the irrelevancy of that decision." Jani detected the flicker in Loiaza's eyes, and knew she'd scored a hit. *You didn't inform Markos you were coming here, did you? Bad Quino.* Nothing like pissing off your host by invading enclaves and issuing warrants without telling him first. "In any case, there are protocols that should have been followed prior to this . . . invasion, which were not. For example, we did not receive a formal request from the Commonwealth government to speak with Doctor Shroud concerning their wish to speak with him concerning his Neoclona holdings."

"Is this the imperial 'we,' ná Kièrshia? Do you speak for the absent ná Gisa as well, or is the act of obstruction of justice yours alone?" Loiaza's mud-brown eyes had hardened to stone. "No matter. Allow me to formally request now that we be allowed to discuss the matter of divestiture of Neoclona holdings with your suborn—"

"Denied." Jani glanced at the other lawyers. All handhelds had been set aside—she had their undivided attention now. "The conversations that have already occurred will be considered to have never taken place. Any documents or other materials that were taken will be returned to Doctor Shroud immediately. You will depart Thalassa now and reapply formally for permission to speak with him."

Loiaza kicked the last shred of social pretense out the window. "This is ridiculous." His voice emerged as a hiss. "You and your Thalassans are medical mishaps, Kilian, not a sovereign entity."

"We're both, actually, which means that Doctor Shroud's skills as a physician as well as his researches are vital to our continued health and well-being. To deny him the right and ability—not to mention the wherewithal—to practice his profession threatens the lives of all members of this enclave. Innocent members. I think the appropriate term for what might follow if you succeed in your efforts to prevent him from continuing his work is 'humanitarian crisis.'" Jani turned her back on Loiaza and held out her hand to the man with whom he'd argued. "I'm assuming you're one of the good guys? Hello. We haven't met."

The man took her hand lightly, as though he feared a shock. "Rudo Sikara, Ms. Kili—ná Kièrshia." His skin was so black it seemed tinged with blue, the reddened whites of his eyes the only outward betrayal of the current stressful interlude. "This is my colleague, James Cossa." He nodded toward the other man, who was younger, lighter of complexion, and even more battered looking.

Jani hesitated as her backbrain sent out a warning barrage. "Sikara and Cossa. I've heard of you." Her gut tightened. "John said he'd hired an experienced firm. He didn't mention it was the most famous in the Outer Circle."

"I am flattered." Sikara's smile was tight. "I wish we could have met before this. That we could have spoken." His voice matched his smile. "Do you have *any* justification for the claims of sovereignty you've just made?"

"I believe I do." Jani lowered her voice as Loiaza and his team strained to overhear. "Last year, the Commonwealth Service ceased efforts to press charges of treason and desertion against two officers because they had begun the process of hybridization. As hybrids, they were no longer considered eligible for the Service. In the end it was decided that they came under the jurisdiction of the Elyan Haárin dominant, ná Feyó Tal, who at the time was considered Thalassa's secular dominant. Since that time, she has ceded the governance of Thalassa to ná Gisa Pilon."

"That should not necessarily be construed as an acknowledgment of sovereignty," Loiaza's nasal voice sounded. "A colonial base may find itself in a situation where acquiescing to local practice is preferable to pursuing a course of action that might jeopardize its future dealings with the native population."

Jani turned on him, once more forcing him to backpedal. "Li Cao would do well to follow the Fort Karistos example."

"This is not a matter of local interest only," Loiaza bit out. "The decisions reached here will have far-reaching implications."

Jani stared at the man until a small vein in his temple

started to throb. "John's your test case. You'll destroy him to keep the rest of the Commonwealth in line. Think you want to hybridize? Remember what we did to the head of Neoclona, and think again."

"Indeed." Sikara stepped up beside Jani. He wore the simplest of black suits and a white shirt, accented by a yellow and green striped neckpiece. "Nasty precedent, Counselor." He arched one graying eyebrow.

Loiaza licked his lips. "Doctor Shroud is a special case."

"So any decisions reached as a result of this 'special case' will never be cited as precedent in support of any other action against another hybrid?" Cossa proved the more expressive of the two, from his more fashionable brown suit to his continued gesturing as he spoke. "Pull the other one, Quino—it whistles the Commonwealth anthem!"

Silence settled like a layer of ash. Then Loiaza turned to Sikara. "Since we have been evicted pending clarification of Jani Kilian's status as godhead—" He glared at her. "We will return tomorrow, Counselor."

"Pending clarification of Thalassa's status, Counselor." Sikara reactivated his handheld and began jotting. "I, meanwhile, will contact Governor Markos. And ná Feyó Tal as well, whose acquaintance I have enjoyed for several years."

Loiaza started to speak, then closed his mouth and beckoned to the other lawyers. They followed him from the room single file, like nestlings trailing after a pissed-off mother duck, dragging the other Justice Ministry staffers and their empty handcarts along in their wake.

"Well," Sikara said as the door closed. "That took a turn I did not expect." He sat on the U-shaped sofa that dominated the space and regarded Jani with tired eyes. "As I said, it would have been nice if we could have spoken prior to this. You compelled us to reveal aspects of our defense that I wanted to keep close to the vest until we had all the facts."

Jani glanced at John, who perched on the edge of an end table, arms folded, staring at the floor. "What difference does it make whether they know this or not? They did what they did—they can't cover it up. They invaded a sovereign state, and they didn't inform Markos before they tramped through his flower bed to do it. They're in trouble."

"Only if Governor Markos's decision concerning Thalassa's status stands up to challenge." Cossa picked up a long-forgotten glass of iced tea, which dripped condensation on his trousers as he drank. "He serves at Li Cao's pleasure. She can pressure him to change his mind."

"And Feyó can pressure him not to." Jani massaged the base of her neck and felt the knot. "We're a long way from Chicago. The clout flows in both directions out here."

"Li Cao will fight—she has too much to lose." Cossa paused to take a napkin that Sikara thrust at him, and wrapped it around the glass. "If she can destroy John, other humans will be dissuaded from hybridizing by the threat of loss of profession and property." His eyes lit. "I foresee a battle the first time a Family member decides to seek treatment."

"Unfortunately, none of them have yet taken the plunge." Sikara gazed over at John. "That we know of."

"I shouldn't have to remind you, of all people, of the concept of confidentiality." John spoke without raising his head. "It's their secret to keep until they start to show." He worked his fingers as he spoke, like a musician warming up. Then he stilled and fell silent.

When it became obvious that his client had no more to say, Sikara stood. "I have known Quino for years. The best way to handle him is to let him think he's winning from the start. He grows smug, and with that smugness comes complacency. And with that complacency comes the tendency to make mistakes." His expression grew wistful. "Ah well. Still a great deal of room for arrogance." He glanced at Jani. "A great deal." He hefted the briefbag that had rested on the floor at his feet. "In any event, this will be a precedent-setting case."

"To the office!" Cossa slung his briefbag over his shoulder and clapped his hands. "Let's go put on the mud clothes."

"My colleague has such a colorful way of expressing himself." Sikara shook his head with mock gravitas. "John, we will be speaking later." He bowed to Jani. "Ná Kièrshia. We should talk soon." The light in his eye sharpened for an instant, as though *soon* meant *before you speak to anyone else about anything at all*. Then he was gone, and his partner after him.

Jani waited until the men left, until the door closed and the silence settled once more. "I'm sorry I was late." She untied the jacket from around her waist, then walked to the sofa and sat. "I was held up at the meeting house and—"

"Do you know what you're doing?" John's voice emerged like a shudder, cold and deep in the bone. "When you open your mouth, do you have any idea what will fall out? Or are you just making it up as you go?"

Jani stilled. *Is this more of what Val warned me about?* She glanced around the demirooms, the courtyard, on the lookout for a familiar head ducking behind shrubbery. *No wonder he made himself scarce.* "I got them out of here, didn't I? It gave you some room to maneuver." She spread the jacket across her legs and stroked it like a pet. "I believe there's enough precedent to support the concept of our sovereignty—"

"Which reinforces the idea that I'm no longer human enough to run my own goddamned company." John stood, slowly, as though movement pained him. "There's a reason why men like Sikara and Cossa are paid a great deal of money to dig poor bastards like me out of holes. It's because they know what to say and when to say it. They don't just blurt. They don't give the game away."

Jani's hands stalled in mid-stroke. "I'm sorry I upset Mr. Sikara. I will apologize the next time I see—"

"You humiliated Joaquin Loiaza. Do you think he's just going to sit back and take it?" John looked toward the courtyard, where a couple of Thalassans fussed over a flowering shrub and pretended not to be eavesdropping. "We were prepared to give up some things," he continued with lowered voice. "We were prepared to let them think they'd won this round. It made me sick to do it, but I had no choice." He started to pace. "It's a dance. I've led all my life, and now I

have to follow, because the steps are everything and if I put a foot wrong, I lose everything."

Jani looked toward the courtyard, where more Thalassans had gathered. Yes, some carried trays of condiments and others table linens, but set-up for late afternoon sacrament usually didn't begin for another half-hour. *But today, there's a floor show.* "Why didn't you just tell me—"

"I'm telling you now." John stopped in front of her. "I should have told you sooner. That was my mistake, and I will pay for it, assuming I haven't already." He bent closer, mindful of their audience. "Some things are not your job. Some things, you leave to those who know what the hell they're doing. Do you really believe you said anything that Sikara and Cossa didn't already know? They were going to wait until they spoke with Markos and prepared him for the onslaught, until they had everything in place. The concept of Thalassan autonomy is a smoke screen. The idea that someone who decides to hybridize risks losing their livelihood, their life's work . . . " His eyes clouded. "That's the more important point." He bit a thumbnail. That was a new tic, one that the angle of his hand revealed had already claimed the index and middle fingers. "Quino's sharp, but as Sikara said, he makes mistakes. This dramatic raid of his was a mistake. You've given him a chance to recover."

Jani sat back, fighting the invisible weight that pressed down on her shoulders. "They won't have time. This isn't Chicago—they're out of their element here."

"They have what they need. A few Service officers. A few colonial officials. If Stash Markos isn't placed under house arrest by sunset, we'll be very lucky." John laughed, a humorless bark. "Of course, they won't call it that. They'll invent a reason to place him in protective custody. A newly discovered assassination plot, or something."

More Thalassans appeared, and the setup for the afternoon meal that Jani always thought of as "fourses" began in earnest. Her stomach growled as aromas of baking bread and various tangy sauces reached her. The animal, demanding her feeding, even as the higher being's gut twisted and she wished she could crawl in a cave and hide. "But if they took your records—"

"That's the documents examiner in you, fixed on paper." John's voice defrosted, a little. "I do keep copies. And the most important things . . . let's just say they're safe, and leave it at that." He quieted. Then he circled around the sofa and strode to the lift. "I'll be downstairs, working. While I still have work to do, and time in which to do it." He nodded curtly to the few Thalassans who offered greetings. Waited by the lift for a few moments, then struck the wall with the flat of his hand and headed for the stairs.

Jani lay back her head and closed her eyes. The hum of courtyard conversation, the clatter of plates and the beeps of cookers, formed a pleasant background noise. Enough to clear her racing mind and quiet her rumbling stomach, purge Meva's laugh and Tsecha's dismissal and John's doubt. But not lulling enough to bring sleep. That escape route had closed to her, provided no respite at all. Instead, she just breathed slowly, in and out, and tried not to think of what tomorrow's meeting might bring.

"Where did you get this ham?"

Jani opened one eye to find Val standing in front of her, holding a filled plate.

"It can't be Virginia, can it? I didn't think Earth would trade with you." He sat on the edge of the low table and plucked strips of baked ham from a pile that included sliced hybrid mango and bean salad.

"It's Hortensian, I think." Jani forced open the other eye and sat up. "Glad you like it." She watched Val shovel in food with the focused abandon of a starving teenager. "Should you be here, considering?"

Val stopped his fork halfway to his mouth, then lowered it. "I begged your excellent Mister Brondt to let me layover. He found me a room, and I showered. Took a nap. Pretended I was at a resort, far away from everything, waiting for the love of my life to show up." He tried another bite of ham, then set his plate on the table. "I have a reservation at some place in Karistos, but as soon as I'd show up, Quino would lock me down. I'd be a prisoner. Who needs that shit? I hid as soon as I saw the skimmers in the driveway." He sighed. "I wanted to see John. I wanted to at least try to make it . . . not seem so . . . "

"Horrible?" Jani leaned forward, hands clenched between her knees to keep from reaching out for Val's neck. "Rotten? Insert your adjective of choice here. If you run out of English, there's Elyan Greek, my Acadian French—"

"All right." Val pressed his hands to his temples, then locked his fingers behind his neck. "How is he?"

"How do you think?" Jani forced a smile at two Thalassans who wandered past. "He went downstairs to work."

"That's John for you. It was the same at Rauta Shèràa. 'John, that last bomb hit right next door!' 'It missed us? Great! Time enough for one more assay.'" Val laughed, a sound softened by memory. "Sikara and Cossa." His brow arched. "John picked the right man. Rudo hates Quino's guts." His eyes closed halfway as he accessed long-buried gossip. "Fight over a girl, back in the Pleistocene. Don't know who won. Can't have been over Quino's wife. He wouldn't cross the street for her." He sniffed, then grinned, one marriage dissected and all was right with the world. "So what happened? With Quino and that?"

"It went—" Jani stopped, then studied Val's handsome face. Close enough to reach out and touch, yet so far, far away. "They came for some documents. Both sides worked it out."

"But didn't Rudo—?" Val's brow furrowed. Then his face reddened. "Oh." He looked toward the courtyard, where fourses had hit its stride, a hundred different conversations bouncing off every hard surface. "I guess—" He coughed. "Yeah." He braced his hands on the table's edge, then pushed to his feet and grabbed his plate. "I have to go." He didn't look back as he maneuvered around the planters and the maze of tables and vanished into the shadows.

Well, I finally kept my mouth shut. "And that didn't help, either." Jani girded herself, then rose and walked into the midst of the mealtime melee. Filled a plate and found a seat away from everyone, the transient on the run, with no time to talk.

Then she went to the library. Dragged a favorite chair out onto the balcony. Found a recording board and a stylus and made notes for the next day's meeting.

CHAPTER 8

Jani wandered upstairs eventually, after the Main House had gone dark but for the graveyard crew. A determinedly nonchalant question to the night nurse awarded her the news that John had retired an hour earlier. Now she stood before the door to their suite, hand on the control, and pondered. *He should be asleep by now.* Years of hospital training had left him a light sleeper, but if she undressed in the sitting room and slept on the couch . . .

The door whispered open and she crept inside. Stepped inside the bedroom just long enough to pull a T-shirt out of her armoire, and stilled when she heard the rustle of bedclothes, the voice.

"Where've you been?"

Jani activated a table lamp, since there was no longer any reason to risk her shins in collision with the furniture. "Library."

"I should've guessed." John worked into a sitting position and activated the bedside light. "I ran into Val in the clinic. He was wandering around, trying to make himself useful. He sounded quite hurt. Said you'd given him the boot."

"He asked what had happened with Quino. I didn't tell him." Jani boosted atop the low dresser. Under normal circumstances, she would have sat at the foot of the bed, then edged closer toward the inevitable, but normal was a day ago. A lifetime ago. "I was practicing keeping my mouth shut."

John hung his head. "I'm sorry for that."

Jani smoothed the T-shirt over her knees, stretching out creases. "I can't do anything. I can't make it stop. Every time I open my mouth, I say the wrong thing. Every time I don't open my mouth . . . same difference." She folded the shirt in half lengthwise, then rolled it from the bottom up into a tight tube. When she finished, she stared at it. In another life she'd have tossed it in her duffel and continued packing, but she wasn't going anywhere. Now when things got tough, she had to stay put. "Every time I do something, it's exactly the thing you don't want done."

John's head snapped up. *"I don't need you to do anything."* He flinched as his own volume battered him, then sagged against the headboard. "I just need you to be there. It means a great deal. To be able to look across a table, across a room, and see you." His face lightened in grim wonder. "I can't recall ever feeling so alone. Even in Rauta Shèràa, after you left the first time. The way I felt then was nothing like the way I felt this afternoon. It hit me like a broadside that I was going to lose it. All of it. That Val would do what he could, but in the end he'd save the company . . . even if that meant shunting me aside." His eyes widened, flashing silver in the half-light.

"He wouldn't have . . ." Jani hesitated. Then she shook out the T-shirt and started rolling it anew.

"Even you doubt him." John looked around the room as though searching for something. Then he fixed on her, waiting until her gaze met his. "This year has been the best of my life. I worked. I changed. I learned so much." A bare hint of a smile. "And you were always there, somewhere. Not side by side with me every moment, but still. Always together, working toward the same goal. It was the way Rauta Shèràa should have been. The way my entire life should have—"

His voice cracked, and he smoothed his hands over the sheet again and again.

"You think I'll leave you if you lose Neoclona?" Jani looked around the bedroom and saw . . . a room. It possessed a beautiful view and held all she had never wanted or needed, and yet . . . *You leave rooms. You close doors, and never open them again.* They were places you passed through, not places you remained. "I once lived out of a Guernsey Station storage closet for two months. I'm adaptable."

"I'm not. Not anymore." John pushed a hand through his hair, the wheaten strands capturing all available illumination and holding it like a miser. "I won't be the same, after they take it away."

Jani set the shirt aside and slid off the dresser. "You'll be what you've always been." She approached the bed slowly, ready to veer toward a nearby chair at the first hint of rejection. "You were a controlling, arrogant, brilliant, driven pain in the ass in Rauta Shèràa. Before you'd built your empire. Before anyone had heard of Neoclona." She paused at the footboard. "You're still controlling, still arrogant, still driven. Still brilliant. Still a pain. In these essentials, you will never change. You'll take what's available and remake it as you always have. You are what you've always been, and will continue to be whilst you breathe."

John managed a grin. "That sounds like something your father would say."

"He does." Jani lowered to the edge of the bed, just within arm's reach. "Mostly to my mother."

"A handful, is she?" John pushed down the sheet, then pulled up his legs so he sat cross-legged. "He and I should get together sometime and compare notes on the Kilian women. I think he'd talk to me. He seems to like me a little more than does your mother." His brow twitched. "Brilliant?"

Jani rolled her eyes. "I thought you'd pick that out of the list first."

"But also controlling, arrogant, driven, and a pain in the ass." John wiped a hand over his face. The first hint of beard glinted across his cheeks, combining with ruffled hair and skewed T-shirt to make him appear agreeably rumpled. "And yet you love me anyway."

"I've been told more than once that I possess my own endearing qualities." Jani shrugged. "One of the reasons we're together is because we can't find anyone else who'll put up with us." She looked over at John, to find him staring her down, lips slightly parted.

"We could've found worse places to land." He reached out and grabbed her by the shoulders, pulling her to him, applying rough kisses to her face and neck and lower still as he peeled away first her clothes, then his. He drove into her almost immediately, going off on his own for most of the journey, not waiting for her to catch up. Too intent this time on finding solace to offer any.

Jani held him until he finished, and cradled him as he slept. So much simpler, sex, even though it only served to delay. Even though it was only half the song, the melody sans the words. But she'd settle for half, accept it and never argue. For her, the words had always been the difficult part.

All was still and quiet, but for John's breathing and the tumult in her own head. She slept eventually.

And she dreamed.

The sunrise horizon glowed orange as Rilas parked her skimmer behind a rock formation, then gathered dried scrub and branches and spread them across it, obscuring it further. Even the smallest risk could not be allowed, for there were dangers enough at times such as this, when the moment had come to act. When the planning ended and the action began.

Once she had hidden the skimmer, she uttered a prayer to Caith and strode to the house. Her slingbag hung from her shoulder, bumping her hip with every stride. Animals fled before her, scuttling beneath rocks as she passed.

The dawn air felt cool, which she did not expect. So much did this place resemble Rauta Shèràa that she anticipated

the same warmth, longed for it. *Soon.* Soon her task would
be completed, and she would be free to leave this godless
world. Her berths had been purchased, as had her new name,
her new possessions. All rested in a locker at Elyas Station,
assembled in pieces by those who did not know that which
they did, and left in their hiding place by another. So eager,
humanish and idomeni both, to perform tasks for payment.
So disinterested, humanish and idomeni both, in the reasons
for that which they did.

*Such is the way of humanish, which the idomeni have
taken as theirs.* So said nìRau Cèel, who knew all there was
to know of these matters.

Rilas surveyed the area around the house, both visually
and with a handheld scanner. She compared the signaling to
that she had compiled on the day she first visited the place,
took note of the minor variations. More small animals had
entered and departed, leaving their food remnants and their
waste. Leaves had blown in through one of the broken windows, piling in one corner of the area she had chosen for
staging. *But no being has entered.* The inevitable disturbances created by a large form walking through a rubble-
strewn, dusty space did not reveal themselves. Since the day
she first examined this house, no one else had visited.

She walked through the shattered entry, then across the
rubble-strewn room to the window. Took one last look at the
grounds, the distant cliffs and the sliver of bay beyond. Then
lowered her slingbag to the floor and knelt beside it. Opened
the flap and set to work, hands moving with speed born of
practice as her mind pondered the details of the task ahead.

She removed the pieces of the rifle strut, assembled it and
balanced it atop the sill. Assembled the rifle itself. Activated
the sight mech, then tossed its satellite into the air to find
its way to the area above the target. Removed one of the
cylinders from its chill encasement and inserted it into the
chamber. Locked it within.

She eased into a half-sitting, half-reclining position atop
the wide sill, edging onto her side so she could lie beside the

rifle. Brought it close and curled around it. Felt the sharp
chill of the rocks through her thin clothing, the edges like
blades digging into her skin, and offered the pain to Caith as
sacrifice, as always.

Pressed the rifle to her shoulder and lowered her eye to
the sight mech. Waited for the secondary to activate, cali-
brate, and send back the first of the signals.

Nothing for a time but blurred images of portions of the
house yard. Then came color. Clarity. The image of the distant road. The houses that lined it. The meeting house around
which workers had gathered and commenced their labors.

Rilas settled in. She was at her most vulnerable now, this
she knew and truly, so fixed on her target that she could miss
any warning signal from her secondary. *But such is as it is.*
Such risk was the tribute she paid Tsecha, the fact that at
some point she left herself as open, as exposed, as he was.

She breathed the fetid air, let it fill her, became one with
the blasted house.

Watched.

Waited.

CHAPTER 9

"Are you worried, nìa?"

Jani looked back over her shoulder at Tsecha. He stood in the middle of the meeting room, hands clasped before him like a headmaster greeting the first class of the term. He wore a tunic and trousers in shades of tan and off-white, topped off by his propitiator's overrobe. The garment's red-slashed sleeves proved the brightest thing in the room, drawing Jani's eye despite her growing nervousness. She tried to recall the last time she'd seen Tsecha wear it. Weeks, possibly months.

Dressed to kill. "I'm waiting for Markos. John and his lawyers think that Li Cao could have him arrested." Jani turned back to the window, which overlooked the street at the point where it angled down toward the beach, on the watch for a flash of reflected sun off a skimmer chassis.

"I would have something to say about that, I think." Tsecha drew up beside her. "I have heard that he did leave his house near to sunrise."

Let's hear it for the Elyan Haárin spy network. "Then he should have been here an hour ago." Jani gripped the window ledge, massaging the rough stone with her thumb until the pain stopped her. "Even if he took the roundabout route and came in from the south, the trip would take an hour, tops." She yawned, then rubbed grainy eyes. John had slept through the night, but she hadn't quite managed. *New dreams for old.* But in this one, the shooter fired.

"Nìa." Tsecha tapped her shoulder. "I see a skimmer."

Jani ran out of the room and through the entry, pausing in the doorway just as the dark blue double-length drifted to a stop a few doors down from the meeting house. Reached beneath her shirt-jacket and undid the clasp of her shooter holster, just in case.

The skimmer's passenger side gullwing swung upward, and Governor Stanislaw Markos emerged into the morning. He looked down the street in the direction he'd come, as if he feared he'd been followed. Then he turned to Jani and blew out a long breath. "Jesus Christ." He seemed at first glance the sort of man one saw on Family fringes, a door opener and holder of the coats, all slicked silver hair and expensive tailoring. But he was Phillipan by birth and colonial to the core, and his lack of affection for Chicago had blossomed over the years into mutual enmity.

"Good morning, Excellency." Jani adjusted her shirt to hide the shooter holster, then walked out into the street. "You look like you've had an interesting morning."

"It was a near thing." Markos's voice emerged guttural, raked by anger and more than a little fear. "Two officials from the Justice annex visited me last night. 'A plot to overthrow your government,' they said. 'You must remain in your home, under guard.' Bullshit. The only plots those idiots know of are those they hatch themselves." He smoothed the front of his cream daysuit and eyed Jani expectantly.

"I think it has to do with John." Jani tried to see who else sat inside the skimmer, but Markos's bulk blocked her view. "And the concept of Thalassan sovereignty."

A corner of Markos's mouth twitched. "I wondered when that would come back to bite me." Then he smiled. "Thank God for friends in high places." He smacked the skimmer roof, and the rear door of the double-length opened. "Come out, Zhenya. We're the first ones here."

The man who emerged paused to stretch, then muttered something to Markos in Elyan Greek that made them both laugh. He stood shorter than average and stockier than was fashionable. His hair had been trimmed in a haphazard bowl that accentuated his broad face, its blond more an absence of color than a brilliant statement, dull as it was and streaked with grey. He wore a loose-fitting outfit in off-white, some new style of tunic and trousers with an open collar and tucks and seaming that betrayed the presence of ventilation panels.

Yevgeny Scriabin. Deputy Commerce minister, and the greatest threat in a decade to Li Cao's hammerlock on the prime ministry. Jani watched him approach, her trepidation an undercurrent, like the first rumblings of food poisoning. *Anais Ulanova's nephew.* The *S* in the Commonwealth-spanning NUVA-SCAN business conglomerate. *Not the sort I'd turn to at a time like this.* "Your Excellency." She extended her hand as he closed in.

"Ná Kièrshia." Scriabin's hand enveloped hers. "I hope that's the correct appellation. I tore through every idomeni language guide I could put my hands on, but didn't find much that proved helpful." His voice was a rough baritone, his accent a mélange of Michigan Provincial seasoned with Old Russian. "Finally, I broke down and asked my driver. He proved surprisingly helpful."

Jani looked past Scriabin to the skimmer just as his helpful driver emerged.

"Mornin', gel!" Niall smoothed the front of his dress desertweight tunic, then set his brimmed lid. "Not used to all this subterfuge and evasive maneuvering so early in the morning. Felt like I was sixteen again, running the White Line in the Wodonga Mountains."

Markos laughed. "A Victorian boy, are you, Colonel?"

"Born and bred, Your Excellency." Niall circled around the vehicle toward them, eyes bright with the thrill of the chase. "Shaped and baked to a crusty turn."

Scriabin cocked his head. "The white line?"

Niall slowed. "The White River, Your Excellency," he

piped a bit too brightly. "Loops around the northern half of the city of Wodonga. My school chums and I enjoyed many a summer rafting trip." His grin at Jani held a touch of friendly malice. "You look surprised to see me." He herded her into the doorway, leaving Scriabin and Markos standing by the skimmer.

"Rafting with school chums." Jani kept her eye on the two officials, who leaned against the skimmer and waited for the other governors. "Make that running stolen goods from the Wodonga shuttleport to where the hell ever."

"We used rafts sometimes." Niall pulled out his case and plucked out a 'stick. "When the jungle got too dense and the skimtrucks couldn't hold the track." He cracked the tip and took a long pull as he slumped against the polished stone. "I know enough about John to fill in the rest. Cao wants him out at Neoclona. I'm surprised it took her this long. What's Parini's role?"

"Stunned bystander." Jani stifled another yawn. "They let him come here to inform John only after the legal surgery had already started. Now he's hiding out in the Main House, trying to pretend he's just visiting and not having much luck."

"If he fights to defend John, he's out, and Cao hands the whole Easter egg over to Eamon DeVries, third in line and incipient gutter sot." Niall sneered, his scarred lip curling to reveal a pointed canine. "Here's your choice, boy. We destroy you a little or we destroy you a lot." Another pull, a drift of smoke. "Smuggling was cleaner. When you overstepped, they just shot you."

"Who shoots, Colonel?" Tsecha poked his head between them and bared his teeth.

"Figure of speech, ní Tsecha." Niall pulled the 'stick from his mouth and hid it cradled in his hand like a schoolboy caught out during recess.

"*Hah.*" Tsecha turned and vanished back into the comparative dark of the meeting house. "Smoke your nicstick, Colonel, before you choke."

"Dammit." Niall stuck the 'stick back in his mouth, then examined his palm for burns. "Look, gel, I know Markos isn't here just to admire ní Dathim's tilework. I've been here for nigh on six months, and I'm not fuckin' blind. Or deaf." He took one last drag, then tossed the spent 'stick into a nearby planter. "I am, in point of fact, the Service representative at this little discussion, as ordered by Admiral General Hiroshi Mako himself."

It's too early in the morning and I'm too tired to be surprised. Jani looked out toward the street, where another skimmer had joined the governor's. "Any danger of Lucien turning up?"

"He's blogged down with transfer paperwork," Niall said as he headed toward the skimmers. "Should keep him busy for the day."

Scriabin hurried to the new skimmer just as the passenger gullwing drifted upward. "You finally made it."

Jani heard an all-too-familiar voice emerge from the vehicle and froze.

"—not since Rauta Shèràa, when we all feared for our lives every moment." Exterior Minister Anais Ulanova, dressed in cool blue, as ever the elegant hatchet, disembarked the skimmer and immediately latched onto her nephew's arm. "Zhenya, you left Karistos too quickly. We lost you—" She stopped when she saw Jani, mouth stalled in mid-word as though caught in the midst of a scream.

Jani heard Niall emit a low, tuneless whistle.

"Tyotya Ani." Scriabin patted his aunt's hand. "I believe you and ná Kièrshia know one another."

Jani bowed as low as her sensibility allowed, which wasn't much. "Excellency."

Anais Ulanova said nothing, even when her nephew touched her arm and spoke in her ear. She simply stared, eyes dark as space and just as cold.

"Minister Ulanova." Tsecha glared Sìah daggers over the top of Ulanova's head at her nephew. "Minister Scriabin should have informed us."

"Ní Tsecha." If Ulanova noticed the tension in Tsecha's manner, she ignored it. "I trust my nephew implicitly, of course, but given the sensitive nature of this discussion, we felt that the presence of a first-level minister would lend more credence to any agreement reached."

"I know what you're thinking," Niall said as he joined Jani at one end of the long table.

"If you did, you wouldn't sit next to me." Jani continued to watch Ulanova, who still hung onto Scriabin's arm then laughed too loudly at something Tsecha said. "Who was the genius who pulled her into this?"

They had adjourned to the largest meeting room, which opened out onto a small garden complete with bubbling fountain. Jani concentrated on the trickling burble in the hope that the sound would calm her, and knew from the roil in her gut that she hoped in vain.

"She's been Exterior Minister for a long time." Niall lowered his voice as the governors from Amsun and Hortensia, Avelos and Wallach, took seats nearby. "She does know the lay of the land out here."

"The first hint of trouble, she'll sell you out to Cao."

"Not as long as her nephew's involved. He's our insurance. If he falls, she tumbles with him."

Ulanova took a seat near the head of the table, next to Scriabin. Since the initial shock of recognition, she had ignored Jani, and seemed determined to carry that standard throughout the balance of the meeting. She greeted Avelos and Wallach like the old friends they likely were, and complimented Markos's neckpiece before directing her attention to the recording board set before her by an aide.

"Looks like I don't rate a personal greeting." Niall sniffed. "I'm crushed."

"That's what you get for sitting next to me." Jani pulled a folded sheet of parchment from the inner pocket of her shirt-jacket and spread it flat on the table. "Feel free to move if you'd rather sit with the popular kids."

"Nah. I've always been a back-of-the-room type." Niall

grinned, the expression altering to a formal smile when Avelos pointed at him.

"So, your Mako's hip-deep in anti-Cao factionitis." Avelos was an angular woman with a voice to match, the light bouncing off her lofty cheekbones and casting deep shadows under her eyes. "Doesn't surprise me—those two never got on. They've been trying to cut one another off at the knees for years."

Niall shook his head. "It's much deeper than that, Your Excellency. There's a fundamental difference in how we view the state of the Commonwealth and her relations with the worldskein. With her colonies."

"The Service is stretched to the brink out here." Wallach, a skinny whip of a man with an unfashionable receding hairline, doodled in the margins of his recording board display. "No one's gotten to the bottom of the dock attacks, and Cèel is threatening to call the Haárin back into the worldskein if any more of their facilities are hit."

"Cèel can call all he wishes." Tsecha had seated himself at the head of the table, hands clasped lightly in front of him, no note-taking device to be seen. "The Haárin will not go."

"Then he'll send his warrior skein to come and get them." Wallach shook his head as a series of interlaced loops appeared on his board. "And who will save our sorry asses from a colonial version of the Night of the Blade?" He glanced across the table at Niall, then resumed his doodling.

"I thank you for raising the subject of defense, Your Excellency." Niall adopted his instructor's voice, world-weary and wise. "His Excellency Minister Scriabin and I, along with those we represent, are also examining this matter from that point of view." He stifled a cough. "Six Common months ago, I was charged with the task of evaluating the situation at Fort Karistos. Over the last two weeks, I have collated my findings. I've concluded that thanks to years of neglect by Chicago, the Service personnel stationed there have evolved in sensibility to the point that they feel more loyalty to their base colony and the mixture of races surrounding it than to their nominal homeworld."

"It's taken you long enough to figure it out." Jani paused as another yawn threatened. *Not now, dammit.* "It's been that way out here for a generation, at least."

Niall nodded agreement. "The decision we're faced with is, do we clean the place out, restaff it with more traditionally loyal forces we can't spare, and alienate the local populations?" He took a stylus from the holder in the middle of the table and rolled it between his fingers. "Or do we work with the situation as it stands, maybe even help it to . . . evolve, then concentrate on developing a close relationship with whoever happens to wind up in charge."

Avelos and Wallach stared across the table at one another, while Markos folded his arms and nodded. "The Service supports secession."

Niall glanced downtable at Scriabin, who nodded almost imperceptibly. "The Outer Circle would remain allied with the Commonwealth—that would be one of the conditions of the separation. But the colonial governments would be granted their autonomy. The forces stationed both here and at Amsun Base would be theirs, to command as they would. To man as they would, be it with humans"—he gestured toward Jani—"hybrids . . . even Haárin." He spoke slowly, his Victorian twang all but buried in careful intonation. "All indications are that Cèel and his Vynshàrau will face a challenge from the Pathen by year's end. Aden nìRau Wuntoi, the Pathen dominant, is ready—he has Oà and Sìah backing, and would be anyone's first pick to assume the Oligarchy. The Pathen and Sìah Haárin are well settled here in the Circle, and we want them on our side *now*. We want friendlies in place so if Rauta Shèràa implodes and civil war spreads throughout the worldskein, our border colonies don't get chewed up in the process." He placed the stylus back in its holder, then worked off his nerves by flexing his fingers. "One war at a time. We can't fight to keep the Outer Circle in check and at the same time take on whatever Cèel throws at us. For that reason, we don't want to risk losing the support of either the resident humans or the Haárin. Or any combination thereof."

Jani made to speak, then paused and pressed her fingertips to the middle of her forehead. She could feel the tightening, and knew it would only get worse. Tracking the Thalassan ball through the diplomatic maze had that effect on her. "You would support the Pathen alliance against the Vynshàrau, knowing Cèel would see this as a threat to his authority, maybe even an act of war." She waited for Niall to nod. He didn't. He didn't look at her, either, which made the sweat bloom along her back. "You'd commit Service troops to this?"

Scriabin nodded. "Yes."

"Troops that you and Mako have no right to commit?" Jani recalled Niall's words during one long ago lunch. *Do you believe in ghosts?* Maybe the bigger question was, did the ghosts believe in you? "The Service taking sides in an idomeni civil war. Am I the only one who's seeing history gearing up for an encore performance here?"

"It would be different this time." Niall's lips barely moved, as though he feared to say the words aloud.

"You, of all people, can sit there and say that to me? We're Exhibits A and B, for crying out—" Jani stopped when she felt the stares from the rest of the table. Took a deep breath. "What happens," she finally said, "when Cao figures out that you're snaking her?"

"She's preoccupied with the upcoming election." Niall sat forward, braced his elbows on the table's edge and gestured toward his ally. "Yevgeny's going to clean her out. He's playing Cao even in most polls, and all his numbers are trending up. In between now and then, we just need to keep Cao out of the loop."

"Thank you for the vote of confidence, Niall, but I take ná Kièrshia's point." Scriabin ignored his aunt's irritated muttering. "The number of like minds on Cabinet Row is significant, and most are not seen to be supporters of mine. Even if I should lose the election—and despite what the good colonel says, odds that I win are even at best—I feel that there will be sufficient push in place to ram the secession bill through."

"Many a slip twixt cup and lip," said Wallach, the resident realist.

"The word's treason." Jani looked around the table, and saw that even Ulanova had grown thoughtful. "Much as I care for some of you, my concerns are other. If Mako gets rousted out of bed in the middle of the night and disappears into some Cabinet Row cellar with the rest of his buddies, what happens to Thalassa? If it becomes known that I aided and abetted a treasonous cause, and with John Shroud stripped of all influence and ability to pull strings due to his expulsion from Neoclona, what happens?" She took note of the lack of surprise at that particular bit of news. *Great Ganesh—did everyone know it was coming but us?* "You'll all be arrested." She clenched a fist and tapped the table. "Meanwhile, Fort Karistos will be restocked with hardcore Earthbound. Thalassans would be split into Haárin or humanish regardless of their level of hybridization—the Haárin would be shipped back to their former enclaves, and the humanish would be jailed. Without medical care, some of them would die. The ones who didn't could be exiled or executed, rejected by their families, or simply stoned in the street like lepers. Thalassa isn't just the only home they have. For some, it's the only home they *can* have."

Scriabin studied Jani for a long moment, then glanced sidelong at Tsecha. "What does Thalassa want?"

"I think the more important question is, why should we care?" Ulanova didn't look at Jani but instead concentrated on her hands, running a fingertip over the edge of one scarlet talon. "What can they offer that makes sustaining them worth the effort?" The single word reply, *Nothing*, hung unspoken in the air.

Jani stared down at her single page of notes. Despite the hours spent on the library balcony, she'd sketched out only a few words, arranged in a list, written in a mongrel Acadian French-Vynshàrau scrawl that no one could read but she. Then she glanced at Tsecha, who studied her in turn with narrowed eyes. *So, nìa?* his look said. Academy examination, but on a different scale, the results the altering of lives rather than student assessments. *Teacher and student, in the class that never ends.* She bit back a nervous laugh, and began.

"Thalassa's bargaining power is that it's the chosen home of a male who is acknowledged to possess one of the foremost medical minds in a generation." Jani traced the first word on the list. *John.* "With some initial support, and a base from which to operate, he can continue to provide the area with a level of economic stability that it otherwise wouldn't possess."

Ulanova raised a hand. "Eamon DeVries—"

"Will wreck Neoclona inside of a year." Jani dug a thumbnail across a word farther down the list, grooving the parchment. *Jackass.* "No one can deny that he's a good device man, but when it comes to the complex dynamics of running a Commonwealth-spanning entity like Neoclona . . . " She took note of the stricken expression on Scriabin's face, and knew she'd struck the right chord. *Or nerve.* "John Shroud, working on the colonial side. Val Parini, on the Commonwealth. A measure of stability during what may turn out to be a tumultuous time." *Friend.* The last word on the list.

"Our Neoclona facility serves the entire colony and provides about one-quarter of the jobs in Unter den Linden and the surrounding area." Wallach sketched something that resembled a tombstone. "I don't want to see that end."

"Neither do I." Avelos shook her head. "I think we can speak for our colleague on Whalen and the heads of the satellites and stations. We need Neoclona as it is today, a strong, *stable* medical care provider and employer."

"This is good." Tsecha bared his teeth. "The Outer Circle Haárin value the opportunity they find here, and wish that John Shroud may continue to thrive so that all remains as it is. We will support your cleaving of the Outer Circle colonies from your Commonwealth."

And we will keep our businesses with you, and continue to run your most profitable ports, and promote the stability of your colonial governments. Jani read between those lines as though they'd been scrawled on the wall in letters a meter high. So did Markos and his colleagues, judging from their soft sighs of relief.

"No one I've spoken with thinks breaking up Neoclona's a good idea. I think a reversal of that particular decision should be easy enough to shove through." Scriabin's shoulders sagged, the first and only sign that he'd felt any tension at all. "Well. It appears we're all in agreement." He looked to Tsecha, who nodded. As one, they pushed back from the table and fell into light conversation while those who used recording boards fingered pads and tapped displays, erasing the contents and purging memories.

What you say here, what you see here, let it stay here when you leave here. Words to keep living by. Jani folded her own notes and tucked them back in her pocket, then looked at Niall to find him grinning at her.

"That was too goddamned easy, wasn't it?" He leaned his head back and stared at the ceiling. "Sad day, when you can't trust common sense."

"It was too easy, but we're all like minds here. The fight comes when Scriabin takes this to Chicago." Jani stood, stretched. Her stomach rumbled, this time from hunger.

"—sabotage." Markos's voice carried from the other end of the table. "Cèel scares me. He's spent the last decade building a network of spies throughout the Commonwealth. He'll find out about this and—"

"Stash." Scriabin closed his eyes for a long moment, then opened them slowly, like a beast roused from slumber. "Cèel's attempts at spy networks have gone and will continue to go the way of all the other humanish practices he has sought to adopt. Subtlety is not his strong suit. I remember when . . ." He circled the table and draped a thick arm around the man's shoulders and steered him to the door.

Jani followed the others outside, sneezing as the sun hit her in the face. "I'm numb."

"Nìa?" Tsecha drew alongside her, arching his brow in a humanish display of puzzlement. "You have that which you wish."

"For now." Niall set his lid, then patted his trouser pocket as the nicotine yearning surfaced. "Keeping it won't be easy."

"It will be a busy time." Tsecha looked out over the bay and bared his teeth. Then he clapped his hands and started after Scriabin. "Minister, I must ask you—"

"Lunch?" Niall glanced at his timepiece. "Make that breakfast."

"Let's go." Jani patted her stomach, then started up the road toward the Main House.

Rilas's heart beat harder as Tsecha moved into her vision field. She willed her breathing to slow, and sighted down until the cross hairs of her sight mech centered on the shorn head and downloaded the target position from the satellite.

Edged the stock away from her chest so the beat of her heart would not jostle the rifle.

Held her breath.

Pressed the charge-through.

CHAPTER 10

"Are you going to tell John right away?" Niall glanced back at Tsecha and the other officials, then unfastened the top clasp of his tunic and dug into his trouser pocket for his 'sticks. "I can't imagine you'd want to keep him hanging."

"I'm torn between blurting everything and holding back. I don't want to get his hopes up." The morning breeze off the water still held a chill, and Jani hugged herself.

"He's a big boy, Jan. He knows how the game is played." Niall puffed out a smoke ring. "Better to give him all the ammo so he can figure it out him—"

"Ná Kièrshia!"

Jani turned to find Avelos running up the incline toward them, dress boots skidding on the gravel.

"Ní Tsecha—" The woman stopped, chest heaving as she pulled in air. "He's ill."

Jani rushed past her and down the incline. Saw Scriabin, Markos, and the others standing clustered near the front of one skimmer.

Scriabin broke away and trotted out to meet her. "He leaned against the skimmer. Said he felt dizzy. We helped him to the ground. He said he wanted to sit."

"Nìa!" Tsecha leaned to the side to peer at her through a jungle of legs. "I am better now. Help me rise."

Jani turned to Niall, who stood at her shoulder and had already pulled out his handcom. "Call John." Then she pushed past the others and knelt beside Tsecha. "*Inshah*, you should sit here until John comes."

"I can stand." Tsecha gripped her shoulder with a hand like cage wire. "I am well—I am—well." He pushed himself into a crouch, then slowly straightened.

Jani moved close so she could support him, then struggled to maintain her balance as he sagged against her. "He's too weak to walk—we need one of the skimmers."

Niall moved to Tsecha's other side and took his arm. "I'll drive, but someone needs to help us get him inside."

"I can—not—" Tsecha pressed a hand to his left ear. "Something—" He worked his jaw, then shook his head once more. "—in—my—ear—" He paused, the look in his eyes altering from puzzlement to alarm. "Nìa?" He tried to take a step forward. "I do not—" His knees buckled and he became dead weight, dragging Jani and Niall to their knees with him.

"I see John." Ulanova's voice emerged tight. "Both him and Val."

Jani counted the seconds as John and Val raced down the road toward them in one of the clinic's skimcarts. Another cart followed close behind, carrying a tech and more doctors.

John leapt off the cart while it still moved. "What happened?" He knelt in front of Tsecha, scanner in hand, and pressed the probe against the idomeni's forehead as he checked his eyes. "Ní Tsecha? What happened?"

Jani tried to shift her weight as gravel pierced her knees like nails. "He felt dizzy. We tried to get him into the skimmer, and he collapsed."

"I—cannot—" Tsecha's voice emerged hushed, hoarse, as though his throat had been coated with dust. "The sky spins—"

Val unfastened a gurney from the back of the cart and lowered it to the ground beside Tsecha. "Ní Tsecha, you're going to feel movement under your legs—we're sliding the gurney underneath." He touched a pad on the side of the floating platform and it vibrated, then thinned. He took hold of one end while the tech took the other, and together they worked it under Tsecha's knees. "Now John's going to help you lie back."

"Relax, ní Tsecha." John placed an arm around Tsecha's shoulders and with Jani and Niall's help eased him onto his back. He detached a larger scanner from the side of the gurney and activated it—the relay to the Main House clinic opened immediately, the green illumin fluttering. "Eccles—stand by for signal."

While John talked to the clinic, Val loosened Tsecha's clothing, then plucked scanner probes from a bag he'd pulled off the skimcart and attached them to the idomeni's chest and scalp. "Eccles, are you receiving?"

"Yes, sir," came the tinny response. Illumins flickered over the surface of the scanner as data was relayed and retrieved. "Visualizing a small hole in the left tympanum—"

"I see some bloody discharge." John inserted a probe into Tsecha's left ear, then checked the scanner display. "Does your ear hurt, ní Tsecha?"

"It feels as though something—" Tsecha tried to touch his ear, but John blocked him, taking his hand and gently lowering it to his side.

"Do you hear ringing, ní Tsecha?"

Tsecha grew agitated and tried to pull his hand from John's grasp. *"I cannot hear."*

"Pronounced deafness in left ear." John tried to speak into the scanner while keeping Tsecha still. "Possible inner ear involvement."

"Perforation due to ear infection?" A few beats of silence. Then Eccles's voice, more hesitant this time. "There's no sign of inflammation or fluid buildup."

"There could have been trauma." John lowered until he spoke into Tsecha's right ear. "Ní Tsecha?"

Tsecha licked his lips before replying. "Yes, John?"

"Apologies for imposing upon your privacy, but did you lave your ears this morning? Did your physician-priest administer any treatment?"

Tsecha tried to shake his head, then winced and gripped the edge of the gurney. "No."

"Could be a tumor," Eccles offered.

"Then why aren't you seeing it?" John rose, his facade of professional detachment showing cracks. "Ní Tsecha, we're going to take you to the clinic for further evaluation and treatment."

"Where is—nìa?"

"I'm here." Jani crouched beside the gurney and took Tsecha's hand. "Not going anywhere."

"The clinic." Tsecha blinked as though dazed. "I do so enjoy visiting . . . " He sighed, then finally stilled and closed his eyes.

Jani kept hold of Tsecha's hand as Val and Niall maneuvered the skimcart alongside the gurney, then hoisted the gurney onto the back of the cart and locked it in place. Then she crawled atop the platform beside him.

"Nìa." Tsecha tried to touch his ear again, then let his hand fall. "I want to talk to John."

John wedged himself atop the platform next to Jani, then waited for Val to pile into the driver's seat and the cart to accelerate before touching Tsecha's arm. "I'm here, ní Tsecha."

"John?" Tsecha reached out to him. "Come where I can hear you."

John moved so he crouched closer to Tsecha's right side. "We're almost at the clinic."

"You will treat me as you did my nìa?" Tsecha tugged on John's sleeve.

Jani tried to read something in John's eyes, his expression. But his self-control had returned en force—she might as well have tried to read a wall.

"I will, ní Tsecha." He nodded, his voice a dark blank.

"You will not allow the worldskein control of me?"

John shot a look at Aris, the idomeni hybrid who served as

the xenomedical specialist and currently rode shotgun while monitoring the scanner outputs. "Except for the damage to his ear, all readings are within normal variation and stable," the male replied, answering his unspoken question.

"*John Shroud.*" Tsecha's voice held a divine rage. "Promise me—you will not allow—"

"I won't allow them near you." John squeezed his hand. "But ná Via, your physician-priest—"

"Not her! Not any of them!" Tsecha struggled to sit up, but the restraints that held him onto the gurney stopped him. "John—you must—" He fell back against the gurney pad, his labored breathing drawing worried looks and hurried scanner evaluations from Aris.

John took a dispo cloth from a dispenser on the gurney footguard and wiped it over Tsecha's brow. "Everything I did for Jani, all the effort I expended . . . " His hand slowed. "All the care—"

"All the *protection.*" Tsecha kept moving his head to better hear. "*John.*"

John looked at Jani, then at Aris. "Are you sure—"

"*John!*"

"I swear. By all in which I believe." John shifted so he could keep an eye on both his patient and the scanner that Aris held. "I will take care of you."

By the time the skimcarts reached the Main House, Thalassans had already gathered near the entry. Niall worked crowd control, then helped open doors and push planters and furniture out of the carts' path. "*Please keep clear,*" he called to the hybrids who hurried across the foyer to meet them. "Wait on the other side of the courtyard, please."

"There's something—" Aris studied his hand scanner. "I see a small mass in the left internal auditory canal."

"A neuroma?" John leaned forward to look at the display. "Why the hell didn't you spot it before?"

"Because it wasn't there before." Aris stared at his scanner, then muttered something and gestured for Val to stop the cart. "It's growing."

"How—?" John grabbed Jani's wrist. "You have to let go."

Jani gripped Tsecha's hand harder, felt him squeeze back. "No."

Niall took her by her shoulders and eased her off the platform. "Let him do his job, gel."

"Son of a bitch." Aris leapt out of the cart and circled to the gurney. "John, it—"

As he closed in, Tsecha's back arched, his body twisting against the restraints. Other doctors joined John and Aris, moving in rapid concert, one-word orders sounding. As they worked over Tsecha, he continued to writhe and shake, his breath coming in gasps, his skin paling to clay.

Then he shivered. Twitched.

Grew still.

"Oh, God." Aris checked one scanner, then another.

Jani tried to follow as the cart with its motionless cargo was driven to the lift, but once more Niall held her back. She watched the doors open, John and Val unfasten the gurney and carry it inside. The doors closed.

Jani sat in the visitors' alcove, repositioning her chair until she had the best possible view of the door to Tsecha's room. The clinic was quiet, seemingly deserted. John had restricted access to medical personnel only, but when Jani snuck down the stairs and through the corridor, she encountered no guards, only a red-eyed nurse who at first seemed about to ask her to leave, then waved her toward the alcove and disappeared into the room.

She flinched when she heard the *click* of the stairwell door, the clip of hard soles on lyno. Relaxed, a little, when she heard the rough Victorian mutter.

"Where the hell . . . ?" Niall stopped in the alcove entry. "There you are, gel. Kid said he saw you come down here." He dragged a chair beside Jani's and sat, balancing his brimmed lid on his thigh. "You know, the kid who's always writing things down and imaging?"

"Torin." Jani paused to rub her eyes. "Torin Clase."

"Torin—that's his name. Nuisance in the making, he is." Niall drummed his fingers on the arm of his chair. "I turned Yevgeny and the others over to Brondt. They needed to call their offices, settle down their staffs." He sniffed. "Head off any press inquiries at the pass." He glanced toward the door and swallowed hard. "Anything?"

Jani shook her head. "Ná Via, his physician-priest, went in about a half hour ago. No one's come out. I contacted Dathim. He was going to tell Meva and Feyó."

Niall nodded. "Bloody hell, Jan." He sat forward, lid still in hand, working his fingers back and forth along the brim. "It's the not knowing that makes it worse."

"Tell me what you don't know, Niall." Jani waited for him to respond, and took his silence for the surrender she knew it to be.

They both started at the distant *hiss* of the lift door. Soft footsteps followed, played out in double time.

"Jani? Jani?" The voice, as rapid as the steps.

Jani's head started to pound. "In here, ná Meva."

The female appeared in the alcove entry. She had dragged on her propitiator's overrobe over a bright purple shirt and orange trousers, and tucked her hair into a messy knot. "Feyó will be brought by Dathim. I am by myself." She looked toward the door to Tsecha's room, then back to Jani. "You saw?"

"I didn't see him fall ill." Jani rose and walked past Meva into the corridor. "When Niall and I reached him, he was already on the ground. He said he felt dizzy." She paced, heart tripping each time she passed close to the room. "His eardrum had perforated. John ordered him brought here for evaluation. Everything seemed under control. Then scanning revealed a tumor. Then he suffered a seizure, or . . . something." She stopped, closing her eyes as the images flashed. The arching back. The shuddering. The stillness.

"Haárin have gathered in the meeting house, and in the temples. They wait." Meva adjusted her overrobe sleeves, her shoulders slowly rounding. "You are not dressed as is seemly."

Jani looked down at her blue shirt-jacket and trousers, now rumpled and dusty. "I haven't had time—"

"He is your dominant." Meva stepped in front of Jani. "You are to be a priest, and I have never seen you wear your overrobe." She had never displayed the idomeni reluctance to look others in the eye, and her auric glare drilled even more deeply than Tsecha's. *"You do not know your gods, and you do not know your clothes."*

Jani clenched her hands, felt her heartbeat strengthen, then slow. "I am not leaving."

"You must wear that which—"

"I am not leaving to change clothes. Not now."

Niall wedged between them, nudging Jani back. "Tell me where it is, gel."

"Right side of the closet." Jani turned away, listened to Niall's footsteps recede, the door to the lift whisper open, then closed.

"You must prepare." Meva's voice at her shoulder. "For whatever is to be."

Shut up. Jani stuffed her fists in her pockets. Sometimes the anger built, a rank combination of the remnants of her augmentation and typical idomeni temper, but taking a swing at Meva would just make a horrible situation worse. "We still haven't heard from John. We still don't know—" She heard the lift door open again, and turned to find Dathim striding toward them, followed closely by ná Feyó Tal.

"Ná Meva." Feyó's voice emerged tight, her shoulders rounding. She didn't like the propitiator any more than did Jani. "I wished you to travel with me."

Meva waved a hand, an imitation of a humanish *Don't bother me.* "I needed to be here. You delayed for too much time."

"There are prayers to be said. This is a place of sickness."

"It is a place of Tsecha. That is why I am here." Dathim leaned against the wall opposite the door to Tsecha's room. He still wore his workclothes, the brown cloth streaked with white tile dust.

Feyó crossed her left arm over her chest as she drew up

very straight, a posture of supplication. Like most of the other Haárin, she had never set foot in the clinic. Her medical matters were still handled by a physician-priest, who labored to keep her soul intact by the usual idomeni blend of modern methods together with prayers and wards against demons, all based on the premise that the injury or illness of one threatened the soul of any other who came in contact with them. Wholeness of Soul, a concept that Tsecha had called "anathema," still formed one of the cornerstones of Feyó's world. "It is not godly."

"You are an idiot, Feyó." Meva turned her back on Jani and fixed on her secular dominant. "Tsecha is here—he fell sick here and needed to be treated *here.* Thus did Via come, *here.* Thus do we all come, *here.*"

"My soul—"

"Would suffer greater damage if you did not come here, to be with him whom you claim to esteem." Meva closed in on Feyó as her own shoulders hunched.

Feyó lowered her arm as her shoulders rounded in a crippling curve. "You dare—"

"Quiet!" Jani pressed a hand to her ear as the sound rattled her aching head, then let it fall when she remembered that Tsecha had done the same thing before those last terrible moments. *I'm going to collapse—I'm going to die.* She gave herself a mental kick. *Don't be a jackass.* "Let's wait for what John and Via have to say." She leaned against the wall beside the preternaturally calm Dathim. *When the tilemaster is the only one controlling his temper, we're in trouble.* She looked across the corridor to the door to Tsecha's room. *John, where are you?*

As if on cue, the door opened and John emerged. He wore a medcoat over his daysuit, shoe covers over his boots. "I—" He looked around as though lost. "We did . . . " He hung his head. " . . . everything. We did everything we could possibly . . . "

From behind him, no sounds. Only silence.

Jani walked to him, sensed his warmth through the chill air, and stepped past him into the quiet.

CHAPTER 11

The air felt cool, weighty, the lights as bright as sunlight reflecting off ice. Val stood over an analyzer—he looked up as she entered. Like John, he had donned a medcoat. Like him, he failed to meet her eye.

Via sat in a chair by the far wall, her head lowered. Aris fed samples into another analyzer, stopping every so often to wipe his eyes.

And finally, in the room's center, a bed, surrounded by blinking plastic boxes, instruments and machines, the body it contained prone, unmoving, another aspect of the silence.

Jani walked closer, each step a labor, the urge to howl like a stab in her throat. Tsecha lay centered like a figure atop a sarcophagus, his face obscured by tubing and sensors, legs straight, arms at his side, the thin bed cover folded down to expose his bare, sensor-dotted chest. His torso, once home to an idomeni's wiry strength, seemed whittled down to faded skin and bone, all muscle, as well as the will and fire that drove them, spent. Extinguished. He looked desiccated now, as though he'd become one with the desert from which he came.

Then she heard the soft pad of footsteps. John's voice filling her head.

"Jani, come over here, please."

She turned and followed him to the door, where Feyó, Meva, and Dathim stood, their stares drawn to the still figure.

"Ná Via?" John gestured to the physician-priest, who rose slowly and joined them. "There is no easy way to say this." He stopped, passed a hand over his face. "He's gone. He cannot breathe on his own. His heart cannot beat on its own. He has no detectable brain function." A shaky sigh, the first hint of the tears to come. "He had a tumor in his left inner auditory canal that we didn't visualize immediately. By the time we did, it had already bulged out into the brain case." He stared down at the floor. "There was blood vessel rupture, and the pressure . . . " He raised his head, eventually. "The damage was catastrophic and irreversible."

"We must do that which must be done." Via's voice emerged soft, its usual strength seeped away.

"He did not believe in it." Meva's eyes never left the bed. "That which you must do. He no longer believed it mattered."

Via sighed, as though she had heard the words from Meva before and expected at some point to hear them again. "I have contacted my suborns, Meva. They have gone to the enclave vaults and broken the seals of Tsecha's chamber. They bring his reliquary. If he had not wished it to be used, would he have preserved it? Think of what you know of Tsecha, who always did that which he would, and answer me."

Meva remained still for a time, before twitching one shoulder in her version of a humanish shrug. "We must ask his suborn." She raised a hand in question. "Ná Kièrshia?"

Jani turned her back on the questioning priest and walked to the side of the bed. An edge of the bed cover had rumpled. As she reached out to straighten it, her hand brushed Tsecha's arm—she jerked back at the touch of soft, warm skin.

"His blood is being warmed by the circulator." John moved opposite her. "His internal thermostat no longer functions."

"He is dead." Feyó smacked the top of an analyzer. "Why can you not say the words, Doctor? Are they not your words to say? Tsecha is dead. Not gone. Not irreversibly damaged.

Dead." She pointed to the door. "Ná Via's suborns will soon arrive. We must proceed."

Jani looked at John, who looked away. "John?" She struggled to find the words, to form the question. "Isn't there . . . ?"

Feyó stepped between Jani and John. "We must proceed. To wait longer is anathema."

Val had been sitting with his head in his hands. Now his head came up, eyes glistening. "*What's the rush!* That's the anathema, Feyó. That you're in such a goddamn rush!"

"Val." Jani stared at him until he got up and strode to the farthest corner of the room to pace. "A soul in an artificially sustained body realizes that the body is dead, and tries to depart. But it's trapped, and as the length of captivity increases, it degrades, fragments. The Vynshàrau believe it. Most of the major sects." She stepped around Feyó, dodging the female when she grabbed for her sleeve. "Tsecha, however, had his doubts, and those doubts must be respected."

"He doubted when it came to injury, to sickness." Feyó set herself in Jani's path, stopping her. "But he is *dead*. Life has left him. I look at him, and I see . . . " Her voice faded, the first hint of blankness crossing her face. The first suggestion of loss.

Jani stepped closer to the female. "Where is the urgency? Is it for his sake?" She twitched her head in the direction of the bed. "Or because you fear what the other Haárin will say? That you mishandled him. That you botched it."

"*Yes!*" Feyó's shoulders bowed so that her neck twisted. "Idiot humanish—do you truly believe such does not matter? He is *Tsecha*. Before he was Tsecha, he was Avrèl nìRau Nema, Chief Propitiator of the Vynshàrau. The guide to the gods for all Haárin. If his soul loses its Way, so do all of ours. If he is lost, so are we all."

Jani felt her scalp tighten, and worked a hand through her hair to ease the ache. "NìaRauta Sànalàn is your Chief Propitiator now."

"She is as nothing. He repudiated her, again and again."

Feyó's voice emerged in a hiss. "He trained you. You learned from him, and you do not understand that which he was?"

I know what he was to me. Jani stood still. "John?"

John cleared his throat. "It's over, Jan." He gestured toward one of the analyzers. "I can show you the scans, the test results—"

"I have seen the scans, and the test results." Via walked to the bedside, her voice lowered to a whisper. "All is nothing. All the physicians could attempt has been tried. Now is the time for the priests." She rested a hand on Jani's arm, a humanish gesture she seldom employed. "His soul is at great risk. The souls of all Haárin are at great risk. We have to proceed."

Jani nodded. Then she shook off Feyó's hand and walked to Tsecha's bedside. Ignored the muttered Sìah curses that followed her, and waited for a more familiar touch. It came, eventually, a light hand on her shoulder. "It's moving too quickly."

"It's a nightmare." John moved in, close enough to lean on. "I keep telling myself to wake up, but I'm not listening."

"Didn't Via see this coming?"

"I asked her. She'd seen no signs of anything like this."

Jani watched the bare chest rise and fall, and knew John had made a mistake. Knew that Tsecha would open his eyes, tear out the intratracheal insert, the sensors, and demand to know why he'd been treated in such a manner, why everyone had been so stupid. "He didn't seem ill at the meeting house. Did I miss something? Should I have—"

"Stop it." John squeezed her shoulder. "Sometimes you just don't see it coming, and when it hits, there's nothing you can do."

Jani nodded. Her head felt as though it floated, her feet as though they didn't touch the floor. Shock, or hangover from her augmentation, or a little of both. "There's nothing—"

"No."

"He's gone."

" . . . Yes."

"Then . . . " Jani turned to Feyó, who had moved to the foot of the bed. "Bring it." She saw the relief in the female's bearing, understood the reasoning behind it, the millennia of religious belief, yet hated her anyway.

"Are you sure?" John's voice in her ear, like a guilty conscience.

"No." Jani shook her head, then closed her eyes to stop the motion. "So many Haárin still consider him their propitiator, even though he isn't. If we don't treat him properly now, the backlash . . . " She looked down at her hands, at the rings she wore, and fought the urge to yank them off and return them to the hands on which they belonged. "He deserves all honor. All ceremony due a chief propitiator. I'll see to it."

"I know." John embraced her, rested his head atop hers. "What do you want me to do?"

"Check the corridor. See if Niall is there. He went to get my overrobe." A voice she didn't recognize, saying things she never thought she'd say.

John opened the door and walked out into the corridor, returning a few moments later with Jani's overrobe in hand. "Can anyone else attend?"

"Come in, Niall." Jani took the overrobe from John and dragged it on. Arranged the sleeves, straightened the hem, and knew herself for the imposter she was. The fake priest, preparing to send the true one upon his Way. "He liked you."

"I—liked him, too." Niall slipped inside and took a place against the wall, straightening gradually until he stood at attention.

"I'll show everyone else out." John released her and headed for the door.

"No." Jani turned to him. "You and Val—you both battled him for so long. His esteemed enemies. He'd want you to stay." She scanned the ceiling. "Does this room have imaging capability?"

John nodded. "Yes, but—"

"Activate it, if you haven't already. It's history. What's more, it's important." Jani looked at John, who stared wide-eyed. "I don't want there to be any questions, ever. No argument that we didn't do this or we didn't do that. I want them to see. I want them all to see." With that, she walked to the foot of the bed and waited.

A few moments later the door opened. Feyó and Via entered silently, bearing the reliquary between them like a pall. It proved to be a simple wooden box, a half meter high and a meter or so long. The wood itself had the ebony hue and tight grain of one of Shèrá's northern varieties, which grew in the mountains and was fed by snow and rain. Strange, that Tsecha had chosen such a wood to hold his scroll, rather than the sandstone of his native Rauta Shèràa.

The two females carried the reliquary over to an empty table on the far side of the room and hefted it on top. Via then left Feyó and beckoned for John to join her in front of the main instrument console, where they had a hasty consultation punctuated by the evaluation of screens filled with data. Then she walked to the bed, her step slowing as she took in the still figure that lay before her. "*É ne lona, Tsecha. É neà lonai . . .* " Her voice lowered to a murmur as she circled to each piece of equipment in turn and evaluated the readouts.

For your journey, Tsecha. For your journey to come . . . A Vynshàrau prayer, a wish that his journey to the First Star would be swift and uneventful. Jani breathed in once, then again. "*É se te lon à kavai,*" she uttered in a priestly singsong. "*É sei te kavao à volai.*" She drew a sharp look from Via for the half-humanish imposter that she was, but she didn't care. *For to journey is to know. For to know is to understand.* Those words, Tsecha believed, for all his doubt and argument. Those words, he had the right to hear because of what he'd been. Those words, she had the right to speak because of what he'd been to her.

"Jani?"

She turned to find Feyó standing behind her, her eyes averted.

"Go to your place." Feyó pointed toward the reliquary.

Jani walked to the bench on which the reliquary stood. She lifted the flat lid, suppressed a gasp at its weight, and maneuvered it carefully to keep it from bumping anything. She sensed stares. Meva's judgment. Via's disapproval. Feyó's more benign concern. She set the lid upon the bench, then looked inside the reliquary. Nestled within lay Tsecha's scroll, the construct that had been made soon after his birth to house his soul after his death.

Idomeni live to die. Jani reached into the reliquary and opened the cover of the bound volume nestled in the padded lining. To her surprise, it felt cold to the touch, rough and weighty. This was the sandstone of Rauta Shèràa, dull umber and gritty, its surface carved with swirling traceries that were the favored imagery of the Vynshàrau. Beneath it lay a face page, blank but for symbols denoting the names of the major gods. Jani looked them over, stopping when she came to a clenched fist, fingers gripping some unidentifiable object. *Caith.* Goddess of chaos, of annihilation. She who destroyed for the sake of destruction.

Bitch. Jani wiped her thumb across the image in an effort to smear it, erase it, give order a little of its own back. But idomeni inks were the finest and this image had been in place for a long time. It remained sharp, bright black against the cream of the parchment. *This round to you, then.* She smoothed her hand over the page, then turned around just as Via took her place at the head of the bed.

The physician-priest paused. Then, leaning forward, she cupped her hands and positioned them above Tsecha's face. After a few moments she straightened and circled the bed once more, this time touching each control pad, shutting down each instrument in turn. When she came to the heart-lung array, she hesitated, then reached out slowly, clenching her hand once before touching the control. What little sound had filled the room ceased. Red indicator lights fluttered across the unit's surface, then faded. Tsecha's chest stalled in mid-rise.

Time stopped, the tick into the next second hanging on
some cosmic balance. Jani looked to Tsecha, strained to see
some movement, some sign that analysis and instruments
had erred and hope had won the day.

But Tsecha remained still and time started again, leaving
hope in its wake.

She looked at John. He stood in the far corner of the room,
against the wall, shoulders hunched and arms folded. He met
her eye for the barest moment before fixing on the floor at
his feet. Val stood beside him, as hunched and cramped as
his partner.

Then she looked to the entry, and saw Dathim and Meva,
tall and still, arms raised above their heads in supplication.

Via resumed her position at the head of the bed, then
waited for Feyó to take her position at the foot. She peeled
away the sensors from Tsecha's scalp and chest. Removed
the intratracheal insert, sliding it out with a sure hand. After
setting it aside, she once more brought her hands together
over Tsecha's face, this time cupped together, palms facing
one another. According to all she believed, she now held his
soul in her grasp, and she moved slowly, as though jostling
might damage it. Straightening, she reached out toward Feyó
and opened her hands. As she did so, Feyó held open her
arms. Via then closed her hands and let them fall, dispatch-
ing Tsecha's soul to the protection of his secular dominant.

Feyó crossed her arms, hollow thumps sounding as her
hands struck her chest. The seconds passed as she stood in
place, eyes closed, hands gripping her shoulders, lips moving in some silent prayer. Then, slowly, she turned to face
Jani, and lowered her arms.

Jani held out her hands in time with Feyó's action. All the
teachings she had read over the months stated that she would
know when she had grasped the soul of the deceased. She
would feel its weight, its presence, sense the pain it had suffered over the course of its bodily habitation, the joys it had
experienced. She would cross her arms over her chest, and
know that she sheltered something most delicate, something

that would journey across the bridge to the paradise of the First Star, along the Way meeting its gods. Along the Way achieving peace.

So she gauged every sensation, every thought bidden and unbidden, and felt . . . nothing. Waited for Tsecha's voice to sound in her mind, commanding her to pay attention, and heard only the thudding of her own blood in her ears. She turned to face the reliquary and lowered her arms, reaching inside the box and placing her hands over the scroll. Counted to four because it seemed a good number. Not too large, yet not too small. Four seconds—plenty of time for a soul she couldn't sense to nestle itself within the recesses of a book whose contents she didn't believe. *Thus sayeth the priest.* She closed the cover of the scroll and, with hands that felt as they always had, hoisted the reliquary lid and slid it back into place. As she bent close to the wood, she caught its faint scent, a blend of dry herbs and fresh cuttings, tinged with cinnamon. The *vrel* blossom Tsecha spoke of so often. A tear spilled, spattering the wood, and she wiped it away.

She placed her hands atop the reliquary, the only finishing gesture she could think of. *Ason ea lon, nìRau. Good journey, wherever you are.* With that, she let her hands fall, and turned to face the others.

Silence dragged on for one beat. Two. Then Via gestured. "We must go now, and prepare—"

"I'd like some time, please." Jani flinched at the sound of her own voice. "Alone with him. I'd like some time. To say good-bye."

"Good-bye?" Via gestured in question. "Farewells have been made. It is at an end, ná Kièrshia. We must take him out of this place."

"His soul rests in safe harbor. As far as you're concerned, he's secure. No evil can befall him." Jani looked down at her hands, the redstone ring Tsecha had given her more than twenty years before. She tilted her hand back and forth, and watched the scarlet flashes. "A few minutes, Via. That's all. Allow the humanish in me some time."

Via gestured a strong negative. "It is not—"

"A few minutes." Jani saw John push off the wall and start toward her, but when their eyes met, he stopped. "I knuckled under to your traditions. You can damn well knuckle under to mine."

Via sliced the air with her hand. "It is not godly. I cannot—"

"Via." Feyó's voice sounded tired, the bowing of her shoulders a result of exhaustion as much as irritation. "We must assemble your staff to take ní Tsecha's body back to the enclave. Such will take time. During that time, it will be watched by a priest."

"She is no—" Via fell silent as Feyó's shoulders curved further. She glanced at Jani, then away, the struggle to contain her own anger evident in the stiff way she held herself.

"His soul is intact, Via. Your duty is discharged." Feyó nodded to Jani. She then ushered the physician-priest out the door, their under-their-breath back and forth audible until they left the room.

"I will . . . go upstairs." John gestured vaguely in the direction of the entry. "Everyone's waiting." He turned to Aris, then jerked his thumb toward the door. He hurried into the hallway, followed by John, Val, and Niall. The door closed.

Dathim and Meva had lowered their arms at the conclusion of the rite, but remained still. When the door closed, Dathim edged toward the bed. "If all is finished, why do you remain?"

Jani dragged a chair to the side of the bed and sat. "What place for the student but with her teacher?" She looked up at the male, who like Feyó appeared drained, expression blank and shoulders bowing. "Why do you remain?"

"To see what you will do." Dathim finally looked at her. "You will pray?"

Jani hesitated, then shook her head. "I'll sit here, and wish that the last few hours hadn't happened. I'll wish that I could turn back time."

"You will wish in vain," Meva said.

Jani nodded. "But I'll wish anyway." She tugged at another crease in the bed cover. Reached out a finger and grazed Tsecha's arm, felt the cooling even though only a short time had passed.

"Humanish are strange." Some animation returned to Meva's face, a flare of impatience in her downward curve of lip. "And you are still most humanish."

Jani raised a hand in surrender, let it fall. Sat quietly as the minutes passed and Meva and Dathim continued to watch her before giving up and leaving the room.

"With idomeni, the soul is the important thing. The body is as nothing. They'll burn it down to a scraping of ash, and won't even collect it. Lave the crematory with blessed cloths, and rinse it all away." Jani tried to think of something else to say, to find the words that defined what she knew in her heart to be indefinable.

Finally, she gave up, and did the humanish thing, and wept.

CHAPTER 12

Rilas replayed the memory of the cart bearing Tsecha surging up the hill and vanishing around a curve of stone. She had seen him gesture, watched as Shroud bent over him, as the hated Kilian held his hand. He had spoken, yes, but what had he said? Had his words been lucid, or, as she most hoped, only the last ramblings of a dissolving mind?

Not that it mattered. She had performed the act she had come to this damned place to execute. It troubled her that Tsecha had not died within moments after the vector found him and transferred its cargo to his brain, but did the timing matter? Dead was dead.

She should not have stayed in the house for as long as she had, watching Tsecha's transport up the hill. She had worked quickly, breaking down the rifle and packing it away. As she left the house, she set off a protein bomb, obliterating all traces of her presence.

I have succeeded.

As soon as she entered the Karistos shuttleport, Rilas stopped before a news display and read the scrolling headlines.

He must be dead. She waited for the words to appear on the screen, for the bustle around her to cease. For the silence.

Stock market values . . . weather . . . a new holoVee detective series . . .

He must be— Someone jostled her and she stumbled forward, grabbed the back of a bench to keep from falling. She straightened slowly, imagined burying a blade in the heart of that clumsy fool. Then she continued down the concourse toward the Haárin wing, and the locker area where her new documents had been hidden. *No more Nahin Sela.* No more damned tiles. She muttered thanks to her blessed Caith.

She hoisted her slingbag, which was nearly empty now. The rifle, the cartridges, the beautiful sight mech, she had coated with protein digester and buried in a remote place off the shuttleport road. Even if discovered, they would prove useless, the biobased mechanics obliterated, only their metal shells remaining. The secondary—

Rilas stopped in mid-stride. *The secondary.* It still hovered above the Thalassan enclave—she imagined its path growing more and more erratic as the signals it sent to the destroyed primary went unanswered. *It does not matter.* Soon its power supply would deplete and it would tumble into the bay. It signaled as biological—no scanning device would track it.

She started to walk again, one step following the next, her feet tingling as though she walked across a high ledge, a sheer drop on either side. *A mistake.* She did not make mistakes—such was why nìRau Cèel had chosen her for this greatest of tasks. *I can make no more mistakes.* Such were an insult to Caith, a temptation to godly wrath.

Rilas hurried down the concourse, then turned down the corridor that led to the locker area. She passed first one Haárin worker, then another. Saw gaps in the ceiling, holes in the walls on either side.

Stopped in front of the entry to the locker area, and found only the hacked-out remains of a doorway, and barrier tape, and an empty expanse where the lockers had stood.

"What is this?" Rilas looked to the workers' dominant, who stood off to one side performing calculations on a handheld.

"Ná." The male nodded to her, a meaningless gesture. "These rooms are being repaired. The plumbing was not as adequate."

"Repaired?" Rilas tried to step past the barrier tape, but stopped as the polymer sensed her presence and beeped a warning. "There is something I must recover."

"All contents have been taken from the lockers and moved to Lost and Found." The male turned his back to her, gaze still fixed on the handheld display. "You go there and present your identification, and you may recover that which is yours."

"Lost and Found?"

"At the end of this concourse, next to the security offices."

Rilas remained in place. Her heart beat harder now. *Identification.* She would display her documents naming her as ná Nahin Sela and recover a bag containing documents for another, for a name she did not even know. *If they searched the bag—scanned it—* They would ask her why she recovered documents belonging to another. They would demand explanations.

I cannot attempt to claim this bag. Nor could she remain on Elyas long enough to purchase new documents, assuming there were Haárin here who produced such. *I have to remain as ná Nahin Sela.* For the first time, she would depart a place with the same name she bore when she arrived. *Such is not seemly.* Even more important, such was dangerous. Too many here knew her as ná Nahin. Those who worked or lived at the enclave in which she stayed. Those she had spoken with at the Trade Board.

But still . . .

Rilas turned and walked back up the hall toward the concourse. Sensed Caith's laughter as she approached the outgoing passenger gates and scanned the displays for the first Haárin shuttle to Elyas Station. As she walked up to the billet counter and presented her identification.

"Ná Nahin Sela." The female clerk looked her in the eye, baring her teeth as she scanned the identification wafer and processed the billet request. "Glories of the day to you."

"Glories," Rilas replied, even as Caith's glee settled as an ache in her soul.

It started on the shuttle. One Haárin with a handheld, and soon the entire craft knew.

Then the news spread, like the voices of the gods.

As a humanish cathedral. If the designer of Elyas Station had ever wished to observe godly quiet in the place she caused to have made, such desire would have been fulfilled this day. Rilas could track the movement of silence through the Haárin concourse as the news of the death of ní Tsecha Egri revealed itself on wall-mounted displays and announced itself from handhelds. Haárin did not yell or cry out as they comprehended the news. Such was not their way, and even years of godless exposure to humanish had not degraded their response.

Silence.

Rilas pondered the quiet along the Haárin concourse of Elyas Station. Relished it. *Tsecha's hold over the colonial Haárin is as an iron band,* nìRau Cèel had told her. *When it first shatters, they will be as lost.* He had bared his teeth at that moment. *Then they will conclude that the humanish in whom they have trusted have betrayed them. At that moment, they will look back toward the worldskein.*

At that moment . . . Rilas stopped before one of the displays, a humanish broadcast that offered a Sìah translation.

" . . . cerebral hemorrhage . . . tumor . . . undiagnosed . . . unusual . . . "

"Hemorrhage?" Rilas stepped closer to the display. "They think it a hem—" She fell silent as the other Haárin gestured her to be quiet, their hands slicing the air, the harsh movements of emotion, distress.

Rilas's heart pounded. *It is not illness—I killed him! I, Imea nìaRauta Rilas, as my Oligarch bade me!* She wondered for a moment at the reaction if she announced such. *They would strike me down, as years ago we struck down the Laum.* They did not yet understand the goodness that had been done for them.

Let them think it illness for now. Rilas stepped away from the group and resumed her walk toward her departure dock, slowing to ponder the displays in shop windows, and to think of the future. *Soon, they will learn it was not a hemorrhage.* Then, the accusations would begin. Against Chicago. Against humanish separatists. The same groups that had been accused of bombing Haárin docks would stand accused once more, would argue for and against the blame, embracing or denying it in proportion to how weak they were, how eager they were to appear strong.

And as humanish argue, idomeni will listen, and realize their errors, and return—

"Hello, again."

Rilas stopped. Turned first toward the concourse, then toward the entry of the shop near which she stood. Saw no one.

"I'm back here."

Humanish male. Rilas clenched a fist. "I do not—"

"You remember me. The other day. The Rose Window." A face emerged from the shadowed recess beside the shop. The dark skin and darker hair, clipped short. Another too bright shirt, this in a yellow that pained the eyes. "I remember you. I never forget a face."

I do not, either. Rilas felt the heat of her soul rise up her throat. *The male who explained gargoyles.*

"I was just hanging around, watching the passing parade." The male looked out toward the concourse crowds, his eyes bleared as though with sleep. "Well, not doing much passing today. Mostly standing around, because of what happened and all. Tragic, just tragic." He shook his head, then leaned against the wall, one hand gripping the brickwork as though he struggled for balance. "Then who do I see window shopping?" He bared his teeth. "'Oh, look,' I thought, 'a familiar face.'"

Ethanol poisoning. Rilas had been trained to deal with

humanish who degraded themselves in that way, but dreaded such. The chemical slowed their reflexes, yes, but the pits of their souls were as tainted as their brains, and such led to messy outcomes. *If I strike him in the abdomen, he may vomit. I would then need to lave. To change my clothes.* Rilas glanced at a timeform. Her flight departed soon. She would not have the time.

"A little friendly advice? You'd look better with your hair unbraided, loose—but then, most females would." The male leaned closer. His breath stank of harsh sweetness. "My name's Neason, by the way." He held out his hand.

Rilas took a step back. "I will inform your dominant that you are drunk."

The male drew back his hand and stood away from the wall. "You do that." His voice altered, from high and light to low, a voice of threat. "Go right ahead and inform that bitch about anything you want. Add your name to the goddamn list." His head moved back and forth as though palsied. Then it stilled. "Did you report me? Were you the one who—"

Rilas raised her right hand and curved it upward in question. "Report?" She tilted her head to accentuate her false dismay. "I said nothing. To anyone."

"Improving relations between the races. That's all I was doing." The male's voice rose. "I told her that, the bitch, but did she listen? Did any of them listen?" He shouted now, spittle arcing from his mouth. "I am a diplomat. Do you hear me—*a diplomat!*"

Rilas turned toward the concourse. A few Haárin had turned from the displays and now looked in her direction.

"A fuckin' diplomat!"

"Silence." Rilas pushed the male back into the darkness. "You attract attention."

"Oh yeah?" He grabbed at her hands, missing his grip as the poisoning slowed his reactions. "Think you know how to keep me quiet, do you?" He laughed, filling the dark recess with the stench of his breath. "You come back here and keep me quiet, then."

Rilas had stepped into the recess. As her eyes accommodated to the darkness, she saw the drink receptacles piled in one corner, the door that she knew led to the station interiors and from there to the humanish section.

"If you come back here, you can keep me real quiet." The male opened the interior door. "Come back here with me and I won't make a sound." He shifted his weight from one foot to the other as he sought to maintain his balance. "That's what you want, isn't it? To keep me quiet." He curved his lips without baring his teeth, that strange humanish expression. "I can tell. You don't want me to say a thing."

Rilas felt her heartbeat slow and strengthen. Her hands clenched. "I do not know what you speak of."

"I'll bet you don't." The male backed through the door opening, beckoning to her with a crooked finger. "Liar. I know all your secrets."

"What secrets?" Rilas studied him now. His build. His weight. The way he moved. *A soft thing. Unfit. Untrained.* "I do not know what you are telling me."

"All you idomeni are so mysterious, but you're no mystery to me." The male looked her up and down. "All I have to do is look at you, and I know all about you. What you want. What you need." He made a sweeping motion with his hand. "Come in here, and I'll tell you everything."

"I must go to my dock."

"I know a shortcut." He tried to grip her arm, and swore as she dodged his hand. "Come on now—be nice."

Rilas watched him, even as the strength of her goddess coursed through her. *He knows secrets.* Had he matched the identity she had used to enter the station with that of Nahin Sela? Had he somehow followed her to Karistos without her seeing him? "I will come with you."

The male bared his teeth. "That's more like it." He stepped aside so she could enter the interior walkway, then turned his back so he could close the door.

As he did that, Rilas let her slingbag slide off her shoulder to the floor. She moved in behind him, her gaze fixed on his rumpled shirt collar, the place where neck and shoulder joined.

Raised her hand edge on.

"Now this is how—"

Brought it down.

The male made no sound. He dropped to his knees, pitched forward so that he struck the wall. Slid to the floor, twitched, then lay still.

Rilas watched him, even as panic touched her and every instinct bade her to flee. Waited, until she saw the liquid puddle around his hip, smelled the stench of urine, and knew him to be dead. What he knew of her, he could never tell.

She picked up her slingbag and shouldered it. Turned the door mechanism and felt the finger of Caith touch her soul as the panel failed to open. She studied the mechanism for a moment, determined the two-handed grip and pull necessary to release the catch, and did so.

Rilas entered the concourse, walking past the groups that still gathered around the displays. The boarding alarm for her ship sounded, and she quickened her pace, thanking her goddess that she would soon leave this most damned of places behind.

CHAPTER 13

"Jan?"

Jani looked up to find Niall standing in the entry. "Via and her suborns . . ." She waved toward the bed, which now lay empty, the covers stripped. "About—I don't know—a half hour ago."

"I saw them leave." Niall's voice emerged scratchy, as though his throat ached. "Yevgeny wondered how you were holding up?"

Yevgeny? Jani struggled to place the name. Then the token dropped. "Scriabin's still here?"

"They all are." Niall managed a weak smile. "It's only just afternoon." The expression faded. "All lifetime in a day." He fell silent. Coughed. "Anyway, he asked how you were doing, and if you could see your way clear to stopping by the library when you're up to it."

"Which in minister-speak means now." Jani tried to rise, and found her limbs had gone to lead. "Give me a minute."

"Of course." Niall stepped inside and let the door close, then dragged a chair next to hers. "Take all the time you need."

There isn't that much time. She plucked a dispo cloth from the dispenser on a nearby cart and wiped her eyes. "What's it like upstairs?"

"Quiet." Niall brushed some nonexistent lint from his trousers. "Everyone had gathered in the courtyard. John talked to them a little while ago. He did well, I think."

Jani imagined John's solemn mien, his voice. Not a combination one would choose to lighten the mood, but in this case they probably struck the right note. "What did he say?"

"That Tsecha died as the result of a brain hemorrhage." Niall exhaled with a *whoosh*. "He didn't mention the undiagnosed tumor—let Via field that one."

Jani thought back to the scene in the room a few short hours before, John showing Via analyzer readouts and instrument displays while she dogged his shoulder, like a stranger at a party sticking to the only person she knew. Did she feel lost amid the brightly lit bustle of a humanish-style hospital room? Did John even try to bring her up to speed, or did he barrel along as he always did, and assume she'd keep pace? "Idomeni often don't treat diseases until they fall visibly ill. But I thought Tsecha had gotten past that."

"Maybe Via didn't." Niall shrugged. "And it backfired."

You will not allow the worldskein control of me?

Jani pondered Tsecha's words. He had included Via in his plea—he hadn't wanted her to take charge of him, either. She shivered, and blamed her chill on the temperature of the room. "Willful negligence?"

"I never thought I'd get to be the one to say this, but now you're thinking like a human." Niall pointed an accusing finger. "I will never claim to understand the idomeni mind-set, but I'm not an idiot. Tsecha was *Tsecha*. A former Chief Propitiator, and, for want of a better term, a defining personality. He grew, but not all of his followers kept up. Not all of them thought as he did. If some of them felt that they still needed to treat him as an old-line idomeni because of what he'd been . . . ? They'd ignore a developing problem until it became a problem, then get caught flat-footed when it blew up in their faces."

Jani hugged herself. As she did, the rough weave of her

overrobe grabbed onto that of her shirt-jacket, pulling it so that she felt wrapped in restraints.

Then she looked toward the bed, and her eyes filled.

"Jan." Niall touched her arm. "You need to get out of this room." He took her by the elbow and supported her as she stood, then guided her to the door.

"It won't help."

"Humor me."

They navigated the twist of corridors. Heard voices, and followed them until they came upon John and Scriabin sitting in the clinic foyer. Their conversation was low volume, but animated, the sort of discussion one saw in hospitals.

John looked around when he heard footsteps. "Jani?" He stood and started toward her. "I thought you'd gone upstairs."

"I was with Niall." She leaned against him as soon as he embraced her. "He told me that His Excellency wished to see me."

Scriabin stood. "I appreciate Niall's sense of urgency, but there is no rush." He had changed clothes at some point, and now wore shirt and trousers in drab tan that looked like they'd been liberated from Dieter Brondt's own closet. "Anais has departed for Karistos, where press and staff await. I will be following her shortly. Stash and the others are conferring with ná Feyó. Colonial impact will be felt most immediately, of course."

"I imagine it's begun." Jani eased away from John, who ran his fingers down her back, then took hold of her hand.

Scriabin eyed her, then tilted his head toward John. "I told John of our discussion this morning, and the outcome. You have lost an inestimable ally, but that does not change the economic reality. We would prefer that the situation here remain as it is. We will do what we can to ensure that." He looked down at his clothes and sighed. "I dread leaving, to tell the truth. Stash's decision to treat Thalassa as a sovereign state reaped unforeseen benefits. You have borders, and your own com system. No one has to talk to the press because you haven't cleared it, and no one can report back to Cao while they're here because your secure system and Chicago's secure system can't talk to one another." He sighed. "I think I could live here."

"Just say the word, Zhenya." John gestured down the hall toward the labs.

Scriabin's eyes widened. "Perhaps not quite yet." He grinned, then hung his head. "Jani." He looked at her, all professional seriousness. "Words cannot express. He was one of the greatest, most influential beings who ever lived, and you called him friend for over twenty years."

"Among other things." Jani fielded Scriabin's startled look. "If you'd known Tsecha for a quarter-century, you would have, too." Her eyes stung, and she inhaled slowly, exhaled, struggled to maintain control. "Thank you."

"Now it's important that we preserve his legacy. This place—" Scriabin gestured around the foyer. "—and sound relations between humans and idomeni." He squeezed Jani's hand, then nodded to John and Niall and walked to the lift.

Jani waited until the farewells had been said and the lift door closed. "I thought we'd have things to discuss." She let go of John's hand and paced around the foyer.

"They're not machines, Jan, and they know you're not, either. They're giving you time. They know what you're going through." John stepped in front of her, forcing her to stop. "I have to go." He took her face in his hands and kissed her hard. "I'll see you later." He nodded to Niall, then headed down the corridor into the clinic proper, disappearing around a corner.

Jani remained in the middle of the foyer. Eventually, she stared down at the patterned lyno, then at the gleaming walls. "I'm going to make some coffee."

Niall fell in behind her as she headed for the break room, which was located just off the foyer. "We could go upstairs. Your mess crew has hot and cold running everything up there."

"I need to do something with my hands." Jani scanned the break room for bodies before entering, and was relieved to find it empty. She walked over to the coffee table and started to assemble the brewer. "Want some?"

As usual, Niall chose a table by the wall, with a clear view of the entry. "Sure," he said as he dug for his nicsticks.

For a few minutes the only sounds were the clatter of metal parts and glassware, the gravel tumble of beans, a metal gnashing, and the gurgle of water. Then came the aroma, like dark brown velvet, swamping out the odor of Niall's clove smoke.

Jani rummaged for cups in the community cupboard. She filled them to the brim, forgoing flavorings or any other additives that might dilute the caffeine. Sat down. Took a sip of coffee, tried to savor the flavor, and tasted only heat and bitterness.

Niall took a swallow, then reached for the creamer. "There's awake, and then there's orbit, gel." He poured half the contents of the small pitcher into his cup. "John would be proud."

Jani sat back, cradling her cup. "I'm wondering if I should change." She tugged at the front of her overrobe. "I know this is priestly garb and should be correct no matter the situation. My mother would consider it appropriate, but to her, white is a color for funerals."

Niall tipped back his chair, 'stick in one hand, coffee in the other. "I see your father in black. With a red rose in his buttonhole."

"Close." Jani took another sip, felt her head clear. "He preferred sprigs of lavender. He said the scent reminded him of his grandmama." She laid back her head. "The looks I got from Via's suborns when they came in for his body. As though I'd committed some grave sin. Spread out dinner on the edge of the bed." The patterned ceiling reminded her of the beach, the swirls of the tile coating like sprays of sand. "My father would've demanded more time. A proper wake, with stories and whiskey and laughter. We'd have had a chance to say good-bye. We wouldn't have felt like road-blocks in the way of those gods I'm supposed to intercede with even though I don't believe in them." She looked across the table to find Niall watching her, eyes dark with worry.

"Why don't you get some sleep?" He extinguished his spent 'stick, then immediately ignited another. "I'll hold off everyone, tell him that you had things you needed to see to."

"Can't sleep."

"Let John give you something."

"It's not the getting-to-sleep that's the problem." Jani's eye fell on the image someone had tacked up on the wall opposite. A forest scene, all green and leafy and shadowed. Quiet. Peaceful. "It's what happens after I arrive."

Niall stared at the smoke as it drifted upward, then he shook his head. "How long?"

"Three months. Maybe a little longer." Jani set down her cup. Plucked sugar packets from the dispenser, and stacked them one atop the other. "You don't have to listen to—"

"You've listened to me enough over the last couple of years." Niall took a long drag. "How many versions have you heard? A dozen? Two? 'What did you do during the War of Vynshàrau Ascension, young Niall?' 'Night of the Blade, sir. Laum blood running in the streets and shatterboxes shredding the air like tissue. Botched an arrest during evac, blew the commander of Rauta Shèràa Base and two of her cronies to bits, then spent the next twenty or so years covering it up.'" He stared straight ahead, the room's soft lighting making his battered face look very young. "'And why is that a problem, young Niall?' 'Because, sir, the man people think I am and the man I know I am are quite different. Because the honors I have since received are as dust upon my tongue. Because I'm living a lie.'" His head tilted toward Jani. "'But I have a friend who tells me that the man I am now is the one who matters.'" He cleared his throat. "Out with it."

"I never . . . even after it happened, I didn't . . . " Jani struggled for the words, wondered if the right ones existed. "The years went by. Nothing. I came here, and I was fine for months. Then . . . " She studied the forest scene again, and wondered at the feel of cool, damp air. "I don't know if it's the heat, or the scenery. Or the fact that this is so much an idomeni place, despite the humanish presence. The voices, that soft rise and fall. The gestures, and the smells, and the colors of the clothes." She paused, debated continuing, and felt the pull of Niall's patient gaze. "The first one. I'm walking down a dune. I can't find my footing, and I keep sliding. There are tents in the distance. The Laumrau tents. I'm wearing drop-dead whites instead of desertweights. I never get to the tents. I never even get to the base of the dune. I just keep walking, and sliding."

Niall remained silent, and waited.

"The second one . . . " Jani tugged at the red-slashed cuff of her overrobe. "I'm wearing desertweights. I have my shooter drawn." She raised a hand, index finger extended. "I'm standing at the first tent and pulling at the flap, but it won't open. It's like the fabric's all one piece—I can't find a gap. Then I freeze, because I know someone's behind me, and if I make any move to turn around, they'll kill me." She felt her heart pound and waited until it slowed. "Then I hear a shooter hum, and it isn't mine, and I know they'll kill me anyway." She flicked the pile of sugar packets, sending them splaying across the table. "Last night, they finally did." She waited for Niall to say something, then looked across the table to find him sitting with a fist pressed to his mouth, his eyes closed.

He lowered his hand eventually and opened his eyes. "Have you told John?"

Jani shook her head. "He'd get Neuro right on it. And who knows what else they'd take out along with the memories? They tend to overcompensate where I'm concerned." She picked up her coffee, then set it back down. "I wish I could drink."

"It doesn't help." Niall's voice emerged quiet, almost a whisper. "You dodged it for all those years. It was one of the things I held onto. Not that it did me any good. But just knowing . . . that if you never had them, maybe eventually I wouldn't have them, either." A twitch of a shoulder. "Doesn't make sense, but not much does. Can you talk to Parini?"

"Val tells John everything. They'd gang up on me like always, tell me it's for my own good." Jani looked at the forest again, but she'd lost the sense of it. Instead, she felt the heat and the dust, and smelled the bay, and saw the body on the gurney. "It happened so fast. He was there, and we were talking, and five minutes later he's on the ground, and ten minutes later he's—"

Niall stood. "I'm getting John."

"No." Jani rose, cup in hand, and walked to the sink. "I'll be all right." She poured the dregs down the drain, rinsed the cup with cold water, held her hand beneath the flow until her fingers ached.

"I need to get back." Niall set his cup on the drainboard. "I sent off a quick missive to Roshi, but I need to prep the one with all the details."

They encountered several clinic staffers in the corridor. Jani fielded words and gestures, meeting sympathy with sadness, and tears with a touch or handshake. And all the while, something roiled within. Restlessness. And anger, looking for a place to land.

Niall ushered her into the lift, then waited for the doors to close. "I'm guessing Pascal sent something to Roshi as well. Maybe I'll intercept it and see what he has to say about me."

Jani forced a smile. "Would anything surprise you?"

"I can think of a few things that would piss me off." Niall flipped his lid from one hand to the other, then ran his sleeve over the smudged brim.

The ground floor proved to be the clinic writ large. Thalassans came from the demirooms, the courtyard, and the offices. Then word traveled, and they hurried down from the three upper levels. The line formed in orderly silence, and Jani walked along it and accepted the words and the hugs and wondered if there was any way to trade all that grief to

Tsecha's gods for five more minutes. For a chance to say good-bye. To say anything at all.

Niall hung by her shoulder the entire time, monitoring her every move. When the impromptu receiving line petered out, he herded her to a table, then filled a plate for her from one of buffets.

"I will call later. I'll go through the office so that I don't wake you in case you're sleeping." He set the food in front of Jani, then unwrapped some cutlery from its napkin wrap and handed it to her. "'His life was gentle, and the elements so mixed in him that Nature might stand up and say to all the world, "This was a man."'" He spread the napkin across her lap. "The end of *Julius Caesar*. Not completely appropriate, but it says what I mean it to say." He kissed the top of her head, then turned and clipped across the courtyard.

Jani ate a little, then passed the time tearing a roll into tiny bits and feeding the lizards that had taken autumn refuge in the courtyard. Eventually, she heard distant thunder, then the rain spatter against the skylight roof. Looked overhead, and watched the roiling dark through the glass.

"You'd think it would be cold, but it's not."

She tore her attention from the rain just as Lucien emerged from the garden shadows. He wore civvies, brown trousers tucked into low boots and a tan shirt with the sleeves rolled up. A slingbag hung from one shoulder, and he had tied a weatherall around his waist. "I thought you'd be back at the base."

Lucien shrugged. "I showed up for an emergency staff meeting. But I couldn't get into the room—my coding hadn't been entered into base systems, and according to regs, I cannot attend certain types of meetings unless I have been entered into base systems."

Jani tossed a bit of bread on the floor, where it vanished amid a rustle of leaves and a flick of green and red striped tail. "You have the right security clearances?"

"Yes," Lucien said with a sigh, "but I am not officially in systems. Pierce's admin told me that initialization can take up to a week. She was smiling when she said it." Another shrug. "I could bitch to Mako, but what would be the point? He's in Chicago—any communication he sends Pierce ordering him to give me access would be lost or garbled. They're experts over there at losing and garbling. It's the Elyan way."

"What did you expect? You know he can't stand you, and you forced yourself down his throat."

"Doesn't matter. I've been keeping myself busy." Lucien studied her through narrowed eyes. "I thought you'd have meetings of your own to attend."

Jani looked around the courtyard, then up toward the walkways, where Thalassans milled, chatted. It could have passed for a normal enclave evening but for the pall that hung in the air. "I've been allowed time to grieve."

"How considerate of everyone." Lucien met her low tone with his own. "I have a skimmer parked out on the beach. If you have some time, I'd like to show you something."

Jani eyed his face, rain-damp and drawn. His clothes and boots, mud-streaked and spattered. He'd been looking for something. Would he have come looking for her unless he'd found it? "I have time." She fingered the edge of one red cuff. "Give me a chance to change clothes."

CHAPTER 14

The Service two-seater coursed over the water like a seabird. Whitecaps swelled close enough to touch, spray mixing with rain to spatter across the vehicle's windscreen. Lucien had shut down all lighting both exterior and interior, leaving as the sole illumination the sickly green safety string that ran along the bottom of the dashboard.

Jani huddled against the heated cushions, fixing on the distant lights of Karistos, their yellow-white flicker like stars against the churning dark. "Does Niall know you're here?"

"I don't think he gives a rat's ass." Lucien's voice emerged measured, his native French provincial accent muted to nothing, a sign that anger and humiliation simmered into stew just below the surface. "I spent part of the day filling out forms. Then we heard the news. I tried to get into the staff meeting, like I said before. When that fell through, I pulled some strings at the Communications center, which for some strange reason *did* have me in systems. Poked around. Intercepted some chatter. Changed clothes, gathered gear, signed out the skimmer, and went to have a look around."

Jani rode the silence for a time, listening to the dull hum of the motor and the occasional splash of water against the hull. "What sort of chatter?"

"Details about Tsecha's death."

Jani's heart tripped as Lucien maneuvered the skimmer off the water and along a narrow strip of rock-strewn shore-line, held onto the armrests and squeezed as the vehicle shuddered and bounced. "What bothered you?"

Lucien remained silent until he had steered the skimmer onto the comparative smoothness of a steep incline. "The speed." He paused as he executed a hairpin turn. "I heard folks mention stroke. Hemorrhage. Aneurysm." He shook his head. "I didn't think that Tsecha would allow any condition he developed to advance until the point of crisis." He tore his attention from the narrow snake of a road to look at her. "John didn't discuss this with you?"

"Not in any detail." Jani folded her arms and concentrated on the road ahead. "We were right in the middle of it. John had to focus on treating him." She felt her face heat as Lucien's deceptively gentle laugh filled the cabin.

"Did he really think you wouldn't find out?" He steered around the final turn and up over the edge of the cliff, his voice shaking as the skimmer fought to stabilize over a stretch of rocky scrub.

"Find out what?" Jani closed her eyes and waited. *They were just giving me time to adjust.* Her gut ached. *They were being kind.* She opened her eyes. *Since when?* She saw the lights of Karistos, brightening the horizon like sunrise. *They wanted to talk to me.* And then they didn't.

The sounds of argument remembered . . .
Why the hell didn't you spot it before?
Because it wasn't there before.
It's growing.

"He was killed." Jani heard her voice echo in her head. A barely detectable sound, like the first pebble in the land-slide.

"I think the word is 'assassinated.'" Lucien clucked his tongue. "How much time did it buy John? A few hours, at most. Now here you are, hot on the trail." His lips curved in the barest trace of a smile. "You're very angry with him now."

"That's none of your goddamn business."

"If you say so." Lucien fell silent, half smile fixed in place, and steered the skimmer over rock formations and across ravines with practiced ease.

Still several kilometers from the Karistos outskirts, there was little to see besides bare land. Jani took note of the odd house that broke up the monotony, but these appeared uninhabited and, judging from their ruined appearance, uninhabitable.

"This area's prone to quakes," Lucien said, as though reading her thoughts. "The land around here has shifted over the years, and some people didn't choose their building sites very carefully." He pointed out a one-story white stone box that had collapsed in the center as though a giant had stepped on it. "A two-meter crevasse opens up beneath your sitting room—there goes the couch."

Jani heard the skimmer motor hum lower in pitch as the vehicle slowed. "You didn't bring me out here to show me wrecked houses, did you?"

"Just one wrecked house in particular." Lucien slowed to a stop near yet another one-story white box, this one half buried thanks to the collapse of a sheltering overhang. "Although I checked out every abandoned homestead in this general area."

Jani popped her gullwing and disembarked the skimmer. Despite having lived the last two years in the thick of Commonwealth society, she still saw things through the eyes of the fugitive she had been. *Secluded, but half the view blocked by rocks . . . couldn't see someone approaching from the direction of Karistos . . . the outcropping offers too good a hiding place for an intruder.* She would have struck the place from her list, but knew she wasn't looking at it the right way. *Look at the place through the eyes of a killer.* The blocked views still bothered her, but the seclusion seemed more desirable now. "Where did they park their skimmer?"

"Up the road a little. There's a niche with some overhanging shrubbery. They broke off branches and used them for coverage." Lucien drew his shooter and activated it. The high-pitched hum sliced the air, highlighting the quiet. "There are a few sets of footprints around the place. Some bits of trash." He stopped in the doorway, examined the interior, then stepped inside. "Careful what you touch. It's been wiped with a protein bomb, and there's still some of the residue about." He drew a lightstick from inside his weatherall and activated it. Soft illumination rose slowly, casting weird shadows on the walls and ceiling.

Jani trailed him into the house. The interior proved even less inviting than the outside. Cracked walls. Rubble-strewn floors.

But at the far end, a window that allowed an expansive view of the bay and the curve of cliffs beyond, trimmed by a wide, rock-strewn sill.

Jani walked to the spot, on the lookout for disturbances in the dust, anything that could serve to confirm her surmise. "They stood here." She stepped around to gauge the view through the window. "Not the best angle."

"The only alternative is the sill," Lucien said as he stashed his shooter. "They would have had to clear the rubble, though, and beyond some smearing of dust, it shows no signs of having been disturbed. It seems the better choice—more stability for the weapon. But standing allowed more mobility, not to mention a better view of the doorway." He reached into his slingbag, removing a fist-sized ball that looked like crumpled metal foil. "Secondary spotter courses overhead, relaying information on the target back to the primary sight in the weapon's eyepiece." He tossed the ball out the window. It hovered for a few seconds, then shot upward like a shooting star in reverse, vanishing into the dark.

"We'll give it a chance to reach altitude." Lucien reached into his bag once more, this time removing a flat, hand-sized display. "A few hundred meters is usually high enough." He flipped open the display lid and motioned for Jani to join him, holding out the device to her so that she could see the screen.

She found herself looking at an aerial view of the Main
House, centered on the balcony outside her and John's bedroom.

"I can zoom in and out at will. I can even record sound."
Lucien touched a spot on the display pad and the secondary
zoomed in. In a blink, the bedroom window filled the screen,
the image sharp enough to discern the outline of Jani's desk
and chair through the gauzy curtains.

"As I mentioned," Lucien said as he deactivated the display and closed the case, "the secondary relays images to the
weapon sight. In addition, the assassin wore an audiovisual
array much like the ones reporters use to record events. In
either case, it serves as an archive. Snipers call them their
'books.' They record what is seen through the weapons sight,
and it serves as proof of the kill." He tucked the display back
into his bag, then walked to the window and waited. Within
seconds the secondary flitted through the opening and settled into his hands.

Jani touched the rough globe. "Why didn't enclave security systems pick up on this?"

"It scans as an organism. Systems would identify it as a
small bird, or a very large bug." Lucien tossed the device into
the air, caught it, then stuck it back in his bag. "Security's a
fiction that dissuades only the laziest killers. If someone really wants to get to you, there's nothing you can do to stop
them."

Jani looked out the window, imagining the scene beyond
the water and the cliffs. Tsecha emerging from the meeting
house and walking across the street. The secondary monitoring him, relaying his image to his killer, who lay watching,
waiting for the perfect time to strike. "You know it was a
sniper. Do you have a name or two that you can offer?"

Lucien hung his head and put his hands in his pockets.
Time passed. One minute. Two.

Jani stepped away from the window and walked around
the room, pretending interest in examining the rubble. She
had known since their days together in Chicago that Lucien's

Service career served as cover for his true profession. He had once arranged it so she found his souvenirs, the items he took from his victims and kept as mementos. A casino chip. A scarf. A whiskey glass. Fifteen items in all, each resting atop a clean, folded cloth inside a dresser drawer. How many had he added to the collection since then?

Lucien raised his head. Cleared his throat. "You know what I do."

Jani leaned against the remains of a smashed couch frame. "I've known for a long time."

"And you love me anyway." He glanced at her beneath his lashes, but his heart wasn't in it—he straightened and started to pace. "What's said here, stays here."

Jani shrugged. "Likewise."

"I'm serious."

"And I never am."

Lucien stopped. Looked about the room, focusing on nothing. "I've never talked about this before, with anyone. What I tell you may not seem important, or vital, or secret, but that's not the point. It's talking out of school." He stopped fidgeting and fixed on her. "We don't do that."

Now it was Jani's turn to remain silent. She listened to the wind whistle through the cracks in the roof, branches scrape against the rough stone exterior. "You know what I am, how I think."

Any other time, Lucien might have offered a flirtatious response, or rolled his eyes in irritation. Not this time. This time, he watched her hands, the way she held herself, as though unsure of what she might do. "I've known for a long time."

"Then you know my answer." Jani patted her trouser pocket, and wished she had taken the time to dig her shooter out from its place in the bottom drawer of her dresser. In this house that had apparently sheltered one assassin, in which she conversed with another, she would have taken some comfort in its presence. "I don't care about your assassins' code of silence, or your fears for your future, or your friends in high places. If you know who killed Tsecha, I expect you to tell me. If you know how to find them, I expect you to help me. If you know and you don't help me, be prepared to deal with the consequences. Do you understand what I'm telling you?"

"The definitions of 'rock' and 'hard place.'" Lucien walked to the window. "I don't know who killed Tsecha. I know the type." He turned and leaned against the wall. The half-light conspired with the layout of the room to shadow his face in a way that obscured his age and left him looking too young. "We all have our specialty. Mine is accidents. Mechanical and systems malfunctions. Vehicle crashes. These are the neatest killings, in my opinion. If executed properly, they don't attract undue attention. They look like tragic mishaps to most people. The only ones who know otherwise are those who know how to read the signs." He looked up, eyes fixed on some middle distance, some event in his past. Some target made. "Some of us specialize in explosives. A few prefer poison." He shook his head. "God knows why." He folded his arms, flexing his hands every so often, as though they pained him. "Then there are some who will only employ projectile weaponry, blades, strangulation, a method that requires them to remain in contact with or close proximity to their target." He straightened, then moved to the side, let his bag slide down his arm to the floor, and perched on the edge of the sill. "That's the sort of killer I believe we're dealing with here."

Jani watched Lucien continue to flex his hands. *He's never been one to fidget.* The last time he showed such restlessness, he had just learned that the Haárin he would meet in the circle the next morning planned to kill him. *He was in danger then—is he in danger now?* Was what he told her that important, or had the mere fact of telling it put him at risk? *Do I care?* "Close proximity to the victim. Close-in weapons. You've just described a Service infantryman."

"Infantry's a *job*." Lucien nudged a small chunk of rubble with the toe of his boot, then kicked it across the floor. "The ones I'm telling you about . . . they consider assassination a calling, like medicine, or the clergy. Every aspect of preparation is ritualized, from the researching of the target to the choosing of the weapon." His eyes narrowed. "The kill . . . needs to be personal." He let his arms fall to his sides, then hunched his shoulders and shoved his hands in his pockets. "Most of us work for money, for position. Tangible rewards, if not always material. It's a job, like any other, for which we receive payment for services rendered. But with them . . . " Again the hesitation, the sense of words being pulled out with pliers. "They see beauty in the act, an affirmation of whatever it is they believe in. I'd be more inclined to believe that one of them killed Tsecha rather than someone with a more commercial bent."

"Why?"

"The risk. Tsecha is the highest visibility target to be hit in decades. The scrutiny will be intense. The investigations. The repercussions." Lucien again glanced at her beneath his lashes, but judging from the edge in his eyes, flirtation was the furthest thing from his mind. "Say that I had been offered the commission to assassinate Tsecha. I know that given your closeness to him, you would become involved in the investigation. If you discovered that I was responsible, you would kill me." His head came up slowly, a trace of the old challenge showing itself in the set of his jaw. "Don't tell me it didn't cross your mind." He cocked his head. "Not even once?"

Not until now. Jani wished again that she'd brought her shooter. "It might have."

"That's my girl. Trust is for other people."

"I'm not people."

"You never were." Lucien looked back down at the floor. "Like I said, I know how you'd react, and that would be taken into account as I considered whether or not to accept the commission."

Jani felt the silence envelop them, the tension crystallize. Even the wind had paused as if to listen. "Was it offered?"

Lucien hesitated. One could almost hear the rattle of an

ancient scale as he weighed his options. "No. The fact that it wasn't eliminates a number of possible customers. I'm on their preferred list when it comes to jobs like this."

Questions surfaced in the document examiner part of Jani's mind. Was there a paper list? If so, who kept it and how did they classify it? Who had access? What sorts of accounts did they set up to bury the payments, the expenses? *Just give me a chance to hunt. A chance to dig.* She focused on the emptiness of a niche cut into the wall opposite, the shadows that defined it. Anything to keep her mind from racing until she could find time alone to ponder. "Wouldn't they think twice about sending you on this job, knowing your connection to me?"

Lucien shook his head. "Our past relationship would provide me a legitimate reason to be here. Ex-lover seeking to rekindle an old flame." The winning smile broke through, only to vanish as quickly as it came. "I had nothing to do with his death."

Jani shrugged. "I appreciate the reassurance."

"You look impressed." Lucien bent over and plucked another fragment of rubble from the floor. He straightened, then started rolling the bit of debris between his palms. "He didn't like me."

"He liked you just fine. He just didn't trust you." *That was one thing he and I had in common.* Jani pushed away from the wall and wiped her hands on her trousers to remove the grit. "So, we're looking for a sniper-type killer who considered murdering Tsecha to be a religious experience. Do you have any names?" She waited for an answer. As time passed and none proved forthcoming, she looked up to find Lucien still seated on the sill, watching her.

"Let me take care of it. Send a killer to catch a killer." He continued to roll the rubble fragment between his hands, the movement growing ever slower until it stopped completely. "It might take some time. Years, perhaps. But I would find them and handle them and no one would ever be able to trace it back to you."

Jani studied his face for some indication of his thoughts. She would have expected him to try to cut her off. *Instead, he goes and surprises me by offering to help.* Not that it mattered. "No, thank you. I want to find them myself."

"Why?" Lucien closed one hand around the stone fragment. "I'm not making this offer because I like working with you. I'm a survivor of too many rides on the Kilian express, and I have the scars to prove it." He opened his hand and tipped it to one side—the fragment slid off and hit the floor, bouncing once before coming to rest amid the dust. "This situation needs to be approached with caution, and when it comes to killing . . . " He sighed. "With you, it's always personal."

"We've had this discussion before." Jani felt the stomach-rumbling irritation that always accompanied one of their arguments. "I have only ever killed for reasons of defense, mine or someone else's."

"Only after you went out and looked for it. Met it. Stared it in the face. Challenged it." Lucien rose abruptly and strode across the room, raising dust with every step. "You think you know killing. You're a fucking amateur. You always lead with your emotions, and there is no place for emotion in this. No place for vengeance." He stopped in front of the shadowed wall niche and braced his hands on either side. "I know what you want. You want to watch them die. You want to look into their eyes and watch the light go out—"

Jani moved for the doorway just as Lucien pushed off the wall. He met her in the middle of the room, grabbing her arm and spinning her around to face him.

"—feel their blood flow over your hands. Savor the look on their face when they realize it was you who struck the blow—"

Jani took hold of Lucien's thumb and bent it back. He released her arm with a muttered curse—as he took a step back, she moved in. Brought her fist around. The raised dome of one of her rings caught Lucien square in the mouth—she felt the shock of a solid punch jar her hand, rattle up her arm. As soon she connected, she backed off, raising both hands and opening them wide. He'd grabbed her first—that entitled her to one shot. Anything beyond that would take them both to a place they'd never been, a place they could never depart once they'd entered.

Lucien must have understood that as well. He remained in the middle of the room, bent at the waist, hands on knees, his breathing ragged.

Jani watched as a single red drop fell from his mouth to the dust below. Then another. Another. She looked down at her hand and saw the brilliant crimson of the stone faded by the dull wash of his blood.

"Well." Lucien touched his battered lower lip and flinched. "That had something behind it." He drew back his hand and studied the red that smeared across his fingertips. Then he straightened, one slow move at a time, like a clockwork figure. "I can't comprehend how you felt about Tsecha. Even if I could remember what that depth of regard felt like, I've never known anyone worth the effort." He reached into his trouser pocket and pulled out a crumpled dispo, which he pressed to the seeping wound. "But I've seen strong emotion take over before, and I know where it leads. You'll get yourself killed. You'll get others around you killed. Because you won't back down. Because you want the blood of Tsecha's assassin on your hands."

"Stop pretending to read my mind!" Jani wedged between a broken chair and a fallen portion of the ceiling. Anything to block her path to Lucien. Anything to keep her from going after him again. "You don't know me—"

"I know you better than he—*Ow!*" Lucien winced and pressed the dispo to his torn lip. "I know you better than he does," he continued, his voice muffled by the cloth. "He thought he could get away without telling you anything, like he did in Rauta Shèràa." He pulled the dispo away from the wound and glared at the staining, then crumpled it and shoved it back in his pocket. "I'm trying to get you to do now what I've always tried to get you to do in Chicago. Understand the situation for what it is. See reason." He stood in place for a time, the angle of the lightstick illumination accentuating the rawness around his mouth, the first hints of swelling. Then he turned and walked to the sill, recovering his slingbag from its resting place and hoisting it to his shoulder.

Jani massaged the back of the broken chair, squeezing harder even as she felt the ground-in grit abrade her skin. "Did you ever manage to do it? Get me to see reason, as you understood it to be?"

Lucien stilled. Looked at her and said nothing.

Jani let go of the chair, brushed the ground stone from her hands. "Well, then . . . " She paused as the screech of branch against rock filled the room, a signal of the storm's growing intensity. "Are you going to help me?" She awaited the answer she knew would never come. "This takes me back. Yes, to my Rauta Shèràa days. I've been stonewalled by experts, Lucien."

"And you remember how that ended." His voice came soft, barely audible above the wind. "A bomb on a transport. All aboard killed."

Storm sounds receded. Now Jani heard nothing but the beat of her heart. "You're saying that was my fault?" She tried to swallow, but her mouth had gone dry. "No one was meant to survive Knevçet Shèràa. We were dead no matter what."

"Not as long as Rikart Neumann remained alive. He was one of the masterminds—if you'd played him right, you could have gotten your people out." Lucien looked in her direction. He even met her eye. "Instead, you shot him."

"That was self-defense."

"Only after you confronted him. Stared him in the face. Challenged him." Lucien pressed the back of his hand to his lip, examined it, then shook his head. "When your parents lived in Chicago, I used to visit them."

Jani nodded. "Mama told me that you liked her cooking. You liked being able to converse in French. Papa knew better. He said that you were too nosy, wanted to know too much about me."

"Yes, you inherited your trusting nature from him, I think." Lucien started for the door, then stopped and looked her full in the face. "You were never any different, even as a kid. Always a punch in the mouth when a touch would do just as well." His lower lip had swelled in earnest now, the gash red and glistening. "And now here you are. Decades have past, the scenery's different, but you haven't changed a bit." He watched her, dead brown eyes unreadable, then walked to the door. On the way, he grabbed the lightstick from the place where he'd set it, shook it to extinguish it, then stuffed it in his bag.

Jani let her eyes adjust to the dark. Then she stepped out from between the chair and the rubble and walked to the window. Examined the rock-strewn sill, then the view through the window, imagining as she did a tiny object descending through the air toward its target. How did Tsecha's assassin feel when they saw him touch his left ear, saw the first hint of confusion cross his face? Satisfied? Ecstatic? Righteous?

"Hold that feeling tight," Jani whispered. "You won't enjoy it for long." With that, she turned, looked over the room one last time, and headed for the door.

The force of the wind hit her as soon as she stepped outside, forcing her to turn her back on it so she could breathe. She climbed into the skimmer to find Lucien checking weather reports on the vehicle's display. He ignored her, putting the vehicle in motion before she had fully closed her door.

They rode back to the Thalassan side of the bay in silence. The rain had eased to the odd spatter by the time the shore came into view.

Lucien steered the skimmer up onto the beach and up the

cliff road to the Main House. Stopped on the edge of the drive circle near the entry and powered down. "I'll say it one last time. Stay out of it."

Jani didn't reply. She disembarked and walked across the pavered circle to the house, gusts of wind whipping the hem of her weatherall as though hurrying her along. Felt Lucien's stare drill the place between her shoulders, but didn't turn around.

CHAPTER 15

Jani entered the Main House to find a confab going on in the middle of the courtyard. Dicter, Val, and John, standing amid the empty tables and sundered buffets of late evening sacrament, voices rising.

Then John spotted her. "Where the hell have you been?" He started toward her, more relieved than angry, the first hints of a smile lightening his face.

Then something he saw behind her caused him to slow. Stop. Clench his fists.

Jani heard the entry door close. Footsteps.

"Stormy." Lucien removed his weatherall and shook it, sending water spraying. "I'm guessing it'll last the night." He hung the garment on one of the wall hooks near the door, but kept his slingbag with him. "Good evening, Mr. Brondt." He nodded to Dieter, while pointedly ignoring Val. "Could I trouble you to let me use your comroom?"

Dieter's brow arched as he took in the state of Lucien's lip. He glanced at Jani, on the alert for any hint of an objection. " . . . Of course, Captain," he said eventually. "Follow me, please." He cast a last, questioning look in her direction, then headed for the lift, Lucien at his heels.

John waited until the lift doors closed. "Where were

you?" He ignored Val's muttered caution. "We were ready to send out Security."

Jani remained still and silent as John drew closer, watching his expression grow more and more grim as he took in her rough clothes, the wet sand that coated her boots. "Why?"

"What do you mean, why?" Val pressed a hand to his forehead. "We were worried sick. We didn't know if you—"

"That's not the question she's asking, Val." John stood hands on hips, and studied the floor. "Not here." He turned and headed across the courtyard toward the enclave offices.

Jani followed, brushing past Val, ignoring his whispered "Please, Jan—" She felt focused, alive, as though she could run for kilometers, go for days without sleep or food. Idomeni rage, a pure distillation of emotion, a force that had built cities and transformed governments and destroyed them just as surely.

She waited in the doorway of an unoccupied office while John checked for squatters, not entering until he gave the all-clear. Waited longer to speak, because so much of what she had to say had already been said, in a clinic basement twenty years before. *Some essentials never change.* Only the circumstances surrounding them.

She walked to a desk on the far side of the room and leaned against it. "When did you know?"

John turned to her. He hadn't looked her in the eye since Lucien's appearance, and he avoided doing so now. "You don't understand—"

"Answer the goddamned question."

John walked over to a chair set against the wall opposite Jani and sat. "The sudden appearance of the mass in his auditory canal. We scanned the area within minutes of his collapse and we saw nothing. We wouldn't have missed it—it was the sort of thing we were looking for." His gaze shifted to some middle distance, memories of the morning playing across his face, mirrored in his clouded stare. "We initially felt it was a neuroma, but those grow very slowly, and this thing grew while Aris watched."

Jani revisited her own memories, carved in her heart and soul with the force of a knife through flesh. John's angry question. Aris's frantic reply. *Why the hell didn't you spot it before? Because it wasn't there before.* She tried to erase the images, the voices, even as she knew that any respite would prove only temporary. "What was it?"

"Preliminary indications are that it was a weaponized prionic. It entered Tsecha through his left tympanum. After it warmed to body temperature, it began to grow." John fell back on his lecture voice, a measured narration devoid of emotion. "It rapidly extruded into his brain cavity and continued to increase in size until it pressed against his brain stem. This led to seizure, followed by unconsciousness, respiratory collapse, and death."

Death. Jani saw the still figure in the bed. Ná Via circling, shutting down the life support systems one by one. "Did he feel any pain?"

"He—" John hesitated, then shook his head. "Once growth began, it was over within seconds. I don't believe he did, no."

"But you don't know?"

"It's unknowable."

Jani brushed away a tear. There were times when she wished John would lie, but those were the times when he never did. "Who else knows the truth?"

"Val. Yevgeny."

"Markos?" Jani's throat tightened. "Ulanova?"

John nodded, after a time. "Yes."

"Niall?" Jani waited as John didn't respond at first, then shook his head. *Because you knew he'd tell me.* "Via?" She waited again, as John stilled and remained silent and slowly averted his gaze. "She's going to figure out that she didn't miss anything, that if it had been a neuroma, she would have seen it long before Tsecha became ill." She recalled the female, normally as aggressive as ná Meva, following John from display to display. Stricken. Confused. "You lied to her. You let her think she screwed up, that she killed him." Then another figure replaced the physician-priest's in her mind's eye. "What about Feyó?"

"What do you think her reaction will be if she learns that Tsecha was assassinated? That one of his beloved human-ish brought him down? Do you think she'll listen to anything that any of us have to say?" John looked Jani in the eye now, leaned forward with hands on knees as he let fly the facts. "She'll look at us and see humanish and the dialogue will stop there." He sat back, the lecture winding down. "The truth will come out. When we're ready. When we've prepared."

"When will that be?" Jani felt the subtle shift in the air around her. "Tomorrow? Next month? Five years? Ten?" She could have been in any of a score of offices in the old Rauta Shèràa consulate, arguing the same points, fighting the same old battles, and losing every one. "Or maybe you and your new friend Yevgeny went behind everyone's back and worked your own deal. You cover up the assassination, and he guarantees you keep your share of Neoclona."

John's face darkened. "You believe me capable of that level of deceit?"

"In your sleep. You'll have all your reasons lined up, and they'll all be very sound. To preserve the Outer Circle alliance with the Haárin. To preserve Neoclona, and the stability it provides. To help ensure that Yevgeny wins the election." Jani stood and paced, anger driving her to move. "And on the other hand, we have what? You lied to Feyó, who is the foundation of the alliance. If she ever discovers that you misled her, you'll lose her. Maybe you're assuming that you'll be well enough established by that point that you won't need her. That's one hell of an assumption, but you're in a risk-taking mood." Her step slowed. "Then you lied to me. But, you've done that before."

John stood and started toward her. "Jani—"

"I could have struck you. When I realized that you knew Tsecha had been murdered and you didn't tell me." Jani saw the look in John's eye as he drew closer, as he gauged her expression. Read the tension as he stopped in his tracks, as reluctant to approach her as she was to have him within arm's reach. "Who did it? Do you know? Is anyone looking for them?"

"You know better than that. Exterior is turning over every rock—"

"Including the ones they put in place themselves?"

John begged the ceiling for respite. "We know of several separatist organizations whose goal is to drive a wedge between Chicago and Rauta Shèràa. Yevgeny is maneuvering Anais into pushing all the right buttons." His eyes chilled. Frost on silver. "We aren't letting it slide, if that's what you're thinking."

You keep saying "we," John. It's like you're already back in the game. Jani felt her fingers curl, the sense memory of a hand squeezing hers. "He knew. That he wasn't right. That he'd been injured, infected. And in his last few lucid moments, he begged you to take care of him." She laughed. "You're taking care of him, all right."

"It needs to be done quietly. Carefully, so that—"

"So that Yevgeny can dig for any connections to Li Cao, and use them to drive her from office. So that everything can be positioned to derive the greatest political benefit possible."

"I know it's not your way of doing things." John put his hands in his pockets, shuffled his feet. The frost melting, a little. "Yevgeny told me about the meeting this morning. He told me how concerned you were about Thalassa, about what would happen to everyone here if relations between Chicago and Rauta Shèràa fell apart. If we're careful, you won't have to worry about that. You can just—"

"Go back to being your pet lab experiment?" Jani touched her hand, outlining where Tsecha's fingers had locked with hers. "Don't worry about anything—John took care of it. He also won back all his marbles in the process—wasn't that bright of him?" She let her hands fall. "Except that you lied to Feyó. That wasn't so bright."

"Any step you take to inform her will destroy everything we've put in place so far." John maneuvered until he stood in front of her. "It's a cracked egg, Jan. A touch could smash it. Think past Feyó to Morden nìRau Cèel. How do you think he'd play Tsecha's assassination? He'd sever diplomatic relations with Chicago and call all Haárin back into the worldskein. Given the circumstances, Feyó would obey. Then Cèel would have what he needs to hold off his enemies and hang onto power, an external enemy at which he can point his warriors." His eyes dulled. "Do you remember the Vynshàrau warriors? I do. Never a shooter when a blade will do the job. Most of what I know about idomeni anatomy and physiology I learned from helping clean up after them."

Jani turned her back and took a slow walk around the room. She had to be careful now, because John had a knack for sounding sensible, for deflecting her every argument and turning her emotion against her. The trick was to avoid looking at his eyes, his hands, his smile. To concentrate on another time, twenty years before, when he'd talked sense and told her not to worry. "If Feyó considered humanish a monolithic entity with a single fixed mind-set, she would never have become a follower of Tsecha. She never would have worked to establish her enclave here. She's capable of discerning shades of grey." She heard her voice, so quiet. So sensible. "Every hour you delay informing her adds months, years, to the time it will take to win back her trust, assuming it's even possible to do so." She checked the wall clock, and the investigator she'd once been sent up a howl. "She has networks of informants in place at Elyas Station. Throughout the Outer Circle. They could provide us information about suspects. Names."

John sighed. "Jan, I really don't think—"

"No, of course you don't. You assume, because it's easier and it's faster and it gets you what you want." She looked at the wall clock again. So many hours lost. So many chances. "We've had this argument more times than I can remember. And every time, I've knuckled under. Not always immediately, but eventually. Not because I came to agree with you, but because I loved you and because in the end that always outweighed everything else." She looked at John only long enough to see the first glimmer of realization cross his face. "Not this time."

"Jani?" John stared, brow furrowed, as though she'd said something in a language he didn't understand. "What are you saying? What—"

Before he could finish, she walked out the door. Thought she heard his words follow her as the panel slid closed—

I love you.

—and kept walking. Grabbed an empty dish cart that one of the kitchen crew had left in the corridor and dragged it over to the lift. Boarded, pulling the cart after her, turning in time to spot John stride across the courtyard into the nearest demiroom, where Val waited.

The lift door opened on the fourth floor. She disembarked, cart in tow. Keyed into her suite. Hers and John's suite.

John's suite.

She dragged the cart through the sitting room into the bedroom, through the bedroom into the closet, and started pulling clothes off hangers. Trousersuits, coveralls. Left the gowns behind because she wore them for John. Grabbed boots and trainers from the shoe rack and tossed them atop the clothes. Rummaged along a top shelf until she found her old Service duffel, and added that to the mix, then turned and ran headlong into a flustered Dieter.

"Jani, is something wr—" He looked down at the cart, then at the empty hangers, then at her, eyes widening. "I'm sorry."

"Is there a spare bedroom?" Jani exited the closet. "Preferably on another floor?"

"There are a few guest rooms on the second." Dieter hurried after her. "But they're very *small*."

"I'm nothing if not adaptable." Jani pushed the cart in front of her armoire and dumped in armfuls of T-shirts, underwear, and socks. "You know?"

"Yes." Dieter's eyes glistened. "First I saw—" He looked down at the mess of clothing. "I overheard Doctor Shroud and Minister Scriabin. Then I overheard some of the discussion in the library."

"That's my Dieter. Eavesdropper extraordinaire." Jani uncovered an old Neoclona pullover in a pile of shirts and tossed it aside. "Would your old connections at Elyas Station be amenable to providing passenger manifests and information on persons of interest?" She waited. "I don't like the sound of that silence."

"They've been ordered not to talk to me." Dieter freed a coverall sleeve that had gotten twisted in one of the cart's wheels. "All that Fred in Docks Management would tell me was that the word came from the main office. He wouldn't tell me which ministry."

Jani nodded. *And so it begins.* The stonewalling, leavened with outright lies. "I need to talk to Feyó."

"Actually, she's on her way." Dieter picked up a bandbra that had missed the cart and landed on the floor. "Ná Meva is bringing her." He set it atop the pile, his face reddening. "They apparently have something to ask you."

Knowing Meva, it's more telling than asking. Jani headed for her desk. "Great." She freed her scanpack, a parts bag. "Scriabin needs to be here as well."

Dieter caught a stack of T-shirts just before they tumbled to the floor. "I will contact his offices, but—"

Jani added a favorite stylus to the pile. "What?"

"I have spoken with Doctor Shroud. Many things have already been decided." Dieter took a deep breath. "Minister Scriabin may not come."

"Tell him I'm meeting with ná Feyó." Jani pulled out a drawer and emptied the assorted tools atop the clothes. "He'll come."

Dieter grabbed the back of the cart and helped her steer it toward the door. "I left Captain Pascal in the comroom. Betty is watching him to make sure he doesn't get into anything he shouldn't." He cleared his throat. "What happened to his lip?"

"I belted him."

"He said he fell."

"Captain Diplomacy." Jani stopped in front the door and keyed it open—

—just as John did the same from the other side. His face lightened until he spotted the laden cart. Then the brightness died. "What are you doing?"

Jani dragged the cart past him into the corridor. There, she found her way blocked by Val, who tried to take hold of her arm. "Get out of my way," she said as she shook him off.

"Jan, please let us—"

"Get out of my way, you self-serving son of a bitch."

Val's face flushed. "You don't—understand."

"I understand all I have to." She veered close as she pushed past him, forcing him against the wall. "You, me, and John in the basement of the Rauta Shèràa clinic. And the goal for the day is keep Jani in the dark and pile on that manure. Mushroom, mushroom. The more things change." She waited for Dieter to catch her up, and together they pushed the cart down the corridor toward the lift.

Dieter helped Jani organize her suits and coveralls in her new room's narrow closet, but fled when they reached what he referred to as her "small clothes."

"Coward." She rolled and folded as best she could, but found that for the first time in her memory, she had more clothes than places in which to store them. She concentrated on sorting out anything faded or frayed, letting her hands work while her mind raced. *Ná Feyó, forgive us—I need your help to catch a killer.*

"Well, this is cozy."

Jani turned to find Lucien standing in the doorway. "I obviously need to get that lock recoded."

"It's still set to the factory default. Which means no one has used this room yet." Lucien looked around the small, sparsely furnished bed-sit and sniffed his disapproval. "Can't imagine why." He wandered by the bed and gave the mattress an exploratory prod. "You'd find out more if you stayed with him. Have you thought of that?"

"He's a past master at keeping things from me." Jani closed the door of her tiny clothes cupboard before Lucien could make any comments about her underwear.

"Yet you always manage to find those things out." He dragged a frame chair away from the wall and sat, dropping his slingbag to the floor beside him. "He loves you. He thinks he's doing what's best for you, but he's insecure enough to want to explain his reasons to you in great detail. That gives you leverage." He stretched his legs until the soles of his boots grazed the cuff of her trousers. "If you played it right, you could have him financing your investigation by tomorrow morning." He glanced at his timepiece. "Make that this morning." He scrubbed a hand through his hair and yawned.

Jani walked to the room's slit-like window and listened to the patter of the rain. "I'll play him, you play Val, and we'll take it as far as it goes?"

Lucien rolled his eyes. "In case you hadn't noticed, Val's not talking to me."

"When did you ever let moral revulsion and self-disgust stop you?" Jani tried to gauge her view, but could discern only a few dim lights through the dark and the rain. "Did you find out anything at Base Communications besides how quickly Tsecha died?"

"You mean like names of possible agents of change? Sorry, no." Lucien folded his arms and hunched. He had circles under his eyes and yawned with increasing frequency.

"Who did you contact downstairs? Mako?"

"I needed to send him an update." Lucien rubbed a hand across his cheek, which was starred with blond stubble. "The first messages should hit Chicago in the next day or two, after which the shit will hit the fan and proceed in our direction at speed." Before he could say more, the door buzzer interrupted.

"Jani." Dieter slid the door open halfway and poked his

head through the gap. "Ná Feyó and ná Meva have been de-layed." His face colored when he spotted Lucien. "I suspect an attempted intervention."

"I wonder if John bothered to contact Yevgeny first, or went over his head and blocked Feyó himself?" Jani picked up a sock that had gone astray and stuffed it into a drawer. "They're going to have fun roping him in. That gang is all generals and no Spacers."

"I'll let you know as soon as anything changes." Dieter shot a last hard look at Lucien, then let the panel slide closed.

Lucien stood. "Come sunrise, I'll be AWOL. I need to get back." He stretched, twisting at the waist, then stilling like an artist's model in mid-pose, allowing a view of flat stomach and line of shoulder that even his bulky clothing couldn't obscure. "What are you going to do?"

Jani waited until he finished his display and turned to face her. "I don't know. I could go into Karistos myself and poke around, but I have a feeling I won't be allowed to leave the enclave." She yawned, felt fatigue press down, draining whatever shock and grief had left behind. "Feyó is my best bet. I need to wait and see whether she can get past John."

"Waiting was never a talent, as I recall." Lucien took one step closer, then another. He'd applied something to his lip that reduced the swelling but not the redness, making it look wine-stained and wet. "Many were the times I wanted to grab a rope and tie you to the bedpost."

"That's garden variety, as your kinks go." Jani stood her ground as he closed in. "I'm surprised you never tried." She felt the hard edge of his hip as he pressed against her, the warmth of his skin through his clothes and the growing firm-ness between his legs.

"I wanted to. So many times, I wanted—" Lucien pressed close as flesh would allow, eyes closed, lips a breath away. Then he stilled, eyes snapping open. "Are you playing *me* now?" He backed away. "I can't—" He raised a pleading hand. "When Pierce isn't locking me out of meetings, he's watching me like a hawk. I don't have the latitude here that I did at Sheridan."

"You'll think of something." Jani ignored his grumbling reply. "Who manufactures weaponized prionics?"

"Government labs. Service labs. A few commercial."

"Could Neoclona pull it off?"

Lucien's brow arched. "You are angry with John, aren't you?" He hoisted his slingbag to his shoulder. "Can I sleep first?"

"If you must." Jani stepped out of his way as he headed for the door. "Think you can free up information on any persons of interest who've passed through Elyas Station today? Dieter's been declared *hybrid non grata*. His old connections won't connect."

"You don't ask for much, do you?" Lucien paced like a trapped beast. "No one knows me here—I'm still feeling my way. I can't promise *anything*." He stopped and leaned close, but this time kissing was the furthest thing from his mind. "Are you listening? I'll do—"

"Just do what you can." She leaned against the wall, just beyond reach.

"Whatever I can. Yeah. Move the fucking world while I'm at it, and after I do that—" Lucien struck the doorpad hard enough to make it squeal, and blew out of the room.

Jani remained against the wall, listening to the receding *clip* of Lucien's boots. Then she crossed to the bed, prodding the mattress as he had before sitting on the edge. Her eyes burned as tears sprang unbidden.

"I don't want to sleep. I don't want to sleep." She lay across the bare pad. Begged Tsecha to forgive her for every question incorrectly answered, every task left uncompleted, each lesson gone unlearned. Prayed to Ganesh for mercy. Closed her eyes.

Heat. The sharp spice of *vrel* blossom.

Vrel *can't grow here—it's desert*. She wore drop-deads

again. Stood atop a hill some distance from the tents. Made ready to walk down when she saw the curtain of sand close in and felt the lash of the wind.

Before she could take another step, the storm struck. Sand sprayed over her, coating her hands, her face. Filling her mouth, her nose. She fell to the ground and spread herself flat, buried her face in rubble, felt the knife edges of rocks cut through her clothes into her skin. The warmth of her blood as it flowed.

The wind buffeted, hard enough to rock her as the sand swept over her like a blanket—

Jani?

—blowing—

Jani? Wake up.

—burying—

"Jani!"

She struck out, connecting with soft hands that enveloped her fist, absorbing the blow. Opened her eyes.

"Jani? Are you all right?" Dieter's moon face filled her view, brow knit, eyes dark with concern. "Ná Feyó and ná Meva have arrived."

CHAPTER 16

Jani changed clothes. Used what makeup she had to erase the effects of the day from her face. Then she followed Dieter out to the courtyard, and felt the pounding in her head start as soon as she heard the voice bounce off the stone and glass.

"—*and I will speak with her.*" Meva loomed over Scriabin like a specter in a horror 'Vee, waving John silent every time he tried to get a word in edgewise. "She was his chosen religious suborn, most against the wishes of many, but such was as he was. And now she has duties to perform, and she must see to them or his soul will be in peril." She paused to draw breath and spotted Jani. "Ah, there you are." She swept toward her, the hem of her overrobe flapping around her knees. "Damned business. They sought to stop us at the border, your damned security, but I drove past. Let them shoot at us—hah! Let them worry over their souls if they do so."

Jani looked past Meva to the nearby demiroom, where Feyó sat on a couch while Dathim stood sentinel over her. From the corner of her eye she could see John raise a hand in an effort to draw her attention, and ignored him. "Ná Meva, I need to explain something to ná Feyó."

"Then explain it."

"It's difficult."

"Ah. Something she will not wish to hear." Meva looked back at her dominant, voice ripe with sadistic gloat.

Jani stepped closer, lowering her voice as Scriabin tried to stare her silent. "Ní Tsecha was assassinated."

Meva turned and looked her in the face. Her amber eyes were a darker version of Tsecha's, and bright as shattered glass. "No. This she will not wish to hear now, or at any time." She pondered for a moment, then headed for the demiroom, beckoning Jani to follow.

"Jani." Scriabin bowed as she approached, his ministerial air at odds with his stance, feet wide apart, shoulders rounded like a brawler's. "Please reconsider your decision—"

"Save it, Zhenya." John glared at her, looking away just as their eyes met. "She's not buying."

Jani walked past Scriabin and lowered into the empty chair across from Feyó. *"May you take what glory you can from this godless day,"* she said in her most formal Sìah Haárin. She looked to the skylight above. The night's storm had passed, leaving behind scattered cloud shimmering in coral and indigo, reflections of the rising sun. *His first missed sunrise.*

"Did we set the ground rules regarding language?" John hovered behind her seat. "I don't believe it's fair to use one that half the room can't understand."

"Deal with it." Jani sat up straight, so the top of her head was higher than Feyó's, as idomeni protocols demanded and Thalassan habit seldom allowed. "Ná Feyó." She took a deep breath, felt Meva's stare like a stick prodding her forward. "John Shroud determined that ní Tsecha did not die as the result of a tumor. He was—"

Scriabin moved in behind Feyó and glared, fists clenched.

"—assassinated." Jani stared back, until he closed his eyes and dropped his hands.

Feyó raised a hand and curved it in question. "Killed?"

"Secret killing, ná Feyó. From a distance, by one unknown." Dathim's voice emerged surprisingly soft. "The humanish scroll I gave you to read, many days ago. *Ministerial Histories*. The last Scriabin Prime Minister was assassinated, as was an Exterior minister over fifty humanish years ago."

"Secret killing." Feyó repeated the words in English as she turned to look up at Scriabin. "Is this true, Minister?"

"Yes, ná Feyó." Scriabin shot Jani a look that should have killed her where she sat. "I am saddened to admit—"

"A humanish killed him?" Feyó's hand fell to her lap. "He esteemed humanish most completely."

"Unfortunately, not all humanish felt the same about him." Scriabin moved to the end of the couch so Feyó could see him more easily. "They misunderstood his desire for closer relations with humanish. They—"

"I understand the beliefs of your separatists, Minister." Feyó's voice emerged stronger and lower pitched, the first hints of anger revealed. "I spoke with ná Via for much of the past day. She showed me ná Tsecha's medical scrolls, the results of all his scans and examinations." The female looked up at John, her grey Sìah eyes chill as old ice. "There was no tumor, Doctor Shroud. Not a cell of one existed. Ná Via is most thorough. Such a mistake she would not have made, and it most pains me that you would lie of such."

Jani waited for John to speak, but he only looked down at the floor, his face darkening in humiliation. "They feared your reaction if you learned the truth."

"Yet I learned the truth anyway, but only because I hunted for such."

"Ná Feyó." Jani fought the urge to lean forward, knew that any humanish posture or gesture now would give offense. "We must find who did this. I debase myself in the service of those who lied, and beg your assistance."

"We have been searching since yesterday, when we first learned . . . " Scriabin's voice trailed.

That's right, idiot. Let Feyó know exactly how long you kept her in the dark. Jani slashed the air with the edge of her

hand, the idomeni gesture of denial. "Not even Exterior has
the reach in the Outer Circle that the Haárin do. We need
their help."

"I do not wish to help you." Feyó's shoulders and back
curved until her chin grazed her thigh and she had to contort
herself to look in Jani's direction. "My security suborns will
act for themselves, and search on their own."

"Ná Feyó." Jani felt her own shoulders start to buckle,
and forced them back. "He was my teacher—"

"You are of them."

"He was my teacher, and my friend. I esteemed and feared
him. He charged me with much, and if you prevent me from
acting as he deemed me to act, you will be as damned as the
one who killed him."

Feyó straightened a little. Her belief in Tsecha and his
teachings had lost her a position at Rauta Shèràa Academy
and resulted in her being made Haárin. As much as she hated
humanish at the moment, she still felt the pull of her late
religious dominant's authority.

"And you wish what, Jani Kilian?" Her voice emerged a
tone lighter.

"To find who killed him." Jani held out both hands to
Feyó, palms facing up, a gesture of supplication. "And show
them the meaning of that which they did."

Feyó uncurved her back and shoulders until she sat upright. "My security knows much of the separatists. Where
they find funding, and the devices they use to destroy our
docks."

"Your security cannot go into the humanish places to find
them, Feyó." Meva lowered beside her dominant. As she
did, one sleeve of her overrobe rode up, revealing a web of
ragged scarring, souvenirs of multiple challenges. "You need
humanish to do such. And such will they do, out of guilt for
killing Tsecha, and for holding back from you."

"Such is true." Dathim gazed toward the courtyard, where
preparations for early morning sacrament were well along.
"Humanish often ponder that which they do. They worry it,

like a pack animal the mouthbar, even though that which is done is done and to ponder it does no good." He glanced down at Jani, then back toward the courtyard. "Will you stay here, ná Feyó? They prepare sacrament."

"We could go to the library." Jani teetered on the brink, sensed the possibility of winning and wondered how much harder she dare push. "It was ní Tsecha's favored room, because of the view of the cliffs, and the bay." She glanced at Meva to find her staring back, nodding slightly as though encouraging her to continue. *Desperation makes for the strangest allies.* "It would be a good place for your investigators to work with Minister Scriabin's. It is clean and—"

"I met with ní Tsecha in the library, many times." Feyó grew quiet once more, repose revealing the fatigue that grooved the skin under her eyes and alongside her mouth, the dullness that had replaced the dynamism, which not even rage could completely restore.

The idomeni in grief. Jani looked again at Meva, who stood and gestured to Dathim. "You will return to the enclave with ná Feyó, then bring ní Galas back here with you." She stepped aside so Dathim could help Feyó rise and lead her out of the Main House before the food odors could drift over from the courtyard. "I will stay to ensure that all is prepared properly."

Great. Jani swallowed a groan as Dieter appeared with two comtechs in tow.

"If you wish to come with us, ná Meva, you can aid us in the preparations." He nodded in acknowledgment of Jani's eye roll of gratitude, and hustled the female away before she could argue.

John lowered to the arm of the couch and started massaging the back of his neck. "Well," he said after Meva had moved out of earshot, "that went better than any of us had a right to expect."

"Get this through your damned head." Jani stood and planted herself in front of him. "You may have hitched your wagon to Scriabin's rising star, but as far as the Elyan Haárin are concerned, you are part of Thalassa. As you go, so it goes, and you almost dragged it right into the toilet!"

John's gaze flicked over her face before settling on some point north of her left ear. "I am more sorry than I can say that I caused ná Via to question her judgment, but don't go and—"

"No. Hybrid or not, you act as humanish, you fall into the humanish camp, and given Feyó's sensitivity right now, that's not where you want to be."

"Thanks." Scriabin thrust a thick finger at her. "We are busting our asses—"

"To clean up after something one of yours did. To the idomeni, the act of one is the act of all, and everyone pays. You don't believe me, ask a Laum, assuming you can find one. Any left alive after the Night of the Blade decamped to the far edges of the worldskein, and those colonies are a little hard to get to—" Jani stopped when the entry door swept open and two all too familiar figures strode in.

"Mornin'." Niall dragged off his garrison cap and tucked it into his belt. He wore desertweights, as did Lucien, who followed close behind, slingbag in hand. They both looked dusty and tired, but to that Niall added an almost palpable anger that revealed itself in his coiled-spring walk and the bite in his voice.

Scriabin read the signs as well. He held up both hands in a gesture of surrender. "Niall, I—"

"Save it, Your Excellency." Niall set himself in front of the man, hands on hips. "I've had an educational morning. I *hate* educational mornings. Being awakened at oh-hell-thirty by a concerned party bent on educating me just fucks up my entire day." He lowered his voice as a few Thalassans in the courtyard paused to observe, but what he lost in volume he made up for in snarl. "So Tsecha was assassinated. Did it occur to anyone that it might have been a good idea to inform the individual responsible for hauling their asses off a rooftop when—not *if*, but *when*—the news gets out and the Haárin decide to retaliate?"

Scriabin's face reddened. "We always have contingency plans in place, Ni—"

"Not here, you don't. This is Elyas, where if you don't dot the i's and cross the t's just right, you get shit. Elyas, where they've decided they don't want to play with Chicago anymore, and where the same Haárin that you are about to piss off royally control eighty-three point four percent of the dock traffic. It's taken me over six months to work out the systems around here, and you think you're going to snap your Family fingers and make shuttles fly while all hell is breaking loose? Well, allow me to be the one to inform you that if the Haárin do go ballistic, the first ones the locals are going to go after are Family with a big F, and that F stands for 'fucked,' so go right ahead and tell me how much you don't need any help getting off-world in case of a political meltdown." He backed off a stride and stood, eyes fixed on nothing, struggling for control and only winning by a hair. "Does Roshi know?" He turned and looked from Scriabin to John and back again, and offered the barest of nods. "We're going to straighten out something right now. Everything that gets sent to Sheridan comes to me first. Everything you tell Roshi, you tell me first. Is that clear?"

Scriabin took a deep, shaky breath before answering. "Perfectly, Colonel."

"Good." Niall brushed past the man and pulled up in front of Jani. "And how was your morning?"

Jani looked past him toward Lucien, who had finished watching the show and now sat in one of the demirooms and hunted for something in his slingbag. "Lucien filled you in?"

"Yeah. You can imagine my joy when I opened the door to find him standing there." Niall took her elbow and steered her toward the courtyard, from whence the aromas of a board-busting Thalassan breakfast emanated. "He figures they didn't tell me because they knew I'd tell you."

"That's what I thought." Jani headed for the beverage table, grabbing a mug from the stack and filling it from the brewer. "He took me to the place he thinks—"

"Yeah, I know. We just came from there." Niall filled two mugs to the brim with coffee and set them on a tray. Then he moved down the line and filled a plate with eggs, bacon, and a tea party's worth of toast and pastry. "We scanned the place fore and aft, incorporated the analyses he ran yesterday. The fact that the place was protein-wiped is about the only red flag we have, but depending on the weapon the killer used, it could've served as the nest. One has to take into account his experience in these matters, I suppose." He led Jani to an empty table well away from the other diners. *"Jesus Christ."* He set down the tray hard, sending coffee splashing. "If I'd known it was assassination yesterday, I could have kicked Station Liaison into overdrive. We could have shut down the private fields and seized passenger manifests for the last fortnight *and* sifted out the probables by now." He sank into his chair. "Now I'm stuck playing catch-up, and I really hate that." He shoved a slice of bacon in his mouth and chewed with intent.

"You can pick Exterior Security's brain." Jani crumbled crisp bread into her vegetable soup. "Scriabin said they've been working since yesterday."

"Exterior Security couldn't find their dicks with both hands." Niall shoveled eggs and bacon between two slices of toast, then spooned chutney over the mess. "I saw Dathim and Feyó leaving as we pulled in." He took a bite of his sandwich, eyeing Jani as he chewed.

Jani tasted her soup, which was bland but filling. She never noticed taste at times like these, a leftover of days spent cadging meals at low-end kiosks, when food was something to quiet the rumble in her gut and keep her going. "I told her. Up until now, she thought it was a tumor."

"You just told her *now*?" Niall covered his mouth with his napkin just in time. "How did that shake out?"

"Things are touchy. She doesn't want to help humanish. Meva helped persuade her, which surprised me." Jani flinched when she felt a finger stroke her upper back, and looked around to find Lucien standing behind her, tray in hand.

Niall nodded toward an empty chair. "Have a seat, Captain. Eat up. We've got a day ahead of us."

"Thank you, sir." Lucien remained standing for a few beats longer, which was enough time to give the hybrids at the surrounding tables a chance to admire him in all his disheveled glory. "Equipment's arriving," he said as he finally took his seat. "Communications arrays. Data scanners. Mister Brondt is directing it be taken to the library."

"It's the designated command center." Jani felt the pressure of Lucien's boot against hers, and responded by pulling away her foot and tucking it behind the leg of her chair. "Neutral territory."

"For now." Niall looked over at the other tables. "What will happen when they find out? Or worse, when an enclave full of Dathims finds out."

"Dathim knows." Jani finished her soup and pushed the empty bowl aside to make room for her coffee. "He's proven remarkably steady through all this." She grabbed a piece of pastry from the top of Niall's pile and dunked it.

"I would think he would," said Lucien, who nursed a crush on the male that had apparently withstood time, distance, and logic.

"Dathim is different." Niall crumpled his napkin and tossed it atop his plate. "What about when the other tilemasters and stevedores and facilities suborns find out? The ones who think with their hands and not their heads?" He glanced at his timepiece. "I need to check in with the base." He shot a look at Lucien that almost qualified as civil. "Ten minutes, Captain."

"Yes, sir." Lucien waited until Niall exited the courtyard. "I had to tell him. I'm the new transfer from Sheridan, which means I have zero pull and no connections."

"You don't have to apologize." Jani wiped crumbs from her fingers, then cradled her cup, savoring the heat. "He needed to know."

"Speaking of needing to know." Lucien tilted his head in

the direction of the other Thalassans. "When are you going to tell them? They need to hear it from you before they pick up any rumors."

Jani glanced at a neighboring table in time to catch the occupants avert their eyes. "I'll tell them."

"When?"

Jani took a sip of coffee and pretended not to hear.

CHAPTER 17

By late morning assorted underlings, uniformed and civilian, hybrid, humanish, and Haárin, populated the far side of the library, hard at work in hastily assembled office areas and communications centers, and separated from their superiors by an array of portable soundshields

Jani hunched in her corner chair and took roll. The triumvirate of John, Val, and Scriabin, sitting atop a scrollcase like the three monkeys. *Hear no truth, see no truth, speak no truth.* The unlikely pairing of Niall and Lucien, precipitated by Niall's need to stay informed and Lucien's desperate bid to breach the inner circle.

And then there's Meva. Jani watched the female ride herd on the other side of the barrier, the gist of her words obvious from the unhappy postures of the group of Haárin comtechs who were the focus of her displeasure. Beside her stood Dathim, as silent and watchful as he had been with Feyó.

I'm not used to quiet Dathim. Jani watched the male stare stolidly into space. *Like a lion watching flowers grow.*

At last Meva finished with the beleaguered technicians and passed through the barrier. "All is as prepared as it may be." She dragged her chair next to a display case that contained some of Tsecha's writings, then motioned to Dathim to set his seat next to hers.

Niall waited until the pair had settled in before speaking. "The shuttleports, both public and private, may already be a lost cause, unfortunately, given the time lag." His voice emerged subdued. He sat by the library window, the bright sun accentuating the shadows under his eyes. "I doubt we'll have any more luck at Elyas Station for the same reason, but we have set a safety emergency in motion just in case. Lockdown of all docks while they check passengers and scan all luggage and cargo. We've also seized all passenger manifests generated since the time of Tsecha's death." Bone and tissue crackled audibly as he worked his neck. "And we've contacted the other stations in this part of the Gateway network so they can initiate their own investigations."

Scriabin looked to John. "Does the weapon give any clue as to where it originated?"

"The vector was an engineered variant of Sussex A, a prionic that infects facility and communications biosystems on long haul vessels." John nodded toward Val, who took the baton.

"It's not a common infection, but it isn't rare, either. It pops up sporadically, usually in older systems that have been stressed over a period of years. In the case of boards, it's transmitted when poorly filtered system waste products are recycled and mixed with nutrient broth, which is then used to feed the system." Val slid off the case and walked about, hands in pockets. Only the fact that he kept his back to Lucien offered the barest hint that all was not as fraternal as it seemed. "A reverse-phase filtration step was added to all ship systems a few years ago in order to extract it from the stream. If someone wanted it, all they'd have to do is infiltrate a ship during a layover and get hold of a used filter."

"Sussex A usually takes months to incubate, spread, and destroy an array." John sat arms folded, eyes fixed on nothing. "You see the occasional drip under a console, and think it's a leaky nutrient cylinder. Suffer through the occasional glitchy communication. Catastrophic systems failure doesn't occur until the disease is well progressed." His voice deadened, made lifeless by too-recent memory. "Whoever designed this variant ramped the virulence exponentially, compressed the cycle from months to minutes, and designed it to specifically target Tsecha's brain tissue. Cranial insertion via the left auditory canal, followed by the apparent formation of a neuroma, a slow-growing benign tumor. This was in fact the payload, an aliquot of Tsecha's blood infested with the rogue protein. Once it reached body temperature . . . well, you all witnessed the result." He paused and glanced at Jani, but looked away when he saw that she watched him. "Ruthlessly elegant work. A weapon coded to Tsecha, indistinguishable from his own tissue until it was too late. Even if we'd realized what it was immediately, we could not have halted the cascade in time."

"We've compiled a list of the labs capable of developing this type of entity." Scriabin blew out a long breath. "Unfortunately, it's quite long."

Jani suppressed a yawn. She longed for coffee. Or better yet, sleep without dreams. "Who benefits? Tsecha's death— who benefits the most?"

Scriabin knocked his heels against the side of the case. "The more radical separatists always blamed Tsecha for doing more than any idomeni to initiate and maintain human-idomeni relations."

Jani shrugged. "Have any of them claimed responsibility?"

Niall shook his head. "The fact of assassination has not yet been made public."

"So the group that engineered this Killing of the Century is going to sit back and wait for us to make an announcement before they pipe up?" Jani didn't wait for a reply. Instead, she wrote invisible notes on her thigh, and sorted through the questions that tumbled in her brain. "Boards are farmed from humanish or idomeni brain tissue. Wouldn't a bug that

had been altered for use on Tsecha have come from an idomeni board?"

Before John or Val could reply, Niall interjected. "If the
Outer Circle is any indication . . . let's just say that the access to docks and ships undergoing repair isn't as well con-
trolled as it should be. Could a human obtain material from
an idomeni ship? Most certainly."

Jani wrote another note. "Could a humanish lab have obtained a tissue sample from Tsecha sufficient to build this
weapon?"

"It wouldn't take much, unfortunately." Val frowned.
"A few skin cells. A single strand of hair with the bulb attached." He sat on the floor against the wall, a position that
let him watch Lucien without Lucien seeing him. "And with
access to even a lousy booster device, they'd be able to copy
and manufacture sufficient genetic material within hours."
Before he could say more, one of Feyó's brown-clad security
suborns crossed over to their side of the barrier.

"Ex-cuse, pl-eease." Her voice shuddered as she passed
through the soundshield, pushing one of the office chairs
ahead of her like an orderly maneuvering a seated patient.
"We must bring ní Galas a proper chair, ná Meva. He cannot concentrate in a soft thing such as *this*." She kicked the
chair with her booted foot, sending it careening the last few
meters until it bounced off the wall. "This one." She grabbed
the sole idomeni-style chair, a rigid, twisted thing, out of a
darkened corner where it had languished since its delivery,
and pushed it toward the shield. "I think he is crazy, and
truly, but he is the one to sit in it so what do I care?" She
launched the chair through the shield with another kick, the
sound-canceling field swallowing the last of her mutterings
as she followed after.

Val winced. "He's really going to sit in that?" He looked
to the other side of the room, where an older male took
charge of the chair and sat on it, pressing against the ridged
and bumpy seatback. "I guess he is."

"The mind-focusing properties of pain." Scriabin sniffed and stared into the distance, a professor imparting arcane knowledge. "Strange for an Haárin to persist in the habit. They usually leave that to the bornsects."

"Ní Galas enjoys to be different." Meva looked Scriabin in the face. "And to show off before his suborns." She bared her teeth as the man's face flushed.

The joys of interacting with the idomeni. Jani glanced at John and Val, who had suffered similarly over the years, and who now eyed their compatriot with a combination of pity and *better you than me.*

"There will be some time lag as we let the investigators do their jobs." Scriabin watched Meva as though fearing another embarrassing interruption, relaxing only a little when none appeared forthcoming. "But in the meantime, distasteful as it may seem, we need to consider how to handle the fallout when word gets out that ní Tsecha was assassinated."

"Cèel will enjoy your fallout." Meva pulled a wafer folio from a shelf near her chair and examined the leather binding. "He hated Tsecha, yes, but he hates humanish more. He would not fight for Tsecha when he lived, but he will claim a great loss now that he is dead." She traced her finger over the gold leaf flower that adorned the binding. "You made a great mistake, and truly, when you hid the fact of Tsecha's killing. You should have announced it as soon as it was known. To hide such is to imply that there is reason to hide. Such does not appear as caution to idomeni, but as treachery."

"We certainly esteem your point of view, ná Meva," Scriabin said, in a tone that indicated he believed anything but.

"You should, Minister. I know the idomeni point of view most well, as I am idomeni." Meva reached out with the binder and tapped Jani on the knee. "You knew better, priest-in-training, but you did not go far enough." She sat forward, gripping the binder in both hands like a threat. "Think as Tsecha. Think as he trained you to think, ná Kièrshia. Toxin. The bringer of pain and change, whom your *inshah* declared his suborn for reasons known only to himself."

Jani felt her skin tingle as all eyes focused on her. "He would not have hidden a murder."

"Good, priest-in-training. You repeat that which I said back to me. Such is what four cycles of Academy training gave you."

Jani heard Scriabin cough, Niall mutter a curse. Felt the anger grow, even more than it had with John. "He would declare it. He would face anyone who questioned his motives, and challenge them if they disputed him."

"Indeed, Tsecha would do such." Meva cocked her head. "But Tsecha is dead." Again she bared her teeth, the idomeni's death's head rictus. "And you are his suborn."

Jani's heart skipped. "I should . . . " She tried to lick her lips, to summon saliva in a mouth gone dry. "I should go to Cèel and tell him of murder." Behind her, she could sense Niall's stillness, his held breath. "To his face. I should tell him—to his face."

"Yes." Meva waved the folio at Jani edge on, like a hatchet. "You wake up eventually. This is most reassuring, and truly."

Jani gripped the arms of her chair. She felt as though the room rocked, as though her world shifted beneath her. "I should return to Rauta Shèràa and explain Tsecha's death to Council."

"And to Temple." Meva sat up, then shoved the folio back into its slot. "Idiot—what else can be done?" She looked to Dathim, who embraced his role as the mummers' chorus and simply nodded. "Tsecha and I talked often of his death. We did not talk of murder, no, but simply of death. Of what should be done after." Her voice quieted. "It is fitting that he return. He was Chief Propitiator of the Vynshàrau, and the souls of all Chief Propitiators since the first have been released on Shèrá." She sat up straighter, in honor of the one she esteemed. "I fear for his soul. It began its journey in this damned strange place, and may not find its Way without guidance." She glared at Jani, her shoulders rounding. "Your guidance, priest. That for which you trained."

Jani ran a hand along the arm of her chair, imagined sand beneath her fingers. "I'm not sure I'd be particularly welcome."

"Knevçet Shèràa—I know of it. We all know of it. Twenty-six Laumrau, killed by you." Meva sat back. "Do you regret such? Do you wish you could return them their lives so that they could take yours?"

Jani felt the stares, and held back her answer. Sometimes, she had to remind herself. That her actions at Knevçet Shèràa, defined her. That in the minds of many, idomeni and humanish, Knevçet Shèràa was what they thought of when they heard her name. "No," she said finally. "Given the same circumstances, I would do it again."

"Kill idomeni at sacrament, as they prayed to their gods?"

"Yes."

"And now you would return to Shèrá the soul of the greatest propitiator. You, the killer of Knevçet Shèràa? Tsecha's toxin." Meva's voice emerged a little less impatient, a little more wondering. "You, who declare knowledge of idomeni, do you question that such is what idomeni would expect from you?"

Silence claimed them. For a minute. Forever. Jani glanced at Val to find him staring back at her, his face gone ten years older.

Scriabin cleared his throat. "We'd be at Cèel's mercy as soon as we crossed over into the worldskein."

"You'll be at his mercy as soon as the news of the assassination gets out." Jani looked back at Scriabin, at John and Niall, and saw them looking at her as Val did. Only Lucien maintained his detachment, his eyes holding curiosity rather than empathy. "If you face him, you have the chance to salvage some seemliness."

"A funeral delegation?" Scriabin studied the ceiling. "I assume Li Cao will be sending one, out of fear if not respect for Tsecha. I assume my aunt can append herself. I'm a little low on the diplomatic totem pole to claim a right to attend in my own name, but I can possibly justify my attendance as a male relative, an escort. Given that I'm Cao's opponent, I'll look like I'm grandstanding, but that can't be helped." He shot an uneasy look at Meva, uncomfortable with discussing the Commonwealth's political weakness in front of her. "I can possibly meet with some of the other bornsect dominants, get the lay of the Shèráin land."

"You may meet with Aden nìRau Wuntoi, and assure him that you will support him against Cèel." Meva fussed with the cuffs of her overrobe. "In exchange, he may receive you in the Pathen meeting house, and his acceptance may compel Cèel to receive you whether he wishes or not. Cèel fears Wuntoi—do not think he does not. The Pathen have always offered the greatest threat to Vynshàrau. It will prove, I think, a most interesting problem for Cèel." She studied the display case next to her chair, Tsecha's writings, one by one. Then, with obvious reluctance, she returned her attention to Scriabin. "You look at me oddly, Minister."

Scriabin smiled weakly. "I am used to dealing with the directness of idomeni, not the duplicity."

"We are most as straightforward, compared to you humanish. What is not as straightforward, when compared to humanish?" Meva laughed, the idomeni's monotonal *heh heh heh* sounding like someone trying to cough quietly. "But now you wish to feel more sure, because you have erred, and are uncertain of your standing. In such a case, our intrigue is enough to upset you."

The silence that fell now was the sort that got under the skin and nettled. Jani tried to force thoughts of her imminent return to Shèrá from her mind, concentrating instead on the work being done on the other side of the barrier, the fact that each analysis, each message sent and message received, brought them one step closer to finding Tsecha's killer. After a time, she glanced at Niall, who had taken his nicstick case from his pocket and now massaged it as though trying to absorb the nicotine through the engraved metal.

"If you would smoke, Colonel, please do so." Meva bared her teeth at the surprised looks that greeted her dispensation.

"I have entered this place so many times. Any godly bornsect would consider me as damned. I only consider myself as ná Meva Tan. What difference?"

Niall didn't have to be told twice. "Thank you, ná Meva." He pulled his case from his pocket and flipped it open. Removed a gold-striped cylinder, crunched the tip—

—and stalled in mid-inhalation as on the other side of the sound barrier cases emerged from bags and pockets, and tips crunched in filtered silence. About a quarter of the hybrids lit up, by Jani's quick count, along with a lone Haárin who ignored the alarmed postures of her fellows and took a pull with the skill of one who'd had a lot of practice.

Niall shifted in his seat. "Well. Nice to have the company." He expelled smoke in a series of distracted puffs. "So, when would this journey be expected to get under way? The transporting of Cabinet ministers over long distances is not a trivial undertaking."

"Does 'as soon as possible' make your blood run cold, Colonel?" Scriabin's voice emerged strong, his Family-caliber composure returned. "I think ná Meva has made it clear that any delay will only make us look worse."

"Can anyone attend this?" Val raised a hand. "If I'm not part of an official delegation, am I out of luck?"

John leaned forward to get a better look at his embattled partner. "What are you asking?"

"I'm asking if we . . . or if I . . . " Val tapped the floor with his fist. "Well, dammit, John, we fought him for years. Then you wind up here, a hybrid, one of the blended race he started talking about during the war. It's all so damned . . . ironic." He stilled, then scooted forward and gestured to Niall, who tossed him his nicstick case. "And I liked the son of a bitch—pardon the language, but what else would you call him?—and I think that we should attend this ceremony." He shook out a 'stick, then tossed the case back to Niall. "Assuming we can." He crunched the tip, then took a long, shaky drag.

Niall examined the case absently, then shoved it back in his pocket. "What usually happens at these things?"

Meva leaned forward and prodded Jani's knee. "Priest-in-training?"

Jani gritted her teeth. Counted to three. "The most sacred place in Rauta Shèràa is the site of the Temple. The dome rotates, and there's an observation port that allows a view of the region of sky where the First Star is located. I would release Tsecha's soul there so it could see the star, and follow it." She recalled a forbidden daytime visit to the dome, the view through the port of the milk-blue skies of Rauta Shèràa. The uproar at the Consulate when her intrusion was discovered. "I think there is some question as to whether they would let me in, despite what you say."

Meva clapped her hands. "It will be a great confusion. Caith will laugh."

Niall looked to Jani and sighed. "Now which one is Caith?"

"The goddess of chaos. She fights a never-ending battle with Shiou, the goddess of order." In her mind's eye Jani saw the page from Tsecha's scroll. The clenched fist. *Second round soon to come, bitch.*

"I wouldn't mind seeing the old bird wing it to home." Niall's voice sounded deceptively light. "Besides, with all these ministers dancing attendance, I don't have much choice, do I?"

Jani studied him for some sign he joked, even as she knew that this was the last thing he would ever joke about. "You'd go? To Rauta Shèràa?"

"Wouldn't miss it, gel." Niall forced a grin, then sealed the deal by blowing a smoke ring. "God knows why. The variety of ways in which this can go south boggles the mind."

"Then you had better enjoy those while you can." Scriabin shot him a grin laced with cool commiseration, their earlier blow-up, if not forgotten, at least set aside for the time being. "They don't allow you the good ones in the brig."

"But they are required to provide you any brand you want

as part of your last meal." Niall's grin proved a little wider, a little colder. "And the one they give you after they tie on the blindfold tastes best of all."

Val rolled his half-spent 'stick between his fingers. "Now isn't that a cheery thought? I wonder if we get our pick, like with our last me—" Before he could finish, Dieter swept through the barrier.

"We've just intercepted a communication from Elyas Station." His eyes met Jani's. "There's been a murder."

CHAPTER 18

Dieter brought up a face on his display. A younger man. Bandan or Phillipan or Earthbound Asian.

"His name was Neason Ch'un." The image flickered, and Dieter eyed the fragrant cloud of board-corroding nicstick smoke that hung just overhead. "His body was found in the interface, the utilities chase-slash-walkway that divides the humanish and Haárin wings of the station. Cause of death was determined to be asphyxiation, resulting from severe trauma to the area between the third and fifth cervical vertebrae." He paused, giving the words one last chew before spitting them out. "Station security believes a drifter responsible."

Lucien leaned against a nearby desk. "That's not the sort of blow you'd expect from a drifter."

"Depends where they drifted in from." Dieter stared at the display. He seemed to have backslid into his former role as station liaison, taken on the look of a mason faced with a crumbling wall and unsure which hole to patch first. "He died yesterday, around station noon. Since the blow was such that death occurred within minutes—"

"Add in the time it takes a shuttle to reach Elyas Station," Jani said, edging closer to the display, "and you have the time Tsecha collapsed."

"At this time, there's no evidence that links this death with Tsecha's assassination." Dieter drummed his fingers against his thigh, then segued into picking his nails. "Ch'un worked for the station as a mid-level vendor liaison. He'd visit shops, talk to the managers, make sure they were satisfied with systems hookups and whatnot." He shuffled his feet. "But the timing bothers me. And as Captain Pascal said, this type of injury is usually indicative of a certain type of killer. A certain type of training." He seemed determined to look everywhere but at the faces surrounding him. "We are still gathering information, of course. We could find out that he argued with a coworker earlier in the day and the matter escalated. We could . . . " He let the sentence fade. Then in the next breath, he straightened, pulled himself together, the professional once more. "Until the matter is resolved, I've requested that the Haárin station dominant keep us informed of developments in this investigation." He turned to Scriabin. "We could use some grease from a ministry, sir, either verbal or written communication to the station chief."

"I'll have my office draw up something within the hour." Scriabin pulled a handheld from his pocket and made a note. "In the meantime, we have ships to outfit, stories to get straight, and a funeral delegation to prepare."

Meva, who stood off to one side, seemed in no hurry to depart. "Feyó will provide all necessary technical and dock support."

"I shall stay here with ná Meva," said Dathim. "I can prepare to depart within minutes. I have no stories to straighten." He glanced at a nearby table, and with the deliberation of a gourmet, plucked a single grape from the bunch some daring soul had sneaked into the area and popped it into his mouth.

Scriabin tore his attention from the placidly chewing Dathim. "My guess is that we'll leave within twelve to eighteen hours. Details tend to sort themselves out rather quickly when Tyotya Ani gets involved." He started toward the shield, then stopped and looked back at Dieter. "Mister

Brondt." He stared at the male for a long moment. "You have the look of someone with more to say."

Dieter pretended puzzlement at first. Then he started to drum his fingers against his thigh again. "The late Mr. Ch'un apparently found it difficult to keep his mind on his job. He had a . . . *thing* for Haárin females. He'd spot one he liked on the security monitors, arrange to accidentally run into them, try to chat them up. A few complained to their dominants, who in turn complained to the Station Liaison office. He'd been disciplined a couple of times. Threatened with suspension. Nothing seemed to stop him. So, today they fired him." He resumed his nail picking. "Idomeni are very strong. Ch'un wasn't particularly fit, and testing indicates that he was drunk at time of death. If he tried to force himself on any Haárin female, he'd be bound to get into troub—" He flinched, then pulled a dispo from a nearby dispenser and wrapped it around his finger. "My apologies for suggesting such without proof, ná Meva." He lifted the dispo, glanced at his wounded finger, and swore.

"Haárin have murdered. For some, it is the reason they are Haárin." Meva never averted her gaze from the image of the late Neason Ch'un. "Your comment would not upset anyone who is sensible."

Jani fixed on Ch'un's image as well, desperate for distraction. *People are murdered at stations every day.* Stations were small cities populated by transients, not all of whom were upstanding citizens. *On the other hand, the postmortem could be wrong. Maybe he just passed out and hit his head.* Maybe. "Did anyone notice anything strange around the time of Ch'un's death? Anyone running out of the chase, acting strangely?"

Dieter had liberated a piece of adhesive from one of the desk drawers and seemed intent on securing the dispo around his finger. "No one reported anything."

"On either the humanish side or the Haárin?"

Dieter glanced up from his self-ministrations. "The Haárin were never particularly forthcoming concerning matters in their side of the chase. Since the dock attacks started, they've become even more reluctant to share."

"With reason, ní Dieter." The speaker was the elder male who had requested the bornsect chair. Along with his penchant for pain-inducing furniture, ní Galas Linai shared Jani's affection for bitter lemon over ice. He sat back, drink in hand, while the others sorted seating arrangements out as best they could. Under John's abrupt direction, techs were routed and relocated and the two desks thus liberated shoved together to form one long table. Dathim found chairs while Val and Scriabin sniffed out a bottle of single malt and assorted finger foods from yet another hidden stash.

Only Lucien and Niall remained off to one side, talking in low and surprisingly civil tones. Niall's responses sounded as abrupt as one would have expected, but those grew fewer the longer Lucien talked.

Meanwhile, ní Galas sliced an Elyan lemon in half, then squeezed the juice into a fresh glass of iced water and slid the drink across the desk to Jani. "It is not unheard of for an Haárin to murder another Haárin. But a humanish? Even with the feeling between us as it is, such would be extreme." He shook his head, then bit into the drained remains of the lemon half, chewing the fruit with evident relish. "Ní Defa Roen is my investigative suborn." He gestured toward a male seated at the next desk. "He has been in communication with the Trade Board offices on Elyas Station."

"The lockdown of Elyas Station has affected only the humanish sections, ná Kièrshia, as would be expected." Ní Defa consulted a recording board. "Trade Board Security monitors all entries and exits of the Haárin transept." He was older, lantern-jawed and conservative of dress, with the pale coloring of an Oà. "Station Liaison has uncovered little information," he added, in a voice that proved a surprisingly pleasant rumble. "They provided us names of the Haárin females who complained against Neason Ch'un, but none of these are of the type who would commit this sort of act."

"We're looking for someone unexceptional—an average passenger with average luggage traveling to an average destination." Jani met Defa's eye. Like his dominant, he didn't flinch—both had lived on Elyas for a long time. "It is possible that the assassin impersonated an Haárin to avoid humanish security and escaped Elyas Station using Haárin transport."

Ní Galas bared his teeth. "An impersonation as one you describe would not last for long."

Jani's eyes stung as memories surfaced. "Ní Tsecha impersonated humanish in Rauta Shèràa twenty years ago." She reached up to wipe away a brimming tear, only to have Niall's silent appraisal stop her. She scratched her ear instead.

"He pulled that in Chicago, too." Lucien had scavenged a handful of nuts from the liberated trove, then returned to his place beside his commanding officer and new best friend. "Two years ago."

"An idomeni would pass more easily as humanish than the reverse. You tolerate strangeness more readily." Ní Galas stirred his drink, dredging up lemon pulp from the bottom. "I maintain that no humanish could remain undetected for long, no matter how well they trained."

Jani counted to three again. For all his openness, Galas exuded an air of patronizing superiority that begged argument. "If Ch'un's murder had happened last week, or even today, I doubt we'd be talking about it. But it happened at about the time Tsecha's killer would have arrived at Elyas Station."

"That's assuming they had departed Karistos within an hour or so of Tsecha's death." Niall activated another 'stick, which led to a second general round of lighting up. "Even with prep in place, that's cutting it a little close."

"If you had just killed ní Tsecha Egri, would you hang around?" Jani sensed the change in the air as soon as she spoke. The stilling of some Haárin, and the hard rap ní Defa gave his touchboard when a command went awry. *If ná Meva*

*weren't here now, what sort of reception would we have re-
ceived?* She wasn't sure she wanted to know.

Galas pondered, then motioned to Defa, who in turn gestured to a female suborn. She joined them at their table, flip-
ping open a portable workstation and starting to key.

"Transferring now," she said, her voice a brittle rasp that
did little to lessen the tension. "We will first examine all images recorded after the time of the humanish male's death, in
the section where he was killed." She made one last series of
entries, then twisted the workstation display so it faced the
middle of the table. A diffuse beam flashed from the panel,
then refocused to form a cylinder of white light. The cylinder in turn unrolled like an ancient scroll, the resulting pane
of light thickening until it formed a milky cube.

The milkiness soon cleared, replaced by the image of a
crowded concourse. Miniature Haárin, their every expression and movement detectable, their voices a background
rise and fall.

Jani rose and circled the table until she faced the concourse image head-on.

"Why isn't anyone moving?" Val sat back, double shot of
whiskey in hand. "They're all crowded around the—" His
face flushed. "They're all watching the holoVee displays."

"Ní Tsecha's death had just been announced." Ní Galas
sat up straight and raised his glass above his head, a combination of a humanish toast and an idomeni gesture of
respect.

"This one," Defa said, leaning forward and pointing first
to one Haárin who moved too quickly from one display to
the next, then another who gestured in anger while talking
to a security suborn. Another. Another. As he took note of a
figure, the female suborn would stop the image action and
home in on it, touchboarding entries as a series of flickers
played across the subject's face and frame.

Jani watched, trying to pick up the cadence of the search,
to see the crowds through Defa's eyes. *I'm looking for
waves. He's looking for eddies. Bare ripples.* She took one

step back from the cube, then another, struggling to see the single star in the nebula.

Then she saw. And it turned out to be a wave, after all.

Defa spotted it as well. "This one." He pointed to a conservatively dressed female who appeared as if from nowhere and walked along one side of the concourse for a time before veering toward the middle. "She does not stop at any of the displays."

"She is not humanish. She is idomeni. She is Vynshàrau." The suborn paused, waiting for another request.

Jani watched the female move along the concourse, passing the clustered Haárin like an iceskimmer moving past floes and bergs. Never once pausing to talk to anyone. Never once glancing at any of the displays. She wore a wrapshirt and trousers in sand and pale grey, topped by a darker grey overrobe. Her brown hair had been gathered into a messy horsetail that on closer inspection seemed at odds with her neat clothing. "Show her again."

Defa looked up at her. "She is not humanish, ná Kièrshia." He gestured toward the workstation. "Proportional evaluation and chroma show her as Vynshàrau." He shrugged. "Darker-skinned Sìah is also possible. Or a blended sect. But idomeni, yes, and truly." He squinted as he leaned closer to the cube and watched their latest subject continue down the concourse until she turned down a gangway. "Vynshàrau, most likely."

Jani fought the urge to wrest the touchboard from Defa's suborn and mash pads until she found the reverse feature. "Why doesn't she stop at any of the displays? She doesn't even slow down to glance at them."

Defa twisted around to look her in the face. "She does not stop—" He turned back around to stare at the image. "She does not . . . "

"Maybe none of them transmitted in her language." Niall now sported a glass of whiskey to go with his 'stick. "Maybe she couldn't understand any of the broadcasts."

"Vynshàrau Haárin is the dominant language, Colonel

Pierce." Ní Galas had started in on the second half of the lemon. "All Haárin understand it."

Defa folded his arms and cocked his head to the side, the cross-species attitude for *show me*. "Why does she behave as this? She should know and truly that she is being imaged at all times."

Jani walked to the window. The sun had risen to mid-morning, a molten gold ball that bleached the sky. "Could we talk to her?"

Defa's suborn tapped her workstation touchboard, shutting down the concourse image. She flipped the display back around, her hands moving over the board with a musician's dexterity. "She is ná Nahin Sela." A few more taps. "A trader in decorative tile. She travels within the fifth cruiser built by Pathen during their last fallow season, and blessed by Shiou. She travels to the worldskein by the usual route, then on to Shèrá."

"We will bid security at Guernsey Station to hold her until we arrive." Ní Galas gestured to another suborn, who opened yet another portable workstation.

"What reason will you give for holding her?" Jani held up a hand in apology as the Haárin stared. "She might refuse to remain behind. She may request her dominant's aide in obtaining her release."

"Order is our reason, ná Kièrshia. A reason acceptable to all godly idomeni, Haárin or bornsect, suborn or dominant." Galas bared his teeth. He radiated contentment now, like a cat that had locked up his quarry and could now torture it at his leisure. "Ná Nahin will remain in place until we arrive at Guernsey Station to question her. Such is her obligation— she will not refuse such." He rubbed his hands together, a profoundly humanish gesture. "She is as ours."

The library huddle broke up an hour later. Galas and his crew fingered four other Haárin for questioning, but none of them interested Jani as much as Nahin Sela and her single-minded walk through the concourse.

Then the scatter began. Meva and Dathim returned to the enclave to inform Feyó. Val and John hied off to prepare the clinic staff.

"And the panic is on." Niall tossed a few under-his-breath orders to Lucien, who shot Jani a last loaded look before departing. "I should have a minimum two weeks to prep for this voyage. Instead I have a grand total of—" He checked his timepiece and winced. "—nine and one-half hours."

Scriabin gave a silent chuckle. "Sit back, Colonel." He clapped Niall on the shoulder. "Witness the effect that Family finger-snapping can have."

"I'm off the hook, then?" Niall offered a crocodile grin. "You won't want an escort to the shuttleport or coverage on your way to the station? No escort to Guernsey, either. And oh, when you reach the worldskein and realize that the news has gotten there ahead of you that it was assassination instead of a brain tumor and a substantial proportion of the idomeni population wants to nail your hide to the nearest surface? I'm guessing your ministry security can handle it."

Scriabin rolled his eyes. "Niall, I was just—"

Niall held up a hand. "Another thing we should get straight right now, Your Excellency, is that this is not a game. You want to play 'my daddy's bigger,' feel free, but you'll be playing with yourself." The chill cast in his eye indicated that he knew exactly what he'd said, that he meant every nasty little double entendre, and would be happy to clarify matters if pushed. "Now, I have a long haul to plan coverage for. By your leave." He turned to Jani, and light in his eyes softened. "I'll check in later." He yanked his garrison cap out of his belt and set it in place as he strode to the door.

Scriabin muttered under his breath as he watched Niall leave. "Arrogant bastard . . . "

"Pot, kettle, black." Jani stood her ground when Scriabin turned on her, eyes wide and face reddening. "He's the AG's colonel for a reason, and he's worried. So am I. We've both lived through idomeni political strife and the Commonwealth's bungling attempts to turn it to their advantage." She waited until the man backed off, until his breathing slowed. "I think he trusts you. In any event, he's thrown in with you for good or ill because he believes it's better for his Commonwealth. It's your job to show that you merit his confidence. Announcing every five minutes that you're the *S* in NUVA-SCAN isn't quite good enough."

Scriabin studied her through narrowed eyes. On close inspection, the sense of the brawler held true, from his wide, broad-nosed face to his blocky build and dockworker's hands. "Anais has filled my ears about you ever since we learned you were involved in this. You helped drive the wedge between her and Li Cao. She's been scrambling to keep a claw in ever since, and not having much luck." He jerked his head toward the door. "Then to add insult to injury, you went and stole her bauble. I should thank you for that. Expensive bastard, our blond captain, and from what I've observed, not worth the cost." His voice held the same quality of question as did every heterosexual male's when they pondered the survival skills of Lucien Pascal. "I would have figured you for smarter."

Jani shrugged. This wasn't the time to discuss the matter of Lucien, and even if it were, Scriabin would never be the man she'd choose to discuss it with. "For all his complicating ways, he possesses a uniquely uncomplicated view of life. Sometimes, that can be a refuge."

"And other times, it can be a trap."

"I could say the same about Family loyalty. Capital F."

Scriabin's head snapped back, in the manner of those who commonly questioned others' choices but never their own. "Tyotya Ani has her uses. She quiets the fears of the hardliners who worry that the Commonwealth is disintegrating. Before they realize what's happening, we'll be in." His voice quieted. "Only an idiot would allow her any real power."

Jani considered the Anais Ulanova she had dealt with in Chicago and couldn't help but smile. "Does she know that?"

"By the time it dawns on her, she will be too committed to

back out. She will have nowhere else to go." Scriabin leaned close. His breath held the bare hint of whiskey. "Stakes, yes, I understand the meaning of the word. Risk."

"You won't face a firing squad if it goes to hell."

"Are you sure?" Scriabin glanced up at the sun, which had just become visible through the glass roof of the courtyard. "We must continue this discussion at another time. Perhaps your captain can keep score." He snorted. "Assuming he can count that high." He offered a curt nod in farewell and headed for the foyer, only to be intercepted by Dieter bearing a clothes bag containing his outfit from the previous day. He grabbed the bag without a word and left.

Dieter stood still for a moment, then turned to Jani. "You're welcome, Your Excellency. Wear it in good health." He tried to grin and failed, his face showing all the fatigue and sadness and worry that marked the mood of the Main House, which was quiet as a church even as noon sacrament approached. "You'll need help preparing. I can have Gena help you pack, and—"

"I think we have more pressing matters to settle." Jani beckoned him to follow her into the maze of demirooms.

CHAPTER 19

Just track the voices. Especially a certain weighty bass, dark as clouded midnight.

John rose when he spotted her, then sank back into the couch when she ignored him. "We're discussing how to handle matters in my absence." He nodded toward Sikara and Cossa, both dressed in staid black.

"Ms. Kilian." Sikara rose and bowed low. "Our deepest sympathies for the loss of your friend."

"Indeed." Cossa matched his partner's bow even as he eyed Dieter, who stood just outside the bounds of the room.

"Thank you." Jani sat on the end of the couch as far as possible from John, a move that drew a raised eyebrow from Sikara. "I don't mean to sound unappreciative, but as John no doubt told you, we will be departing for Shèrá later this evening." She motioned for Dieter to join them. "This is Dieter Brondt, my suborn. He will act for me in my absence, and I would like him to take part in this conversation." She sensed John's glare, his desire to interrupt trumped by his reluctance to anger her more than he had already. *Yes, I've just hijacked your legal team. Try and stop me.* "I assume John told you that ní Tsecha was assassinated?"

Sikara nodded. "He informed us yesterday afternoon, yes."

Jani looked at John, only to find him intent on his hands. *You told your lawyers before you told me.* She tried to speak, but a rise of anger choked her. *You told your goddamn lawyers!*

"We actually did want to consult with you concerning your assessment of the current situation." Cossa removed a recording board from the briefbag at his feet and activated it.

You mean you want to know whether John's back-door arrangement with Yevgeny Scriabin is still viable? Jani took one deep breath, then another. "If things remain unsettled—" She stopped, then tried again. "That may work in John's favor. A solid source of money in a troubled region does wonders to calm shaky nerves." She watched Cossa transcribe her every word, and wondered if he really hadn't already considered the point. "If there's war, all bets are off. Feyó may take her Haárin and go home, or she may stay, and Cèel would send warriors to collect her. Or Li Cao could send Service troops to drive her out." She shot a look at Dieter, who had dragged a chair into their circle and now sat and watched her expectantly. "I'm glad you brought up the subject, Mister Cossa. Are you still taking clients?"

The two lawyers looked at one another. Then Sikara took over. "We represent cases involving matters of business. Bankruptcies. Dissolutions. Mergers."

Jani nodded. "I admit that Thalassa isn't a business. More a medical condition wrapped around a state of mind. It consists of this house, some surrounding homes and outbuildings, a few crisscrossing roads. A lot of land—the original surveys are stored here in our offices. Governor Markos allows us some autonomy. I think the operative word is 'allows.'" She paused, and heard only the intermittent *click* of Cossa's stylus. "I will be gone for several months. I need to leave some bastards in place to make sure that my home is still here when I get back."

Cossa stopped writing and slumped back. "Thanks. A lot."

"Settle down, James." Sikara sat back more easily and folded his hands, the pose of a man prepared to listen. "I think we've just been paid quite the compliment."

Jani nodded. "When we numbered only fifty or so, I once spent a few days making up sets of fake documents for everyone. A safety net, in case of disaster. Birth certs. ID cards. I even reconfigured inset chips, though I don't think they would stand up to full-bore ministry-level analysis. Now the place has grown too large, and I no longer believe that scattering the inhabitants to the four winds is a viable strategy." Her jaw cracked as she swallowed a yawn. "Thalassa is in a grey zone. In case of war, I want it to be protected. I don't want Thalassans to wind up in prison, or be forced to revert to their original humanish or Haárin state if they don't want to."

Sikara's eyes half closed, as though he listened to music. "The issue I see is one of jurisdiction. Mister Cossa is human, and a Commonwealth citizen, as am I."

"Isn't it our decision?" Jani looked from the senior partner to the junior, searched for any hint of encouragement, and saw only professional blandness. "Can't Thalassa grant you the right to represent us?"

"Perhaps." Cossa studied the tip of his stylus. "How have legal matters been handled in the past?"

Jani looked at Dieter, who shrugged. "We haven't really had any legal matters that required special handling. Internal disputes are handled . . . well, internally. Discussion between the parties, sometimes heated." She leaned against the arm of the couch and propped up her head with her hand. Ached for sleep, even as she dreaded the prospect. "Externally—"

"Externally, all major dealings, including purchases of land, goods, and services, have been handled by Neoclona attorneys working on my behalf." John's voice emerged warm, patient. He didn't look at Jani. He didn't have to. *Go ahead and kick me out of bed,* his tone implied, in a wavelength she had come to know all too well. *I still own you.*

Cossa once more took notes. "So your primary source of wherewithal is Neoclona?"

"Over the last several months we've actually started to develop into something more than an extension of John Shroud's ego." Jani paused until Cossa cleared the large smudge he'd scratched across his board and Dieter stopped coughing. "We're leasing a couple of docks from the Elyan Haárin, and one from a Karistos holding company. We've leased ships, and have begun exporting our food culturing technologies to other colonies. Ná Gisa Pilon, our dominant emeritus, is heading that project." She hesitated, pondered wording, ignored John's mouthing of *dominant emeritus*. "And we've entertained the odd inquiry regarding our willingness to house large amounts of cash."

Sikara's eyes opened wide. "Funds laundering?"

"That, too." Jani rocked her hand in a so-so gesture. "Numbered accounts, mostly. Since we're outside Commonwealth jurisdiction here, I can understand the appeal."

"We are considering the numbered accounts," Dieter added, eyes still watering.

"Conservative projections are that these nonmedical ventures will earn sufficient to support this enclave, even allowing for an explosion in population, within four to five years—" Jani stopped when Sikara held up a hand.

"In event of war . . . "

"In event of war, there are no guarantees about anything." Jani sniffed the air as the aromas of noon sacrament wafted. "But people will still need to eat, and some will still want places to park their funds that the Commonwealth can't touch."

John started to laugh. "This is ridiculous, pie-in-the-sky—"

"If Misters Sikara and Cossa can tie up matters in the Commonwealth courts long enough, we'll have enough money to buy you out." Jani avoided looking John in the eye. "Hell, Elyas already considers us an autonomous entity. We could just declare that the Commonwealth has no jurisdiction and nationalize you now."

Cossa's stylus stopped in mid-word. "That's actually . . ." His brow arched. "It's a ballsy move—"

"That would get quashed by any—" Sikara tapped his

chin with his fist. "The decision concerning jurisdiction would likely end up in the Commonwealth Court."

"If a procolonial autonomy figure like Yevgeny Scriabin won the prime ministry and packed the bench with like minds?" Jani finally looked at John, to find him glaring at her, gripping his couch cushion in a white-knuckled clench.

"Not often the patients wind up buying the hospital," said Cossa, driving in the knife just a little deeper.

Sikara looked from John to Jani, and cleared his throat. "I won't ask. It's none of my business *yet*. I will only say that I do not handle divorces and have no intention of starting now." He grew quiet, his lawyer brain already mulling the possibilities. "That being said, my partner and I will evaluate your overall situation. Whatever our decision, Mister Brondt may feel free to call on us at any time during your absence."

Jani looked at Dieter, who nodded. "We have the wherewithal to retain you."

John thumped his thigh with his fist. "Does the term 'conflict of interest' enter into this anywhere?"

Sikara's chin came up. "We are looking after your interests, John, in a manner that isn't so dependent on the outcome of a Chicago-run general election. If your share of Neoclona was successfully nationalized, you'd retain control of all research and medical facilities, and Thalassa would begin to acquire some sort of . . . national identity, for want of a better term." He looked to Jani for confirmation, and frowned when she took her time nodding her reply. "You would likely lose some control of operations and decisions concerning expansion and whatnot, but it would beat the hell out of two percent, give us your ball, and go home. If I were you, I wouldn't dismiss it out of hand."

Dieter stood and clapped his hands silently, a *let's go* gesture that implied how eager he was to flee the room. "I can give you a quick tour of our offices on your way out. We have a retired attorney and a paralegal organizing matters."

"Yes, I'd like that." Cossa stood, stuffing his board in his bag as he nodded to John and Jani, then hurried along, as eager as Dieter to exit stage left.

"I'll catch you up in a moment, James." Sikara stood. "Safe journey to you both." He held out his hand to John, who shook it eventually, then bowed to Jani. "As I stated before, what's going on between you isn't yet my business. I would prefer it remain that way. Remember that you're on the same side. We will be blazing new legal trails here, and Chicago will throw every mud-coated roadblock in our path that they can devise. A united front is essential if we are to succeed." He straightened his jacket, adjusted the fan fold of his pocket square. "It is about control, in my experience. The money loses meaning—a fight over seashells could prove as deadly." He started after Dieter and Cossa. "When in doubt, try acting as adults. And remember what you're working toward."

John waited until the man was out of earshot. "And I thought Val was a sandbagger."

"I want this place protected. These people." Jani heard the rise of voices behind her, and turned to the courtyard to find it filling. Those who sat at tables stood and looked toward the demiroom, while the overflow filled the perimeter of the space. "If it's a choice between your pride and their lives, it's not really a choice, is it?"

"I am not going to let you steal my life's work."

"Who's stealing? You'll still have it. You'll still be able to work, but you'll be working for Thalassa, not Neoclona. Does the name change matter that much to you?" She started toward the courtyard, then stopped and looked back to John. "If it does, what the hell are you doing here?" She left him smoldering and entered the courtyard to find that someone had already set out an empty crate for her to use as a dais. She stepped atop it and faced the crowd. Sensed their confusion and the questions and, most strongly, their fear.

"I'm guessing from the looks on your faces that you've heard a little and inferred a lot." Jani paused, tried to grab words out of the air, and decided the hell with it. Words were not her gift. All she could think of to say was the bare truth, and bare truth stabbed like blades. "Ní Tsecha was assassinated. We don't know who did it. No group or individual has yet claimed responsibility. We'll find them. That's all I can say." She felt the pressure of shocked stares, unspoken questions, the first glimmers of anger. *Stay with me, please.* She put her hands in her pockets, then took them out. Looked toward the upper floors and saw more Thalassans standing at the walkway railings, watching her.

"Tonight, Doctor Shroud and I will be leaving for Shèrá as part of a funeral delegation. We will be taking ní Tsecha's soul home." Jani pulled in a shaky breath. "The fact of the assassination is not yet common knowledge. It will disseminate over the next few days, and the reaction will be swift and profound. Only humanish assassinate. The worldskein will blame the Commonwealth, and even though Morden nìRau Cèel cast out ní Tsecha and declared him Haárin, he will still proclaim grievous injury. He—" She stopped herself. Now wasn't the time for a history lesson, even though part of the history was hers. "What I'm trying to say is that things will become very difficult. Elyans may pull away from us. The Haárin may, as well. Sides will be taken, and we straddle the line here." She sensed the further quieting as the realization settled over them. The silencing of the silence.

"Questions?" Jani fielded shock, the loss for words she knew all too well. "Talk to me, to Doctor Shroud. To Dieter Brondt, who will serve in my absence. Talk to one another." She started to step down from the crate, then stopped. Every speech needed an ending, and she'd never possessed the knack for those. "We have sustained a great loss. But we will survive it, and grow, and thrive. We will do it in Tsecha's name, and in spite of those who would stop us." She stepped down, and soon found herself surrounded, the questions battering like shot. *How? What?*

Why?

She answered as best she could. Tried to comfort, although she had never possessed the knack for that, either.

Looked past the bodies that crowded her, and saw John doing the same on the other side of the courtyard.

Then someone handed her coffee, and someone else led her to a seat, and they sat and talked some more and tried to eat and she wondered if maybe, just maybe, they would be able to—

"Hey!"

—get through this without a—

"Fight!" Dieter hurtled past her, dodging around tables toward the shadowed far end of the courtyard.

Five minutes. Jani pushed back from the table, sending her chair flying, and took off after him. *We lasted five fucking minutes!* She slid to a stop behind him as he struggled to push into the scrum. Three bodies, maybe four, a punching, kicking, biting mass of bright clothes and fists and elbows.

"Knock it off!" Dieter deflected a blow to his chin, grabbed the back of a collar and yanked. *"Break it up now!"*

Jani circled to the other side. Grabbed the back of a shirt, a handful of hair. Took a wild punch to the breast and struck back hard, heard the howl and rode it, felt the sensations rise. The cold burn of the flesh. The song in the blood. Brought back her fist again and—

"Jani?" Dieter shouted from the other side of the pile. "Jani!"

—lashed out, connected, felt the blessed warmth spatter across her skin. Caught hold of cloth and hair and pulled, lifted a body clean and slammed it against the stone wall. Heard the *hmph* of expelled air, the wheezing intake of breath, a curse. Caught a fist with the flat of her hand.

Recognized the face through the rage and the red.

"Do you want to fight me, Jemmie?" She saw the answer in the young male's widening eyes. That she was the Kilian of Knevçet Shèràa, and of other things whispered of, but not known for sure. That she leaned against him with all her weight, one arm braced across his shoulders, a knee against his leg and a fist in front of his balls, and that whatever advantage he'd enjoyed due to age or anger or strength, he'd just lost it.

Jemmie shook his head as he tried to wriggle out from under. "You said—humanish assassinate. Humanish killed ní Tsecha!" He struggled to point with an arm immobilized by her pressure on his shoulder. "He's humanish!" He twitched his hand toward another young male who Dieter worked to free from the mess.

"That's *Bryan*." Jani paused, put her head back, breathed. "Are you saying that Bryan killed ní Tsecha?" She watched the two look at one another, then away. *Bryan and Jemmie.* They'd arrived at about the same time, did the program together. Worked in the greenhouses. Together. "You've both been here three months. At this point, he's only a little more humanish than you. You're practically the same." She edged back, let Jemmie step away from the wall. "If you're thinking of telling me that it makes a difference that he began as humanish and you began as Haárin, I would beg you to reconsider your argument. You both chose to be made Thalassan, and you did so for a reason. Have you forgotten what it was?" She gave Jemmie's bright blue shirt and aqua trousers a once-over. "Or did you just do it for the clothes?" She watched Jemmie's face redden as the nervous laughter spread through the crowd of onlookers. *Humanish enough to be embarrassed.* Well, that was a start.

"You'll do nothing."

Jani looked around to find the third member of the scrum looking up at her from the floor. One eye had already swelled closed and his lip glistened raw red. *Owen.* He'd come with his father. They'd been there from the start.

"You're up against the Commonwealth, and their Families, and their money." Owen coughed, spit blood and phlegm. "They'll hide whoever did it, and if you fight them, they'll crush you."

Jani stood over him silently, staring him down until he broke contact and hung his head. Then she held out her hand, waited until he took it, and pulled him to his feet. "Humanish or Haárin—it's all the same in this. We will be questioning Haárin who were in the vicinity at the time we believe the assassin passed through Elyas Station. To see if they saw *anything,* if they know *anything.*" She looked at each of the fighters in turn, then at the rest of the crowd.

"We are working together in this, ná Feyó and ná Meva and I. Colonel Pierce. Governor Markos. The colony of Elyas, the Haárin enclave and Thalassa." She shook her head. "If ní Tsecha could see you now, what would he say? You know what he would say, and he'd be a hell of a lot less diplomatic than I am." She stepped over blood-smeared flagstones on her way back to the central courtyard. "Why are we here? Because some of us were ill, and the blending saved us. Because some of us believe that the blending is the future. Because we want to live longer and watch the changes and become that which we are meant to be." She turned back to the three chastened brawlers, stopping them in their tracks. "Don't ever do this again!" Then she walked back to her table and her cold coffee. Sat down and breathed slowly and tried to silence the pounding in her head.

"You're the one who did the number on Owen's lip. That's two in less than a day. Thanks for the assistance, but from now on, let me break up the fights." Dieter sat across from her, a mug of tea in hand. "I left them in the care of angry home-parents." He slid back the lid of a sugar bowl and plucked a couple of cubes, dropping them into his tea. "And so it begins."

"Might be a good idea to introduce *à lérine.* It'll help release the steam." Jani drank her coffee, and wondered if it would keep her awake until she boarded the shuttle. "We were bound to need it eventually."

"Let them challenge one another?" Dieter slumped and stared at her. "We'll spend the next three weeks hosing the blood out of here."

"I don't see an alternative." Jani picked out a roll from the breadbasket, tore off a chunk and dredged it through a dish of herbed oil. "The idomeni in them will crave the structure. And it will prepare them in case any of the Elyan Haárin decide to express their opinion and start offering challenges."

She tasted mild grassiness and wished it would burn, blister, keep her awake. "Talk to Dathim. He can recommend some friendly Haárin who can serve as trainers. I guarantee they won't put up with any crap."

Dieter drummed his fingers along the side of his cup. "Someone could die."

"Not likely, given we're right atop a damned clinic." Jani fielded Dieter's stare. "I doubt anyone is going to assassinate one of them." Another chunk of bread. More oil. "We've reached the one-day-at-a-time stage. Start with some organized violence, and see how it goes." She looked up at the skylight, the sun already grazing the edge as departure time grew closer. "Forgive me for leaving you with this, but I have no choice."

Dieter sipped. Shrugged. "There will be washouts, as in any trial by fire. Some may need to return for medical reasons, and maybe they'll eventually see sense. The rest of us should come through stronger, more united." He forced a smile. "Your home will be here when you return." Then he looked past Jani and the smile wavered. "Pierce."

"Brondt." Niall dragged a chair next to Jani and sat. "I seem to have walked into the middle of something." He looked across the courtyard to the scene of the fight, where the guilty parties mopped the floor under the watchful eye of Owen's father. "I wanted to let you know the details so far."

"Snapping Family fingers?" Jani managed a grin.

"Shut up." Niall staged his own raid of the breadbasket. "Shuttle services to Elyas Station are being provided by Exterior, but you'll travel as far as Guernsey on a Commerce cruiser, the *Madelaine*. Pascal and I and a few other of my staff will be claiming billet privileges on both your shuttle and your ship. After we hit Guernsey, it will be our turn. We'll be giving you a ride as far as treaty allows. Then it's back to the *Madelaine* for the balance of the journey to Rauta Shèràa."

"A Service vessel?" Dieter's brow arched.

"A carrier. The CSS *Viktor Ulanov*, who history indicates

wasn't the worst Prime Minister we ever had, and who was less of a bastard than others of his family, small *f*." Niall smeared butter on black bread, then swiped a cup from a nearby place setting and filled it from a carafe. "Roshi's orders."

Jani calculated message central transmit times in her head. "He can't have received your messages already."

"He can when he's already halfway here." Niall grabbed another slice of bread, then offered a grinning "thank you" to a young female who slipped him a plate of ham. "He was already on his way out here to assess the Fort Karistos situation personally. He'll reach Guernsey about a week before we do." He folded the meat into the bread and dredged it all through a dish of hot mustard. "It's the general feeling that it's the best way to protect the embassy. Let Cèel see a little of what we have." He took a bite of his sandwich, nodding as he chewed.

Dieter tossed back the last of his tea, then stood. "Your gear won't pack itself." He circled the table and headed for the stairway.

"Don't forget the small clothes." Jani smiled as he turned and shook his finger at her.

"Think you're up to it?" Niall refilled his cup, then scanned the table for something else to eat.

Jani didn't have to ask what he referred to. *Rauta Shèràa in our sights.* She twitched a shoulder. "You?"

"We'll find out, won't we?" The filtered sunlight struck the side of his face, highlighting a throbbing vein and a bunched jaw muscle. "Sleeping well?" He didn't wait for an answer. "Might've been better for your overall health if you'd avoided the spat with your medical team."

"It was more than a spat." Jani broke off crumbs of bread and tossed them into the oil dish.

"I know. Pascal filled me in. I'm having a hard time adjusting to receiving my updates from him." Niall touched his lower lip. "I did notice a spot of imperfection on that face you seem to think so much of." He paused. "So why'd you hit him?"

Jani dropped the last chunk of bread into the oil. "Can I just say that he got on my nerves and leave it at that?"

"Much as I'd like to believe you've finally come to your senses where he's concerned, no." Niall gave up the hunt for further sustenance and dug out his 'sticks. "Like I said before, he thinks they didn't tell me that Tsecha was assassinated because they thought I'd tell you. Why would that worry them?" He exhaled twin streams of smoke, watched it drift upward. "Of course you'd be upset. And you'd want to find out who did it. Not really a stretch. Did they think you'd try to take over the investigation? I thought you were remarkably well-behaved in the library." He set his nicstick case spinning on the tabletop, and it flashed back sunlight like a beacon. "Pascal said he told you to let a pro handle it."

Jani laid back her head. Sleep called again, and she struggled to ignore it. "Handle what?"

Niall swept his case off the table and back into his pocket. "It's bad enough adjusting to working with Pretty Boy. What's bothering me even more is that I find myself agreeing with him. Half the Outer Circle is on this case, Jan. Leave them to it. Let the courts, or a discreet professional, take care of the killer." His timepiece beeped and he grumbled. "Can I use your comroom? I need to send Roshi an update. Take what I said to heart, please?" He made as if to rise, then sat back slowly. "Please?"

Jani watched him slump, the energy seep away, until he looked as tired as she felt. "Niall?"

He dropped his spent 'stick in a refuse dish and watched the last curls of smoke. "You first."

Jani waited, while around her Thalassans talked and tried to laugh. "I'm caught in a sandstorm. It buries me."

Niall nodded. "My long-range misfires, blows a hole in my chest. I look down, and I can see my heart beating. Then it stops." He stood. "First one in months. Maybe I'm not so sorry that Pretty Boy woke me up early this morning after all."

"You don't have to go."

"You're going."

"I don't have a choice."

"Neither do I, gel. If we need to pick embassy personnel off the rooftops, I have to be there." Niall put a hand on her shoulder and squeezed. "Do things right this time." He released her. "See you on the tarmac."

"Yeah." Jani watched him maneuver across the courtyard to the lift and step aboard the cabin. Watched the doors close. "This time." She finished her coffee and headed for her room.

Packing went quickly. Anything that she had left behind in John's suite was retrieved by a solemn Dieter, who considered all the diplomatic possibilities and made sure that the trouser suits outnumbered the coveralls, then added a few gowns to the mix as well. That task completed, they adjourned to the offices, where Jani affixed signatures, discussed contingencies, and wrote the letter formally requesting that the firm of Sikara and Cossa act on the enclave's behalf "in any and all legal matters."

The sun had begun its downward trek as she walked out to the beach. Imprinted the view in her mind in case she never saw it again. After a time, she heard the footfall behind her. The weighty quiet. "He loved it here."

Dathim drew up beside her. "We have put him aboard our shuttle. We leave at sunset. Feyó says little, so Meva speaks for both. She does that well." He wore brilliant green and yellow, his ears arrayed with small hoops of gold, his brown hair freshly shorn. "You said you would show his killer the meaning of that which they did." He looked down at her, eyes gleaming in the fading light. "You will kill them."

"Yes." Jani saw a glimmer in the distance, growing larger with the passing seconds. The Exterior shuttle, approaching at speed. "Are you going to try to talk me out of it, too?"

Dathim looked back out to the water. The lion, ever quiet, ever watchful. "No."

CHAPTER 20

"Glories of the ship's day to you."

Rilas looked up from her solitary game of pattern stones to find another of the passengers standing before her table. A female, attired in the most seemly manner. Hair braided in a breeder's fringe. Trousers, shirt, and overrobe in shades of palest green and sand.

The female bared her teeth, and kept her eyes averted. "I am ná Bolan Thea." She spoke Vynshàrau Haárin laced with gesture that was almost bornsect in its complexity. "You wish an opponent?"

"I—" Rilas looked down at her stones. They had transitioned to yellow and green spirals, and she had only three stones left to align to complete the required arrangement when ná Bolan interrupted. Now, as she watched, the pattern altered to cross-hatching lines. She had been so close—

"I have lost you your game!" Ná Bolan crossed her right arm over her chest, a most formal gesture of apology.

"Such is not important." Rilas cast a final look at the stones before sweeping them off the table and into her cup. "I am ná Nahin Sela, and I do wish discourse. Since we departed Elyas Station, I have spoken to no other passengers." She looked about the games room, empty but for herself and ná Bolan. "One ship-cycle past, yet all still remain in their rooms." She handed the other female the cup, then smoothed the table covering so the stones would tumble cleanly and lay well.

"They pray. They send transmissions to the worldskein." Ná Bolan shook the cup and cast the stones. "Ní Tsecha Egri is dead, and they ponder that which comes after." The polished rounds scattered across the table surface, the first pattern developing almost immediately. Left-hand spirals, a difficult design to manipulate.

Ponder? Rilas watched her new opponent arrange the stones, hands moving with a quickness that rivaled her own. "They worry greatly, I most believe. Many considered ní Tsecha as their propitiator."

"I did not." Ná Bolan completed her arrangement just as the spirals altered direction "What status had he, the first Chief Propitiator to be made Haárin? He was anathema." She then used her handheld to record her points and her time. "NìaRauta Sànalàn is my propitiator."

Rilas fought the desire to bare her teeth as she collected the stones into her cup and shook them. So good after so long, to hear the words of a godly Haárin.

She cast her stones. X marks. The simplest design. She bared her teeth and arranged the pattern, hands moving as quickly as they had when she assembled her rifle. "I have won this round!" She activated her own handheld and entered her scores. "We shall play a series—"

"Ná Nahin?"

Rilas looked up to find a ship's security dominant standing before her.

"Glories of the ship's day to you." He bared his teeth. "You will accompany me, please, to the security workroom." He stepped back from the table, then paused, waiting.

"Detained?" Rilas leaned against the high seat the dominant had offered her. "There are issues with my documents? With the business I performed in Karistos?"

The dominant did not respond, but wrote a note on a piece of parchment with an inking stylus. As the other dominants on this Sìah Haárin cruiser, he dressed much as a humanish. Trousers and shirt of dark green, the uniform color of the ship. Around his neck, a strip of knotted cloth decorated with blue and green whorls. He wore his brown hair clipped short, which left visible the silver hoops that arrayed both earlobes from top to bottom.

Unseemly. But security just the same, which meant that she needed to answer all questions and appear cooperative at all times. Even the godly act of disputation would be forbidden her, since Haárin who worked too long with humanish saw such as an attempt to evade and obstruct rather than as the blessed discourse that it was.

Rilas tried to climb onto the seat, but one of its legs proved shorter than the other three, which sent it tipping to the side each time she set her weight upon it. *Ungodly.* The male sought to disquiet her with his silences and his broken furniture, this she knew as surely as she knew her robes and her rings. She had spent season after season training against such. It could not be unexpected.

As though he had heard her thoughts through the air, the dominant stopped writing. He set down the stylus, then picked a hand light from a tray of writing tools and shone it upon the parchment, setting the inks. Then he sat back, hands clasped before him on the desk. "When we arrive at Guernsey Station, you will present yourself to this office. From here, you will be escorted to the Haárin Trade Board offices located at the station."

"I ask again, ní—" Rilas checked the front of the male's shirt, then the top of his worktable, in search of a plate or disc bearing his name. She had seen such on the other ship dominants and suborns. Why did he not offer the same information? "Why am I to be detained? Are my documents not in order? Is there a question of my actions on Elyas?"

The male took a documents slipcase from the stack on

the side of his desk, and removed the parchment contained within. "You are a broker of decorative tiles?"

"Yes, ní—" Rilas fought to straighten, to relax her throat and lighten her tone. "Yes. I am a tile broker."

"How long was your stay in Karistos?"

"Two Elyan days."

The male nodded, a maddening humanish gesture that could mean anything or nothing. "When we arrive at Guernsey Station, you will be met by ná Calas Pélan, who is security dominant for the station. She will advise you of whatever you are entitled to know. You will be housed in suitable rooms, and communications will be sent from ná Calas's dominant to yours conveying our sorrow at the disorder of this interruption." His hand paused in its movements. "Who is your dominant, ná Nahin, so that we may process the notification with godly haste?"

Rilas hesitated. Ná Nahin Sela was a tile broker of Rauta Shèràa, and thus had nothing to hide. She needed to behave as such. "My dominant is ní Kolesh Metán. His business rooms are within the Trade Board in Rauta Shèràa." For this, she and nìRau Cèel had planned. Just as every godly Haárin acknowledged an Haárin dominant, so did she, for each of the Haárin she had ever pretended to be. And just as she had played the part of many Haárin, so had her dominant. The male owed his life and allegiance to nìRau Cèel, as she did. If he were ever contacted, he would respond as was appropriate to his skein and standing.

"We shall initiate contact with ní Kolesh." The male dragged the input board across the desk until it rested before him. "The Trade Board is well outfitted with rapid communications, thus we will seek to contact him immediately." Another worthless nod. "We shall address the skein dominant as well, and present our regrets over any delay."

"The skein dominant?" Rilas felt her heart quicken once more. "Such would be an interference."

"Such is the most formal of protocols, ná Nahin." The

male's hands stilled in their labors. "I only seek to placate. To acknowledge your concerns and address them." He began inputting once more. "If reparations are due the skein of tilemasters, we of the security skein will make them, and truly."

Rilas watched the male work, and pressed a hand to her stomach, her roiling soul. *I could kill him before he knew I had moved.* And before she had reached her rooms, his skeinsharers would be on her, and all would be as lost. *But all will be as lost in any case, for the dominant of the tilemasters' skein will not know of ní Kolesh.* His name existed in the roll, but he had no formal presence as a tilemaster. *They would seek him and not find him.* "I would request that you delay contacting ní Kolesh until I have done so."

The male tilted his head to one side, but since he did not alter his posture or raise either hand, it meant only more nothing. "Why, ná Nahin?"

"Because there is discord between ní Kolesh and the tilemaster dominant, unto the edge of challenge, and I most fear that any interruption of business will aggravate this discord further." Rilas paused to breathe, and felt her heart slow. Yes, if one accepted order, the gods protected one, and granted one cleverness. "Such contact as you wish to make would compel either ní Kolesh or the dominant to offer challenge, and such is not seemly. I as a suborn should not be the one to provoke such. The provocation should originate between them."

The male sat back and lowered his hands to the desktop. "And if I notify ní Kolesh, he may take the news to the skein dominant himself, and the challenge, if it is offered, may be offered in a more orderly manner."

"Yes." Rilas drew herself most straight. "I am gratified that you understand."

"I understand why I am most content to no longer live within the worldskein." The male folded his hands one over the other and rested them upon his knee. "I believe that given the tension between ní Kolesh and his dominant, it would be more fitting if you contacted him yourself. That way, you could explain the circumstances most fully, and determine between you the best method to approach the skein dominant."

Rilas bared her teeth. Her heart beat as slowly as if she slept. Those who worshipped the beauty of Caith would always be assured a well-illuminated path. "Such a solution would be most gratefully accepted, and truly."

Rilas restrained herself as the communications suborn instructed her on the use of the headpiece and showed her more times than was necessary the order of activation of the various relays and feeds. She knew more of the workings of such communications than any suborn. *But a tile broker would not know of such matters.* Thus did she remain silent, and gesture gratitude when the suborn completed his useless teachings and departed the cubicle.

The security dominant so readily allowed me this. Rilas stood before the recording screen and prepared herself to speak. *Does he believe that I will say something of interest to him?* She fully expected that he would intercept her message, or perhaps have it relayed directly to his workrooms. *He thinks himself most as humanish.* Crafty. Devious. *Do you believe, you with no name, that you are the only idomeni who is this way?* One of the first lessons nìRau Cèel had taught her was how to adopt humanish ways, to defeat the enemy by becoming as they were.

Across the narrow cubicle, the screen indicators altered in countdown. Rilas stood straight, tilted her head to the right in regard, curved her right hand and brought it level to her chest.

"Ní Kolesh." She bared her teeth. "Glories of the day to you." She elevated the pitch of her voice. "With regret I tell you that I will not be able to attend our planned meetings at Phillipa Station. I will be detained at Guernsey Station for an unknown span of time. I am to be asked questions by ná Calas Pélan, security dominant of the Guernsey Haárin. I have not been told that which these questions concern."

She stopped, held her breath and listened, even though the cubicle was enclosed, soundproofed so that no one outside could hear that which was spoken within.

"Such is all I can say, ní Kolesh, for such is all I know. May our ventures be blessed by Shiou in spite of the efforts of Caith to hamper our path. Blessings of future days grace you, and all who labor for you." With that, Rilas gestured farewell, and stepped out of range of the display. She had done what she could, which was more than could have been hoped. She had notified nìRau Cèel of where she traveled and who would detain her. She prayed to Caith that by the time she arrived at Guernsey Station, some order would have arrived from Shèrá releasing her from having to respond to ná Calas's questions. *But if such is not forthcoming . . .* Another method of interference would suffice. She could think of several that would affect an older station such as Guernsey. Provided access to the proper materials, she could construct the devices herself.

Rilas pressed the cubicle door pad, waited for the door to open fully. Stepped out into the corridor and followed the path to the games room. She found ná Bolan Thea still seated in the same chair, executing a complex solo game with three sets of stones.

"Have you committed crimes, ná Nahin? Is that why security dominants demand to speak with you and take you away from your games?" The female bared her teeth. "Nahin the criminal. I shall warn everyone of you."

Rilas clenched one hand. Imagined Bolan's neck and the blow required to break it, then stopped herself. *Ná Bolan is a godly Haárin, and such is her way.* The combative, challenging way of idomeni. The way she, Imea nìaRauta Rilas, would have recognized had she not been so concerned with humanish-acting security dominants who did not comprehend the custom of nameplates.

"I am indeed a criminal." Rilas bared her teeth and sat, and prayed to Caith for a disaster to befall Guernsey Station.

* * *

As the ship-cycle passed, more and more Haárin ventured out of their cabins. Rilas remained among them, and behaved most as that which she was supposed to be. She studied business dispatches prior to mid-afternoon sacrament, participated in movement sessions in the gymnasium and in discussions in the ship's veranda. Through ná Bolan, she met others. They filled the games room and discussed ní Tsecha's death in between the clatter and toss of the stones.

It did not surprise Rilas overmuch when the male security dominant who had questioned her earlier entered the games room. Their ship was small. They would be bound to encounter one another. Even so, she felt relief when he did not acknowledge her and sat at another table. *Nahin the criminal*, ná Bolan announced, and she accepted the mocking with bared teeth. Cast her stones. Arranged her designs. Kept her scores.

Rilas won several rounds, and played until the corridors darkened, a sign of the ship-night. She left the loud ná Bolan and the others behind and returned to her rooms. Entered. Paused in the doorway and studied the worktable, the altar alcove, the laving room and bedroom beyond. Could detect no sign that someone had entered during her absence and searched her belongings, yet trusted the sense she had acquired over many such journeys and accepted that someone had. The male security dominant, possibly. One of his suborns, more likely.

Rilas walked through the rooms, one by one. Took note of objects and their locations and positions. *Twenty ship-cycles until Guernsey.* She prayed to Caith for the time to pass quickly, even as she knew what awaited her there, and realized that she might be praying for the lesser choice.

CHAPTER 21

"Kilian says Haárin to be questioned in connection
   with assassination."

Rilas read the title of the Guernsey newssheet once, then
again. Then she studied the image of Kilian that had been
placed next to the text, looking her in the eye as she would
never have done if they stood together in the flesh.
Godless eyes. Anathema. The sickly green, pale as Oà,
too light against Kilian's dark skin.

"Humanish or Haárin—it's all the same."

Rilas crouched before the image display, one hand fixed
on the controls. She had obtained a copy of the newssheet
as soon as it had been received by the ship relay, replayed
it constantly, as every idomeni had done since it had first
been released. Argued over it on the ship's veranda, in the
games room, the movement room, as they had argued over
the news of ní Tsecha's assassination, released only a short
time before.

"Humanish or Haárin—it's all the same."

Morden nìRau Cèel's response had been swift, his godly
aspect broadcast throughout the worldskein to the Commonwealth beyond. *The Kièrshia is anathema*, he had entoned,
shoulders rounded and voice deepened. *Idomeni do not kill
in such a secret way.*

But then the stories emerged of deaths that occurred
within the circle as the result of godly challenge, of knives
that had slipped and blood that had flowed too well.

Such is different, and truly. Rilas deactivated the display,
watched Kilian's eyes darken to blackness. *Each slip of the
blade is the will of the gods.* If a soul heard the call of the
gods, its duty was to answer. Any action that assisted it upon
its way served as part of that reply.

"All is anathema." Rilas paced. They would dock at
Guernsey within half a ship-cycle, and still she had heard
nothing from ní Kolesh, not even an acknowledgment of her
message. *They have notified ná Calus, and I will not be questioned.* But if this was the case, why had not the nameless
ship security dominant informed her? Why allow her to wait,
and wonder?

She sensed the tension grow in her limbs and knot the
core of her soul. Now was not the time for the games room,
even though she had arranged to meet with ná Bolan. Now
was not a time for the stones.

She removed her overrobe, trousers, shirt. Greyed blue
and sand they were, colors of the gaming room and veranda,
made of cloth which possessed a delicate sheen and a light
hand. Walked to her storage chest and removed sand-shaded
trousers and sleeveless shirt and put them on. Bound the fasteners. Knotted the ties. Heavier cloth, this, dull to the eye
and mended many times.

Rilas looked down at her bare arms, gold-brown skin
darkened by Shèráin sun and crosshatched by the pale ridges
of old scars. Flexed her hands, watched the muscles work.

"Time for the blades." Wooden ones, most unfortunately.
But such would have to suffice.

* * *

"She proclaimed such at the meeting house on Elyas." The male, a young Dahoumn, pale and blocky, executed a complex turn of wrist that caused his blade to spin as a fan. "She stood atop a stage, as humanish do, and proclaimed while all about her shouted and clapped their hands."

Rilas worked her blade in a solitary exercise, close enough to the Dahoumn to hear him, but far enough away to seem separate from his group. All were younger, pale, shorter Dahoumn and darker, taller Sìah, and most disordered. They did not work their blades in unison, and bumped and banged into one another repeatedly.

"After she proclaimed, humanish challenged Haárin, and forced them to lave the circle afterward, to clean away their blood," said another of the group, a Sìah female. "The walls as well . . . or walls and floor . . . or just the walls?"

"It's all the same," sounded a female voice. A humanish voice.

Kilian's voice.

Rilas flinched. Her hands dropped. The end of her blade caught on the edge of the floor pad, stopping her motion in mid-twist. Pain radiated up her right wrist and along her arm, a thin line of flame. Her hand spasmed and the wooden blade spun out of her grasp, through the air and into the midst of another group, striking an elder male in the face before clattering to the bare floor.

The male covered his nose with both hands even as the blood flowed through his fingers and down the front of his tunic. A few Haárin shouted, while one ran to the communication array and pressed the switch that summoned the ship's physician-priest.

Rilas turned to the group of youngish, who stared at the blooded elder, their blades at all angles. One began to laugh, until his neighbor elbowed him in the pit of his soul. Another, one of the females, had positioned herself behind the others, ducking so she could not be seen.

"What has happened?" Another of the elder male's group stepped between Rilas and the youngish. A male of middle years, Sìah or light-skinned Vynshàrau, breeder's fringe gathered in a knot and tied with a cord, arms so hacked with scarring there seemed no clear skin left. "Answer."

"She lost control of her blade." The young Dahoumn male pointed to Rilas. "Demand answers from her."

The male turned. "So?"

Rilas gripped her injured wrist and stared past the male to the Dahoumn. "One of them spoke in the Kièrshia's voice, and another laughed."

The male stepped around to the rear of the youngish gaggle, where the guilty female all but crouched as an animal to hide herself. "Do you find the Kièrshia's voice an amusement?" He gripped her by the wrist and pulled her upright. "She who accuses all idomeni of anathema? You imitate her?"

"I did not—" The female looked toward Rilas. "We did not mean—"

"Stop cowering!" The young Dahoumn faced the scarred male. "Ná Lia did nothing wrong. She—" He pointed at Rilas. "—she listened to private talk. The blood is her fault."

The doors opened and the physician-priest entered together with a suborn. They hurried to the elder male, who had been led off to the side of the room by others in his group and now sat on the floor, head tipped back to squelch the bleeding from his nose.

"You distracted her." The scarred male released ná Lia, then pushed her toward the rest of her group. "If you speak loudly enough to be heard, you will be heard, and others will act as they will when they hear you."

"That is for them. We shall still say that which we will, and laugh at that which we will." The young Dahoumn broke away from the rest and faced the scarred male, moving around him as though they stood within the circle. "We did not laugh at ná Kièrshia's voice. We laughed at the expression on her face when she heard it." He pointed again to Rilas, looking her in the eye as he did. "As though she had seen a demon. Such was how she appeared, and truly."

The scarred male looked toward Rilas.

Warrior skein. Rilas began to straighten, and forced herself still. Whatever the male may once have been, whatever honor he may have earned, he was now Haárin, and she would show submission to no Haárin.

"Ná Kièrshia is the cause of fear in some." The scarred male turned back to the Dahoumn. "She is anathema."

"All is anathema." The Dahoumn laughed. "Ní Tsecha is dead. What difference? He was anathema. Such was all we heard, that he was a shame on all idomeni. Now he is dead, and such is anathema as well, and all cry out at the sadness of it, the sadness of the death of one we called anathema." He picked up a discarded wooden blade and inscribed a circle in the air. "A humanish would tell you to make up your minds. He is Tsecha, or he is not. He is great, or he is not. We mourn and honor him, or revile and forget him. We hate him and all for which he stood, or we do not."

The scarred male kept the Dahoumn in his sights, turning with him. "NìRau Cèel has said—"

"Cèel is a hypocrite!" Ná Lia found her voice once more. "He exiled ní Tsecha, and made him Haárin. But now ní Tsecha is dead, and he calls him great."

"Great now that he is dead," the Dahoumn said. "Great now that he cannot write, or speak." He stopped his turning of his blade and stilled. "Great now that Cèel does not have to listen to him any longer."

All had gone quiet in the room. Even the physician-priest and her suborn had stilled to watch the two males circle one another. Meanwhile, the Dahoumn's friends had moved to one side of the room, the scarred male's to the other.

Rilas backed toward the far wall, away from both groups. The Dahoumn's arms showed pale and lightly scarred, as nothing compared to those of the other male. Such would prove an unseemly challenge, unbalanced and graceless.

The scarred male's shoulder rounded. "Why do you speak against nìRau Cèel? Humanish killed ní Tsecha. He did not."

"He wished to. He would have executed ní Tsecha if he ever returned to Shèrá. Some say—" The young Dahoumn began to circle again. "Some say that Cèel paid humanish to kill ní Tsecha. Thus could he condemn the killers even as he rejoiced that the killing had been done."

None moved. Even the elder male who bled over his shirt listened.

"Who are these 'some' who say this?" The scarred male's voice deepened in anger. "Who?"

"Many." The Dahoumn stilled once more. "Many say this."

"Such is—"

"Anathema?" The Dahoumn bared his teeth. "A humanish would say that if all is anathema, then nothing is."

The silence that followed was disturbed by the physician-priest, who aided the elder male to his feet and guided him to the door.

Rilas followed them, straightening and lifting her chin as though requesting the injured male's pardon. But as soon as she stepped into the corridor, she left them behind. Rounded the corner and—

—collided with ná Bolan, who stifled a cry of surprise.

"Ná Nahin?" The female curved her right arm in profound question. "What is this?"

"We must leave." Rilas continued down the corridor. Prayed the physician-priest would not come after her, or the scarred male, or any of the Dahoumn's idiot companions. "There will be a challenge fought, and it will be a mess. I do not wish to witness such."

"Shall we play the stones, then?"

"Yes." Rilas massaged her wrist. The joint felt hot to her touch. Tender. Not a break, but a sprain, or a tear of a tendon. She could provide an ice wrap herself, pray over it herself. She did not need to see the ship's physician-priest, who would ask her why she lowered her hands, why she let the blade drop. *Because I heard the Kièrshia's voice.*

And first the priest would laugh. Then she would ask, *Why do you fear ná Kièrshia?*

Because she knows.
But what does she know?

"Ná Nahin?"

Rilas felt the hand on her arm. "Ná Bolan."

"You are not well."

"I am most well, and truly."

Bolan removed her hand and gestured reluctant agreement, a tilt of head and sweep of arm. "We dock at Guernsey
in a short time. Will you disembark?"

"Yes." Rilas closed her eyes, heard Caith's laugh. *I shall
allow myself one round of the stones.* Then she would present
herself to the security dominant, the male whose name she
did not know, even after twenty ship-cycles and numerous
encounters in corridors and in the games room. The male
who had searched her rooms and found nothing. *He will give
me good news.* He would tell her that she would not be questioned on Guernsey, that she did not even need to leave the
ship. That she was free to travel on her way.

She paused as Bolan coded open the door to the games
room. Followed her inside, and found the security dominant
seated alone at a table, casting stones.

"Ná Nahin. Ná Bolan." He gestured to the empty chairs
next to his own. "Join me in a game before we prepare to
dock."

Rilas walked past the chair he pointed out and sat across
from him. "You have received a message for me?"

"Yes, ná Nahin." The male bared his teeth, then handed
her the cup of stones. "Your play."

The Haárin concourse of Guernsey Station had no gargoyles,
no stained glass or transepts. Instead, there were white and
grey walls and battered grey flooring, kiosks and shops and
hallways as bright and crooked as the snow-coated branches
of winter trees.

Rilas walked beside the security dominant. He had not
allowed her to leave his presence since their meeting in the
games room, arranging for one of the ship suborns to collect

her possessions, and remaining with her throughout the approach and docking sequences.

"This way." He pointed down yet another corridor, this one marked with plaques covered in Sìah script. "The office of ná Calas is here—" He stopped as a rumble like thunder sounded, shuddering through walls and floor.

Then came the sirens, like the screeches for beasts.

"There has been an explosion." The dominant grabbed Rilas by the arm. "We must find a shelter and—"

The door of ná Calas's office opened and a female emerged. A most familiar female.

Rilas slowed, hands clenching even as her wrist ached.

"Ná Bolan Thea?" The security dominant gestured toward Bolan, a vague wave of the hand that meant nothing. "You have knowledge of ná Calas—" He stopped, then looked at Rilas, his lips moving, saying something . . .

A shadow moved in from the side. A male, dark-clad, his arm raised. The security dominant turned toward him, but too late. Brought up his arm, but not high enough to counter the blow. Fell where he stood, groaned and shuddered and stilled as the blood seeped from his battered skull and puddled around him.

Rilas watched his soul leave him. Then, slowly, she raised her eyes.

"NìaRauta Rilas." Ná Bolan spoke with a voice not hers. Gone was the querulous tone, the high pitch of the suborn, replaced by depth and strength and the chill of snow.

Rilas sensed the male at her back. "Why? I am going to him freely." He gripped her injured wrist, and she gasped.

Then Rilas felt a sting, a sensation of warmth travel up her arm. A cessation of pain. Tried to pull away and found she could not move at all. Looked to the female she had known as ná Bolan Thea, the female she had not known at all, as her knees weakened and her vision tunneled and her whisper roared in her ears. "Freely . . . I go . . . freely . . . "

CHAPTER 22

Jani opened her eyes and checked her bedside clock. *Six hours out. Guernsey Station, here we come.* She pushed off her bed cover, shivered as the chill air hit her, and dragged it back on. Waited for the sensation to leave, the light-headedness that came from too little sleep over too long a time. Waited a little longer, and knew she could wait forever for her head to clear and her limbs to feel like parts of her body again and not dead weight. Pushed the cover off again and sat up.

The entry buzzer twittered. She ignored it. It twittered again, a mechanical imitation of a songbird.

"Jan? Are you awake?"

Val? She shook her head, wondered if she still dreamed. Things had remained cool between them over the first half of the voyage, their sole interaction the odd greeting during inadvertent corridor encounters.

"I'd like to talk to you for a minute." Val gave up on the buzzer and switched to tapping on the door panel. "Jan?"

What could you possibly have to say to me? And did she want an answer to that question? *No.* Did she really think she could avoid it for long? *No.*

Did she long to hear another voice right now besides the

one in her head? *Oh, hell.* She slapped the door pad on the bedside end table.

The panel swept aside and Val stuck his head in, looking first to his left, then to his right, as though he expected crossways traffic. "We missed you at breakfast." He stepped inside, a casual vision in blue and brown. "Jeez, this place is small." He stopped and looked around the one-room cabin, then paced the sitting area, which was separated from the sleeping area by a strip of carpet and wishful thinking. "My bathroom's bigger."

"I think Anais took charge of the assignments." Jani stretched her legs and grazed the edge of the carpet with her toes. "I'm probably lucky she didn't stick me in the engine room."

"Or an airlock." Val sat in the sole chair, a straight-backed thing with balky ergoworks. "This is bullshit—why didn't you ask for something else?" He grimaced as he tried to work into a comfortable position.

Jani looked around and shrugged. "I've lived in worse."

"Yes, but that's not your life anymore, is it?" Val drummed his fingers on the chair arm, then looked toward the corner near the bed, and the small desk that held a workstation and stacks of wafer folders. "Working?"

"Researching separatist groups. Going over dossiers." Jani stood and walked to the closet, dragging the bed cover with her and wrapping it around her shoulders. "Niall got me some information."

Val eyed her makeshift robe and shook his head. "Don't tell me—you can't adjust the temperature in here, either."

"OK, I won't tell you."

"That old bitch." Val swung a leg over the arm of his chair, shifting it back and forth to avoid kicking a nearby table. "Are they going to let us go wherever we want on that carrier? Like, all the way to the other end?"

Jani dragged out a set of coveralls, then tucked them back inside, opting instead for wrapshirt and trousers in dark blue. *Going to ride on a carrier.* Probably time to stop dressing like she actually had lived in a ship's engine room for three weeks. "I think we'll be limited to a transient VIP area, which, if distant memory serves, is usually one section of a single deck. Unless we're escorted. They don't want civilians wandering around, getting into trouble."

Val sighed. "I could use some trouble. Some nice, attractive trouble that didn't run my heart through a grinder." He laid his head back, watched her dress through half-closed eyes. "You know, one of the best things about owning my own ship is having the freedom to pick my travel companions." He looked away for a moment. "Barring the odd billet privilege." He frowned. Sniffed. "I think I'm paying for it now, because so help me Jesus, the absolute last people in the Commonwealth that I would choose to long-haul with are Anais, Yevgeny, and you know who." He groaned. "*God.* Anais has a cackle that could shatter crystal at fifty meters."

Jani finished tying the sash of her shirt, then stood on her toes so she could check herself in the half mirror. "I wouldn't know. She never laughs when I'm around."

"No, she doesn't, does she?" Val gave a mean little grin. "I think we'd fail every group dynamics evaluation on the books. Anais and Yevgeny pretty much talk to one another. You know who spends all his time either working in the Service area or showing off in the gym. John's like you, spending way too much time in his cabin. I always call it his tiger-in-a-cage mood, pacing and pissed as hell. I finally pulled it out of him a couple of days ago. Did you have to be quite so brutal?"

"He'll still have his work. Overall ownership changes, is all. Does that really matter?"

"Yes. A little. Maybe more than a little. He thinks it's payback for not telling you about Tsecha."

"Maybe he should stop thinking about himself so damned much."

"Yeah." Val massaged his temples. "Then there's you and Niall, two people I could long-haul with any time . . . " He studied the ceiling. "He's drinking. You know that?"

Fuck. Jani glanced at Val in the mirror. *Of course he can tell. It's his job.* "It's not as bad as it could be."

"How bad does it have to be?" Val folded his arms and nestled into the chair, as though he intended to nap. "He covers it pretty well, and his staff protects him when he doesn't. But it's going to get worse the closer we get to Shèrá, and on top of that he'll be on a carrier with his precious Roshi, which means he'll be under even more pressure." Again, the half-closed eyes, the deceptively casual observation. "You're no better off than he is, though in your case the problem isn't liquor. You're not sleeping well, though. Anyone can see that." He worked into a sitting position. "John was the one who mentioned it to me. He said that when he'd bring it up back in Thalassa, you'd brush him off. He thought maybe Meva was getting under your skin."

Jani folded her sleep shirt and stuffed it beneath her pillow, then sat down so she could put on her boots. "Did he send you here?"

"Would it matter if he did?" Val hesitated, then shook his head. "Not to worry. Mine is a solo effort." He sat forward, elbows on knees and hands clasped between, so friendly and expectant. "What you say here, stays here. You know that."

Do I? Jani rested a booted foot atop her bed and wiped away smudges with the corner of the sheet. "I'm fine."

Val watched her. Waited until she met his eye, then waited some more, his brightness fading as the realization settled. That she wouldn't tell him. That if he pushed her, she'd lie.

"Well . . . " He stood slowly. "It is good to be trusted by those you love."

"Likewise." Jani took what grim satisfaction she could in his blush, in the way he suddenly couldn't meet her eye.

"We had our reasons, Jan." He walked to the door, head down.

"You always did."

"Yeah, well—" The tweet of the entry buzzer cut Val off, and he struck the door pad with his fist.

Niall pushed past the panel before it opened completely.

"There's been an explosion at Guernsey. One of the Commonwealth docks." He wore dress blue-greys, the shine of his badges and designators providing sharp contrast to the dullness of his skin and eyes. "It's bad."

Jani rose slowly, whispered the question she had grown to dread during her time in Rauta Shèràa. "How many?"

"One hundred twenty-six confirmed dead." Niall turned to leave, then hesitated. "And climbing."

Val left to track down John, who was arranging transport to the station to aid the medical team. The rest of them gathered in Niall's office, a converted conference room restocked with desks and workstations and alive with the bustle of staffers, their commander's desk serving as the hub.

"Service Station liaison believes it was a small pulse bomb." Niall called up a holo of the dock area schematic, which formed above his desk. "Structural damage was significant in the immediate area." He stuck a stylus in the middle of the image and inscribed a circle around an area that encompassed a large gangway some distance from the main concourse. "No breach, thank God. The sealer layer did its job."

"Looks well off the beaten path." Scriabin walked around the image, taking it in from every angle. "Why so many dead?"

"The starliner *Capria* had just docked. Emergency due to mechanical issues." Lucien pushed aside a stack of files and sat atop his desk. "Passengers were in the process of disembarking when the bomb exploded."

Jani lowered into a chair. "The gangway was full . . . "

"Yeah." Niall turned off the imager, and the schematic faded. "The station is in full shutdown. Instead of docking there, we will hook up directly with the *Ulanov*." He nodded toward Scriabin. "Luckily, your pilot has carrier experience. Otherwise we'd have had to ship one over who did."

"Minister Ulanova and I will need to port over to the station in any case." Scriabin paced. "We have people there. We need to ensure that supplies can get in, arrange transport for family members."

Niall nodded. "We can see to that as soon as station security gives us clearance. For now, we need to—"

The door opened and Anais Ulanova swept in. She wore somber brown and carried a rolled newssheet in one hand. "Horrible. Just horrible." She ignored Jani, shot a venomous glare at Lucien, then focused her attention on Niall and her nephew. "Could it have anything to do with this?" She unrolled the newssheet and laid it on Niall's desk.

Scriabin strode to his aunt's side. His brow arched as he read. "'Kilian says Haárin to be questioned in connection with assassination.'"

Jani sat up straighter as all eyes fixed on her. "I never spoke to a reporter. I haven't given an interview in months." She stood and walked to the desk. Tried to read the article, only for Ulanova to wedge in front of her, blocking her.

The woman stabbed the sheet with a carmine-tipped finger. "It states that you gave a speech to your enclave informing them that ní Tsecha had been assassinated, and that several Haárin were being sought in connection with his death."

"I would like to read it without benefit of translation." Jani shouldered her aside, then checked the byline and the banner. "I don't know that reporter, and I've never spoken to anyone from the *Amsun Star*." She read each sentence once, then again, her heart tripping as the truth dawned. One of her Thalassans had talked. *I didn't tell them not to.* Because she hadn't thought it necessary, because she never spoke to a reporter if she could avoid it.

Scriabin's voice emerged tight, mounting anger laced with disbelief. "You informed your entire enclave that Haárin would be questioned in connection with Tsecha's assassination, and it never occurred to you that one of them might talk to a reporter?"

No. Jani looked across the desk at Niall, who blew out a long breath, then shook his head. "They had a right to know what happened. A right to know the truth. I was leaving them behind to face who knew what? Sanctions? Attacks? I had to tell them why. I couldn't let them find out from someone else."

"Goddamn it." Scriabin's face flared. "Relations with the worldskein are all but severed. Our border colonies are in danger, and some of us are risking our lives—"

"And I had an enclave to keep a lid on." Jani felt the anger rise, swamping out the fatigue and uncertainty. "Haárin hybrids getting into fistfights with humanish hybrids because a humanish killed Tsecha. Haárin and humanish who were friends ten minutes before."

"Strictly speaking . . . " Niall waited until he had everyone's attention. "The article isn't incorrect," he continued at lower volume. "We are talking to Haárin about Tsecha's assassination. Nowhere in that article does it state that we think an Haárin killed him."

"Don't be disingenuous, Colonel." Ulanova jerked her head toward Jani. "Thanks to her lack of judgment, we have this wrenching disaster to contend with."

"What has this article to do with the bombing?" Jani caught the glitter in Ulanova's eyes, saw the thin-lipped smile form. "You're saying they're related?"

"Of course they're related. You say that Haárin played a part in Tsecha's assassination—"

"That's not what I said."

"—and humanish are killed in revenge." Ulanova breathed hard, cheeks flushing. "Anyone with any intelligence can see that this is the case."

"You're saying the Guernsey Haárin are responsible?" Lucien avoided looking at his former patroness, concentrating instead on the state of his cuticles. "And they've been so peaceful to this point."

"This stupidity would drive anyone over the edge, no matter how peaceful they'd been to this point." Ulanova reclaimed the newssheet and rolled it into a tight tube. "First, Zhenya and I will go to the station. Observe the damage. See to our annexes." She turned to Jani, finally looking her in the face. It was all there, reflected in the woman's shining black eyes. The history between them, the hatred and the humiliation and the loss. "Then I will go to Hiroshi Mako and request that you be sent back to where you came from." She turned on her heel and walked out, head high, triumph radiating like an aura.

Scriabin waited until the door closed. "I'll do what I can." His crisp tone indicated that it wouldn't be much. "We'll talk more after we return from the station." He followed after his aunt, his posture bowed and his step slower, the brawler who had taken a hit from an unexpected quarter and couldn't shake it off.

Jani leaned against Niall's desk. Felt all eyes upon her, Niall's and Lucien's and the rest of the staff's. Struggled to find her voice. "They know it was a bomb?"

Lucien slid off his desk and walked to her. "They've found a few pieces."

"And you think my remarks triggered the attack?"

Niall swore under his breath. "Did you hear me say that?" He stepped around his desk and stopped in front of her. "Did you plant the bomb? Did you detonate it? Then you're not responsible. Don't let that bitch get to you."

Jani nodded. "I should go over."

"Why?" Lucien shrugged, ever the pragmatist. "What can you do?"

"I'm still a documents examiner." Jani patted the place on her hip where for years her scanpack had hung. "I think Guernsey Station has two, total, and they're probably going in five different directions about now." Long ago memories surfaced. The smells. The images. "We're always needed at times like this."

"Why? You—" Niall paled. "Oh, Jan, no."

"I have to." She stared him in the eye until he looked away.

Scriabin's pilot docked the *Madelaine* with the *Ulanov* with practiced ease. From the juncture point, Niall escorted Jani down tight winding corridors to the carrier shuttle bays, where medical teams and repair crews stood waiting for transport to the station.

"Station staff is overwhelmed in more departments than one." Niall patted the pocket containing his nicstick case, then eyed the NO IGNITION SOURCES sign and let his hand fall. "Are you sure you want to do this? Because we have dexxies of our own whom we can send over."

Jani turned her back on Niall and walked around the bay. Heard his muttered, "—and I may as well argue with a god-damned wall." Felt the stares of the Spacers as they studied her, recognized her, and started talking. She had taken time to change clothes, switching out the delicate tunic and trousers for coveralls in drab dark grey. Her old Service duffel hung from her shoulder, nudging her hip with every step. Inside were her scanpack, tools, and spare parts. A verified copy of her Academy certificate, just in case anyone questioned her.

Her shooter, just in case.

"Ma'am?"

Jani turned to find a baby-faced corporal with a recording board eyeing her expectantly. "Jani Kilian. I'm part of the Shèráin mission." *For the time being, at least.* "I'm a documents examiner, and I wondered if they needed help with close-outs at the station?"

Before the corporal could reply, one of the med techs piped up. "They do. I heard one of the doc techs say that they're falling way behind. The station dexxie was going to put out a call."

"Looks like you won yourself a seat on the next nonmedi-cal shuttle, ma'am." The corporal glanced past Jani toward Niall, who hovered grim-faced like a doubt-filled father of the bride, then back at her board. "If you follow me over here, we'll scan you in."

Jani followed her to the ID scanner. Stood still for the retinal, ear, and palm scans, and hid a smile as the diplo-matic sigil popped up on the display alongside her confir-mation. *Thank you, Stash Markos.* She held onto her duffel and passed on through to the boarding chute into the shuttle, then turned in time to see Niall step around the scanner and hurry after her. "Diplomatic immunity works even better than scanproof compartments."

"You're armed, aren't you?"

"I'm sorry, Colonel?"

"Goddamn it." Niall followed her up the single aisle to a pair of empty seats. "What are you up to?"

"Nothing." Jani opted for the window view. "I wouldn't lie to you, Niall. Not now." She inserted her duffel into the grapple rack under her seat, then buckled herself in. "I know this isn't a good time, but when can we talk to Nahin Sela?"

"I knew you were going to ask that." Niall fastened his own seat harness, then pressed a hand to the back of his neck. "I told Pascal to use his charm and see if he can get through to the station liaison, but I think they'll tell us that they have enough on their plate for the moment."

"He's proving useful, isn't he?"

"I don't want to talk about it."

Around them, seats, grapples, and overhead racks filled. Then came a series of warning *pings*, followed by wave after wave of shudders as the boarding chute detached, the airlock sealed, and the hangar door swept open. Jani looked across the aisle to the starboard observation port and the view beyond, pitch-black tempered by a spray of stars. Felt the acid rise to the base of her throat and her stomach threaten rebellion as the shuttle directionals activated and the craft elevated then drifted to the side, freeing itself from its mother carrier and the bulk of her gravitational field.

Jani glanced at Niall, who sat with his head resting against his seatback, his eyes closed.

"I always like that floaty feeling when you first break away." He sighed. "Like sleep without the dreams."

"You can have it." Jani swallowed carefully. Breathed slowly. Looked out her portside observation port and saw only the gunmetal bronze surface of the carrier, fretted by seaming and welds and the odd bleached splash mark that developed when the destructive flash of the debris shield flared brightly enough to oxidize the surface coating.

"You ever pull carrier duty?"

Jani shook her head. "Never asked for it. The Academy degree pretty much guaranteed a slot at Rauta Shèràa Base." More recollections surfaced. The entire damn voyage was proving one long gantlet run down memory lane. "And I'd heard stories about carrier duty."

"The old Service." Niall grimaced. "I remember her well."

The shuttle began its swing around to the far side of the station, a maneuver that finally allowed Jani a clear view of the immensity that was the CSS *Viktor Ulanov*. Ten football fields in length and at least three in height, a sloping, featureless throwback to older style vessels that Service wits had christened "space whales." In the distance, the winking lights of her escort destroyers and caravelles, arrayed in uncloaked patrol like worker bees guarding their queen.

"Roshi's making a point by taking her into the worldskein." Niall leaned forward to take in the view, eyes alight with pride. "This is called a carrier group, Morden nìRau Cèel, and we've got thirty-three at home just like it."

"The idomeni have carrier groups, too." Jani sat back. Ships had never impressed her during her Service days, and the feeling hadn't changed with time. "Been years since I did close-outs. I'd hate to think that I can anticipate lots of practice."

They passed the undamaged side of the *Capria,* an ornate silver bird outfitted with useless but attractive turrets and masts. Every so often a Service hullwalker, welder in hand, would float into view before disappearing on the other side of the ship.

Then came the darkness of Guernsey Station itself, a kilometers-long grid that dwarfed even Service carriers.

"They're going to drop us off on the other side of the main concourse, where there was no damage." Niall settled back in his seat. "The hospital, all the waiting areas, they're all on that side as well." He licked his lips. "The morgue."

Minutes passed. Then came the clicks, hisses, and barely detectable bumps of docking. Another series of *pings,* followed by still silence. Then, as if on cue, everyone unsnapped their harnesses and gathered their belongings.

The first thing that struck Jani as she entered the main concourse was the quiet. The area had been evacuated after the blast, passengers, vendors, and other personnel shunted off to station annexes to wait out the emergency.

"It happened down there." Niall pointed to a gangway entry halfway down the concourse, which had been sealed off with flex paneling and a semicircle of emergency cones. Station security paced the area, pulse rifles lowered but ready to be brought into play at any time.

Jani looked down a nearby gangway, a long, bare tunnel capped at the far end by the ship juncture. "It was like dropping a grenade down a well, wasn't it?"

"Pretty much." Niall muttered under his breath. "It wasn't your fault, all right?" He nudged her elbow. "The paper pushers are all down here."

Jani followed Niall down a corridor that ran between lines of darkened shops and kiosks, then into a large room filled with desks, the only sounds the rustle of parchment and the occasional beep of a scanpack.

"I think you can take it from here." Niall waved her on into the room, then let the door close.

Jani walked to the nearest desk, where a woman in a green station uniform ran her scanpack across an identity card. "I thought you might need some help."

The woman looked up. Her brown eyes were dull, her dark skin ashy from the shock of too much, too fast.

Then she fixed on Jani's face and her jaw dropped. "Jani Kil—" She stood. "If you're here to take charge—" She motioned toward her chair.

Oh, please, no. Jani shook her head. "Just show me a stack."

"Oh." The woman stared at her desktop for a moment, then looked up. "Beah Lynn, Station Documentation."

Jani reached into her duffel and pulled out her scanpack case. "I'm traveling on the *Ulanov*. I heard you were short-handed."

"Yes." Lynn led her to an empty desk in a far corner, glancing over her shoulder every few steps as though making sure she was still there.

Meanwhile, the stares from the surrounding desks. The buzz of voices.

"Jani Kilian—"

"Two of Six—"

"Academy—"

"Tsecha—"

"Knevçet Shèràa—"

"Here." Lynn pulled out Jani's chair, then transferred a stack of document slipcases from another desk. "These have all had prelim and collate. They just need to be closed."

Jani sat. Removed her scanpack from its case and ran a hand over the scuffed black surface, then touched the device's underside, activating it. Took the top slipcase from the stack and started to undo the clasp until she realized that Lynn still stood by the desk.

"I just want to say—" The woman rolled her eyes, struck her thigh with her fist. "Twenty-five years ago the Helier Express ran a series of stories about you and the other humans who attended the Academy. I saved them all, and I read them over and over." Her face lit, despite the fatigue and the hell that surrounded them. "But yours especially, because you were a colony kid, like me, and I thought that if you could make it—" Her eyes filled. "I became a dexxie because of you, and now you show up to help." One tear spilled, then another, and she turned and ran back to her desk.

Jani watched the woman until she sat and resumed her work. Then she undid the clasp of the slipcase. Removed the contents and spread them out on the desk. Identity cards. Three credit chits. She read the names, examined the faces. *Albee.* Mother and daughter. They'd each named the other as their emergency contacts.

Jani adjusted her scanpack settings, then ran the device over the cards, sending a burst of energy through the inset chips. Fried them, canceled them out so they couldn't be used, so that relatives could show them, along with the d-certs, as proof of demise.

D-certs. Death certificates. *And all the old terms come back into play . . .*

"You're really Jani Kilian?"

Jani glanced at the young man at the desk next to hers. "Yes."

"Wow."

. . . as dust upon my tongue . . .

Another slipcase. Thicker, this one. *The Denischevs, from Hortensia.* Father, mother, and two sons, ages fifteen and twelve.

Scan. Cancel the paper like the bomb canceled the lives it represented.

The Seligs, from Helier, Guernsey Colony. Husband and wife, ages eighty-four and seventy-eight.

The d'Abos of New Indies. A family of three, mother, mother, and daughter.

"You don't have to do this."

Jani looked up to find Val standing in front of her desk. He had dragged on a disposable coverall, probably to cover the bloodstains. "I have to do something." She took another slipcase from the stack. "And I've done it before. One of the duties they don't tell you about when you sign up for the scanpack and make the appointment to have your brain cells farmed." She sorted out the d'Abos' lives atop the desk. "How are you doing?"

Val twitched a shoulder. "'Bout what you'd expect." He pulled a dispo pack of nicsticks from his trouser pocket. Shook one out, then showed the pack to Jani. "The colonel will be glad to learn that I do occasionally buy my own." He bit the tip, took a long pull. "John told me to take a break."

"Is John taking a break?"

"You're kidding, right?" Val pulled over a chair from an

empty desk and sat. "Word is that as the Guernsey-based emergency services arrive, we'll start backing off. Six-eight hours. Then off we go."

"Val?"

Jani and Val looked around to find John standing in the side entry to the room. Like Val, he wore a disposable coverall, only his didn't cover everything.

"Sorry. We need you again." John looked in Jani's direction. "What are you doing here?" His chill, dark voice. The voice he used for strangers, and those he knew whom he didn't like.

Jani pointed to the documents on the desk. "Help with close-outs."

"Hmm." John stepped aside so Val could walk past him into the corridor. "The next time you wonder why we don't tell you things, remember this day."

"*Dammit, John.*" Val grabbed his arm and pulled him out of the room.

Jani stared at the door after it closed. Then she completed the close-out of the lives of the d'Abos, and moved on to the next slipcase. Then the next. The next.

"Jani?"

This time it was Lucien who stood over her desk, kitted out in fresh dress blue-greys, his brimmed lid tucked under his arm.

"Mako wants to see you."

CHAPTER 23

Admiral General Hiroshi Mako's office was located aboard the *Ulanov*, in a suite replete with galley, dining room, and a bar. The glossy top of his truewood desk was clean but for a comport, stylus stand, and holos of his wife and children, the paperwork the purview of the staffers who swept in and out with the silent dispatch of temple acolytes.

Mako himself stood in front of one of the observation ports that dotted one wall, a browned, bald stump of a man, arms folded, dress blue-grey tunic pulling across broad shoulders. He turned as Jani and Lucien entered, revealing a round, high-boned face that bore a few more lines, a few more shadows, than when Jani had last seen him in person over a year before.

You've aged since Chicago, Roshi. But then, hadn't they all?

"My sympathies on the loss of your friend." Mako's voice emerged a gravel growl, the roughness exacerbated by the ship's dry air. "He was . . . one of the great ones." He made as though to say more, but was interrupted by Niall, who emerged from the galley bearing two steaming cups.

"Would you like coffee, gel?" He handed one cup to Mako. "They've got everything back there but the coffee plantation itself."

"No, thanks." Jani chose a chair on the side of the room opposite Mako's desk. Sat on the edge, back straight, duffel at her feet. Lucien settled for a seat in a far corner, like the low man that he was, while Niall opted for a cushy lounger close to Mako.

The man himself walked around the desk and perched on the edge, setting his coffee untouched beside him. "Anais spent the better part of the morning apprising me of your culpability in the Guernsey matter." Mako tilted his head toward Niall. "My colonel has since expressed his opinion, which differs significantly." If he fought the urge to raise his voice, he hid it well. Instead he sounded tired, as though this was the latest disaster in a snakebit campaign. "You should've realized that what you said would leak out. A remark like that is just the sort of thing a reporter would latch onto to create controversy."

Jani felt the anger rise, clearing her head for a blessed moment. She hadn't been able to concentrate since leaving the station, her mind a muddle of emotion and half-formed thoughts. "I said it before. I'll say it again. They had to hear it from me. They needed enough time to prepare for any reaction. Any retaliation."

"I've messaged back to my team at Karistos to start digging." Niall sipped his coffee, then set it aside and dug for his 'sticks. "The fact that the article appeared in the *Amsun Star* is a red flag. I fully expect to learn that Exterior played a major role in funneling that remark to the press, at which point I will kick that bitch's bony ass." He exhaled a smoky sigh. "You made yourself one hell of an enemy, gel."

Jani looked to the corner where Lucien sat, and pondered the skills of those who always seemed to land on their feet. *But such is not my way.* She sketched a word on the leg of her coverall. Another. "Sensitive bunch, this group that carried out the bombing. They read that Haárin will be questioned in connection with Tsecha's assassination, and they get all shirty and kill hundreds of their own. When do you think they'll claim credit? All the groups I researched are very keen about claiming credit, but this group is different. What's taking them so long? Think they're saving it up for a threefer? One more tragedy and they win a brand-new skimmer?"

"Jani?" Niall stubbed out his 'stick and moved to the edge of his seat, ready to rise. "Are you all right?"

"Where's Nahin Sela?" Jani pointed to him. "You sent Lucien to find out about her."

Lucien stood. "I'm awaiting a call-back from the Guernsey Merchants Association. They seem to have a better relationship with the Haárin than we do." As if on cue, his handcom buzzed.

"Take it here, Captain." Mako's voice held the same brand of wary disgust that Niall's did when he spoke to Lucien, aversion to the man coupled with grudging acknowledgment of his talents. "We'd all like to know what they have to say."

Lucien activated the handcom. Listened for a moment. "Nahin Sela's disappeared. The ship security officer who was escorting her to the Haárin office is dead." He shook his head in response to the unspoken question. "The Haárin office is in a completely different section of the station. It was unaffected by the bombing." He paused to listen. "Three ships broke away before the Haárin closed their side of the station as a safety precaution. Two were larger passenger vessels that responded immediately when asked to submit passenger information. The third was a smaller courier-class vessel that ignored attempts at contact, cloaked, and vanished, presumably on its way to the GateWay."

"So let's shut the GateWay down." Niall glanced at a wall clock. "We have three station-hours to initiate."

Jani wrote another word on her knee. "The idomeni have a GateWay out here, too. Samvasta."

"It has a reputation for instability." Niall chuckled with a complete lack of humor. "Half the ships that enter it don't come out the other end."

"I heard those same stats twenty years ago." Jani stood

and walked to the observation port. Looked out into the star-spattered dark. Imagined Nahin Sela, hunkered down in a cabin, awaiting the jump through a balky GateWay and wondering if she would punch through to the other side. *I certainly hope not.* "Beyond the wording in various treaties, do you have any reason to believe that Shèrá hasn't repaired it?"

"We do keep an eye out for those sorts of activities," Mako said dryly. "It's one of the reasons we're here." He tapped his comport. "Ask Vice Admiral General Vega to stop in when she has the chance."

The four of them looked at one another. Then Jani sat in front of a coffee table and inscribed across the top. Words. Numbers.

Niall opened the drawer of a side table and removed a stylus and a sheet of letter parchment. "Here, gel." He put the stylus between her fingers, then slipped the parchment beneath her hand.

"Only humanish assassinate." Jani pondered the stylus, a curving sweep of silver much like a Sìah blade. "Except when they don't." She wondered why she hadn't thought of it before. *Only humanish assassinate.* Just as only humanish ate in public, smoked, drank bitter lemon on the rocks. *We are all the same in this.* She'd said it herself, but grief and loss had prevented her from seeing the facts for what they were.

She looked at Lucien. "The sill provided the better view."

Lucien nodded, slowly at first, then faster as he figured out what she was talking about. "Yes, but standing allowed the assassin a greater ability to maneuver. Remember?" His voice came soft, light. A voice for animals, children, and absent-minded older relations. "The rubble on the sill wasn't disturbed."

"You said the dust was smeared."

" . . . yes." Lucien nodded as slowly as he spoke. "Possibly they set something on it, a gear bag or a weatherall.

Analysis of the scans of the area may indicate what exactly laid there."

"An idomeni who lay on that sill would feel the sharp edges of the rubble through their clothes. The mind-focusing properties of pain." *Focus*, she wrote on the parchment. "And they'd have the better view."

"An idomeni assassinated Tsecha?" The first flare of surprise entered Mako's voice. "An idomeni named, perhaps, Nahin Sela?" His tone sombered. "So the dock explosion—"

"Diversion. To keep us from getting our hands on her." Jani looked to Niall, who watched her with wide, worried eyes. "She didn't have to watch the monitors because she already knew what happened." Pieces slotted into place, one after the other. No need to force them. No need to change them in any way. Because this time they *fit*. "Because she drove what happened. She killed Tsecha."

"Jan?" Niall's voice came so gentle that Mako turned to stare at him. "That's a leap. I'm not saying you're wrong, because you know the idomeni better than any of us, but it's a major leap to take Sela's walk down the concourse and her disappearance now and extrapolate assassination."

"It's more than that." Jani set aside the stylus and parchment. "Wholeness of Soul. Tsecha had spoken out against it many times. It was the subject of his last treatise, which he published just before he died." She stood, returned to her place by the observation port. "It's a major tenet of the major idomeni religions. The idea that injury to a body also damages the soul that inhabits it, and that any sort of prolonged, grave illness or injury so endangers the soul that it is preferable to let the body die than to attempt to save the life." She closed her eyes, remembered that last argument in his workroom. They had argued so much, toward the end.

"Jan?" Once more, Niall's voice, bringing her back.

Jani opened her eyes, looked out to the black. "Tsecha had come to feel that the concept of Wholeness of Soul was no longer acceptable, that those propitiators and physician-priests who espoused it were anathema. He felt that the hu-

manish practice of doing all possible to preserve life was
the one idomeni should adopt." She studied her hands, the
animandroid left and real right. One was nourished by rose-
pink carrier, the other by blood. Other than that, they looked
identical, felt and sensed the same. "A body can suffer hor-
rendous injury, and the life can still be saved. I'm living
proof of that. But the brain must remain relatively uninjured,
because we haven't yet figured out a way to restore it, to
rebuild it, in the way we can a limb, an organ. Nerves."

Niall sat back, the events of that day replayed in the way
his shoulders sagged, in the pain in his eyes. "My God."

"Whoever killed Tsecha made sure that he couldn't be
saved by destroying his brain. But they left the rest of his
body uninjured, intact but for a punctured eardrum." Jani
turned her back on the starscape, leaned against the wall, felt
the chill through her coverall. "That brand of cruelty would
only, in my opinion, have been practiced by one to whom the
original principle meant a great deal. And who had come to
hate Tsecha very much."

Mako passed a hand over his face. "Do you know what
you're saying? Do you?" His comport beeped, and he struck
it with his fist. *"What?"*

"Vice Admiral General Vega is here, sir," the disembod-
ied voice meeped.

"Bring her in," Mako bit out. "You're saying Cèel had
him killed." He twisted around to glare at Jani. "No one else
hated him so much."

Jani nodded. "I know."

The door swept aside and one of the hot-and-cold-
running aides escorted Alex Vega into the office. She was
a tall, stocky Felician, as old as Mako and just as seasoned,
brown skin a sharp contrast to the silvery braid that wound
her head like a crown. The *Ulanova* group was hers, and if
the presence of her supreme commander aboard her flagship
unsettled her in any way, that upset didn't show in her calm
brown eyes.

But she knew tension when she stepped in the middle

of it. She stopped in the center of the room and regarded each of them in turn before fixing on Mako, who kicked any preamble to the curb and started in with the most important question of the moment.

"Is Samvasta GateWay operational?"

"No, sir." Vega's voice was mellow. "It's not."

Niall raised a hand. "Has Shèrá made any attempts to repair it, ma'am?"

"Oh, they've tried. We detect their soundings and send out cancellation waves. They have not been able to do more than the most preliminary surveys." Vega's tone altered from Felician caramel to vinegar. "Is someone going to tell me what the hell is going on?"

Mako gestured toward Jani. "Vice Admiral, I don't know if you've ever met Jani Kilian."

Vega focused on Jani with narrowed eyes. "Anais Ulanova does not have anything good to say about you. I'd normally consider that a recommendation, but she blames you for the Guernsey bombing."

"She's full of shit." Niall carried his coffee to the bar and tossed it into the sink.

Mako looked ceilingward. "I can bring you up to speed on the twists and turns later. At the moment, the most important issue is whether an idomeni courier can evade capture by bypassing Guernsey and punching through Samvasta GateWay."

"Only if they want take a substantial risk that they will not come out the other end." Vega's face reddened. It was clear that she wanted context and she wanted it yesterday, but she didn't dare blow up at Mako. "I will not send anyone to patrol that area. We lost two tracer pilots last month when they approached too closely just as the boundary destabilized without warning. They vanished. There was nothing left."

Niall added ice to half a glass of colorless liquid that Jani hoped was water. "We could stick Anais Ulanova in a drone and shove her into it, see what comes out the other end."

"That's enough, Colonel." Mako closed one hand into a

fist. Opened it, then clenched it again. "Ms. Kilian believes that an Haárin named Nahin Sela assassinated ní Tsecha Egri at the behest of Oligarch Cèel. Sela was to have been held at the station for questioning, but during her transfer to the Haárin offices, Cèel's agents detonated the bomb as a diversion. While all attentions focused on the *Capria,* they killed Sela's security escort and took Sela aboard a courier, which vanished soon after breakaway. We wonder if they might attempt to punch through to the worldskein via Samvasta GateWay in order to avoid capture."

"So the idomeni have adopted the practice of selective elimination." Vega watched Jani all through the course of Mako's explanation. "All I will say is that they are taking the risk of their lives if they attempt to punch through at Samvasta."

"So what if the GateWay is only marginally functional?" Jani watched Niall drain half his drink in a single swallow, and knew it wasn't water. *Mako and Vega are too agitated to notice.* Unfortunately, there was someone else in the room who wasn't. She glanced at Lucien, a figure half in shadow, eyes fixed on Niall. "What if marginal is sufficient?" She heard her voice ring inside her head, and paused to breathe. "Nahin Sela has been ordered home by the fastest route possible. Her escort has no choice but to take the risk."

"The circumstantial evidence does seem to be piling up." Niall finished his drink, then set the glass in the sink. "What about Neason Ch'un?"

"Nahin Sela killed him, too. Why, I don't know. He saw something. He bothered her. He attacked her." Jani tried to inject warning in the look she gave Niall, but he regarded her blankly, all alarms missed or, more likely, ignored. "She screwed up. She didn't fade into the background, as killers are supposed to." She avoided looking at Lucien, who had returned to his corner, forgotten by everyone else. "She attracted attention."

"So Cèel sends his goons to bring her home, and they

slaughter over three hundred humans as a cover." Mako slid off his desk and paced. "We have no proof. Niall is right, it's all circumstantial." He stopped in front of Jani, their past fractured relations as visible in his eyes as those with Anais Ulanova had been in hers. *Forget that now,* the look said. *Help me anyway.* "Can you give me proof?"

I don't need proof. I know. But courts needed proof, as did admirals general and cabinet ministers. So she answered in the only way she could, as much as she hated to say the words. "I don't know."

The VIP section's observation port proved an artful arrangement of twin spindle lifts that corkscrewed up the two sides of an enormous span of clear metalloceramic, then opened out onto a narrow catwalk that spanned the width of the pane.

Looks like about a two-story drop. Jani tore her attention away from the dimensions of the indoor balcony and looked toward the station. The damage to the *Capria* was more visible from this angle, shiny pink hull sealant smeared across the side of the ship like blown bubble gum.

She heard the observatory door open, footsteps. The sound of the left-side lift ascending. Looked toward the one-person capsule just as it opened and Lucien stepped out onto the catwalk. "What are you doing here?"

"I could ask you the same question." He stopped just beyond arm's reach and looked toward the *Capria.* "Does it help to stare at it?" He waited for her to answer, mumbled something in French when she didn't. "Pierce said Anais is full of shit. Why don't you believe him? Don't you trust him anymore?" He stared at her until he drew her eye. "I saw him take that drink in front of Vega. A dumb risk. He's not doing well, is he?"

"I'd say you'd been talking to Val, if you and Val were talking." Jani kicked at the balcony railing. *I need a map of this tub.* She had tried to corner Niall after the conclave in Mako's office disbanded, but he shook her off and she had tried to follow. *It took him one flight of stairs to lose me.* In a pulse-driven city with officers' clubs, bars, and liquor stores on most every deck. "He shouldn't have come. He should've stayed in Karistos."

"He couldn't. He has to turn the clock back twenty years and make it right—" Lucien tried to dodge, but before he could, Jani kicked his leg out from under him. He hit the balcony floor hard and she followed him down, planting her knees on his chest, pinning his shoulders, rendering his arms useless. He tried to kick out a leg and twist so he could throw her off, but every time he tried, she pushed down with her knees, immobilizing him.

After one last failed attempt, Lucien struck the floor with his fist. "Uncle." Then he laid back his head and smiled. "You scoot up a little bit, we could have some fun."

"While you're on this tub, you keep your mouth shut about Niall, and your two-bit psych eval to yourself." Jani pushed herself off him and scrambled to her feet, ready to kick hard if he came after her.

"I'm always the target." Lucien sat up. "You want to batter the world, but the only one you can put your hands on is me." He worked into a crouch and stood, then set about straightening skewed badges and brushing the creases from his tunic. "You'd kill to protect him, wouldn't you? He'd do the same for you. I think if he ever got his hands on Anais, he really would stuff her in a drone and send her down Samvasta GateWay." His voice held the childlike curiosity that it usually did when he pondered emotional connections. "What does that feel like?"

"You want a lesson in humanity, take a class. They've got a branch of Chicago Combined on this damned thing."

"I just find it fascinating is all. When you first met him, he gave you the creeps."

"I didn't know him." Jani edged down the railing, intent on remaining just out of Lucien's reach. *I don't need this now. I really don't.* "Some relationships improve over time."

Lucien ignored her insult. "It's all gotten messy, hasn't it? Tsecha's death. This bombing. And you think you know what happened, but you can't prove any of it. And Mako needs proof, and unless you can give him something, he may just start thinking you're lying. He may even start believing those things Anais is saying about you, despite what his colonel tells him." He leaned easily on the rail. "And that's not even the worst of it. If Cao catches on about the secession deal, we just might see Family members jailed for the first time in memory. As for the non-Family members, who knows what might happen? Rebellious Service officers, for example." He looked over the side to the poured poly floor ten meters below. "This balcony isn't nearly as high as the one in Thalassa." He looked at Jani and his gaze sharpened. "The view's the same, though."

Jani tried to walk past Lucien to the left-side lift, but he stepped in front of her. She turned and headed for the other lift, but he circled her, blocking her again.

"I'm here." He edged closer. "I've been here for weeks."

Jani feinted to one side, then stepped back as he blocked her again. "A sympathetic ear."

"An ear. When did you ever give a damn for sympathy?" Lucien started to laugh. "You know what's funny? I've actually missed this. Arguing with you. What sane person would miss arguing with you?" He shook his head, and wiped his eyes.

Jani turned her back on him and looked out at the stars. Sometimes, she found it easier to argue with Lucien if she didn't look at him. *I don't love him.* No, but love and sympathy and other of the finer emotions had never defined what passed between them. "When did you start thinking of yourself as sane?" A cheap insult, but with some luck it would irritate him enough to drive him away.

She stared at the stars. Tried to count them. Waited for the sound of the lift door, the sign that she was finally alone. Waited for any sound at all. When the silence continued, she turned to find Lucien studying her.

No, that wasn't the word. His expression—rapt, grave—she'd seen it before. In the half-light, after he'd undressed her, run his hands over every part of her, made ready to do all those other things to her that he did so well . . .

"You never change." His voice emerged rough, as though he'd just returned from the same memory. "And I keep coming back for more, again and again and again—" He moved in, resting his hands on her waist, pulling her closer without seeming to apply any pressure at all. Kissed her cheek, lips barely brushing her skin. Maneuvered her gently to the other side of the balcony, blocking her view of the *Capria*, because if she opened her eyes and saw it, she'd make him stop, and he couldn't have that.

So simple. Jani closed her eyes. Savored the growing ache between her legs as his lips moved across her neck, the trip of her heart as he fingered the front of her shirt and touched the topmost fastener. *Simple answers to simple questions.* Did she want him? *Yes.* Did she trust him? *Never.*

Did she want to forget, even for a little while?

Yes.

Could she afford to?

Jani opened her eyes. Took what was there, to remember later. The sense of his body as he pressed her against the railing, the hardness and the heat. The softest scents of male and musk. The crisp feel of Service cloth and the silken touch of hair that seemed lit from within.

"This is pretty much what you did with Val, isn't it?" She touched Lucien's cheek, stroking it until he raised his head. "The air of defeat. 'Here I am—why do I bother?'" She brushed a nonexistent smudge from one orange collar tab. "Well's run a little dry, has it? You're starting to repeat yourself."

Lucien blinked. Then his eyes widened. *"He told you?"* He released her as through she burned. "That pathetic—"

"Not the details." Jani walked to the left side lift capsule and hit the door pad. "Anyone who's watched enough bad porn could fill in the details." She entered the tiny booth as soon as it opened. Hit the Down pad. A simple task, as long as she didn't look back. "You chose your path, Lucien. Deal with it."

She rode the lift down. Pushed out of the small capsule as soon as the door opened, like an animal freed from a cage. Felt Lucien's stare track her as she walked across the observatory and out the door.

She walked until she found a vend arcade. Bought a map of the *Ulanov* from a kiosk. Found a build-your-own-sandwich shop, inserted enough tokens to cover a double order, and poked through the vend coolers, assembling as she went. *Ham—cheddar—mustard—* She sprinkled a handful of peppercorns across her ham slices, then fixed them in place with a generous swathe of mustard. Spread pickles on both sandwiches, added tomato slices, and on Niall's a dollop of potato salad. Arranged the food on a couple of dispo plates, then piled them on a tray.

She consulted the map again. Stuck to stairways and primary corridors. Crossed from the VIP wing into Officer Country. Turned the corner onto the row of Transient Officer suites, and almost collided with Mako, who was headed in the opposite direction.

"Kilian." Mako looked at the tray and his eyes softened. "I think he ate lunch, but that was some time ago." He had changed into casuals and carried a battered gym bag. "I stopped by to see if he wanted to take a break, work out . . . " He blinked, leaned against the wall. "What is it?"

Jani tried not to look too closely at Mako. He stood more than a head shorter than she, and in his grey T-shirt and blue pull-on pants looked more like an old man headed out for a day of beachcombing then the supreme commander of the Commonwealth Service. "What do you think?"

Mako rubbed his bald scalp, shook his head. "I don't know how many times I told him, 'Niall, you saved the Service the cost of three courts-martial.' We'd have fried them anyway."

"They were Family."

"We'd have fried them anyway." Mako's eyes brightened with fight. "I'd have made sure." He glanced at Jani side-long, as reluctant to confide in her as she was to listen to him. "I told him he didn't have to go on to Shèrá. Before you showed up with Pascal, I told him. The way he looked at me, as though I'd kicked the last skid out from under." He stared down at the floor. "Talk to him. Because he can't—" He pushed away from the wall. "He can't go on in the direc-tion he's headed. Not here. Not now." He edged past her and disappeared around the corner.

Jani stood in place for a time. Finally studied the map again, and started down the corridor. Checked nameplates until she found N. PIERCE. Hit the entry buzzer. "Niall?" She waited, then hit the buzzer again. "I need to talk to you." She watched the red entry light, waited, waited. "Niall?"

Long moments passed. Then the light flipped to green.

Jani palmed into the cabin to find the lights dimmed. She closed her eyes, then opened them, hurrying their adjustment to the half-dark. Saw the shadow in the far corner, seated in a chair, obscured by smoke. "Have you been drinking?"

"Yeah, but like I told you, it doesn't help." Niall's voice emerged slurred. "We're leaving a cruiser behind as a show of force. Fort Helier is on alert. Guernsey ComPol are round-ing up members of human separatist organizations. If what you say is right, it's all a waste of resources and manpower. I always like feeling useful." The tip of his 'stick glowed as he took a pull. "Is that a tray?"

"I made sandwiches." Jani held out the food like a child displaying a craft project. "Ham and cheese."

"You *cooked*?" Niall shook his head. "Constructed." His voice emerged hushed. "For me?"

"Do you want it or not?"

"I'd be . . . loath to eat it." Niall cocked his head. "Might have it bronzed."

"Fuck you, all right?" Jani walked to the table beside Niall's chair and plunked down the tray, coughing as the clove smoke raked her throat. "Eat." She took her plate, hied to the opposite side of the sitting room and fell onto the couch.

"You sound like my dear Roshi." Niall took the sandwich in hand and peeled back the top slice of bread. "I've never seen potato salad used as a filling before."

"My papa makes mashed potato sandwiches." Jani bit into her sandwich and immediately hit a peppercorn. "You fry up the mashed with butter and onion. Dice in some bacon." She savored the sinus-clearing capsaicin rush. "Grill the bread first, or it sogs up fast."

"I can imagine." Niall broke off a corner and bit carefully. "Thank you, gel." He chewed. Paused. "Been dreaming much?"

Jani mined another peppercorn from the depths. "A little."

"You know the drill. Tell me yours and I'll tell you mine."

Jani nodded. *First, there comes simple. Then there comes hard. And then there comes this.* "It's been the same one the past few nights. I walk into the Laumrau camp, pull back the flap of the first tent, and no one's inside." Sweat trickled down her back, and she blamed the pepper. "Then I turn around, and there they are. All twenty-six of them, shooters drawn." She laughed, a dead bark of a sound. "It's a short dream."

Niall set his plate aside. "Mine's old. It's the one where I'm just about ready to take out Ebben." His voice softened. "And she stops running, and turns, and points at me. 'Sergeant Pierce,' she says, 'a good Spacer only shoots the guilty.' So—" He exhaled with a shudder. "—I set aside the long-range I'm holding, and take out my sidearm, and activate it, and—" He held his hand to the side of his head, index finger extended. "—I—" His finger twitched.

Jani waited until Niall lowered his hand. "You haven't had that one for a while." Another peppercorn, because the burning made her feel alive. "Three more weeks of this crap."

Silence settled until the warning klaxon sounded, announcing thirty minutes until breakaway.

CHAPTER 24

Stillness. Stillness and warmth and the sound of running water.

The security dominant, whose name she still did not know, yelling at her, his words as shatterboxes in her head.

Quiet, and the sense that one would never move, ever again.

"She wakes, nìRau."

Rilas opened her eyes, then closed them against the glare of white that struck as the light of a sun. *Ceiling.* She clenched her hands, felt the rumple of cloth. *Bed.* Pushed up with her elbows. Tried to sit up—

The bed seemed to shudder, as a shuttle upon reentry.

Her soul screamed. She twisted to one side as the acid heat rose in her throat and freed itself, as she convulsed again and again.

"All will be well, nìaRauta."

She felt a hand on her shoulder, supporting her as she leaned over the purge receptacle. After she finished, she fell back onto the bed, felt a cool cloth move across her forehead, over her mouth. Heard prayers, the wishes of a physician-priest that her patient remain in the esteem of the gods.

She is not my priest. She did not recognize this female's voice, this touch. Even so, she thanked her. Drank from the cup she held to her lips, laid back as she bade. Accepted the frozen cylinder placed beneath her neck as the greatest of gifts.

"The sedative affects some idomeni in this way. Even treatment does not counter it. The gods forgive your unseemliness, Rilas."

Rilas raised her head. Blinked away the tears that had filled her eyes, and looked toward the figure at the far end of the room.

"Imea nìaRauta Rilas, survivor of Samvasta GateWay. The gods are with you, and truly, and would forsake me if I did not honor such courage. Thus have I come in person to welcome you home." Morden nìRau Cèel sat near the entry, in a chair so low he seemed to rest directly upon the floor. "In between meetings. So many meetings. And the arrival of the humanish. So many arrivals."

Rilas pushed so that she sat upright, even as the physician-priest struggled to push her back. "I was coming to you freely."

Cèel gestured apology. "Unfortunately, nìaRauta, others sought to interrupt your coming. Thus were we compelled to ensure that your journey home was not impeded."

"An escort, nìRau." Rilas shifted to and fro, struggling to see around the physician-priest, who stood at the foot of the bed and operated the levels and adjustments. "Such would have proved adequate." The edges of her vision blackened and she sagged back.

"You cannot sit up too far, or you will sicken again." The priest returned to her side and held her down, then rearranged cushions under her head. "I have raised the front of the bed as far as I will."

"Raise it higher."

"You are too ill, nìaRauta. Your reaction to the soma is too profound—"

"Raise it higher."

"Do as she bids, nìaRauta Ansu." Cèel stood, then arranged the sleeves of his overrobe. "She will not rest as you wish until I have told her that which she believes she needs to know. Such is as she is. This I know, and truly."

The physician-priest straightened, but whether she did so in supplication to Cèel or the gods, Rilas could not surmise. After a few moments she walked around to the foot of the bed and pressed the adjustments. The front of the bed rose, and Rilas motioned with her hand for it to continue.

"Enough." Ansu stopped the elevation at the quarter point. "Any higher and you will faint." She glanced back at Cèel, then gestured her leave-taking and departed.

Cèel walked across the room to the single narrow window, which had been barred on the outside. "Ansu is my own physician-priest. She believes and truly that she is bound to care for all Vynshàrau as she cares for me." He bared his teeth, then turned to observe the view. "The Haárin ship bearing Tsecha's reliquary arrives within the next two sun cycles. The Cabinet ship on which Kièrshia travels arrives soon after. I would prefer to blast it out of space rather than allow it to dock, but such would constitute an incident, and our hands must appear as clean." His voice emerged guttural, deepened by anger and the demand for obedience. "They will search for you, and they must not find you. You must remain here in this hospital until they depart."

Rilas raised a hand to her ear, then felt along her temple to her eye.

"I have your book, nìa. NìaRauta Ansu removed it as you slept." Cèel offered a posture of regard, tilting his head to the right, raising and curving his right hand against his chest. "I viewed Tsecha's collapse. I regret that I could not also view his death, but such is as it is." He turned to her. "You have earned the greatest esteem of all Vynshàrau. Of all idomeni." He once more gestured gratitude, then left the window and walked to the entry. "Now I must take leave of you. You will be cared for here until the ungodly depart." He paused and bared his teeth. "Or are expelled, when we convince them that the words of the Kièrshia are as nothing and that only humanish assassinate." He walked to the door and placed his hand upon the pad.

Rilas struggled to boost herself up on her elbows, stopping to swallow each time her soul rebelled. "NìRau?"

The door had already swept aside—Cèel put out a hand to stop the panel from closing. "Nìa?" His voice once more emerged deep, a sign of his impatience.

"I was returning to you." Rilas eased back against her cushions. "There was no need for this. No need to humiliate yourself by witnessing my illness. No need to—" She did not say it aloud. Such was ungodly, and as suborn, it was not her place to say it. *No need to humiliate me.* An Haárin thought. Such was her dismay that the memory of living as one corrupted her mind.

Cèel stood silent. Then he stepped through the entry. "They would have captured you, nìa. Such could not be allowed." He let go of the panel and it swept closed.

Ansu visited Rilas several times over the course of the next cycle. She oversaw the preparation of her sacraments, escorted her to and from the altar room. When she arrived after mid-afternoon sacrament and asked if Rilas wished a walk in the hospital gardens, she met no argument, for Rilas did not believe herself able to refuse.

They walked in silence for a time. Despite her unease, Rilas allowed herself to enjoy the heat of the Shèráin sun, lost to her for so long. She strained for any noise in an effort to determine her location. Voices and traffic meant the City Center. The rhythmic echoes of mallets against anvils meant Temple, where metallurgist-priests forged the ceremonial blades.

She sniffed the air. Salt tang meant they were near the bay, while faint sulfur and ammonia marked the blessed greenhouses—

"You are so quiet, nìaRauta Rilas." Ansu looked her very

nearly in the eye, as though she conversed with an esteemed friend.

"I am relishing the sun, nìaRauta Ansu." Rilas bared her teeth, then turned her head so Ansu could not see her face. *She studies me.* She felt a quickening in her soul. *She reports to nìRau Cèel of me.*

"I met ní Tsecha Egri only a single time, many seasons ago." Ansu folded her arms and tucked them inside her over-robe sleeves. "NìRau Cèel had appointed him ambassador to the Commonwealth, and I was to offer instruction to his physician-priest prior to their departure for Earth. He insisted upon attending our discussions, which was most unseemly." The priest's shoulders rounded in memory. "He corrected me, several times. I suspect he partook of humanish foods, so much did he know of their effect on idomeni."

"He was anathema." Rilas stopped before a *chala* shrub and bent low to one of the fragrant white blooms. "He lived with humanish, and died on one of their worlds, bereft of the esteem of the gods or of any godly idomeni. His fate was most deserved, and truly."

"There is talk that the half-humanish will release his soul here. Such is not a thing I care to witness." Ansu lowered to a bench and smoothed her hands over her sand-hued overrobe. "NìaRauta Sànalàn should officiate at such a ceremony. As Chief Propitiator, she intercedes for all Haárin. Even the godless ones." She fell into silence, and continued to pass her hand over her overrobe even as the cloth lay smooth as parchment.

Rilas straightened and walked to a flowering tree. Blessed *vrel*, its flowers as brilliant red as fresh blood. *NìaRauta Ansu, you who considers all Vynshàrau yours to care for, why do you spend so much time caring for me? Why do you stay with me, sit with me, talk to me of Tsecha?* She bent close to the bloom, taking what pleasure she could in its beauty. *Am I your only patient but for nìRau Cèel? Have you no other duties to see to?*

"Tell me of your journeys, nìaRauta." Ansu raised her

hands and heightened the pitch of her voice in wonder. "NìRau Cèel has told me that you have traveled to many worlds for him."

Rilas stepped back from the tree and turned to the female, who sat with her back to her, hands in her lap, her neck fully exposed. Clenched her hand, then let it relax. "Indeed, nìaRauta Ansu, I have traveled." And she described some of her journeys to the priest, because she had nothing better to do. And because she believed, and truly, that she had no choice.

Alone in her room at night, Rilas thought too much of the Haárin security dominant whose name she did not know.

She had watched death before, both that which she brought on and that brought on by others. Killed before with her hands, many others besides the idiot humanish, felt bodies shudder and go limp as they released their hold on their souls and became waste to burn or bury. But she never thought of those others. Never saw their faces in dreams. Never heard their voices in her head when all about had gone quiet.

Yet now she continued to think too much of the Haárin security dominant whose name she did not know. Recalled that last godless look of his, directly in her eyes. Saw his lips move, and pondered the words he had spoken. English. Of all languages, why an ungodly humanish one?

It had taken her some time to work out that which he had said. She had resorted to writing out the sounds phonetically, matching them with the few humanish words she knew until she identified the language.

Realized that he had spoken English to her because he did not want ná Bolan and her suborn to understand.

She looked down at the paper she held, scrap parchment recovered from a trash pile and now covered with her script.

Hee. Whel. Keel. U.
Hewel keelu.

He well kill—

And then, as though an illumin had activated, she understood, and wrote those final words.

He. Will. Kill. You.

Even now Rilas wondered if she had misheard him, if he had said something else. If he had even spoken at all, and the soma had addled her memories.

But at night, in the silence, she heard him, his words as clear as if he spoke to her in the hospital garden.

He will kill you.

She had not thought of those words until her second night in the hospital. The library contained nothing of interest, no newssheets or transmissions. The Haárin ship bearing Tsecha's reliquary would arrive the next day, but at the hospital no one knew of anything. Rilas's questions to suborns met with disclaimers and denials, and Ansu claimed no interest. Thus was she left to imagine the carved wooden box, the bound scroll it contained, the godless spirit that called it as home.

Then, later, as she lay in her strange bed and pondered the darkness, she imagined other things. Tugged at the edges of her bed cover, suddenly chill despite the blessed warmth.

He will kill you.

"The Kièrshia had asked for the Guernsey Station Haárin to stop me." Thus had she begged for help from her dominant, who in turn had gone for aid to his dominant. To Cèel.

But ná Bolan Thea joined me soon after departure from Elyas Station. Which meant that the female had been sent by nìRau Cèel to follow her to Elyas, that she had watched for her return to the station, and bought billet on the appropriate ship.

Rilas lay still. "NìRau Cèel had placed spies, as he always has." Her dominant, who had taught her to question as no suborn ever had. Who had taught her the worth of untruths, of speaking one thing and planning another. Who had taught her the value of suspicion.

He did not ask what happened at Guernsey. He did ask of the humanish death. He did not ask what I had done to draw the interest of the Elyan Haárin. He had not asked her to explain anything.

Words of his returned to her. Words he had spoken long ago, when she asked him of another of his suborns who had not returned home after completing a task. *Do I ask this blade why it cuts? No. I use it, and I set it aside when I no longer need it.*

And Rilas lay in the quiet dark and pondered her suspicions and knew. That the Haárin whose name she did not know had known who she was and who had sent her. That he had known that which she had done. And that he had known also what awaited the blade after it had performed its owner's bidding, a knowledge that had come to the blade much too late.

He will kill you.

She lay in the darkness, and imagined.

CHAPTER 25

"Let's run through this one more time." Niall pinched the bridge of his nose. "Meva walks down the aisle first, ahead of the reliquary." He sat across a breakroom table from Jani, untouched vend alcove coffee at his elbow. "But you won't walk with her?"

"I told you before, I have no standing with Rauta Shèràa Temple." Jani had plucked a lemon from the fruit bowl and started to peel it, piling the bits of rind on the table in front of her. "Meva and I have been messaging back and forth about this for the last two weeks—where were you?"

"Studying station plans. Working out routes. Ensuring you don't get killed anywhere between the docks and the embassy. Minor details." Niall rubbed bleary eyes. "So you're just going to let Meva leapfrog you? Tsecha considered you his suborn, not her. She has no business escorting his reliquary."

"The more important issue is Tsecha's status. He merits every honor possible, and he won't receive them if I'm seen anywhere near that procession. Besides, it would reflect badly on Feyó, and she needs all the boost she can get right now."

"Ah-hah." Niall took a packet of crackers from a dispenser

and peeled it open. "Feyó and Meva did see your interview-that-wasn't. I wondered what the reaction to that would be."

It was good, and truly, priest-in-training, that you were not present when ná Feyó read your words. "It didn't go over well." Jani pried out a section of the fruit and popped it into her mouth. Felician lemon, green as emerald and sour enough to bring tears to a hybrid eye. "Meva had to explain repeatedly that questioning didn't equal accusation. She said Feyó accepted her reasoning, eventually. But given all the tensions, we felt that shunting me to one side during the official ceremonies was the best option." Another wedge. A cough to add to the tears. "It seemed the best way to make up for John's and Yevgeny's delay in telling Feyó that it was assassination. You can't allow her to lose face within the worldskein if you expect her support for Outer Circle secession."

"Your circumspection is commendable." Niall took a cracker from the packet, but instead of eating it, he broke it into bits, then laid the bits out on the tabletop and moved them around like game pieces. "It's also out of character, which worries me no end."

Jani ignored him, hunting through the spice dispenser until she found the pepper. "After Tsecha's soul is released, Meva technically becomes the propitiator and can walk behind the reliquary when it's transported to its final interment in the Temple catacombs." She sprinkled pepper on the lime and took a taste, savoring the added bite. "I would like to see that, but there's no way they'd let me down there."

"Who gets the honor of letting the old bird out of his cage?"

"It's all Meva." Jani pulled off another lemon section. Sprinkled pepper. Chewed. Swallowed. Wiped her eyes. "It's the least awkward solution. Temple feels that the honor of a former Chief Propitiator will thus be maintained, and Tsecha's soul will be able to proceed to the First Star without further impedance."

"If they wanted to maintain honor, they shouldn't have

kicked Tsecha out of the club in the first place." Niall continued to rearrange cracker pieces. "I'm not just arguing for the sake of arguing. In a reasonable world, you would walk in front of his reliquary. You would officiate at the release of his soul."

"In a reasonable world, he'd still be alive." Jani returned the pepper to its slot and hunted for a new taste. *Ginger? Onion salt?* "Meva told me that Feyó told her that she still hears his voice." A sprinkle of ginger on another section of lemon. More tears. "I need to let it be. It's not the fight I want to fight now."

"You do understand that hearing you preach caution makes the hairs on the back of my neck stand up?" Niall swept cracker remains into the tableside trash receptacle, then freed a 'stick. "Know what I think? I think you're laying low. You don't want to attract undue attention while you hunt for Nahin Sela." He blew a smoke ring, then watched it until it dissipated. "I'm not saying I don't believe you. But we've looked. For three weeks we looked for any sign, any hint, any trace of evidence. Then we messaged ahead to embassy security and had them look."

"They were most thorough, I'm sure." Jani flicked a piece of lemon peel into the trash receptacle to join Niall's crackers.

"The request came from Roshi. Damned right they were thorough." Niall took of sip of his coffee and grimaced. "Take it from this old Victorian—if Cèel has one-tenth the brains I think he has, Nahin Sela will never be found. She died when her ship tried to punch through Samvasta, or she's sleeping the big sleep at the bottom of Rauta Shèràa harbor. If Cèel felt merciful—excuse me whilst I laugh—she's at some idomeni version of a resort doing whatever the hell it is that idomeni do for fun. But wherever she is, we can't get her, because there is a very powerful and ruthless male whose status as Oligarch depends on her continued absence." He stood and walked to the sink, cup in hand. "Galling as it is to admit, I think the bastard won this round." He poured the coffee down the drain, let the water run. "You ready?"

Jani didn't have to ask what he referred to. *Ready to enter Rauta Shèràa Station again? See the city from the shuttle windows? Walk out of the shuttleport and feel the heat and smell the flowers and the bay? Ready to stare your past in the face and remember?* "I found images of Rauta Shèràa in the library. Started slow, and worked my way up. I got to re-visit all my old haunts. The old bazaar. The walkways along the river. Amazing how little has changed. I bet I could still trace my old route from the humanish enclave to the Academy and not get lost." She wrapped the lemon remains in a dispo napkin and tossed the wad into the tableside receptacle to join the ghosts of Niall's crackers. "I'm as ready as I'll ever be. You?"

"Glad I've had enough to keep me busy is all I can say." Niall leaned against the counter. His face had grown greyer since they'd departed Guernsey, his cheeks more sunken. His uniforms hung. Over the last three weeks, he had smoked too much, eaten and slept too little. But he hadn't taken a drink since the night of the *Capria* bombing, a struggle that had left its mark in the form of haunted eyes and a shortened temper.

"So." He drew up straight. "We disembark *after* Meva and the reliquary, after we give the crowd that's come to greet Tsecha's wooden box a chance to clear out. Shuttle to the surface, where skimmers await. On to the embassy enclave, where we hook up with everyone else. You're wearing your shooter vest?"

Jani tugged down the front of her grey wrapshirt, revealing the silvery lacework beneath.

Niall nodded. "Embassy security's providing the bulk of the ground coverage. They have a decent relationship with the Station Haárin, if not the bornsect Council. They seem to know their collective ass from a hole in the ground."

"Praise, indeed." Jani tried to draw a smile, and managed, a little. "I'll be fine."

"Yeah." Niall reached into his pocket. "I want you to plug this in." He pulled out a small metal flat that looked like a smaller version of his nicstick case. "It's an ear bug." He flipped up the top and shook out a small, milky disc. "We'll be able to remain in touch at all times. You'll also be able to hear all the chatter, know what's going on."

"I've seen these before." Jani took the bug from Niall, then walked to the sink. "Got anything to plug up the other ear?" She activated the tap and wet the disc, then massaged it between her fingers until it softened and expanded.

Niall drew a jittered breath. "Don't think that hasn't crossed my mind."

"Cèel isn't interested in killing me." Jani inserted the bug into her right ear, shivering as she felt it expand and fill the canal. A momentary muffling of sound, then a return to clarity. "He excised his particular thorn."

"Proof, gel." Niall motioned toward the door. "Can't take him down without proof." He waited for Jani to draw alongside, and they walked into the corridor just as the approach klaxon sounded.

"One hour to go. I'll walk you to your cabin, then go on to the bridge." Niall's step slowed. "'And so we return to that place of war. To that place that summoned our blood.' To damned Shèrá."

"I've been waiting for a quotation." Jani fought to keep her voice light, even as her chest tightened. "They've been thin upon the ground of late."

"Listen to you." Niall smiled. "Henry the Fifth. One of my favorites. Especially the part where he rallied his men before the Battle of Agincourt. They were outnumbered, exhausted, that morning of St. Crispan's Day." His expression turned grave. "'In peace there's nothing so becomes a man as modest stillness and humility. But when the blast of war blows in our ears, then imitate the action of the tiger. Stiffen the sinews. Summon up the blood.'" He looked at Jani, beautiful eyes dark with the memories of what they'd seen twenty years before. "'Once more into the breach, dear friend. Once more.'"

* * *

Jani took one last turn around her spacious sitting room as she waited for the *Madelaine* to dock. This leg of the journey had passed more easily than she feared. Only the odd mealtime had proved a challenge, between John's and Anais's determination to ignore her existence and Lucien's refusal to follow their example. This time around, Val had interceded in the matter of cabin assignments, snagging her a two-bedroom suite complete with working thermostat, as well as an office. The ability to access secure networks and Cabinet-class libraries and archives had allowed her to pass the time in productive seclusion. She had searched the records of shipping companies and research facilities in areas of the Commonwealth with a history of idomeni infiltration. The Outer Circle. The Jewelers' Loop. Hunted through manifests and invoices and directories, on the lookout for the materials that might have been used to manufacture the weaponized prionic, and for scientists who might have constructed it.

Proof, gel. Niall's words rattled in her head. The haystack needle. The one-in-a-billion shot. *If I had more time . . .* She told herself that, even as she knew. Even as she feared.

. . . the bottom of Rauta Shèràa harbor . . .

"But that's too good for her." Jani sat in a lounger, and waited for that mildest of bumps that would tell her the *Madelaine* had docked at Rauta Shèràa Station.

She yawned for the first time in days. She had managed to sleep, even as the dreams came. Convinced herself that any night during which she didn't die counted as a good one, and so managed to find some rest about half the time. Sent message central transmit communications to Dieter at Commerce expense, and viewed the replies until she could recite them by heart. *A few more fights . . . brought in Dathim's friends . . . the training is going much as you'd expect.* Dieter's skills at saying everything and nothing with the same words came into play repeatedly. She tried to read the truth in his eyes, in the way he'd lower his head as he spoke, as though exhausted. Trying to deduce, even as she dreaded what she might learn.

Nothing in the newssheets, at least. No unrest in Karistos. Some problems in Meteora, its smaller sister city to the south, but those proved to be related to the local ComPol's mishandling of a political corruption investigation, not the aftershocks related to Tsecha's death.

It's like reading tea leaves. Trying to divine truth over great distance with little concrete information. To compensate, the imagination ran roughshod, dragged the rest of the mind to places it didn't want to go—

"*Jani?*"

She flinched. Slumped and swore at the ceiling, her heart pounding. *Dammit, Niall.* She touched her ear, activating the bug. "*What do you want?*"

"*Could you please come to the bridge.*" Not a question, but a veiled command, delivered in a voice gone tight enough to string a violin.

Jani slapped the door pad. The panel opened to reveal a vision in dress desertweights, brimmed lid tucked beneath his arm.

"There have been developments." Lucien stepped to one side, eyes fixed straight ahead, and waited for her to precede him down the corridor.

"The station stopped all shuttle flights at midnight, Rauta Shèràa time." Niall hesitated, then shook his head as the feed from his ear bug claimed his attention.

Jani heard the same string of chatter, saw from the distant look in Lucien's eyes that he received it as well.

Felt the cold sweat bloom and trickle.

"An update for we the deaf would be nice," Scriabin snapped. He wore tunic and trousers in Commerce dark green, an unfortunate contrast to his reddening face.

"Tsecha's welcoming committee is currently estimated at a quarter million inside the station proper." Niall paused again. "Could be three hundred thousand. The ones who couldn't make it here are lining the Rauta Shèràa streets. Estimates there have topped the two million mark, but I understand that number is swelling as I speak." Another of his aides whispered something in his open ear, and his expression darkened. "Two point five million, and still climbing."

"They came to see him home." Jani smiled, felt a swell of pride nudge aside the fear. "Even though Cèel tried to marginalize him. Even though Temple declared him anathema and tore his writings to shreds."

"I wouldn't read too much into it." Ulanova entered the bridge, a flicker of black-garbed flame, her usual uniform of ministry burgundy set aside in deference to idomeni religious protocols. "Idomeni see things as they are. Whether for or against Tsecha, they would turn out, simply to watch." She surveyed the narrow, instrument-lined room, gaze sliding past Jani and pausing on Lucien before settling on her nephew. "The embassy has sent an escort to clear our way through the mess, surely? There's no need for us to remain on board for hours to come."

"I want to see it." Jani turned to the bridge's small monitor, which currently showed a view of the gangway, populated by a quartet of embassy security guards. "Can we see it on the port?" She nodded toward the semicircle of clear metalloceramic that served as the bridge's window.

"Why can't we watch in person?"

Everyone turned to find Val standing in the entryway.

"It's been ages since I passed through the place, but there have to be areas at one end of the concourse or the other where we can stand and not get in anyone's way." He glanced at Jani, looking away before she could grin, the eternal coconspirator.

"I would like to watch as well." Scriabin fielded his aunt's glare. "It's history, Tyotya. I want to be able to tell my children that I saw it firsthand."

"We are in the human section of the concourse." Niall shot a glare at Val that should have dropped him on the spot. "We would have to move to the outlet in the idomeni section, along with all those poor souls who have flown up here for the sole purpose of protecting you. I don't believe that standing in full view of a small city's worth of idomeni is the best course of action for a group of humans—" He redirected his glower at Jani. "—or one hybrid in particular to take, given the circumstances and the prevailing mood."

Ulanova favored Niall with one of the few smiles she'd allowed over the course of the voyage. "I agree, Colonel. I believe—"

"I'd like to watch, too." John stepped inside, casting an edgy glance in Jani's direction before looking away. He wore her favorite daysuit, the pale blue-grey that matched his eyes. "If we're just going to stare at a display, well, we could've done that in Thalassa."

"Yes." Niall fit three weeks of ramping tension into a single word. "You could have."

"You're outvoted, Niall." Jani heard the twitter in her ear, felt her heart skip. *Three hundred fifty thousand.*

"No. I'm in charge of security. My vote trumps everyone's." Niall muttered a curse as the same number fed into his ear. "Look, I liked him, too. But we could be looking at a riot here."

"I'll hide behind someone." Jani read Niall's eyes, the pleading and the question. *Are you that eager to walk out there? To take that first step?* No, she wasn't. But what choice did she have? "Let's go."

Niall led them to the exit, muttering all the while, every angered inflection broadcast into Jani's ear. *"I didn't know you knew those words,"* she whispered, and watched his face flare.

Then Lucien squirted ahead while Niall moved behind. Shortcut code streamed into Jani's ear, names and locations and positions and conditions, so quickly that she couldn't identify the individual words. The inner door slid aside, then the outer door, and with as much formality as a stroll down the Thalassan beach, they walked out onto the gangway.

CHAPTER 26

"My God." John stopped at the point where the gangway opened out onto the human concourse.

"Nothing's changed." Val drew up beside him. "Not a thing."

Jani wiped her hands on her trousers as the shiver of nerves and fear and anticipation washed over. Glanced at Niall to find him fixed in place, as shaken as the rest of them.

"Damned place always was a beauty." He spoke softly, as though to himself, before switching back to security jargon.

"Yes." Jani nodded. Compared to the baroque excesses of Elyas and the jury-rigged clutter of Guernsey, Rauta Shèràa Station was as airy and elegant a public thoroughfare as ever existed. Sand-colored walls curved upward, carved at the peak to form a lattice like interlocking fingers from which skeletal metal chandeliers hung at regular intervals. The walls themselves had been equipped with illumination insets that provided most of the lighting, and made the space glow like a windowed room on a sunny day. In niches along the walls came the only shots of color, arabesque panels in green, blue, and worked metal.

Lucien's soft French crept into Jani's ear, as though he

lay beside her in bed. *"It's like a cathedral without the pews or the altar. No snack kiosks. No shops. No holos of ministers or the celebrity of the moment."*

"You've never been here?"

"No."

"It affects newcomers that way." And the not-so-newcomers, as well.

They stepped out as one and started down the causeway. Lucien remained in front, Niall to the rear. *"—like herding kiddies through the dinosaur exhibit—"* Jani picked out his voice amid the stream. *"Keep 'em moving and don't let them touch anything."*

Few humanish populated the place, since without the shops and eateries, there were no magnets, no reasons to hang around. They soon reached the end, which abutted an even larger cathedral that was the main concourse, near the spot where Tsecha's reliquary would emerge. Val glanced at his timepiece, then stood on tiptoe and checked out the crowd. "Can't we move out a little more?"

"Perhaps you can." John shook his head. "I'll have to make do with the sidelines. Hybrids have no rank here. I crouch near the front, I'll get hammered for commanding status I don't have. It only looks like a scrum out there. There's strict organization according to skein, sect, and degree of outcast."

"Have you ever noticed that idomeni . . . smell?" Lucien sniffed, then grimaced. *"I never noticed it before. It's weird. Faint, but highly annoying. Sickly sweet, like dead flowers."* He eyed Jani sidelong. *"We won't discuss the heat. We're lucky that cooling cells in desertweights are standard now."*

"I don't recall inquiring after your comfort." Jani tensed as a murmur rippled through the concourse, all heads turning toward the far end.

Val stepped over to them. "I just overheard Niall talking to one of his staff. Meva has just disembarked." He looked crisp and cool despite the unhumanish heat, as did his pale yellow daysuit, which also must have come equipped with cooling cells, given his lack of apparent discomfort. He remained at Jani's elbow and ignored Lucien, who for his part didn't seem to notice.

Jani edged as far out into the concourse as she dared. The place was about two hundred meters long, and filled from wall to wall with idomeni but for a narrow aisle that cut through their center. She looked behind her, saw Scriabin standing a few meters back. Ulanova leaned on his arm, as fixed on the unfurling scene as any of them.

Jani turned back toward the concourse just as something in the air . . . changed. She felt the charge, the tension. *The priest has come home.* Her eyes filled, tears spilling even as she tried to blink them away.

After a few moments a familiar figure became visible through the crowd. Meva, dressed as neatly and conservatively as Jani had ever seen in pale tan trousers, shirt, and propitiator's overrobe. Her waist-length hair, which she normally wore in a messy knot, had been braided and looped into a breeder's fringe as weighty as the wigs of ancient Egyptian figures. She walked slowly, her back straight as a plumb line, her head high. She'd encounter Haárin first, some dressed in jewel tones, others in palest earths and pastels. Farther along, she'd meet the bornsects who had come to pay their respects, but here, she met those whom Tsecha had led, those whom he had instructed, inspired. If she spotted Jani, she gave no sign, keeping her eyes fixed straight ahead as she passed by and continued down the concourse.

"How can so many beings stay so damned quiet?" Niall, his voice in Jani's ear as hushed as a child's.

Jani watched Meva until another change in the air caused her to look back from whence the female had come. At first she saw nothing. Then, through the crowd, it became visible, a box of plain, polished wood that floated through the air, a meter or so above the floor.

"You never mentioned pallbearers, did you, gel?" Niall's voice again. Questioning child.

"No, I didn't." Jani watched as the reliquary veered toward

the middle of the concourse as though guided by an invisible hand, then continued its haunting progression. As it passed the midway point, one of the Haárin standing at the front of the crowd raised both arms above her head in a posture of abject supplication. A few rows behind, another Haárin raised his arms.

Then another.

Another.

Finally, the rest of the idomeni, Haárin and bornsect, raised their arms in one upward sweep, the whisper of cloth the only sound as arms brushed and sleeves fell back, revealing traceworks of challenge scars. They stood, still and silent, as the reliquary continued on its way, a shadowed square, dark and dead amid the lightness and life.

Jani looked at John to find him standing somber, arms at his sides. He eyed her sidelong, his face reflecting the same question she asked herself. *What do we do, except watch? How do we show how we felt?*

John nodded. Then, moving in unison, they straightened, lifting their arms above their heads as the idomeni had. Val stared. Lucien simply watched.

"Dammit—you're not supposed to attract attention. You're supposed to—" Niall's voice cut off as Jani plucked the bug from her ear and shoved it in her pocket, then raised her arm again. A few Haárin glanced in her direction, but most watched the reliquary until it vanished from view. Then they slowly lowered their arms.

Jani lowered her arms as well, and waited for the crowd to disperse, to follow the reliquary, to walk to their shuttles.

But they did none of those things. Instead, they remained where they stood, and looked once more toward the far end of the concourse. Toward her.

The silence weighed, heavy as a grieving heart. The idomeni stood still, and quiet, and waited.

"You took it out, didn't you?"

Jani turned to find Niall at her shoulder.

He touched his ear, then looked past her toward the assembled. "Fucking hell. Not a one has budged." He glared at Jani. "*Dammit.*"

"You must get us out of here, Colonel." No more smiles as Ulanova shook off Scriabin's restraining hand and dogged Niall's elbow. "We'll be overrun."

"They're waiting for you." John's voice, quiet as shadow.

Jani looked him in the eye for the first time since they had departed Guernsey. Felt his surprise. His uncertainty. "I know."

Niall pointed to his ear bug. "Station Haárin are asking whether you intend to join the procession. The place is at a standstill and they have incoming craft that may need to be diverted if things don't shake loose soon."

"If she walks out there now, she declares herself ní Tsecha Egri's successor." Ulanova raised her own supplicant hand to the heavens, then let it fall. "In spite of her origins. In spite of the fact that she possesses no standing within Temple or the Haárin hierarchy. That would be a supreme display of arrogance, even for her."

Scriabin, silent to that point, walked over to Jani. "They could attack you. If they did, we might not be able to get to you in time."

"I don't think they'd do that." Jani tugged at the front of her shirt, then passed a straightening hand over it. "I think they're just waiting for me to make up my mind."

"So you are forced by circumstance to declare yourself Tsecha's successor," Ulanova bit out. "How convenient for you."

Jani took the ear bug from her pocket and reinserted it. "If anyone challenged me, I'd have to fight." She looked at Niall. "We didn't work this out ahead of time, but I'd like you to be my second if that happens."

Niall's eyes softened despite his irritation. "You know my answer, gel. What would I have to do?"

"Guard the edge of the circle to make sure I don't step outside it. Declare the challenge at an end if I'm too injured to continue."

Niall nodded. Swallowed hard. "We'll be close around you. We do have Haárin security in the crowd. Overhead scan. Interference patterning."

"Got anything that will stop a half-meter short sword?" Jani patted his arm. "It will be their call. How they perceive me, whether as Tsecha's suborn or . . . something else." She turned, and walked toward the concourse. Sensed a different sort of ripple radiate through the crowd as she approached, one that produced the occasional whitecap.

Jani tried to walk normally, even as the soles of her feet tingled and her knees threatened to buckle. She caught a whiff of the aroma Lucien described, the flower-sweat of idomeni packed shoulder-to-shoulder as far as her eye could see. Felt their heat as she walked the narrow gantlet, the full-face stares of the bolder Haárin.

"Keep going, gel. I've got your back. You're twenty meters in."

One hundred eighty to go. A lifetime in a few minutes. Jani imagined Tsecha's reliquary in front of her, leading the way. Touched the stones of her rings, drew strength from the chill hardness. Met the eyes of an elder female who bared her teeth, and bared her own in return. Slowed as an Haárin male stepped out of the crowd and strode toward her. Stopped as he reached beneath his overrobe and pulled out a blade as long as his forearm and brought it around in a long, slow arc.

Jani continued forward, reached out, gripped his wrist with her left hand, the hilt of the blade in her right, and twisted. Held the freed blade above her head—

"Let me the hell go!"

—then turned to find Niall standing stricken a few strides to the rear, a station Haárin hanging onto his arm. "I'm fine, Niall." Then she turned back to the male and handed him back his blade as the crowd surged forward and closed in behind her, bearing her along like a wave.

"What the hell was that?" Niall's voice rang in her head, as shaken as ever she'd heard it. *"What in bloody hell—"*

Lucien's voice broke in. *"I think it may have been the Haárin equivalent of asking for an autograph."*

"You think so?" Niall's sneer could have curdled milk. *"Well, fuck that—"*

Jani plucked the bug from her ear again. The crowd altered the farther along she walked, the brightly colored garb of the more militant Haárin giving way to the subdued coloration of the conservatives.

Then, near the end of the concourse, palest colors only, the braided fringe of the breeder the only hairstyle to be seen. *Bornsect.* Lighter Oà and Sìah, darker Denas and Pathen.

"Glories of this strangest of days to you, Kièrshia!" A male voice, speaking lightly accented High Sìah. But the words came from a Pathen male, who stepped forward and held out his hand to Jani. He was shorter and broader than Cèel, than any Vynshàrau. His skin was the yellowed black of old bronze, his shirt, trousers, and overrobe sun-yellow slashed with white. "And to the one you bring home to his rest."

Aden nìRau Wuntoi. Jani stopped, stood up straight, prayed her High Sìah was up to the challenge. "Glories to you as well, nìRau Wuntoi." She felt the pressure from behind as idomeni crowded inside her humanish comfort zone, the bones grind as Wuntoi gripped her hand in his.

"Favored of ní Tsecha, who believes and truly that his own Haárin killed him." Wuntoi bared his teeth. "Did you fear to meet his fate when you walked out into this place?"

The bracing bluntness of idomeni. Jani waited until Wuntoi released her hand, until the silence stretched to snapping and she knew she had his attention. "Have idomeni grown so fond of secret killing that I must worry, nìRau?"

Wuntoi raised his right hand, curving it in question. "No godly idomeni believes in such. You would have nothing to worry of from one of them." He cast her a glancing look in the face, his brown-on-brown eyes as chill as Lucien's. "From an ungodly, you would need to worry, as all idomeni would need to worry, and truly." With that, he stepped back into the crowd, and was swallowed up by his suborns.

Jani felt a push in the small of her back and started walking again. Parsed Wuntoi's words over and over, damned her sketchy High Sìah and wondered if she had heard properly. *He thinks it's possible an idomeni killed Tsecha. He accepts the idea.* Her heart hammered as she reached the end of the concourse and the station Haárin closed in, separating her from the all-enveloping welcoming committee and delivering her to a hidden alcove, where an enraged Niall waited, bracketed by Lucien and Scriabin.

Jani held up her hands. "No blood. No chance of injury." *Except when Wuntoi shook my hand.* "Cultural differences, Niall."

"Is that what we're calling it now?" Niall started to pace, then stopped and stood, glare fixed on some unlucky point in the distance. "No more crowds. No more knives for fun. And you will put that bug in your ear and leave it there—do you understand?"

"Wuntoi greeted you." Scriabin's eyes held surprise and a sharpness akin to envy. "The Pathen dominant. What does it mean?"

"I think it means that he accepts the possibility that an idomeni had Tsecha killed. He referred to an ungodly idomeni whom we all need to worry about. Was he speaking in general about the unknown idomeni who killed Tsecha, or was he just trying to turn us all against Cèel?" Jani leaned against the alcove entry, longed for nothing more than a comfortable seat on a shuttle, a chance to breathe. "I don't know where he learned humanish doublespeak, but he's damned good at it."

"I wonder if Cèel knows his feeling, or if it will take him by surprise?" Scriabin pointed down, in the general direction of Shèrá. "I doubt seriously that he will be expecting it."

"Assuming that's the case." Niall relaxed a little, and even managed a grin. "Cèel is going to start shitting little green apples any time now."

Scriabin's lip twitched. "He's made of fairly stern stuff, Colonel."

"Then it'll hurt that much more." Niall took Jani's elbow and steered her toward a walkway that led them back into the humanish concourse. "Let's go. Our shuttle received expedited clearance, which I swear comes courtesy of your new friend Wuntoi. Everyone else has boarded."

"Welcome back to Shèrá, Niall," Jani said under her breath.

"Maybe." Niall shook his head. "I may not understand cultural differences, but I know a power struggle when I see one. Your new friend drew a line in the sand, gel, and you're it."

Jani eased out of Niall's grip as they reentered the humanish concourse. Shivered, and blamed the coolness of the air.

CHAPTER 27

Jani walked out of Rauta Shèràa shuttleport's humanish section and gasped as though someone had punched her in the stomach. It was just past the height of summer, and the heat was as she remembered, a palpable oppression that seemed to close in on all sides, a challenge even to her hybrid tolerance. The sky, cloudless and milky blue, played home to the errant drift of seabirds and the more focused streakings of the swallow and hatchlike birds that called the city home and built nests in eaves and gutters. In the distance she could see the same spires and towers, the domes of the Trade Board, Council, and Temple.

The air smells the same. Walk anywhere in Rauta Shèràa, and you'd smell flowers. Near the port, the blooms of choice had always been *camalas*, fist-sized clusters of pink-trimmed white trumpets with a scent that always reminded Jani of cinnamon. She walked over to one of the shrubs, which had likely greeted her during her first arrival, twenty-five years before, and sniffed. *Still cinnamon.* A little sharper than she recalled, and maybe her hybridization was to blame.

The shuttleport itself, a cottage version of the orbiting station, also looked much as it ever had. She'd walked its corridors as a callow teenager, a Spacer and diplomat, a fleeing war criminal. *Now I'm back to diplomat.* Technically. She knew some who would argue the designation, herself included.

"What do you think, gel?" Niall drew up next to her. He held his nicstick case in one hand, ready to light up as soon as he entered the refuge of one of the embassy triple-lengths that abutted the curb. "Stuff of nightmares?"

"When I first came here, I thought it was one of the most beautiful cities I'd ever seen." Jani watched as Scriabin and Ulanova slipped into a skimmer bearing the ambassadorial crest on the door. They were followed closely by John and Val, who boarded a vehicle branded with the familiar caduceus. "Then reality started chipping away."

"The only things that struck me were the heat, and that I couldn't smoke outside the enclave." Niall nodded toward a Service blue skimmer. "Roshi got here a day ahead." He guided Jani toward the vehicle as though afraid she'd bolt.

Jani stepped into the passenger cabin, shivering as the chill, dry air washed over her. Sat on the edge of the bench seat and let her eyes adjust to the comparative darkness.

"Glories of this strangest of days. I fear Wuntoi is a master of understatement." Mako regarded her from the opposite bench.

"Understatement of the year." Major General Callum Burkett, commander of the Service Diplomatic Corps, snorted a laugh. "We've been in damage control mode ever since that damned article of yours reached us. Then we watched the arrival, which will henceforth be capitalized in all reports and formal précis. Morale did a one eighty within minutes. That little thing with the sword got a nice round of applause." He glared at Jani from his seat in the opposite corner of the cabin. "Is it ever easy with you?"

"Hi, Callum." Jani smiled. "How's Jeanina?"

"My lady wife is just fine, thanks, and don't change the damned subject." Burkett was the image of the middle-aged officer, tall, rangy, and sharp-featured, a darker tan and older eyes the only outward signs of time's passage. He and Mako wore the same uniform as did Niall, dress desertweights replete with cooling cells and special seaming to permit ventilation. "If your plan is to keep Cèel off balance, you're doing a helluva job. If your plan is to keep the rest of us off balance, stop it right now."

Conversation ceased as the front passenger gullwing opened and a familiar figure slipped in next to the driver. "All luggage has been scanned and loaded, sir." Lucien just had time to glance over his shoulder at Jani before the darkened privacy barrier slid into place.

The skimmer pulled away from the curb, then gradually accelerated, driving Jani back against her seat. She took in the view through her window, the wide avenues of the central city, the blockish buildings of white and tan stone, walkways filled with crowds of bornsect and Haárin.

"The reliquary just arrived at the Haárin enclave." Burkett emitted a grumbling sigh. "He was one of the most irritating beings I ever had the misfortune to meet, and I wish I could have told him how much I—" He turned his face to the window. Swallowed hard. "You had to like him, didn't you? You couldn't help yourself."

"Someone could," Mako muttered. After that they fell silent, the only sound to reach them the announcement by their driver as they approached the gates of the humanish enclave.

Burkett poured himself coffee from a large upright brewer, then returned to the couch. "We expected Cèel to be challenged by Wuntoi sometime in the last month or two, but Tsecha's death caught the Pathen completely off guard, as it did all of us."

After entering the humanish enclave, they had been taken immediately to the embassy, a four-story expanse of tan stone that dominated the enclave's central cul-de-sac, which like the other buildings in the place had been constructed according to idomeni protocols. Only the triple-wide entryway broke the smoothness of the facade. Windows were reserved for the rear views, which looked out over a series of gardens laced with artificial streams and surrounded by high brick walls. The feeling was one of enclosure, of shuttering away, which couldn't have been a coincidence given Cèel's opinion of humanish.

Jani sipped coffee. After their arrival, they had been deposited in one of the larger sitting rooms, there to wait for the others in their group. The decor had been chosen by someone who shared Anais Ulanova's taste in furnishings: brocade-upholstered couches and chairs, dark woods, and silk and velvet-covered walls. No reds or burgundies, since those shades would have conflicted with idomeni religious prerogative. But there were plenty of other rich tones to make up for the omission, jewel shades of blue, green, and purple, with a gold mine's worth of gilt thrown in to provide contrast. *Winter colors.* The sight of them combined with the humanish room temperature to make Jani shiver all the more, as though they'd brought with them the stiff winds and dry, cold air of a Chicago winter.

"Wuntoi is biding his time now." Mako had eschewed coffee and, despite the early hour, gone straight to the liquor cabinet and the vodka. "Too much news tumbled in too quickly. First the death, then the news of assassination and the rage at humanish when the news proved true." He sat sprawled in a corner lounge chair like a disgruntled bear and stared into his frosted glass. "Then came your article, and the fallout, both expected and . . . not so." He regarded Jani with the same sharp wonderment that Scriabin had at the station. "None of us believed the idomeni would have ever accepted the possibility that one of their own could have done the deed. Not a one."

"Tsecha's influence." Burkett sat back, eyes fixed on nothing. "I sensed the strength of it increasing with every passing day, especially among the Haárin." He glanced down at his cup, then frowned and set it aside. "But the Haárin don't have the power around here—that's Cèel and the Council and Temple hardliners, and they're hammering on the rest to dissolve diplomatic relations with us, recall the Haárin from their humanish enclaves, and seal their borders." He rose and walked to the liquor cabinet, pulled another frosted glass from the tiny cooler and filled it to the brim with vodka. "Wuntoi would love to accuse Cèel of planning Tsecha's assassination, but first he needs proof, and human-style criminal investigation methods are in their infancy here. Service Investigative has reported that they've fielded a few hesitant probings, but nothing has come of them, and when we try to reach out, the idomeni pull back, lock down." He raised his glass, studied it for a time, then sipped. "Which means that, unfortunately, we are forced to sit, and wait."

Silence claimed them. After a time, Jani shifted in her seat as the stares shifted to her. "How is Cèel responding to the undecideds?"

"With some old-fashioned threats." Mako tossed down the last of his vodka. "He's said that he will win any civil war—the Vynshàrau are the most populous sect in this region, numbering twelve million or more, and as head of the warrior skein, Cèel commands a fighting force of over a million, not including Haárin. He'll treat those who fought him as he treated the Laum years ago. Pathen, Oà, Sìah. Every sect that questioned him would be wiped out. It would make the Night of the Blade look like a playground melee. He'd decimate his people, and call it the will of the gods."

Jani looked to the door and drummed her fingers on the arm of the couch. "So what's our ambassador's opinion of all this?"

"Dear Ava Galina." Mako sneered. "In over her head and sinking fast. Takes her direction from Cao, who so far is doing her usual fine job of ignoring the obvious."

"So now she's closeted with Scriabin, who may be trustworthy, and Ulanova, who damned well isn't. What are they discussing? Escape plans?" Jani looked to Niall, who had taken a seat in the far corner as soon as they arrived and had remained still and silent ever since. "Do you have escape plans?"

"Coordination with Fort du Lac and Phillipa Station. We have combat shuttles squirreled away down the road, on what passes for our base, and the *Ulanov* twiddling its thumbs just beyond Shèráin space. We would bypass Rauta Shèràa Station entirely, of course." Niall straightened, his air of gloomy introspection dissipating now that he had a definite problem to focus on. "Given the quality of Shèrá's orbital defense array, which is unfortunately damned good, and assuming Cèel's normal level of vindictiveness, I'd say we'd be lucky to evac ten percent of the enclave."

As that bit of news settled over the room like a dark cloud, the door opened and Scriabin lumbered in. "You all made it here—good. I gather from the general air of despondency that you've been apprised of the situation." He walked to the liquor cabinet and became the third customer for the vodka. "Ava had little to add. No official statement from Cèel concerning your arrival, but he supposedly called in the Haárin dominants for an emergency conclave as soon as the images hit the displays." He grinned at Jani. "The dominants who were here, at any rate. Most of them were at the station, welcoming you." He leaned against the cabinet and raised his glass to her. "So, Cèel is rocked back on his heels for the first time in a long while, and to that I say, *Nazdrovya*." He gulped the vodka, then hefted the empty glass, eyes fixed on the fireplace on the other end of the room.

Jani set aside her coffee and wished she were still humanish enough for liquor to have the desired effect. "I'd have Service Investigative talk to ní Galas, Feyó's security dominant. Station and enclave Haárin are much more advanced than the locals when it comes to criminal investigation, and they've had over a month to investigate the assassination."

"I filled in Callum concerning the missing Nahin Sela," Mako offered. "He believes that the Rauta Shèràa Haárin enclave investigators, however backward, are withholding information."

Burkett's face darkened. "It would certainly shed a great deal of light on some of the oddness that we've seen these last few weeks. If they suspect that Nahin Sela is being hidden somewhere in Rauta Shèràa . . . "

"It's their humiliation. If one of theirs killed Tsecha, they want to solve it themselves." Jani stood, tense muscles protesting every movement. "If I could beg your indulgence, I would like an hour or so to settle in. I'm guessing the day's schedule is pretty well packed."

"We're all within a stone's throw of one another, in any case." Burkett downed the balance of his vodka, then set the glass upside down on the table. "We'll talk to Feyó's investigator and go from there." He looked to Jani and blew out a sigh. "One hour at a time. That's what we're down to."

"Maybe I should develop a taste for vodka." Jani acknowledged the scattered weak laughter with a short bow. Only Niall, who knew her best of all, eyed her unsmiling, with the wary stare of a man who knew that somewhere there was a shoe teetering on the brink.

By the time Jani reached her suite, a three-room corner expanse with views of the gardens, her luggage had been deposited and was in the process of being unpacked by a pair of officious aides. She grabbed her duffel before either of them could put their hands on it and headed down the hallway in search of the nearest stairwell.

"Hello."

Jani froze in mid-stride at the sound of the unfortunately all-too-familiar voice, then slowly turned.

Lucien had arrived at the embassy the same time she had. Yet judging from the crispness of his dress desertweights and the fresh-scrubbed shine on his face, he'd already showered, changed uniforms, and performed whatever other ablutions served to eliminate every trace of long-haul fatigue. *When Cèel bombs the enclave, he'll die with his mirror-finish boots on.* "You're staying here?" She

looked past him down the hall and tried to divine from which
room he might have emerged. "I thought you had to stay at
the base."

"No room. It's just a dink place—provides embassy security and some firepower, and that's about it. Between Mako's
people and Pierce's crew, they're hanging from the rafters."
Lucien shrugged. "Such are the sacrifices we make when
called upon."

Jani felt the heat move up her neck as his innocent look
sharpened and altered into something focused and . . . not
so innocent. She turned, started back down the hall. "I have
to go—"

"You're all everyone's talking about. Your entrance. Your
unspoken announcement to one and all that you're taking up
where Tsecha left off." Lucien hurried past her, then stepped
in front of her, cutting her off. "They're replaying the images
over and over and over—"

"Until it backfires. Then I'll be on everyone's shit list
again." Jani tried to elbow past him, but he grabbed her by
the shoulders and pushed her against the wall.

"Does that mean I'll finally have some company?" Lucien leaned in until he pressed the length of his body against
hers. "Someone to talk to? Have dinner with? Someone
to—" He abandoned the preamble and kissed her hard,
bruising her mouth as his hands burned their own path
along her buttocks and up her back before finally moving
forward and settling on her breasts, cupping and massaging
and teasing—

Jani tried to push him away, but each touch, each sensation, unlocked memory and need and desire. Craving. To
quench a thirst long denied, ease the ever-growing tension
and allay the fear and soothe the quickening ache between
her legs. *Simple.* Take that one simple path, if only for a little
while. "I don't have time." She tried to shift away from him,
but he'd laced his legs through hers and pinned her against
the wall and all she could feel were his lips and hands and
the press of his erection through his uniform and her pound-

ing heart and the slow trickle of sweat down her back. "I bet they have imagers in the corridors."

"Not in the private wing—the residents would riot." Lucien paused, his breathing rough, his hands stilling, hovering, a devil's promise on hold. "Your room?"

"Aides unpacking the luggage."

"I've got Facilities working on the shower." Lucien turned the handle of the nearest door, prying open the panel and releasing Jani just long enough to peek inside. "Oh, look. Housekeepers' closet." He arched an eyebrow. "Blankets. Pillows." He took her hand and led her through the gap, then pushed the panel closed and wedged the inside handle in the locked position with a long-handled scrubbing brush.

"You've done this before." Jani leaned against a narrow worktable.

"I've done everything before." Lucien slipped the duffel off her shoulder and tossed it in the corner. Pulled her shirt out of her trousers and opened the fasteners, peeling open the front of her bra along the way and applying a quick lick-and-tease to her nipples before undoing her trousers and sliding them down.

Jani reached for his tunic, but he pushed her hands away and undid it himself, slipping it off and laying it carefully across a shelf. His T-shirt, he pulled off more quickly, and it stayed where it landed.

"I don't think this table will hold—" Before Jani could argue load capacity, Lucien swept a shelf's worth of pillows to the floor and lowered her onto them. Kissed her again while his hands found their way everywhere, excited her everywhere, brought her to the edge before easing off ever so slightly. Then with a flick of hand and a twist of hip, he undid his trousers and slipped inside her, moving, then stopping, then moving more quickly and stopping once more, the same ebb and flow again and again until he couldn't stop himself anymore and he buried his head in her neck and whispered things to her that he hadn't said since Chicago and called her things he'd never called her before and she wrapped herself around him and raked her nails across the small of his back and rode his sharp gasps and choked moans and matched them with her own.

Then held him as he slumped against her and relaxed in a way only he could, loose-limbed as a cat after a surfeit of cream.

Her breathing slowed, eventually. The ability to form sentences returned. "If the housekeeper comes in here for towels, they're going to get a hell of a shock."

Lucien laughed, a deep, warm sound that wrapped around Jani like the pillows. "You think they haven't learned to knock before entering a room in this place?" He slid off her onto his side. "You haven't worked in many government buildings, have you?"

"Not with you." Jani scrutinized the ceiling for a time, then looked at Lucien to find him studying her in turn, head cradled on his arm, eyes half closed.

"Six weeks." His voice emerged tight. "Wasted. And why? We could have—and it isn't like you and Shroud were still even—" He rolled over on his back. "Who the hell knows?" He muttered something under his breath, then closed his eyes.

"You could sleep in here, couldn't you?" Jani sat up. Tried to stand until her trousers hobbled her and she fell on her ass and finally lay back and yanked them up.

"What are you doing?" Lucien sat up, a vision of randy dishevelment amid the white-on-white toss of pillows.

"I have to get out of here." She recovered her bra and shirt from the floor and put them on.

"You just—" Lucien stood, pulling up his trousers in one easy motion, a man who had never been hobbled by his clothes in his life. "Wait a minute." He collected the rest of his uniform and dressed. "Dammit."

"I need to get to the Haárin enclave." Jani tried to remove the brush that held the door closed, yanking on it twice before Lucien nudged her aside and removed it with a twist of his wrist. "I need to talk to Meva or Dathim or Galas or somebody."

"Do you trust the security of comport communications around here?" Lucien didn't wait for her to shake her head. "Then you have to leave the enclave, and you can only leave the enclave in an authorized vehicle driven by a licensed member of the embassy staff." He smiled and waved his hand in her face. "Hello. Me, again."

CHAPTER 28

Jani waited in an alley beside the embassy building while Lucien signed out a skimmer. She had returned to her room to collect her overrobe in case she needed it, but instead of donning it, she rolled it up and stuck it in her duffel. She didn't want to be recognized now. She didn't want to be followed. She just wanted to find out what, if anything, Galas had discovered about Nahin Sela.

A sedate four-door in Service blue-grey appeared at the end of the alley. Lucien disembarked and walked around to the passenger side to see to Jani's door, then used the exercise as an excuse to kiss her neck.

"Do you know where we're going?" He inserted himself into the cabin and steered onto the enclave access road, then tapped a blank display in the middle of the dashboard. "If I can avoid using the mapping system, that's one less way they can track us."

"I remember where the Haárin enclave used to be." Jani felt her heart trip as they floated through the gates, the skimmer shuddering as it switched from the humanish to idomeni skimtrack system. "From what I've seen, they rebuilt the city exactly has it had been before the war. I should be able to find it."

They drifted through the streets. Jani recognized old
landmarks, buildings she had used as guides when she first
arrived at the Academy and hadn't known enough Laumrau
or Vynshà to understand the street designators.

"Where's the Academy?" Lucien maneuvered into the
slower lane so he could sightsee.

"We won't pass that—it's about ten kilometers north of
here." Jani felt her throat tighten, and struggled to will the
sensation away. *It looks the same . . . all the same.* The parks
and the art-filled niches in the walls of buildings otherwise
so featureless they looked like molds a child had made with
wet sand and a bucket. "First you'll pass the Council dome,
then the Temple dome. Then there's the Haárin enclave. Then
you pass all the dominant temples for the gods. Shiou's is
the largest, followed by Caith's, which is what you'd expect.
Then there's a riverwalk, and on the other side of that—"
She fell silent. She'd had nightmares, yes, and hadn't wanted
to return to this place. What she hadn't expected was that
part of her would have . . . missed it all, the crowded streets
and the sand-hued monotone and the flowers and the heat
and the distant smell of the bay.

"It's a little like Thalassa." Lucien had slipped into ab-
sorption mode, where he watched and memorized and said as
little as possible as things burned into his brain. "Thalassa's
brighter, and there's that undercurrent of Karistos attitude,
but still." He sat back, still on point but a little more relaxed.
"I know why Tsecha liked Thalassa so much."

"Yeah." Jani fixed her attention on the view. They'd just
passed the street leading to Caith's temple, a squat, ugly
edifice with a dome of tarnished silver. Sedate clothing
and breeder's fringes gave way to the occasional sheared
head or burst of rebellious color, the entire scene clicking
into place when an all-too-familiar figure emerged from
the crowd.

"Pull over." Jani waited until Lucien edged out of moving
traffic, then pushed up her gullwing and waved. "Dathim!"

Dathim strode toward the skimmer. "Hah—I came to see

you as well." He pulled up the rear door and piled into the backseat.

Jani turned back to face him. "Are you sure you want to be seen with me?"

"What difference?" Dathim folded his arms and sat ramrod straight, the top of his clipped scalp grazing the cabin headliner. "Cèel watches us and listens to us and what difference? Hell with him." He looked out the window, then bared his teeth. "We go to the river and talk there. In the open where all can see."

"So that's the Academy?" Lucien stood atop a stone bench and gazed across the river toward the congested scattering of white buildings large and small that stretched from the main avenue down to the bay. "It's smaller than I thought it would be."

"It's about the size of a ministry compound." Jani looked at the place where she'd spent four of the more harrowing years of her life. "One of the smaller ministries." She stepped up next to Lucien. "The library is the largest building—you can see the gold dome. The rest are classrooms, a few labs. The scanpack brain farming is performed at Temple because it's a medical procedure, and all those labs are staffed by physician-priests."

"Humans don't attend anymore?"

"No. There were a few classes after ours, but then the war came—"

"Your overrobe—where is it?"

Jani turned to find Dathim glaring at her.

"You should wear it." He folded his arms. "He died for it, and you traveled here because of it, and you should wear it."

Jani looked out over the riverwalk. The time for midday sacrament approached, and most idomeni had retired to their altar rooms, leaving the usually crowded walkways sparsely populated. "I didn't want to be recognized."

"Then you should not have followed him. You should not

have come here. You should not have walked behind the reliquary." Dathim grabbed her duffel from beneath the bench and held it out to her. "Meva is outraged. She will yell at you when she sees you again. Put it on."

"You're a bully, ní Dathim Naré." Jani yanked open the duffel fasteners and removed the overrobe, shook it out and pulled it on. "Now we better get out of here."

"Now we must talk." Dathim sat down on the end of the bench, hands on knees, like the town chatterbox. "Ní Galas does not trust his secure communications at the enclave, either. He told ná Meva that it would be much the same as if he went to Council and spoke to Cèel directly."

Jani leapt down to the ground and perched on the rim of a planter. "Ní Galas has been busy?"

"Ní Galas has been to the Trade Board. He showed the images of Nahin Sela to all he met." Dathim gestured disgust. "They are all godly idomeni who do not look others in the face. They had never heard of Nahin Sela, and did not recognize the hair or the clothes, so they could not say if they knew her." He held up his index finger and pointed at Jani. "But there was one female. A bornsect. She did not know of Nahin Sela, but she did know of Imea nìaRauta Rilas." He lowered his voice, a concession that said all anyone needed to know about the quality of the information. "Rilas is a member of Cèel's household. She has been thus for many years. The female said that she is absent much, and spoke sometimes of travel."

Jani pushed away from the planter and stared at the river. "Galas will not be permitted to speak to Rilas."

"A fact which he knows." Dathim lowered his voice even more. "Meva has petitioned Cèel for permission to request that another bornsect speak to Rilas. Wuntoi, or another of the sect dominants."

Jani turned slowly. "Meva has already asked Cèel—" She fell silent when she looked past Dathim to the sloping lawns beyond.

"Oh, shit." Lucien stepped down from the bench and headed along the river to the nearby charge lot. "I'll get the skimmer."

They weren't a large crowd of Haárin, a few hundred or so. But judging by appearances, they were the gamiest, all shorn hair and garish colors on the males, horsetails or loose hair on the females, some of whom wore long skirts instead of all-pervasive trousers.

So quiet. Like the crowds in the station. *What do they want me to say?* Did they expect her to preach, like some of the ministers her papa listened to when he entered one of his "loud religion" phases? *Sermon by the River.* She swallowed a nervous laugh. *I don't even believe in your gods.* What could she say to them that they would want to hear?

The Haárin remained standing, because she was the propitiator and the level of their heads had to remain above hers as a show of respect.

Out of the corner of her eye, Jani saw Lucien maneuver the skimmer up to the top edge of the slope. A dash across a short stretch of lawn, a few quick strides, and she'd be free.

Instead, she crossed her ankles and lowered to the ground. Slipped into Vynshàrau Haárin, because that's what most of them were.

"Ní Tsecha missed Rauta Shèràa. Humanish have a term—homesickness—a longing for the places where one lived as a youngish, where one grew up. He used to tell me stories . . . "

"They were just stories." The embassy security guard grinned. "The one she told about Tsecha when he was young and studying at the Temple school and made this confetti bomb—ohmigod—" She finally took note of the less than enthused audience reaction, and fell silent.

"The Haárin were orderly in the extreme, sir." The second guard shook his head, disbelief stripping the years from his face. "They just followed us to the van, and one of them opened the door for her, and another held out his arm so she could climb in. I mean, Christ on a cracker, if Cèel calls that a riot, I'd hate to see—"

"Thank you, Sergeant—that will be all." Niall waited until the pair filed out before planting his elbows on the desk and burying his face in his hands. "If I were to ask you what you were thinking, would I want to hear the answer?"

Jani sat across from him. She'd removed her overrobe and hung it in her closet, then showered and changed into the more embassy-appropriate dinner attire of a severe black trouser suit. "They expected me to say something, and I didn't know what else to talk about."

"You shouldn't have been out there in the first place." Ulanova sat against the far wall next to her nephew, who sat with arms folded and his head down. "Of all the self-aggrandizing, egomaniacal, inflammatory—" She fell silent and pressed a hand to her forehead.

Lucien, who sat off to one side, well away from the center of the action, raised his hand. "In my opinion, sir, ní Dathim planned for this to happen." He spoke softly, his voice steady, determined to soldier on whether anyone listened or not. "He shamed Jani into putting on her overrobe, even though she expressly informed him that she did not want to be recognized. We felt that since the time for midday sacrament was near, no idomeni would be out on the river. The local hardcore Haárin, however, have apparently stopped following prescribed meal times, a fact we had no way of knowing."

Niall plucked a stylus from the desktop holder and tapped it against the blotter. "You shouldn't have been out there, period. As matters stand, Cèel is threatening to pull all driving privileges for embassy personnel—"

"Ní Galas took Nahin Sela's image to the Trade Board." Jani spoke quickly, trying to fit it all in before anyone interrupted. "One of the bornsect females recognized her as a bornsect named Imea nìaRauta Rilas, a member of Cèel's household."

Niall's tapping stopped. "Why didn't you tell me this sooner?"

"Meva plans to petition Cèel to allow another of the born-sect dominants to talk to Rilas." Jani met Niall's tired eye. "That crack you made about the bottom of the bay just might come to pass."

"What about the bottom of the bay?" Scriabin lifted his head.

"Niall is of the opinion that if Cèel hasn't already killed Rilas, he plans to do so soon. When the threat of exposure is sufficient." Jani avoided Niall's eye even as she cast credit his way. He'd freed a 'stick, and now sat glaring at her through a haze of smoke, like the villainous interrogator in a cheap holodrama. "Meva's petition to allow another bornsect domi-nant to speak with her might be enough to force his hand."

"And then we lose the only being who can testify to Cèel's culpability?" Scriabin sat up, fingers drumming on knees. "Is it too late to ask Meva to withdraw her petition?"

"This is Meva we're talking about." Niall's voice emerged desert dry. "She's a handful even by idomeni standards, and we have no diplomatic bludgeon with which to compel her to cease and desist."

"Meva can be a pain in the ass." Jani ignored Scriabin's just audible, "Pot. Kettle. Black," and Niall's arched brow. "But the concepts of trial and conspiracy and culpability don't apply here. Cèel would never stand trial as we know it. The only penalty for a crime like assassination is the same we've seen before with the Laum—another sect ascends to *rau*, and the sect that had been in power is obliterated. That blanket condemnation doesn't apply here. We're only inter-ested in Cèel. We're blazing a new trail."

"Is this your way of telling us to trust Meva?" Niall's voice took on an avuncular lilt, as it sometimes did when they spoke in private. "You don't like her, but you trust her?"

"The two aren't always mutually exclusive." Jani took a deep breath. "Why don't we ask her to meet with us so we can discuss this?"

* * *

Meva was contacted. She proved very eager to arrange a meeting, as there were several things on her private agenda that she felt needed an airing.

"Priest-in-training, you call yourself. *Hah*. You do not even wear your overrobe. The greatest ceremony in which a priest can participate, the transport of a soul. And you do not even wear your overrobe!" Meva had taken charge of the chair in front of Niall's desk. She still wore the same conservative clothing, including overrobe, that she had during the procession, but the overall effect had acquired a rumpled aspect. Some hair had escaped the tight braiding of her breeder's fringe, sticking out at odd angles. A few of the beads that decorated the braid ends had gone missing as well.

She looks like she got caught in a wind tunnel. Jani stood against the near wall, arms folded. Imagined finding Meva trapped in such a device and hitting the activation pad herself. "I didn't want to attract attention." She ignored Ulanova's mutter.

"You are a priest, *priest*. We are that which we are. To hide such is not even anathema. It is simply stupid." Meva sat back and fixed her attention on Scriabin, who had abandoned the seat next to his aunt for a chair next to Niall's desk. "As for my petition, why should I withdraw it? I wish to speak with Rilas. If I cannot do so, a bornsect dominant may do so in my stead. Aden nìRau Wuntoi proved most agreeable to my request, and truly."

"Well, he would, wouldn't he?" Scriabin picked his nails, which over the intervening hours had crossed the border from neat to ragged edged. "It's in his interest to keep Cèel off balance."

"It is in all our interests to keep Cèel off balance, and truly, Minister."

"Yes, but at the same time, ná Meva, it is still taken for granted that a human assassinated ní Tsecha. If Rilas vanishes, never to be found, humans lose their last best chance to prove that one of theirs did not commit that crime." Scriabin's face darkened, as though the conversation dredged up images of that day. As though they replayed in his mind. As though he wanted them to stop and knew they never would. "No one will know the truth."

Meva's expression softened, a little. She sat up straighter, her voice lightening. "The gods know, Minister."

Jani read the answer to that in Scriabin's eyes. *Your gods aren't our gods, Meva.* They didn't affect elections. Didn't quell colonial unrest, or allay the suspicions of Haárin who had lost docks and goods and ships to bombings, followed by their dearest priest.

Then there's the Capria. Meva's gods didn't affect a damned thing where that was concerned.

"Tomorrow, much will be decided." Meva bared her teeth. "Kièrshia will confront Cèel with Tsecha's assassination. She may demand of him then that we be allowed to question Rilas."

Jani fielded the expressions of alarm that focused on her. "That is why I came along, remember? To officially inform Cèel that Tsecha had been assassinated."

"That was when we felt no doubt whatsoever that a humanish had committed the crime." Scriabin picked his nails with renewed vigor. "Now we have doubt, and given our delicate position here, we're not really in the position where we can accuse our host of planning the murder of his most vocal critic."

"Why not?" Meva didn't raise her right hand to chest height and curve it, but let her voice carry the question. "Off balance was the term you used, Minister. To keep Cèel off balance is the only way to drive forward that which is to be."

Scriabin and Niall glanced at one another, a library's worth of enclave evacuation plans transferred in one look, their likely failure in the next. "I think that tomorrow," Scriabin said, eyes still on Niall, "we make our appearance. We swallow whatever insults, whatever threats, Cèel flings at us. And we bide our time, and continue the search for nìaRauta Rilas, for any evidence that Cèel planned Tsecha's assassination. When we have the facts, then, and only then, do we move." He finally looked at Meva. "Do I have your pledge, ná Meva, that you will not do anything to escalate the tensions between Cèel and the Commonwealth?"

Everyone held their breath as Meva sat silent, meeting Scriabin's concern with a bland gaze and an air that Jani remembered all too well.

I could talk to Tsecha until I couldn't talk anymore. And he would still do what he planned, because he was right and she was wrong and any discussion of the matter was simply an irritating way to pass time. *I told him that his treatises would anger Cèel.* The signal time in her life when she would have enjoyed being wrong.

"I will do nothing to irritate Cèel, Minister," Meva said finally.

Niall nodded. Scriabin closed his eyes. Even Ulanova reacted, her shoulders sagging as though tension seeped away.

Then Jani looked to the back of the room, where Lucien sat. Once more in the shadow. Once more, apparently forgotten. He stared back, eyes narrowed, bullshit detector cranked up to the most sensitive setting. *Perhaps they believe her,* the look seemed to say. *I sure as hell don't.*

Meva stood. "Now that you have forced pledges from me, I must return to the enclave. Early evening sacrament approaches, and I believe and truly that there might be cake." She ignored the assorted farewells and thank-yous, her eyes meeting Jani's as she turned and walked to the door.

"I'll walk you to your skimmer, ná Meva." Jani pushed off the wall and followed after her. "So you can yell at me some more."

"I can never yell at you enough, ná Kièrshia." Meva waited in the doorway for Jani to catch her up, and together they walked down the embassy corridor to the entry.

"You lied to Scriabin." Jani lowered her voice as one of the guards emerged from her office to open the door for them.

"I told him that which I will do, which is nothing." Meva shrugged. "You will do that which you will do. Whether it is that which we discussed in Thalassa, or something else which I do not know, you will do it."

As they approached Meva's skimmer, the driver-side gullwing swept up and Dathim emerged. "Did you yell at her for forgetting her overrobe, Meva?"

"Yes, Dathim. But I do not know, and truly, whether it mattered. Whether it had any effect." Meva stood aside while Dathim raised her door, then pushed away his hand as he attempted to help her into the cabin. "Tomorrow, Kièrshia."

"Tomorrow," Dathim echoed as he slammed the door, then circled the vehicle and inserted his formidable frame into the driver's cockpit.

"Enjoy your cake." Jani raised a hand in farewell, and received a flicker of hazard lights in reply. Turned, and found Niall standing at the top of the steps, watching her.

"Well, that was interesting." He sat on the top step and dug out his 'sticks. "Think Scriabin made any inroads?"

"She said she wouldn't do anything to upset Cèel. I think we're stuck with taking her at her word." Jani sat down beside him. Dusk was just beginning to fall, the undersides of the clouds purpling and the sky fading. *Rauta Shèràa sunsets.* She'd enjoyed them at one time, when they didn't carry with them the promise of worse days ahead.

"How are you doing?" Niall leaned back on his elbows, 'stick dangling from his lips, releasing puffs of smoke with each word.

I have never felt more lost, more helpless. More restless. I have never come closer to regretting my life. Jani whittled the words down to a shrug. "I was about to ask you the same question."

Niall sat up straight and wiped off the elbows of his tunic. "Have you been to the base?" He waited until she shook her head. "It's completely different in appearance—new buildings, new skimtrack layout. But the square meterage is the same, so if you remember where things used to be, you can still ... figure out where ... " He pinched the end of the 'stick, then broke it in half. "There's a certain area I avoid, let's put it that way. Otherwise, it's all just bunky." He flipped the halves one by one into a nearby planter. "You?"

"I haven't tried to sleep yet." Jani watched a trio of swallowlike birds flit silently across the skimway and vanish into the trees. "I feel as though it all happened yesterday, that I've only been gone a moment." She savored the weaker warmth of late afternoon sun. "I don't know what's going to happen."

"Pretty standard with you, isn't it, gel?" Niall tried to grin and failed. "We're as ready as we can be. Now all we can do is wait. Always the fun part."

"Yeah." Jani stood, swept grit from the seat of her trousers. "You going to the reception?"

"Wouldn't miss it." Niall stood, stretched. "Probably be the last party we have around here for a while."

Rilas tried to sleep, but the words of Ansu's suborn returned, again and again—

And then she proceeded through the concourse, nìaRauta, after ní Tsecha's reliquary ... and so many waited for her ... and she spoke by the river of ní Tsecha ... and the Haárin listened, and laughed ...

—and again and again.

It seemed as though she had spent an entire season in this room, in this bed, but when she stopped to count the number of sacraments, the times Ansu had visited, she realized that only two sun cycles had passed. *They have drugged me.* She suspected such after the first cycle had passed, when she slept longer than she ever had. Until after sunrise the next day, which was something she never did.

They will keep me here until the humanish leave. Even though she would have pledged to nìRau Cèel to remain silent, to leave Rauta Shèràa, to travel to the islands of the Dahoumn and remain there until she grew most old.

I came to you freely.

But such did not seem to matter to nìRau Cèel, because the anathema was here, and the Haárin followed her, and listened when she spoke of the outcast Tsecha.

Rilas opened her eyes to find Ansu standing over her.

"You are awake, nìaRauta?" The physician-priest stepped back from the bed and crossed an arm over her chest in alarm.

"You are surprised at such, Ansu?" Rilas sensed the female's dismay at such casual address. "You are most as your most esteemed patient, Ansu. You greatly prefer the formalities."

"Such are godly behaviors, Imea nìaRauta Rilas." Ansu stressed the full form of Rilas's name as a form of scolding. "We should all strive to follow such at all times." She lowered the rail on one side of the bed just as the door opened and a suborn entered pushing a skimchair. "Now, we shall go outside for a short while, because it is a godly day, and truly." Ansu took Rilas by the arm and pulled her until she sat up. "The warmth will enliven you."

The withholding of your drugs would enliven me. Rilas tasted the unseemly sourness that spread over her tongue and wondered what Ansu had given her. Not soma, for she did not feel ill in the pit of her soul. Instead there was exhaustion, and the inability to concentrate, and a weakness in her limbs. She tried to sit up, to move onto the chair as Ansu bade. But her knees buckled and her heart fluttered and even the suborn wondered at her growing weakness as he pushed her chair onto the veranda, and the clear sky, and the godly sun.

"You shall drink this, nìaRauta Rilas." Ansu poured liquid from a flask she carried into a small cup. "It is a Sìah concoction which will enliven you, and truly."

"Thanks to the gods for such, nìaRauta Ansu." Rilas watched as Ansu's shoulders lost their slight curve of displeasure, and knew what she had to do from this point on.

Speak as one who would cooperate, even as she behaved as she had to in order to regain her strength and save her life.

Rilas held the cup to her lips, allowed the barest touch of pale brown liquid to skin. Then she waited until Ansu had turned her back and tipped the cup, spilling the liquid to the ground.

CHAPTER 29

Mako tipped the last of the wine into his glass, then crooked his finger at the steward, who removed the empty bottle and set another, already opened, in its place. No decanting. No sniffing or pondering the bouquet or the origin of the grapes. The first order of the evening was to get just drunk enough, and Hiroshi Mako was already halfway to goal.

Guests sat at a scattering of tables that had been set out in the garden. John and Val arrived together, but adjourned to opposite sides, Val sitting with Ulanova and her coterie and John opting for the Service table at which Niall, Burkett, and Mako held court. Lucien, who had been sitting there, rose as soon as John sat down, and walked from table to table, chatting and cracking socially acceptable jokes while looking for a place to land.

Jani watched it all shake out from her suite window. Wished she had the option of a good drunk. A night with Lucien in an actual bed. A chance to forget. The tension permeated the air like the scent of the bay, infiltrated her every thought. *What do you expect me to do, Meva?* What could she do to make things better? How could she keep from making things worse? *And Meva's not helping.* "*Do that which you do."* Which was what, exactly? Breathe? Yell? Shoot someone?

Jani watched the dinner seating settle out. Watched Mako empty the latest bottle into John's glass, then call for another.

Offered a prayer to Ganesh, checked herself one last time in the mirror, and headed downstairs.

"Jani, get over here!"

Jani abandoned the tiny two-chair table in a darkened corner near the stone wall and braved the walk through the gantlet to join an old friend beneath the trees.

"It's so good to see you!" Brigadier General Frances Hals threw her arms around her and hugged her hard enough to hurt, then pushed her down into the chair next to her. "Cal Burkett has locked me and my staff in the embassy basement for the duration. We're prepping paper for treaties and agreements, and hoping like hell that some of them get signed." She was a short, compact woman of middle years, dark of hair and medium complected, a New Indiesian who had worked her way up the documents ranks to become Service Diplomatic's strong right hand.

"He didn't tell me you were here." Jani pointed to the star adorning the collar of the woman's white tunic. "About time."

Frances touched the designator and her face lit. "Thanks." Then her expression clouded. "I'm surprised that poor man can still remember his name, truth be told. This place is a pressure cooker." She looked to her other dinner partner, and some of the animation returned. "Captain Pascal was giving me his eyewitness account of what happened at the riverwalk. My God."

Guess you finally found a place to land. Jani shot Lucien a *shut up* look, which he fielded with an arched brow and a *Who, me?* shrug. "It was an experience." She gave the wine bottle a last look of longing before taking a lemon wedge from the appetizer tray and squeezing it into her iced water, and was trying to think of something innocuous to talk about when a blocky shadow fell across their table.

"Is there room for another?" Scriabin sat before anyone could reply. "To spend one meal not discussing politics would seem like a month's vacation at this point, wouldn't it?" The ground rules thus set, he proceeded to hold forth on everything from wine to olives to the best places in Chicago to buy blintzes and handmade shirts, with occasional interjections from Lucien and encouraging noises from Frances.

Wait staff served and cleared, served and cleared. A salad. Soup. Some sort of fish. All struck Jani's hybrid palate as bland in the extreme, but she ate because she had to and because the company was good and she could feel herself relax even as the night wore on and the next day drew nearer.

Then someone suggested music, and someone else rolled out a synth box, and soon the strains of some band or other sounded. Then Val took over, pushing tables out of the way and pulling a feebly protesting Ulanova onto the floor. A few more couples followed. Word spread, and soon people wandered over from the base and the working part of the embassy, drawn by the open bar and the music and the chance to let off steam that had been building for months.

"Ma'am?" Lucien stood and offered Frances his best recruiting poster smile. "Care to take a turn?"

Frances drank him in, her eyes alight with the effects of the wine and appreciation of blinding male beauty. "Don't ever tell my husband," she whispered to Jani as she took Lucien's hand and followed him onto the floor.

Scriabin watched them for a time and shook his head. "He is an utter waste of talent and training, but I don't know a minister in Chicago who wouldn't kill for ten percent of his charm." He turned back to Jani, arms folded across his barrel chest. "I know you better than you think, you know." He sat back, crossed his legs ankle to knee. "I remember the uproar when my uncle Acton learned that his boy Evan had dropped the family standard and hooked up with a colonial

girlfriend. There the dear scion was, in the alien wilds of
Rauta Shèràa, ignoring all attempts at communication. Acton had already earmarked my cousin Alyssa for him, and
you did not cross Acton van Reuter once he'd made up his
mind." Grey eyes dulled. "My mother tried to play peacemaker. 'Let the boy have his fun,' she said. I think that deep
down, she knew what Evan was, and she didn't want him for
Alyssa. Not that Alyssa was any prize, but even she didn't
deserve Evan. But mother's efforts came to naught, to the
regret of many." He picked up a knife and speared a wedge
of cheese from the dessert platter. "I'm sorry for all that happened. I would have paid a great deal for the opportunity to
see you take on the old Hawk."

Jani looked around the garden. The noise level had
ramped up, taken on an edge. Laughter had grown too shrill.
There would be at least one fistfight before it ended. Affairs
broken and begun. She'd attended enough parties with Evan
to know the signs, had even thrown a few herself under his
guidance. *He lived for this.* Oblivion achieved in noise and
seen through the bottom of a glass. Then came Knevçet
Shèràa, and that final, brutal cleaving. "I'm sorry that the
eradication of the Twelfth Rover Corps and the deaths of a
score of good Spacers came between you and this entertainment."

Scriabin stilled, knife held upright and cheese beneath his
nose for an assessing sniff. Then he grinned, and bit. "See?
That quality of moral anger, tossed out as an afterthought.
I'd have paid much. Not sure if you would've won, mind.
At least not in the long run. Not many did who possessed a
ghost of a conscience." He chewed thoughtfully, then speared
a slice of apple and commenced the same examination he'd
given the cheese. "Did you love Evan?"

Jani looked to the Rauta Shèràa sky for respite, but the
light from the party lanterns overwhelmed the stars. "Worse
than that. I trusted him."

Scriabin winced. "I am sorry." He set the apple aside, put
down the knife. "You will have to forgive my aunt her out-

bursts. She senses this is her last chance to regain former glory, and she sees it slipping away."

Jani looked past Scriabin to the dance floor, where Ulanova still partnered with Val. She smiled brightly at his every joke and comment, but every so often her gaze would drift to Lucien and sharpen. "Did you volunteer to act as her keeper, or did you draw the short straw at a Family meeting?"

Scriabin ignored the question, shifting his chair so he could watch Mako and Niall, who still sat with John and talked, expressions serious and tones low. "Roshi is worried about what tomorrow may bring, as are we all. You have my word that if the worst happens, I will do all in my power to protect Thalassa."

"Can you do anything for Niall?" Jani watched Niall shake his head at something John said. They could have been arguing politics, or opera, or interpretations of *Hamlet*. "They'd call it treason. They'd execute him."

"What do you think are my chances of dragging him from Roshi's side, if it comes to that?" Scriabin sighed. "I would do my best for them all, but they would have to help." He allowed a knowing grin. "Besides, Hiroshi Mako is many things, but suicidal isn't one of them." He rose just as Lucien and Frances returned to the table. "Until tomorrow, ná Jani. Ná Kièrshia. She who tells stories to Haárin by the river." He bowed to Jani and Frances in turn, ignored Lucien, and strode back inside the embassy.

"I think that's supposed to be a hint." Frances glanced at her timepiece and sighed. "When the ministers start decamping, that's the sign that a career-minded officer needs to take to her bed."

"Or someone's bed, at any rate." Lucien didn't sully the remark with a nudge or a wink. He simply left it to hang in the air, to be ignored or picked up as the listener saw fit. "I need to get going as well. Guess who pulled desk officer duty? Three guesses. First two don't count." He bowed to Frances, then leaned down and kissed Jani with all the gentle, patient promise he had set aside earlier in the day.

"God help me, Jani Kilian." Frances watched Lucien walk across the floor and disappear into the embassy maw. "How do you keep your head straight with him around?"

Jani felt a tingle along the side of her face, and looked toward Mako's table to find John watching her. "Sometimes I don't."

"Do tell." Frances checked her timepiece again. "And after all this is over, you will tell. When we have some time to breathe."

Jani hesitated. Then she stood and hugged Frances tightly. "Thank you."

Frances sniffed. "We all do what we have to, girl." Her voice emerged husky, and she covered it with a cough. "Get a good night's sleep."

After Frances left, Jani sat down again, tired and worried, yet loath to leave the music and the sounds of other people having fun. She turned over her unused wineglass and filled it. Took a long drink, tasted the bland sourness of watery grape juice, and pushed the rest aside.

"John said that he has to work on something that would give hybrids a chance to get in on the fun."

Jani smiled as Val sat down next to her. "Hello."

"I've been hearing the most amazing stories about you." Val studied her, then shook his head. "Or perhaps I shouldn't be amazed anymore." He wore one of her favorite evening suits, a rich forest shade that brought out the green in his eyes.

"Those stories may not seem so amazing after tomorrow." Jani took a sip of lemon water to strip the wine taste from her tongue. "We'll see."

Val watched her for a time, then looked toward the dance floor. "Niall said that this party has a Last Days of Empire edge to it. Mako told him to pull his head out of his ass for five minutes and loosen up, but he was three sheets to the wind at that point. I don't think he meant it."

"Did Niall have anything to drink?"

"Not a drop." Val made a point of studying his hands. "How are you?"

"Business as usual. Everyone's pick for Diplomat of the Year." Jani looked to the dancers again to find John intertwined with a lissome redhead in civilian wear. *And so it goes.* "You?"

A breeze sent the lanterns rocking. As Val watched his business partner dance, the light played across his face, accenting the lines and hollows. "He's sorry, you know." He picked up a fork and dragged it across the table, leaving grooves in the cloth. "He wishes he could take it back, what he said at Guernsey Station, but he doesn't know how."

"And so he has Valentin Parini, his eternal apologist, stop by to feel things out while he feels up the embassy staff." Jani laughed a little too long, then forced herself quiet. "It's over, Val. Your services as peacemaker are no longer required. Let it be."

Val shifted as though he sat on a tack. "I'm sorry." He looked toward the floor again, and fixed on a sharp lieutenant with black hair and a crooked smile.

"I can look after myself, you know." Jani smiled as Val blushed. "Go have fun." She squeezed his hand as he kissed her cheek, then left her to go hunting.

Ulanova had long since departed. Val laid claim to his lieutenant and escorted him to Mako's table, the panicked expression on the young man's face a sight for the ages.

Jani sat, and listened to the laughter and the shouts and the music, to the growing disquiet that pushed all else aside. Then she rose and went on a hunt of her own.

Jani followed Ulanova's aide into a sitting room. Left to her own devices, she paced the perimeter, studying the framed paintings and wondering why the peach silk walls didn't make her feel warmer. Paced some more. Studied more brush strokes and compared the quality of frame gilding. She expected Ulanova to make her wait, and wasn't disappointed. She was well into her fourth detailed examination of a Russian provincial landscape when she heard the door open.

"What do you want?" Ulanova remained in the entry, one hand gripping the jamb. She had exchanged her severe trouser suit for a flowing crimson skirt and white wrapshirt, and had freshened her hair and makeup.

If we were still in Chicago, I'd guess dinner on Gaetan's patio. Or the opera, or some other formal occasion. Of which there were damn few to be had in the humanish enclave in Rauta Shèràa. "I don't want to talk to you any more than you want to listen to me, so I'll be brief. If you back out of this and leave them to twist, I will dredge up every crime you ever committed, every misstep you ever took, and hang you with them."

Ulanova's face flushed. "You have nothing."

"Only experience." Jani smiled. "And a very good source of information." She hesitated as she wondered if she could possibly be wrong, and then realized that it had been as obvious as the sky overhead. "Could I please talk to the desk officer, ma'am?" she asked in her best imitation of a new recruit. "I understand he's here."

Ulanova stared. Then the first flicker of triumph brightened her eyes and she smiled. "Darling?" When nothing happened, her voice took on an edge. "I don't think there's any point, I really don't."

Another moment of stillness. Then Lucien emerged from the next room. He'd loosened his tunic collar and held a glass of wine.

Jani started to laugh. *Like a cat, from house to house to house—* She forced herself calm. "I'd like to talk to him, please."

Ulanova headed for the security call pad. "Go to hell."

"Excellency." Jani held out a hand. Heard her papa's Celtic lilt in her voice and wondered how she'd managed to dredge it up. "Even the condemned get a final wish granted."

Ulanova stopped and stared, mistrust and puzzlement warring on the narrow battleground of her face. Then she smiled again, because that was what her kind did when they felt they'd won. "Ten minutes, darling." She waved a heavily ringed hand in Lucien's general direction and swept into the adjoining room.

"Got that, darling?" Jani walked up to Lucien and clapped her hands under his nose, took what pleasure she could in his flinch. "Ten minutes." She backed away before she caught a glass of wine in her face. "How did she foist you off on Mako? That's what I want to know."

"Mako trusts Scriabin to keep her in line." Lucien's voice emerged low and tight. "Taking me on was part of the deal they devised to shut her up."

Jani leaned against a chair. Fatigue had caught up with her, and her knees felt weak. Or maybe it was just self-disgust, and growing anger too great to control. "What she does to Niall, I do to you. If he's arrested, I'll see you're arrested. If he's condemned, I'll do all I can to ensure that you take his place."

Lucien stared into his glass, then set it down on a table so hard that it splashed. "You're bluffing."

"You think I wouldn't trade you for Niall?" Jani saw his eyes narrow and knew that he'd guessed her answer.

"You don't have anything negotiable." Lucien shook his head. "No information to offer in exchange."

"But you told me so much when we lived in Chicago." Jani shrugged. "When I had time on my hands, I even confirmed some of it."

Lucien took a lid off a candy dish, then set it back in place with a clatter. "I do have safeguards in place."

"To use against me?" Jani caught the slight twitch of his head. "Oh, you don't, do you? You actually trusted me. That's sweet. Maybe you really do love me after all." She jerked her chin toward the adjoining room, where no doubt Ulanova listened with clenched teeth. "Your girlfriend's waiting. Time to drop those well-tailored trousers and earn your keep." She headed for the door. Heard the footsteps behind her and tried to dodge, but Lucien was younger and faster and pissed off to boot. He grabbed her arm and spun her around, ducking out of the way as she swung her fist, then pushing her against the wall with all the force he hadn't spent on her earlier.

Jani made ready to propel off the wall. Brought her fist up once more. Felt the idomeni in her whisper for blood. Then her eyes met Lucien's and she saw how his shone. How bright his face, like a young boy's, his breathing hard and fast.

He took a step toward her, then hesitated. "I can be out of here in an hour." His voice had dropped to a whisper. "Two at the most."

As though someone flipped a switch, Jani felt her own heart slow, her head clear. "You've always played both sides." She straightened her skewed tunic. "You always told me that you did me more good than harm, that you were my insider, but it was all just talk. You were just covering your ass. Shoring up your fallback. Making sure you'd have a soft place to land no matter what happened. No matter who won. You never risked anything you couldn't afford to lose. People, idomeni, humanish, and hybrid are in danger for their lives now. Risking everything to change worlds. You don't deserve to breathe the same air." She walked to the door, twisted the handle so the workings screeched, and shouldered through the gap into the corridor.

"Is that supposed to hurt me? Make me regret my wasted life?" Lucien followed her into the hall. "I'm not an idiot! Do you hear me? I'm not one of your damned fools!"

Jani pushed past the door into the stairwell, down the stairs and through a safety door into the night. Music still sounded from the garden. Voices and laughter. Noise. Nothing but noise.

CHAPTER 30

Rilas knew that Cèel had ordered Ansu to kill her. Three times that day, Ansu had brought her the same drink as before, the pale brown brew that was supposed to enliven her. She assumed that she should still pretend to feel tired, that such would be Ansu's excuse to drug her further. *Then when I am too lethargic, they will drown me, or send me downstairs.* A natural death. An accident.

They should have sent another such as me to perform this task. It was an insult to treat the one who had killed Tsecha in such a way as this. Rilas could hear Caith's laughter in the night as she pondered the injustice.

"Glories of this night to you, nìaRauta Rilas." Ansu entered the room bearing the tray that held the pale brown poison. "I trust you enjoyed your time outside and you are no longer as tired?"

"You ask me the same thing each time you visit, Ansu, and each time my answer is the same." Rilas raised an arm, let it fall. "I still am most tired. I am this way because you seek to poison me."

"Poison?" Ansu set down the tray on a table, took the

top off the decanter and poured. "No, nìaRauta, this is a tea brewed from blessed leaves . . . "

Rilas slipped out of the bed. Ansu thought her drugged, and would not expect rapid movement. Would not expect her to behave as she had been trained. She crept across the floor, bare feet silent on the tile. Closed in behind Ansu. Raised her hand, then brought it down where neck met shoulder, as she had with the humanish male.

Ansu fell just as hard. Twitched a little more. Died just as quickly.

Rilas stripped off the physician-priest's clothing, working quickly in case bladder or bowels released and soiled them. Overrobe first, the most important thing, followed by shirt and trousers. Boots.

That unseemly task completed, she dragged Ansu's body to the bed and hoisted it atop. Covered it, making sure to turn her face from the door and tuck the covering high enough to obscure all aspects of her appearance.

Rilas then straightened the overrobe, picked up the tray and departed the room. Few idomeni walked the corridor, and none regarded her in any way. She set the tray upon a rack designed for such things and walked to the entry. Her heart beat harder as the door opened and she passed outside, felt the blessed night air in her face.

I will go to the Trade Board. She kept many things in her workroom there. Things given her by Cèel, and other things that he would not expect her to have.

The streets between the hospital and the Trade Board were much as they always were, filled with merchants and brokers, even in the middle of the night. None noticed her, for which she gave thanks, as the coarser Haárin traders were known for stopping physician-priests in the street and requesting remedies for various ailments.

She entered the Trade Board, passed from corridor to stairway to corridor, ever upward until she reached the last ring of workrooms at the base of the dome. She had never told anyone of this place. The door operated by a simple touchlock that was not connected to the board array, which meant that no one knew when she entered or departed. She had originally taken the workroom in order to practice secrecy, the possession of knowledge known to her and her alone. As the time passed and she grew more familiar with the concept, she began to store things in the room as well. Weapons. Documents. Clothing. Remains from previous tasks that she had been ordered to destroy but had not.

She kept them as secrets instead.

Rilas unlocked the door. Opened it and activated the illumination to a low level. Stepped over boxes and crates until she came to that which she sought.

The projectile rifle, similar to the one that she had used to assassinate Tsecha, lay in pieces. She assembled it quickly, then removed the packet of ammunition from the bottom of the crate and inserted one cartridge into place. Took the secondary from its container and activated it, confirming that it communicated with the sight mech.

Then she set the weapons aside and lay on the floor. When morning came, she would show Cèel how wrong he had been to mistrust her. How ungodly it was to have treated her as he did.

I did as you bade. She closed her eyes. *I would have come to you freely.* Now such did not matter. Whether he wished her to or not, she would come to him all the same.

They gathered in the embassy drive at the base time of oh-eight, which on this day fell approximately one hour after early morning sacrament.

Jani smoothed the front of her overrobe, a needless exercise that spoke to nerves more than wrinkled cloth.

"Good morning." Scriabin left Lucien and Ulanova by their triple-length and strode over to her, his the clear-eyed gaze of a Family politician who had learned long ago how to pace himself. "Slept well, I trust?"

"Well enough." Jani turned her back on Lucien and forced a smile.

"We've heard word of a little bit of a dust-up around Temple, but it isn't expected to interfere with the conclave." Scriabin pulled out a set of sunshields from a small slingbag and donned them. "We will leave in ten minutes or so."

"I guess that means all our drivers can still drive?" Niall drew alongside Jani and glared at her over the top of his sunshields. "You haven't delivered any more sermons, have you?"

"It wasn't a sermon." Jani thought she sounded calm enough, but Niall and Scriabin shot each other looks that she read as easily as though she could see their eyes through the shields.

"We'll be going in Roshi's skim. I'll leave my shooter there since I can't carry it into the damned place." Niall started toward the starred triple-length, beckoning Jani to follow. "Everything OK, gel?" he asked when they moved out of Scriabin's earshot.

Jani looked to the sky, still streaked with early morning cloud. "The time is out of joint."

"Oh bloody hell. When you start tossing the quotations around, it's all over but the last rites." Niall pulled a case out of his trouser pocket. "Here." He handed Jani a new ear bug. "Because I have a feeling that you lost the last one."

"Can't use it." Jani tried to hand it back to him. "I need water to prep it."

"Fountain right over there." Niall led her to a small grassy side yard where a brass dish burbled merrily away. "If you have trouble inserting it, I'll be happy to find you a plunger." He stood silent guard as she prepped and inserted the bug, then whistled a verse of the Service anthem as he led her to Roshi's skimmer.

The cavalcade departed the embassy, sweeping through the enclave at speed, then slowing to a grind as they merged with the inevitability of well-ordered idomeni traffic. By the time they reached the entry to the Council enclave, Feyó and Meva had already arrived. They stood next to their skimmer, bracketed by Dathim and Galas.

"Something has happened." Feyó looked toward the Council entrance, where a greater than normal number of brown-garbed security guards had arrayed themselves. "But no one will tell us. Security dominants only stare when we speak to them. It is most unseemly."

Meva turned and started toward the Council entry's triple-wide doorway, beckoning for Jani walk with her. "Feyó told me that she again saw ní Tsecha during sleep. He bared his teeth. I wish I could have such dreams. Such a sight I used to see each day and did not think of it. Now I think of it constantly, and wish I could see it again." She quickened her step so she could walk next to Jani, a blip in the steady state of idomeni hierarchical protocols. "I viewed images of you speaking of him to the Haárin. Such was a good thing, and truly." She touched the sleeve of Jani's overrobe. "Do you know that which you will say?"

Jani shook her head. "No idea."

Meva bared her teeth. "Good. If you do not know, then Cèel cannot possibly guess, which means he cannot prepare."

They continued along the walkway, up the steps and through the entry, side by side.

Rilas awoke. Removed Ansu's clothing and donned the rough garb of a building worker, wrapping the braids of her breeder's fringe in a length of cloth and binding them to her head so she would look as a shorn-headed Haárin. Packed the ammunition and the secondary in a worker's slingbag, then broke down the rifle and packed that as well. Opened the workroom door and looked both ways. She heard nothing, saw no one. The workrooms at the base of the dome were not of the best, and not many used them. She was alone, of that she felt most sure.

She walked down the corridor to the stairway and down, down and down to the street. Busy as always in the morning, both bornsect and Haárin, workers and brokers and merchants, entering and leaving. She blended with them, as she had been taught.

A pair of brown-garbed security suborns walked past her. She thought nothing of such—Council and Temple lay near and many security labored there.

Then she saw another pair, and another, and knew. That Ansu's body had been found and Cèel now searched for her. She bared her teeth at the thought. *You did not wish to see me, nìRau, but now you wish to see me a great deal.*

She walked as a tired worker, her gait plodding, and headed north toward the Haárin enclave. She saw fewer security suborns as she neared the place, which she expected. Haárin took charge of their own. They also did not work well with Cèel's security, who demanded much and provided little. She doubted, and truly, that they knew anything of the search for her.

She approached the enclave entry. Walked past the gate sentry, who did not look up as she passed. Down the first lane of houses, in search of one that was empty.

A small house, with a window that faced the bay.

All she needed was a window. The secondary would do the rest.

She set the bag upon the floor. Assembled the rifle and inserted the ammunition cartridge. Activated the secondary and loosed it, watched it flit upward until it vanished. Activated the sight mech and waited for the blinking green indicating that the two had interfaced.

Rested the rifle barrel within the window corner. Looked through the sight mech and saw the Council grounds.

Click

The line of windows that faced the gardens.

Click

Through the windows, into the Council chamber beyond. Rilas curled around the rifle. Held it close.

Waited.

* * *

Jani entered the Council chamber. It was a multistoried space, the masonry cut by windows on the side facing the bay, tiered seating lining the other three walls.

Tsecha brought me here once. He had still been bornsect in that time before the war, had still used his born name of Nema. How that name had sounded along the corridors when the other Council members realized that the propitiator of the Vynshà had brought one of his humanish inside the blessed space.

At least it was not Temple, one of the councilors had said. That fact hadn't helped.

Jani matched the room she remembered with the room she stood in now. The same pale sand walls and tiled floors, the Sìah chandeliers and artwork of all the major bornsects. The bombs had missed it, a miracle, given the battering the Vynshà inflicted on the city before they entered it on that last night. The night the Laum lost the right to call themselves "rau." The night eighty-five percent of their bornsect population died. The Night of the Blade.

"It is most as it was," Meva said as she paused next to her. "Most as I recall." She stared out the window at the bay, then followed Feyó to the seating.

Jani looked to the entry on the other side of the chamber. First would come the line of suborns, lowliest first. Then the dominant aides, followed by the Sub-Oligarch and the Speaker to Colonies. Then would come Cèel.

Jani's heart tripped and slowed as the first of the suborns filed through the entry and the councilors walked to their seats and the humanish groups broke up and scattered to their preassigned positions. She walked toward the tiered seats where the propitiators gathered. *I accused his killers. I walked behind his reliquary.* Wore his rings, and his robe. Held his soul. *I have the right.*

Jani felt the stares, heard the questioning mutters, as she stepped over the lowest, highest rated, tier and on to the second. She triangulated according to her relationship with

Tsecha, the size of Thalassa, and the status due to her Vynshàrau blood. The number of times she had fought in the
circle. Given all that, the fourth row seemed fair. Three rows
lower than Meva, who watched her silently. Not presuming
much, but not giving anything away, either. Pushing just
enough, as was her way.

"Kilian?"

Jani sat, then looked down toward the floor to find a
flustered-looking Scriabin trying to lean over the seats to
talk to her without falling over any agitated priests.

"What the . . . ?" He almost placed his hand over his
mouth, but stopped in time and put it behind his back instead. "What are you doing?"

"This is my place, Your Excellency." Jani spread out
her overrobe as she saw a few other propitiators had done,
expanding her personal space a little more. "Given all I've
done and what I am, it is an appropriate place, and truly."
She bared her teeth. "Go sit down." She flicked a finger in
the direction of Ulanova and the others, who stood in the
middle of the floor and looked on in alarm.

"Do you know what the hell you're doing?" Scriabin's
face reddened. "Do you?"

"I do that which I do, Your Excellency. I am that which
I am." Jani folded her hands in her lap and turned her atten-
tion to the entry in time to see the Speaker to Colonies enter.
"Go sit down."

"What the hell are you doing, gel?" Niall's voice in her
ear.

Jani didn't reply, didn't hunt for Niall's face among the
many. She ignored his intrusion as she ignored Scriabin's
continued bids to get her attention, and waited.

Morden nìRau Cèel had always cut an imposing figure. A dour warrior who stood over two meters tall, dark
as Vynshàrau but with the green eyes of Sìah. He had led
the Vynshà armies and their Haárin cohorts during the final
stages of the War of Vynshàrau Ascension, had spent the last

weeks of that war in the hills that ringed Rauta Shèràa. First he'd directed the bombings that shattered half the city. Then, on that last night, he had ordered the Haárin to swarm over what remained, blades in hand, and slaughter the Laum who remained.

Such is what they do, what they had done for thousands of years. Such is how idomeni wage war. And the human-ish side of Jani still reeled from the memory. Of the lines of Laum, standing in line as for bread or billets, their shirts open, waiting for the sword.

Cèel walked directly to his low seat in the front row of the Vynshàrau section, crossed his ankles and lowered to the floor. His status thus announced, he finally looked around the chamber. His gaze settled first on Feyó, who had taken a seat in another tier with other Sìah Haárin, then on Meva. He gestured to her, baring his teeth when she curved her shoulders in reply.

Then he looked toward the humanish seats, which had been scattered throughout the chamber with no rhyme or reason that Jani could discern.

Two reasons I can think of for that. She fussed with an overrobe cuff. *One is symbolic—dilute the hated human-ish.* The other made tactical sense—split the enemy. Prevent them from conferring, comparing notes. Offering one an-other moral support. She watched Cèel as he continued to scan the seats, once, then again, then again. As though he searched for someone. His gaze moved over the propitiators' tiers and he stilled. Cocked his head.

Then his shoulders curved as though they cramped, and the voice that made John's sound like air through a tin whistle boomed.

"You dare! Anathema! Half-humanish thing!" High Vyn-shàrau, replete with gesture, curve of hand and twist of arm and neck, the click and clatter of translator headsets being jammed into place serving as background music.

Jani glanced at the headset that hung from a hook on the

seat in front of her. Realized she didn't need it. The Vynshàrau sounded as Acadian French to her ears, a language of dreams, basic as breathing. *"I am that which I am and I sit where I will."* She pitched her voice low as a show of aggravation and lack of respect, but didn't curve her shoulders just yet. *"I killed Laumrau as they took sacrament, contaminated godly ceremony with humanish action. Humanish filth."* Her heart beat strong and her limbs felt as the air as rage that had built since Tsecha's death took hold. *"But I was humanish then. Such was my excuse."* She bared her teeth. *"What was yours, Morden nìRau Cèel? For killing ní Tsecha Egri as he stood upon a road, forsaking godly challenge and the cleansing act of war? What excuse had you to kill him secretly, in such a way that sickens even humanish?"* Finally, she let her shoulders curve, until her back twisted so she could barely see over the priest who sat in front of her. *"If I am anathema, what are you?"*

The inside of the Council chamber played across the sight mech. Rilas fixed on the edge of the dark head, the curve of neck that she knew as well as her own. Then Cèel moved back, beyond the scope of the secondary, the view blocked by a section of brick.

Rilas twitched the settings on the sight mech, forcing the secondary higher until it cleared the section of wall. If she had planned better, she would have stolen a hair from Cèel's head, a drop of his blood, and typed the secondary to him so it would sense him as the one made for Tsecha had sensed its target. *If I had planned . . . if I had known.* But she could not have known. Betrayal was, Cèel had taught her, a humanish failing.

She twitched the setting again. Again.

Cèel rose, his back a crippling curve, and started across the floor toward Jani.

"You think if you rise, you lose standing?" Jani stood,

straightening her spine as much as she could. *"I can stand before you and still call you what you are."* She stepped over the bench, then down to the next, then down to the floor as Cèel scrabbled toward her.

Rilas fixed on the dark head. Held her breath.

Pressed the charge-through.

Jani heard. A muffled bang, as though a bird struck a window.

Glass, clattering to the floor. A splash of blood.

A beat of silence. Then the humanish screams, the idomeni cries.

Security dominants surrounded Cèel, who pressed a hand to his face, blood seeping between his fingers. Humanish security herded their charges away from windows and idomeni leapt down from the tiered seats.

"Jan!" Niall ran to her. "Get over—" He grabbed her wrist and pulled her to the side near the main entry, where Scriabin and the others stood clustered.

"Who do you think fired that shot?" Jani tried to pull out of his grip, but he had her like a manacle and all she could do was follow.

Galas stood talking with Burkett, his hand locked around Feyó's wrist just as Niall's was around Jani's.

"Galas said that there was an unusual amount of activity on the Council security frequencies earlier this morning." Niall continued to herd Jani toward the wall. "He tried to eavesdrop, but he was blocked. Tried to tap an old source, but all he could get was that there was an accident at the Temple hospital. A physician-priest died in an accident."

"Who sends out hot and cold running security guards because of accidents? They were stacked two deep in front of the entry when we arrived." Jani gripped Niall's fingers with her free hand and tried to pry them open. "Look at Cèel."

Niall turned just as the male pulled a security dominant

to one side, started talking in a manner stripped of gesture. "Jan, he's just been through an assassination attempt—"

"Those aren't the moves of an Oligarch who's just been shot at and is taking instruction from his security team. Those are the moves of a ringleader directing the show."

"He's a warrior, for chrissake."

"He knows who shot at him, and he's pretty sure where she is, and he's telling his security dominants where to find her." Jani tried to bend her arm to break Niall's hold, but he countered that move as well. "They kept Rilas at the Temple hospital. She escaped. She killed a physician-priest in the process." She sensed others move close to her. Only Ulanova hung back, her bitterness like armor. "They know where she is and they're going to track her down and lock her up or kill her. We need to get to her first."

"Well where the hell is she?" Niall looked to the heavens. "In this whole damned city, where in hell?"

"She feels a closeness to Caith," said Galas, who now grappled with a squirming Meva. "Such was what the others on the ship stated when they were questioned at Guernsey."

"Caith's temple is north of here, the same direction as the shot came from." Jani smiled. "I know where it is."

"I'll take you." Lucien turned away from a grasping Ulanova and maneuvered next to Jani.

"We'll take her." Niall looked toward the main entry. "If they'll fuckin' let us out of here."

They moved toward the main entry, found it blocked by Haárin and humanish and the guards who'd herded them there.

"There's a side door." Jani reversed and hurried up a narrow corridor that ran alongside the chamber. "Tsecha and I once escaped through it when some councilors took exception to my presence."

"Can't imagine why that would have happened." Niall stepped in front of her. "I'm going first, just in case."

Jani fell in behind him. On the way, they passed a wall decorated, as most were in the place, with sets of blades, foursomes and pairs, arranged in squares or crossed like X's.

Jani took one of the shorter blades from its hook and slipped it into her belt, then followed Niall out the door.

CHAPTER 31

Rilas dropped the rifle, left it where it fell. Grabbed her bag. Ran. Out of the house, into the street. She had never missed a target. Never.

The blessed sun—she felt its heat, even as it failed to warm. Her heart pounded and her hands felt as though she had washed them in snow. *He will kill me now.* Cèel knew she had killed Ansu, knew she sought to kill him.

She slowed as she came upon Haárin. Rough clothes, as bright in color as birds and insects. Ungodly. They watched her pass, eyes on her face. She turned away.

But not in time.

"You!" An elder male strode after her. *"Tileworker!"* He waved for her to approach, a humanish gesture that made no sense, relayed no mood or status of request. He could ask her anything. She would not know what to expect until he did so.

"My friend and I—" He waved toward another male, who sat on a chair on front of a house, and bared his teeth when she looked toward him. "—we have a wager. I say that all tileworkers use hand-axes instead of short picks. He says otherwise. We are stopping every tileworker we see to ask them, axe or pick."

Rilas forced a humanish shrug. "Hand-axe," she said, and turned to go.

"*No.*" The elder male stepped in front of her, blocking her path. "You must show us."

They claimed a compact two-door from one of the embassy drivers. Stopped by Roshi's skimmer so Niall and Lucien could recover their weapons, and sped through the Council gate just as it closed. Jani drove because she knew the city best.

"Where are you going?" Niall flinched as they coursed down an alley that allowed only a hand span's clearance on either side.

"Caith's temple." She zipped along a tight roundabout, causing the skimmer to tip up on its side and drawing mutters from the rear of the vehicle.

"*You'll lose contact with the skimtrack.*" Lucien braced his hands on the cabin wall and his seat. "This isn't a damned sports skimmer."

"I spotted at least twenty-five security folk headed into the Trade Board as we passed." Niall ignited a 'stick. "Do they think she shot at Cèel from there?"

"I doubt it." Jani slowed as the alleys grew even narrower, the buildings closer together, blocking the sun and making it seem at times as through she drove through a tunnel. "Her Nahin Sela identity was based there. I'm guessing that others were, too. Cèel is going to bottle up anyone who can identify her and shake loose as many records and other physical evidence as he can."

"So where does that leave us?" Niall sat forward, checking each alley and dead end. "If he destroys all evidence and captures the killer, what have we got?" He turned to her. "What are you going to do?"

Jani saw the tarnished silver dome in the distance, the temple of Caith. Kept driving, and said nothing. Touched her right ear, activated the ear bug, and heard the Vynshàrau spill into her head. "Cèel's security is using one of your streams."

Niall touched his ear. His brow arched. "They must think Rilas has the ability to eavesdrop on all of theirs, so they hijacked one of ours." He frowned. "You understand what they're saying?"

Jani nodded. "They think the shot came from the Haárin enclave." She paused, smiled. "They're headed toward Caith's temple. They're going to capture her there."

Niall unfastened the top of his shooter holster. "Let's go."

Rilas stood with her hand on the opening of her slingbag.

"You must show us—axe or pick." The elder male edged to one side or the other each time Rilas tried to walk around him. "You could say anything."

"Why would I do such? It is not godly."

"Hah. She speaks as a bornsect." The other male bared his teeth again. "The bornsect tilemasters use picks."

"Are you a bornsect?" The elder male tugged on Rilas's sleeve. "In clothes such as this? In an Haárin enclave?" He laughed, a guttural hacking sound.

"I do not have to show you what I use." Rilas pulled away as the elder male sought to grab her sleeve again. Broke into a run when he sought to chase her, and heard their jeering as she turned off that street and onto another.

Cèel knows where I run to. Rilas knew that bornsect security waited outside the Haárin enclave, that they patrolled the streets around the temples. She reached into the bag, gripped a shooter, held it fast.

Past the meeting house, the workrooms, the schools for the youngish. She drew near the enclave gate and quickened her pace.

"It's so goddamned dark here." Niall looked out at the claustrophobic press, the tarnished metalwork and dark woods and streets with barely enough room for one being to pass another. "Who lives here?"

"Those who serve Caith. Propitiators. Trainees. Temple maintenance." Jani eased the skimmer into an alley.

"This is not a search." Lucien watched the scene outside his skimmer window and shook his head. "They aren't cordoning off the streets. They aren't going house to house."

"I see bodies scurrying across rooftops." Jani pointed to a figure that vanished in the shadow of an overhang. "They're herding her as unobtrusively as they can. They know where she's going. We just need to get there first." She powered down the vehicle and opened her door.

"What are you doing?" Niall looked around. "This isn't Caith's temple."

"I need to slip through the net." Jani lifted the overrobe's draped shawl collar over her head like a hood, hiding her short hair and obscuring her face.

"Dammit, Jan." Niall pushed open his door and struggled out. "You can't meet her like this. She's desperate and she's armed." He circled around the front of the vehicle. "Jan?" He stopped, turned in one direction, then the other. "What the fuck—"

Jani backpedaled down an alley narrow as a knife slice, listened to the garbled mix of Vynshàrau and Niall's voice through the ear bug. Heard Lucien, and realized he wore a bug as well. *And he understands Vynshàrau.* But not as well as she did.

"She ducked down that alley." Lucien's voice held resignation, anger. *"We'll never find her now."*

"We should've stopped her." Niall's voice now. *"Dammit."* Sounds of him getting into the skimmer, slamming down the gullwing so hard that the sound echoed.

Jani crept down the alley. Found another. Another. Candlewax and wood oils. The damp that found a home in the dark and the shadow. She smelled them all, remembered them all. From a quarter century before, when Tsecha had brought them here, the six humanish he had chosen above all.

Caith is a damned thing, but she serves some purpose, for you cannot have order without its opposite. But for Caith, blessed Shiou would have no reason to be. They had all called him *inshah* then, and hung on his every word.

She stopped at the end of an alley that opened onto a
wider road. Across the road, a blackened building with a
double door entry, topped by a tarnished silver dome.

In the distance, faint sounds. The hum and whine of skimmers. The never-ending Vynshàrau pouring into her head.

Running feet. Growing nearer.

Jani reached into her pocket, closed her hand around the
hilt of the blade, and waited.

Caith called to her. Rilas heard her voice in the pound of
blood in her ears, the pain in her knees, her weakness. She
ran through alleys, walkways, avoiding the larger streets
down which the security skimmers coursed.

She could see the blackened temple dome, the most
blessed of sights. Quickened her pace even as she knew her
heart would burst. They would keep her here, protect her
here.

Then from the corner of her eye, she saw. A propitiator,
head covered, emerge from an alley and walk across the narrow street toward the entry.

"Inshah!" Rilas forced the cry even as the strain tore her
lungs. *"Inshah—ha'alan elas!"* Teacher—wait for me.

The priest slowed but did not stop. Rilas ran to her.
Reached out to grab her overrobe, to bid her to stop, to raise
her arms before her and beg for protection.

"Inshah! Ha'alan elas! Inshah!"

The propitiator turned, too quickly. Rilas caught sight of
the pale eye. In the way of the fighter, she looked down at the
propitiator's hand, and saw the darkness where none should
have been.

Tried to stop. But could not.

Felt the blade—and saw—the face—

Jani braced and staggered back as Rilas barreled into her. Felt
the blade go in, and jammed it deeper. In and up, toward the
heart. The female's eyes widened even as they clouded. Her lips
moved even as blood trickled from the corner of her mouth.

"On your Way, you will pass a shade that awaits the soul of the greatest idomeni." Jani felt wet warmth down the front of her overrobe as Rilas slumped forward and her blood flowed. "And when you pass it you will say, ní Tsecha Egri, I am Imea nìaRauta Rilas, who killed you." She gripped the back of Rilas's headcloth and yanked her head up, stared into the snake-boned face, the dulling eyes. "Because every murdered being deserves to see the face of the one who killed them. Such is orderly." Her eyes burned and her voice keened through a tightening throat. "So says the priest." The female's body slumped again, and Jani felt her last breath leave.

"Let her fall."

Jani looked up to find Lucien standing a few strides away. Behind him, Niall, still running.

"Let her fall." Lucien took a step forward, then pointed to the ground. "She's dead. Let her drop."

Jani pushed Rilas off her shoulder. The female fell back, her weight and the angle of her collapse yanking the blade from Jani's hand.

She felt their eyes on her. Niall, sad, resigned. Lucien—

I know what you want. You want to watch them die.

—the professional—

You want to look into their eyes and watch the light go out.

—shaking his head in disgust, then walking to the body and commencing an odd search, feeling her hair, her ears, down the back of her neck. "There's nothing here. Her book is gone. They must have removed it after they captured her."

While Lucien searched the body, Niall picked through the slingbag. "There's enough firepower in here to blow out a wall—why the hell didn't she use it?"

"She thought she'd entered refuge." Lucien stood, then pulled a dispo cloth from his trouser pocket and wiped his hands. "Perhaps she didn't think she needed it."

"More fool her." Niall continued his search. "What do they look like?"

Lucien held up his hand, thumb and forefinger five or so centimeters apart. "Like an imager, but a little larger. It's more sensitive, more complex. Adjustable."

"Anything like this?" Jani pulled the bug from her ear. It splayed across her hand, soft and cool and clear, like something from the sea.

Lucien shook his head. "Not really."

"Will it do in a pinch?" Jani closed her hand to keep the bug from drying out. "From a distance, will he be able to tell?"

Before Lucien could answer, Niall pointed toward the far end of the street, now blocked by a cluster of skimmers. Security guards emerged and walked toward them, shooters raised. "Cavalry finally arrived."

Jani ignored them, bending to Rilas's body and pulling at the blade. It didn't budge at first—she grasped the hilt harder, almost lost her hold because of the blood, pulled again. A muffled *click* sounded as the blade came free, broken, a third of its length left behind.

"What has hap—" The security dominant stopped when he saw the knife, the blood, the overrobe.

"You will take me back." Jani wiped the blade upon the sleeve of her overrobe, then returned it to her pocket. Stepped around the body, past Niall and Lucien, to the end of the alley and the waiting skimmers.

The Council guards opened the gate to them, the entry, then flowed in after them and closed and barred the doors.

Jani entered the chamber. Saw that they all watched her. Scriabin, so pale. Ulanova, uncertain. Burkett. Frances. They stood against one wall with the other humanish, spectators at another civilization's turn of fate.

The crowd parted until no one stood between Jani and Cèel. He stood at the far end of the room with the other Vynshàrau, had fallen silent upon Jani's arrival. Between them, worked into the floor with squares of faded red stone and tile, a circle about five meters in diameter. A circle in which an idomeni fought both as Nema and as Tsecha. A circle that had once been stained by his blood.

Jani pulled her ear bug from her pocket and raised it above her head, shifting her hand so the light struck it, so Cèel could see it.

Cèel stood rigid, eyes fixed on some spot at her feet. Then, slow as a rising sun, he raised his head and fixed on the bug.

"In the name of my teacher, whom you killed, I challenge you." Jani could barely hear her own words for the roaring in her head, wondered if Cèel heard them at all.

Then she saw him nod once.

The sense of the idomeni changed then, from on edge and uncertain to sure and precise, as actors in a familiar play. Bornsect and Haárin fanned out and moved to seats assigned based on skein and standing, leaving humanish to mill about like sheep in a pen until Feyó and Galas took them in hand and led them to appropriate places.

"Jan." Niall moved in beside her. "I keep you in the circle and I declare the fight ended if you can't go on." He wiped a hand over a face gone grey. "Dammit, is this—"

"Kièrshia?"

Jani turned to find Dathim standing behind her, Meva at his side.

"He will kill you." Dathim spoke as softly as ever he had. "He is of the warrior skein. He is larger, stronger, faster, and more skilled. He had fought in the circle many times." He stepped forward. "I will fight him. I will—"

"It's not your fight, Dathim."

"I was his suborn as well as you!"

"I was his student. He was my teacher." Jani slipped off her bloody overrobe, handed it to Niall. "If he kills me, use it. Break him with it." She turned toward the circle. Blood sang in her ears. Sweat tingled her scalp. She sensed the room as brighter, thought for a moment that the illumination had intensified. *No—this is how it feels to fight as Haárin.* An augielike focus. A sharpening of the senses.

He will kill you.

"Then I will see his face." She started to walk toward the circle, found her way blocked by a male bornsect. Taller than Cèel, and even more scarred. She stared him in the face, and he looked to the side, revealing a gnarl of an ear, half of it sliced away. He pushed a tray of blades at her and pointed to the one she should take, the one that Cèel as the challenged had chosen. A curved Sìah, a sleek crescent with a barbed tip. She picked it up, then walked past him and stepped inside the circle.

Cèel waited on the other side. The scarred male took his place behind him, whispered in his ear.

Jani saw a propitiator out of the corner of her eye, gesturing prayers and invocations against demons. Sànalàn, Tsecha's suborn, who betrayed him.

Keep your prayers. She said her own. To Ganesh. Remover of obstacles. *Guide my hand, Lord.*

She crouched as Dathim had taught her, bent forward at the waist, one leg ahead of the other, arms outstretched to take the hacks of her opponent's blade. Then she tucked her arms in a little to protect her sides, her ribs, and stood on the balls of her feet so she could move more quickly. As if it would help.

He will kill you.

Knife fights never lasted long, especially mismatches.

Cèel moved in first. A short stab that nicked Jani's left wrist, sent rose-pink carrier dripping to the floor. She stepped in it as she tried to parry, felt her boots slide.

Another quick move by Cèel. Another hack, to her right arm this time.

Jani brought up her blade as Cèel backed off, caught his right wrist, sent the blood spraying to the tile. Heard no cries from the assembled. No cheers. Because this was not that sort challenge. Because sometimes knives slipped, and all knew that this would be one of those times.

Another circling. Another thrust parried. Another. Another.

Then Cèel stepped in. Brought his blade arm around just as Jani brought her knife up. Struck her wrist hard, metal on skin and nerve and bone.

Jani's hand flew open as pain sang up her arm. The blade flashed flame as it tumbled through the air.

Cèel closed in. Gripped her around the waist with his free hand as though they danced. Jani brought up her knee to strike him in the groin, but he lifted her like a doll, shifted her so she struck his thigh instead. She looked him in the face to find he looked in hers as well, eyes like new grass frozen in ice. Then he bared his teeth—

—and sound receded—time—each heartbeat a year—

—and drove in the blade—

—warmth flowing through her skin—spreading—pressure—no pain—her heart—heart—

"Nìa!"

—looked past Cèel—outside the circle—saw a figure—shorn head—bared teeth—

"Nìa, you must—"

I must.

Her hand brushed her pocket—she felt the hardness of the broken blade—drew it out just as Cèel released her and stepped back and—

—she stepped forward—brought up the knife—sliced down—sliced back—

Heard Cèel howl. Felt his blood splash over her. Watched him fall back, hand clutching his thigh, blood flowing like a river, spreading across the circle.

Looked down. Saw one knife in her hand. Saw the other, in her gut.

"Nìa!"

Yes, inshah?
Stepped forward into the tunneling black—

That is most stupid, nìa, and I want to hear no more.
Inshah?
Yes, nìa?
Someday you'll be the death of me.

CHAPTER 32

Breathing . . . breathing . . .

Pain.

Jani opened one eye, then closed it as the room light battered her. Heard movement off to the side. "Hmm . . . "

"Jani." A deep voice. A voice of bedsides and cloudy nights. "Don't try to move."

"No—" She paused to summon saliva and lick her lips. "—prollem." She raised a hand that weighed at least a hundred kilos and rested it atop her chest. " . . . Heavy."

"Yes." John lifted her hand and placed it back atop the bed, squeezing it before releasing it. "Cèel stabbed you in the abdomen. The blade curved up—he nicked your left lung, and your heart." A pause. Sounds of shaky breathing. "You're healing now."

"I got him . . . too . . . " Jani nodded. Tried to nod. "What . . . happen . . . ?"

"Not now. Get some sleep."

Sounds of a chair being dragged across the floor. The creak of old ergoworks.

Jani pried one eye open, then the other, saw a shape backlit by the glare of a bedside lamp.

"Let me adjust this—" Niall ramped down the brightness, then leaned close. "Shroud doesn't know I'm here, so I need to make it fast." He looked at her stomach, the padding of sensors and bandages, and winced. "He said that you're far from a hundred percent, so you weaken fast and can't catch your breath and feel like an elephant's sitting on your chest."

Jani held up two fingers.

"Two elephants." Niall grinned. "Has anyone talked to you? About the fight?"

Jani tried to shake her head, stopping when the room spun. "Cèel—stabbed me. I stabbed—him. It was—a tie."

Niall's breath caught. "One of the news services got it all. Don't know how they snuck a relay past bornsect security, but they did. The gel who imaged it spent the next hour in the can throwing up everything down to her shoes, but—she did good. It's a bloody damned thing to watch—the son of a bitch grinned like a skull right before he—" IIc pressed a hand to his mouth, then slowly lowered it.

Jani reached out, touched Niall's arm with the tip of her finger. "I hit him—" She paused to breathe. "—too."

"Yes, yes." Niall glanced back toward the door as he took her hand and patted it to try to settle her down. "The thing is, Jan, you . . . hit him in the groin, his femoral artery and—" He squeezed her hand. "—he bled out in the circle. In a minute, he bled, and it was—" Another shaky breath. "He's dead, Jan. Cèel's dead."

"I would just like to state for the record that this is bullshit." Val held Jani around the shoulders, propping her upright until the bed headrest rose up to meet her. "It's only been two days. We told you that she needed at least a week."

"Doctor, if this wasn't so important, we wouldn't intrude." Scriabin sat at the foot of the bed. He wore full diplomatic rig, Commerce green tunic bearing every medal and award he'd ever received. "Hurt much?"

"Only when I laugh." Jani tried to sit up higher, and

stopped when the elephants began to tap dance across her rib cage. "Judging from the expressions on your faces, I doubt we'll be doing much of that, so I'm—probably safe."

"Niall admitted that he told you." Mako shook his head. "He thought someone should have told you in the operating room. He thought you'd be able to hear, and it would cheer you up." He clucked his tongue. "My Niall . . . can be the bloodiest of bastards."

"Which is why he'll be your Niall until the stars go out." Jani brushed off Mako's glower. "So I went into the circle with a second knife." She touched her thigh where her trouser pocket would have been, where the blade would have rested. "I remember pulling out a knife. I remember stabbing him. Nothing particularly lucid."

"I can't say I'm surprised." Val sat on the end of the bed, opposite Scriabin. "I wasn't particularly lucid afterward, and all I did was watch."

"Did Council lodge a protest?" Jani looked from one face to the next, sensed the need to speak combined with the reluctance to say what needed saying. "It wasn't exactly a fair fight, was it?"

"No, it wasn't."

Everyone turned to the door.

John filled the entry like a pale guardian, his med-whites rumpled, his face a mask. He glared at Mako and Scriabin, but saved his sharpest look for Val, who started to grumble an explanation before deciding silence the better course.

Then John looked at Jani, and his expression warmed, a little. "Cèel was the better, more experienced fighter. He did not enter the circle in the spirit of challenge, but with every intention of killing you. Everyone who witnessed that fight knew that."

Jani detected the jittery undertone in the so-familiar bass. "How much did you see?"

"Everything." John hesitated, then walked to one of the analyzers that ringed her bedside and studied the readout.

"Niall contacted us as soon as you offered challenge. We saw . . . everything."

Jani waited as the silence stretched. "Are you going to tell me what else happened, or do I have to bribe an orderly to snag a copy of the image?"

"I would wait a few years to look at that, if I were you." John remained fixed on the readout. "Cèel's physician-priest wasn't there. We found out later that Rilas had killed her during her escape from the Temple hospital. There were other physician-priests present, but half a minute or more passed while they shook out their hierarchical underwear, and that was a half a minute or more that they didn't have. Our best trauma people would have had their work cut out for them. You couldn't have struck a better spot if you'd aimed." He shot her a look filled with wonder and the barest hint of cold-blooded admiration. "Then they started on the prayers. I think I recall someone cutting away Cèel's trouser leg to look at the wound, but I confess that my attentions were fixed elsewhere by that point."

Jani watched as the physician who had pieced her together from char and ashes, who had brought her back from the brink any number of times, returned to his pondering of readouts. "John, did they . . . ?"

"Do I think they let him die?" John raised his head, his eyes bright. "Good God, is there any doubt?" He jerked his chin toward Val, who nodded. "They went through a few of the motions, but they didn't do a damned thing that mattered."

Scriabin cleared his throat. "Well, there was the issue of Wholeness of Soul—"

"As convenient an excuse as any. If pressed, I'm sure Temple can justify every move they made. And every move they didn't." John laughed. "He went too far. The other sects wanted him out without matters getting too messy. Saw an opportunity, and made the most of it. Assassination by medical negligence. The history scrolls of the idomeni are no doubt filled."

Jani looked from John to Val and back to John. For all their professional disdain and outrage, there was one point they continued to skirt. "Could you have helped?"

The silence radiated like cracks in old glass. Man and hybrid looked at one another, decades of closeness whittling down hours of discussion to the arch of an eyebrow, the twitch of a lip.

"You weren't much better off, you know. We had our hands full." Val looked at the floor and shrugged. "They wouldn't have let us near him anyway."

"Besides, it's not as though he'd have thanked us. Saved by a humanish and a hybrid—I'm sure if you'd have set out the choice before him, he'd have chosen death." John turned back to the analyzers and concentrated on touchpad entries. "But it's a moot point. As Val said, we had our hands full with you."

The room seemed to chill as the truth revealed itself in the humanish manner. In veiled looks and words left unsaid. In the arch of an eyebrow and the twitch of a lip. *Yes, we could have tried, but we didn't. Because you came first. Because we saw the look on his face when he drove in the knife. Because he had Tsecha killed. Because the bastard deserved it.*

Mako walked to a side table and poured himself water from a carafe. "Remind me to never get on your bad side, Shroud." He lifted the glass in Val's direction. "That goes for you, too, Parini." He drank, his stricken expression broadcasting that he would have preferred vodka and even that might not have helped.

Jani waited until the shockwaves settled to the occasional ripple. "So what happened after they carted away the bodies?"

"A firestorm." Scriabin stood and paced. "The Pathen strong-armed a Council vote with a speed I didn't believe possible outside of Chicago. Aden nìRau Wuntoi is the new Oligarch. The Pathen have ascended to *rau*."

"I didn't think a bornsect could ascend to *rau* on a vote."

Val moved to the window and perched on the sill. "What happened to the civil war part?"

"Peaceful transfer of power isn't the norm, but it has happened." Jani picked her muzzy brain for appropriate bits of idomeni history. "The sect that ascends needs to have built one hell of a consensus, but we knew the Pathenrau had been working on that for a while."

"After Council refused to allow Cèel's suborn the right to ascend, they kicked all Vynshà out of Council and Temple." Scriabin stood and paced at the foot of the bed. "Some of the Temple dominants are arguing that Cèel's planning of Tsecha's assassination was so profoundly antithetical to all that is idomeni that it taints all Vynshà." He slowed. Stilled. "And that all Vynshà must pay."

"Pay how?" Jani heard the dread in her voice. "How are they supposed to pay?" But she knew the answer. One night twenty years before, she had witnessed the answer. *The sin of one is the sin of all—*

Then her gut clenched and she doubled over, slumping to her side as the spasms started and her heart skipped.

"I'm going to have to ask you all to leave." John turned her over on her back, fingers flicking over the sensors. "*Now.*"

It was a still night, the moon obscured by cloud—
Jani sat in the hospital's small garden and watched the fish in the ornamental pool, the melodramatic phrasing of the *Colonial Times* playing in her mind's ear like the narration it was. The story had begun with the last days of the War of Vynshàrau Ascension. The reporter had mined every accessible archive and even a couple that technically should have been out of bounds.

Bornsect tradition held that all members of a sect shared in the decisions of their dominants. Therefore, when it became evident that Laumrau dominants had conspired with members of the Commonwealth government and Service to imprison humanish in the hospital-shrine located at Knevçet Shèràa and to subject them to mind control experimentation,

*the sin of the few became the shame of the many, and the
many accepted that the sin was theirs as well.*

"And since all the Laum sinned, all the Laum paid." Jani
worked to her feet, one eye on the relays that studded her
right arm and transmitted her vital signs back to the handhelds that John and Val carried with them at all times. "I
think there are a few isolated settlements left. A few Laum
left alive to pass along the tale, and the warnings."

"Teaching idomeni history to the fish?"

Jani turned to find Lucien standing in the garden entry.

"I wanted to visit earlier, but Val warned me off." He
walked in, brimmed lid tucked under his arm. "I figured
my best bet would be to sneak in and take my chances."
He stopped just beyond reach. "It's sheer insanity outside
these walls, you realize that? Vynshà are gathering in the
streets and Wuntoi is ready to send out the Haárin to bottle
them up."

Jani lowered back into the chair. "No one tells me anything. Scriabin and Mako were here yesterday, but John
ordered them out after—" She patted her chest just over her
heart. "They're going to slaughter the Vynshà. It'll make
the Night of the Blade look like a skirmish."

Lucien took a seat on a nearby bench. "What did you expect?" He picked up a branch that had fallen from one of
the dwarf weeping willows and poked the water, sending the
fish scurrying for shelter. "That's how they've operated for
thousands of years. It's insane. A dominant commits a crime,
and the entire sect gets thrown over the side. If humans did
that, we never would have lasted long enough to make it
out of the caves." He hit the surface hard enough to make a
splash, then tossed the branch into the water and watched it
bob and float.

Jani watched him out of the corner of her eye. *Duplicitous
bastard.* Yet here he was, the only one who seemed willing
to tell her what went on beyond the hospital gates. "What's
the official Commonwealth position?"

"That it's an internal idomeni matter."

"Like hell it is." Jani heard her cardiomonitor emit a warning *beep*, and breathed slowly until it settled. "What happens to the Vynshà Haárin?"

"That's still being discussed." For the first time, Lucien seemed anxious, clenching his hands and shifting restlessly. "Dathim's under a sort of house arrest until they decide."

"What do you mean, 'sort of'?"

"I think they were afraid to come out and tell him." A quick smile, which soon vanished. "They finally settled on having Meva suggest to him that he should remain within the confines of the enclave. She's technically under house arrest as well. Feyó is trying to intercede for them, but she isn't having much luck." Lucien clapped the tips of his fingers together. "They'd kill Dathim and Meva because they're Vynshà, even though they're Haárin?" He made a drifting gesture with one hand. "If you'd kept your mouth shut and let me handle it, none of this would have happened. Rilas just would have disappeared."

"You couldn't have gotten to Cèel."

"He rode in a skimmer on occasion, didn't he? Idomeni tech isn't all that different." Lucien sat back, smoothing his hands over his thighs, then dragging his brimmed lid onto his lap and tracing a thumbnail over the gold braid. "That's what they're all saying. That you had to get in everyone's face. Again. You had to broadcast. Again. Everyone knew you were coming. Everyone knew what to expect. You said things that should have been kept quiet. You did things that upset people. And now everyone's stuck. Because it's all out in the open, they have to act in certain ways. Instead of an easy transfer of power to a Vynshà who would have been more amenable, millions are going to die. Because you couldn't keep your damned mouth shut." His hands stilled. "That's the difference between you and me. I do the job, and I know how to keep my distance. I don't get involved. I don't get emotional." He paused, eyes fixed on the fish, which had begun to emerge from beneath stones and logs and swim about again. "I just do it."

"Does anyone bother to consider that Tsecha wouldn't want this?" Jani paused to breathe as her heart monitor once more beeped a warning. "He was Vynshà. They're his people. Do you think if he were alive now he'd let this happen?"

"He's dead." Lucien shrugged. "What he'd think doesn't matter."

"So it's come to that already?"

"Ani is saying that history is repeating. You did the same thing at Knevçet Shèràa. Drew down fire. You killed Rikart Neumann, and because you did that, Acton van Reuter had to act, had to order Evan to take care of you. You force people to do things they don't want to do because you don't know when to lay low. When to lay off." Lucien tugged at his lid's gold braid too hard, ripping it away from the brim. He swore under his breath and massaged the cording with his thumb, trying to work it back into place. "You always have to push."

"You've made your point."

"Have I? Is it really getting through?"

Jani watched him set his lid back on the bench beside him, then lean forward again, hands flexing. "Lucien?"

He raised his head and looked at her. His eyes glittered like the stones that lined the bottom of the pond, dark and cold and devoid of life. *"What?"*

Jani sighed as she felt the last piece in a long running puzzle slip into place. *I always knew it would come to this.* Always knew that someday, the man who had spent his life playing all sides of the game would eventually make a choice. "Speaking hypothetically, of course, because it's all I can do to get up out of this chair. But if I were to attempt to run out of this garden right now, I wouldn't make it to the entry, would I?"

"Ani prefers Feyó." Lucien fixed on the fish again. "Feyó knows something of how humans operate, but she's not an expert. Ani thinks she'll have an easier time manipulating her if you're not around." He smiled, shook his head. "No, that's not all of it. Ani hates you and wants you dead."

Jani nodded. Odd, that she didn't feel scared. That she

didn't feel angry or betrayed. That she didn't feel the least urge to fight for her life. *I'll be able to apologize to Tsecha in person for destroying his people.* And to the d'Abos, and the Seligs, and the other passengers of the *Capria*. As for the pain or the sensations, well, she'd died often enough to have felt them all at least once. The only thing she had yet to experience was that last letting go, and odds were that it would slip right past without her realizing. *Paying forward for the millions.* Yes, it was right. Yes, it was just. Insufficient repayment, but all she had to offer. All she had to give.

"I've risked everything I ever wanted, everything I ever earned." Lucien picked up a stone and hurled it into the midst of the fish, sending them darting back to the rocks as water splashed. "And every goddamned time, I'd have to stand there and listen as you told me that whatever I did, it wasn't enough. Not enough risk. Not enough blood. You're not running for your life this week, so you can't be serious. What the hell else do you want from me?"

"Not a thing." Jani shook her head. "Not anymore."

Lucien bulled on with no indication that he'd heard. "I can't be what you want me to be—I'm not made that way. I can't say what you want me to say. I can't feel what you want me to feel." His voice dropped to a whisper. "I don't love you."

"I should have realized when you told me all about assassins who needed to get close to their victims that you were trying to tell me something. If I made a list of all our encounters since Elyas, I would guess that each one was an opportunity you let slip. The clinch on the catwalk—that was your best shot, I think. Overcome by guilt over the *Capria,* bit of a push and over the railing she went. Clear case of suicide. No wonder Anais seemed so upset each time she saw me. I wasn't supposed to survive the journey here, was I?" Jani took as deep a breath as she dared, then slid to the edge of the chair. "Well, you'll do the job good and proper now, and you'll be set for life. Ani will never question you again. Hell, she'll probably write you into her will." Using the chair arms

for support, she worked to her feet. Then she undid the collar of her pajama top and pushed back the collar of her robe,
exposing the area around her neck.

Lucien straightened. "What are you doing?"

"Would it be easier if I turned my back?" Jani turned to
face the garden entry, then reached up and tapped the place
where her neck and shoulder met. "I've done this before, so
watch where I'm pointing. Edge of your hand, right here."
She lowered her hands and clasped them in front of her, then
stilled. Strange how she'd never felt so calm. She had no
trouble keeping the cardiomonitor silent. "I'll keep looking
straight ahead. The sun's in just the right position—I won't
even see your shadow. One hard shot, Lucien. All that stands
between you and everything you ever wanted." *And between
me and everything I deserve.*

Nothing, for long seconds. Then she heard him rise, the
crunch of the soles of his polished tie-tops against the stone
rim of the pond. Sensed him close in, as she always could,
and shut her eyes.

Felt him grip her shoulders and ease her around to face
him. Opened her eyes as first he pulled her pajama top closed,
then straightened the collar of her robe. He didn't look her in
the face. He barely looked at her at all.

Then, his ministrations completed, he rested his hands on
her shoulders for a scant moment, before letting them slide
away. "Happy now?" He stood before her, head bowed, then
circled around her and started toward the other end of the
garden.

"You—" Jani inhaled. This time her heart skipped, stuttered.
The edges of her sightline blackened and her knees buckled.

Lucien caught her before she hit the ground, and lowered
with her. Held her, drew her closer, and pressed his lips to
the place were her neck and shoulder met.

"So you're going to kill me after all." Jani heard the
cardiomonitor start to skitter. "You've just settled on your
weapon of choice."

"I learned from an expert." Lucien's arms tightened as he hugged her closer.

"Damned fool."

"No argument there."

"Let her go."

Jani saw John push through the garden gate, Val at his heels. She sagged against Lucien, felt the hybrid lawn prickle through her pajamas. "He's not doing anything."

"There's something wrong with her." Lucien released her and scuttled backward as Val and John linked arms beneath Jani's legs and behind her back and hoisted her up. "She's not her usual self."

"If you had a twelve centimeter gash in your gut courtesy of a Sìah barbed blade and a hole in your heart that didn't want to close, you wouldn't be your usual self either." John glared at Lucien as he and Val maneuvered Jani back to her chair and lowered her into it. "Perhaps you'd like to experience the sensation firsthand?"

"John." Jani laid her head back. "Shut up."

"Jani, you can't afford—"

"Just shut—" She grabbed the front of his medcoat and shook as hard as she could. "—up."

"That sounds more like—" Lucien fell silent as both John and Val turned on him.

Jani looked past her twin guardians to her singular—what was he? Ally? Lover? Never a friend. *Just . . . Lucien.* "Do you have a skimmer?"

Lucien nodded. "I can get one."

Jani slapped the sides of her chair, then jerked her thumb at the garden gate. "I have to go to the enclave and get Dathim and Meva out."

"You're not going anywhere," John said as he checked the various analyzers on the chair.

"I'm going to the enclave to get Dathim and Meva." Jani stared at the side of John's face until he finally looked at her. "Then I want to talk to Wuntoi."

"He's been advised not to talk to you." Lucien stood off to one side, hands behind his back.

"Then we're going to have to persuade him otherwise." Jani tugged on John's sleeve. "John."

"You're in no condition." Val picked up the standard while his colleague fussed with a balky readout.

"Just give me something to get me through."

John's head came up, eyes blazing. *"That's not how I work."*

"Just get me through the next twelve hours. If I can't get something started by then . . . " Jani took John's hand and squeezed. Felt the initial resistance, the slow softening.

His eyes brimmed. "You were all I cared about."

"I know. That was the problem, wasn't it?" Jani leaned close enough to kiss. "Whatever it takes. Please."

CHAPTER 33

"The dominant's name is ná Dena Lau." Scriabin read the name off his handheld display, and did a decent job of pronunciation. "Ava always found her quite reasonable, but now that she has a possible death sentence in her future, all bets are off. Word is that if she cooperates with Wuntoi, he'll exile her enclave instead of killing them."

Jani pondered the view through the skimmer window. City Center appeared much as it always had, the walkways filled with both bornsect and Haárin, all proceeding in an apparently orderly manner.

"Jan?"

Jani touched her ear. "I'm here."

"I'm with Galas . . ." Niall paused, said something to the Haárin male. *"We're north of the Temples, near the site of your Sermon on the Park Bench. Lots of Haárin gathered here, and more streaming in from the surrounding streets."*

Jani looked to the north, past the domes and spires of the City Center. Imagined Niall guiding the small two-seater along the river, Galas riding shotgun. "Any Pathenrau security?"

"A few. No warriors, though. Galas said that he heard they were calling up a few brigade equivalents from the southern encampments in preparation for—"

Jani waited. Tapped her ear a few times. "Niall?"

"In preparation for the slaughter." A shaky sigh. *"Jesus Christ, there are kids out here. Youngish. Some of them can't even walk yet."* Another pause. *"We're going to get started here. Feyó's crew has shown up. What's your timing?"*

Jani checked the view. "Coming up on the enclave now." She tapped the bug, shutting it down. She didn't want a stream of Niall-speak interrupting her, distracting her. She still felt tired, despite the stimulant John had reluctantly given her. *As for the wound . . .* She reached beneath her shirt and touched the bandage, a mass of sensor wrap and healing accelerants that sent out signals, she felt sure, to anyone with a handheld who wanted to know the state of her heart.

"You all right?"

Jani looked over at Val, who watched her from the other end of the seat. "I'm fine."

"Then why do you keep touching it?"

"Just to drive you crazy."

"Already there." Val entered a notation in his handheld. "Bobbing along like a ping-pong ball in your wake."

"I know the feeling, Doc." Scriabin looked up from his handheld and gazed out the window. "She makes Tyotya Ani seem meek and retiring."

"You can both shut up any time now." Jani scooted to the edge of her seat as the embassy double-length floated to the curb. The driver's side gullwing swung up, releasing a uniformed Lucien, who hurried around to her side of the vehicle and opened the door.

Jani emerged, taking Lucien's offered hand and holding on tight because she needed the support. Continued to lean on him as she slowly straightened while trying to ignore the pull of bandages and healing tissue. Her propitiator's over-robe, a clean backup she'd salvaged from the depths of her luggage, unfurled to her knees.

A crowd gathered, Haárin and bornsect both, ripples of hushed speech propagating as she walked to the enclave entry. *I don't look too bad for someone who died three days ago, do I?* She squeezed Lucien's hand, and he released her and stepped to the side, far enough away so that she appeared fully ambulatory, but close enough to catch her in case the unthinkable happened and she collapsed.

She reached the gate just as ná Dena emerged, a middle-aged female wearing the headwrap and rough clothes of a laborer.

"Glories, Kièrshia." Dena spoke Low Vynshà Haárin, a language stripped of gesture. She looked Jani in the eye as well, her Vynshà gold laced with amber and streaks of brown. "I know why you are here. I can do nothing. NìRau Wuntoi compels. I must obey. Ní Dathim and ná Meva must remain until all is decided."

Jani started to speak, then stopped as cold sweat broke out and flecks of light shimmered in her sightline. *Not now, goddamn it.* She bent forward at the waist. Hunched her shoulders. Prayed as she never prayed before that Dena would interpret her posture as growing rage, not an attempt by a weak half-humanish to remain standing by any means possible.

Saw the brown-streaked gold flicker, and knew her prayer had been answered, at least for the moment. "Blood trade, Dena. You hold them for Wuntoi, he lets your enclave leave Shèrá. But if you leave, and Vynshà here die, all will know you betrayed. All will know, because I will tell them." She heard Lucien shift his feet, and knew he understood enough of what she said to glean the threat. *Too harsh? Too bad.*

Dena's shoulders started to curve. "Tell what you will, to who you will. NìRau Wuntoi said that they were of ní Tsecha, and ní Tsecha died."

"So?" Jani parsed Wuntoi's words, searching for the slant he'd given them, the meaning that would have convinced Dena to imprison her own.

Then it hit her like a blow. Her heart stuttered. *"He told you they helped kill ní Tsecha?"* She drew up straight without thinking, looked to the sky, felt the pain across her midriff like the swipe of claws. "They both lived here once." She rounded her shoulders again, stepping away from Lucien as he edged closer. "You knew them."

Dena nodded. "I know of Meva." The harmonics of irritation in her voice indicated that she had known Meva all too well.

"You know she studied ní Tsecha's writings, that she followed him."

"Yes, ná Kièrshia, but—"

"You know ní Dathim, the tilemaster?"

"All know ní Dathim." This time the tone was softer, kinder.

"You say this. Yet you believe that this ní Dathim who you know would participate in secret killing? That ná Meva, who one can hear through walls, would do so as well? Ní Dathim would face you in the circle and strike you down—" Jani poked Dena in the chest hard enough to jostle her. "—and ná Meva would talk you to death, but she would never strike in secret."

"NìRau Wuntoi will slaughter us as we did the Laum." Dena's eyes darkened. Yes, she was of an age. She may have witnessed. She may have even participated.

"Wuntoi will slaughter—no one." Jani stopped to breathe. "Give them to me now, and I will guard you as I guard them. I will guard all Vynshà as I guard them."

Dena looked to the street, the idomeni who crowded from three sides. "NìRau Wuntoi will hear you," she said in halting English. "But will he listen?"

Jani nodded. That was the sticking point, the one thing in all this that she could work for, but not guarantee. "If I can't save you, I'll die with you. This I swear, on Tsecha's soul."

Dena stood quiet, her eyes fixed on nothing. Then she gestured to her suborn, a hulking male who gestured affirmation, then reentered the enclave. A few minutes later he emerged, Dathim and Meva in tow.

Meva grabbed Jani's sleeve and made as if to speak, but Jani shook her off. "Get into the skimmer," she said in Sìah

Haárin. "Before they change their minds." The two followed Lucien to the vehicle, piling into the rear seat while Jani walked toward the crowd. They pushed forward as she approached, a few raising their arms above their heads in displays of abject respect.

"I have taken ní Dathim Naré and ná Meva Tan." Jani spoke High Vynshà, every word replete with change in posture and gesture. "They were ní Tsecha's, as was I. Now they are mine. I care for that which is mine." She paused, until the tension ramped and it seemed as though the air itself would shatter under the stress. "Line the streets from Council to the river, where I met some of you four days past. Do this in the time after mid-afternoon sacrament. I will await you there." With that, she turned and swept back to the skimmer. Waved off Lucien's offered arm, maintaining her show of strength until he closed her gullwing after her. Then she slumped forward, arms crossed over her stomach, while Val knelt on the skimmer floor in front of her, handscanner at the ready.

"John is going to have a fit when he sees these numbers." He checked her vitals, then dragged a slingbag from beneath the seat. "What was that all about? A meeting by the river? Who are you expecting?" He pulled out an injector already loaded with a cartridge, pushed up Jani's right sleeve and pressed the device to her skin. "You can't take much more of this, you know? If John doesn't come up with the right protein soon, we're going to have to open you up again."

Meva and Dathim sat on the opposite bench seat, crowding Scriabin on both sides. Dathim watched the medical ministrations with the skeptical eye of an owner who wondered if his horse would make it through the race. "The Vynshà will not die as did the Laum." His voice was a rumble. "They will take as many with them as they can."

"No one will have to die. Not even me." *I hope.* Jani sagged against the seat as whatever Val dosed her with took effect. "Now here's what I need you all to do . . ."

The skimmer pulled away from the curb, its progress slowed to a walking pace by the idomeni who crowded in from every side, touching the vehicle as it drifted past, like a talisman.

By the time they reached the river, Niall, along with Feyó's crew, had completed their end of the project. The awning they'd erected on the edge of the river proved a drab thing in dark grey, which Jani suspected had been creatively reappropriated from Rauta Shèràa Base stores by a certain colonel of her acquaintance.

"Afternoon, gel." Niall strode beneath the awning, clipwrench still in hand. He tossed the tool aside and helped Val and Scriabin maneuver a skimchair out of the skimmer boot, eyeing Jani all the while. "You've looked better, you know."

"I've felt better." Jani sat in the chair as soon as Val activated it. "Is she here?"

Niall stepped back outside and motioned to someone standing alongside the awning. "Your turn."

A shadow moved along the fabric wall. Then a small face framed with dark brown curls peeked around edge of the polycloth.

"Come on in, gel. She only bites if you bite first." Niall gripped the young woman's sleeve and tugged her inside. "This is Bailey Schiff, an enterprising stringer for Chan-Net, who has already imaged one event of the century and is ready to move on to bigger things."

"It's good to—" The young woman held out a hand to Jani, her eyes widening. "—meet. You."

"Thank you for agreeing to this." Jani gave Schiff's hand a squeeze, because the young woman looked like she needed it. "If this goes according to plan, you won't have to do anything." *We won't think about what will happen if it doesn't.* "All you'll have to do is stand near my chair."

"And an exclusive interview after it's over," piped Schiff, her nervousness evaporating like morning dew in the Rauta Shèràa sun.

"And an exclusive interview after it's over." Jani turned her chair around and motioned to Lucien. "You should get going."

"Are you sure he'll be there?" Lucien's voice emerged tight, his business-as-usual facade showing its first crack. "You never contacted him. You never asked for a meeting."

"If he looks out the window, he can see what's going on." Jani heard a rise of voices, looked out to the river to see that the crowd had doubled in size in the few minutes since their arrival. "He'll be there."

"From your mouth . . . " Lucien lapsed into French as he returned to the skimmer and got in.

Jani watched him pull away. Saw Meva's face in the rear window and raised a hand. Felt a flicker of relief when the female bared her teeth and waved back.

"Ava received a communication this morning." Scriabin grabbed a folding stool from a stack and shook it open. "Li Cao is still insisting that this is an idomeni matter."

"I'm sure she has her reasons." Jani edged her chair behind the draped fold of the awning, then rolled up her sleeve so Val could give her another injection.

"If you pull this off . . . " He shook his head and concentrated on positioning the injector.

Jani winced as the injector pinched, sighed as the drug warmth wandered up her arm. Watched the street that stretched from the enclave to the river, already obscured by the idomeni who gathered there. "Did you bring it?"

Val sighed. "It's right here." He reached into his sling-bag, pulled out the plastic hospital dispo bag and handed it to her.

"He's coming." Niall appeared at the front of the awning. "Pascal picked him up at the front of the Council building. He drove him as far as the enclave, then let him off. Dathim and Meva are leading him here."

"Through the crowds?" Jani smiled.

Niall touched his ear, listened for a moment, then nodded.

"It's just like it was in the station. They've closed in on both sides—there's barely enough room for him to pass."

"Well, time to get ready for company." Jani shifted her weight so the chair tipped forward and stood.

Niall gaped.

It had taken Val the better part of the day to find the clothes Jani had worn the day she killed Rilas and Cèel. They had been bundled into a biohazard bag during her pre-surgical prep and avoided the incinerator through sheer happenstance. Permanent bends and ripples had been created in the shirt and the front of the trousers by Jani's and Cèel's dried blood. The overrobe, streaked with Rilas's blood, had fared a little better, but still looked like something that had been used to wrap a butchered animal.

"Jani?" Scriabin licked his lips. He'd watched her remove the garments from the bag and put them on, and still hadn't recovered. "Do you think it wise to greet a new Oligarch while wearing clothes soaked in his predecessor's blood?"

Jani bared her teeth. "Welcome to Shèrá, Your Excellency."

Jani walked out from under the awning and across the river walkway to the end of the avenue. As she did, idomeni closed in on both sides, both bornsect and Haárin, Vynshà and Sìah and Oà, as well as the odd Pathenrau rebel, gold-bronze faces like shots of night amid their lighter-skinned brethren.

Aden nìRau Wuntoi walked toward her, shoulders curved in anger, Dathim and Meva serving as escort, the crowd closing in behind him and bearing him along. He slowed when he registered Jani standing at the end of the walkway, slowed even more when he saw the clothes she wore.

When they reached the end of the walkway, Dathim and Meva turned as sharply as Spacer recruits, coming to a halt beside Jani. That left Wuntoi standing by himself, an arm's length distant, idomeni pressing around him from three sides.

"The reason?" His English was unaccented. He had been working toward Pathenrau ascendance for a long time.

"One should always look into the faces of those you would kill." Jani turned and pointed toward the awning-covered enclosure. "Now we shall go, and talk of them." She waited for Dathim and Meva to walk ahead, then fell in behind them, allowing Wuntoi his place of precedence bringing up the rear. *With the Vynshà hard on his tail.* She held back her grin without much trouble. She still felt the tightness around her chest, the weakness and cold sweats. Val had rigged a cardiopack over her heart that would inject the appropriate drugs and proteins in case it misbehaved, and had hidden in the backseat of the double-length, a mere twenty-five meter dash away in case of medical crisis.

They entered the enclosure. Everyone rose, Scriabin immediately surrendering the stool, which was of the proper height and style for an Oligarch. Wuntoi smoothed his over-robe around him and sat, a lifetime's practice with bornsect furniture allowing him the balance to situate himself with nary an unseemly wobble. He looked around the sheltered space, then settled in, gesturing dismissively toward Jani's skimchair. "You sit in that chair because you are weak."

"Physically?" Jani shrugged, ignoring the pull of her incision and the heft and drag of the cardiopack. "Mentally is another matter, and unless you wish to challenge me, it is the mental with which you will have to deal."

"A second knife." Wuntoi looked toward the crowds, who had encircled the enclosure as closely as Feyó's security would allow and now sat on the lawns and watched them. "Unseemly."

"So is attempted murder within the circle. But knives have always been known to slip, and idomeni often die who are not meant to." Jani replayed scattered moments in her mind. The moment when Cèel knocked away her blade. When he drew her in like a lover and rammed his own knife into her gut up to the hilt.

"I am here at your bidding, because you were favored

by ní Tsecha. And because you are weakened, and I pitied you." Wuntoi fixed his gaze at a point over Jani's shoulder, on the border between disrespect and regard. "What do you want?"

Jani caught Niall's eye as he clenched his fists and arched her brow. *Calm down, Colonel.* Wuntoi was making a show of putting her in her place, but buried between his lines lay a certain inevitable conclusion. *He didn't have to come here.* He could have ignored her invitation-that-wasn't. Left her with a hatchery's worth of egg on her face, surrounded by idomeni who would wait and wait until they finally realized that ní Tsecha's toxin had provided them nothing worth waiting for. *You don't want to accede to the dictates of Temple, Aden nìRau Wuntoi. You don't want to slaughter the Vynshà.* All she had to do was provide him a way out that allowed him to fend off his propitiators, and she'd have an ally for life.

All she had to do . . .

"I know, and truly, why you wish to speak with me." Wuntoi shot the cuffs of his overrobe. "Temple has dictated that which they wish me to do. The sin of Morden nìRau Cèel is too great to be set aside. It must be shared by all Vynshà. As they all partake of the shame, so must they all pay the cost of it." He pointed to Jani. "You comprehend such. You, who helped damn the Laum."

Jani nodded, struggled to ignore the ache in her chest. "I will never forget the Night of the Blade." The escape from the consulate hospital basement, the dash through the streets to the shuttleport, and the realization that something horrible was unfolding before her eyes. "Ní Dathim Naré fought for Morden nìRau Cèel then. He was one of the Haárin who came down from the hills and rendered the justice of the gods upon the Laum."

Hearing his name, Dathim turned to them, raising a hand in greeting and baring his teeth.

Jani ignored him. "Thinking back, I wonder at the decision. The vast majority of the Laumrau had no knowledge of their dominants' collusion with humanish, or of that which occurred at Knevçet Shèràa." She inhaled, smelled heavy bay air and imagined it light and hot and desert dry. "Do I believe that a laborer here in Rauta Shèràa shared the guilt of the dominants who planned, the warriors who surrounded the hospital and would have killed me and my suborns if I had not killed them first?" She shook her head. "I do not. I argued of this with ní Tsecha, as I argued with him of many things. When he died, he had repudiated the concept of Wholeness of Soul, a tenet of major idomeni faiths. I have no doubt that if he had lived, he would have repudiated the slaughter of the Laum as well."

"You have no doubt." Wuntoi rocked his head back and forth, the panspecies *sez you* gesture. "But you do not *know*."

Jani pointed to the crowd seated on the lawn outside. "They are here because of their esteem for him. Because even though he is dead, they believe that he can deliver them. That his wisdom will find voice here, and change minds." She sat back, ignoring the flutter in her chest. "Forget that there are also Sìah out there, and Oà, who supported Pathenrau in their ascension. Forget that there are also Pathenrau, who see fit to disagree with the decisions of their dominants." She breathed in, breathed out. A glorious thing and truly, to breathe. "The Vynshà who are out there now did not wish to see ní Tsecha dead, and they should not be made to pay for the crimes of those who did."

Wuntoi remained silent. His slouch had straightened somewhat. He didn't seem quite as angry as he had when he'd arrived. Maybe she was getting through. Maybe . . .

"Prime Minister Li Cao and her suborns are content to allow idomeni to decide this matter." Wuntoi folded his arms, and looked for all the world like a negative image of Evgeny Scriabin. "Why do you butt in?"

Jani glanced at Scriabin, who seemed fixated on the state of his fingernails. "It is in Li Cao's interest to trade with the worldskein. It is in Li Cao's interest to encourage worldskein support for the Outer Circle colonies, so that she can hold back her own material support and expend it in other ways." She felt Scriabin's stare burn a hole in her cheek, and ignored it. "It is not necessarily in Li Cao's interest for the worldskein to be united and strong, and a worldskein that has just slaughtered millions of its own and lost tens if not hundreds of thousands more in the resulting rebellion against this slaughter, is not united. It is not strong."

Wuntoi fixed his bronze glare on Scriabin, whose face had reddened to sunstroke levels. "Humanish do not care. If they have nice tilework, and trueleather, and Sìah metal sculpture, they will not care about the history of those who produce such."

"Maybe." Jani gestured to Schiff, who paled and swallowed hard, but managed not to faint. "Yet they will record. They will transmit. They will remember." She bared her teeth. "Now, when most humanish think of idomeni, they think of ní Tsecha, who looked them in the eye when he spoke with them, and made them laugh, and behaved in ways they understood. If the slaughter goes ahead as planned, ní Tsecha will be forgotten, and when humanish think of idomeni, they will think of blood in the streets and the hacked bodies of youngish, and Rauta Shèràa will come to mean anathema. Humanish will move on, together with hybrid and Haárin, and bornsect will be left behind to fester in a pit of your own making."

"You say this to me?" Wuntoi waved his finger under Jani's nose. "You are sitting there in clothes that are stiff with the blood of those you killed."

"Vengeance. Self-defense." Jani once again pointed to the crowds on the lawn. "Slaughter." She shrugged, lowering her arms slowly as her sightline darkened. "It's a fine line, granted, and not always logical. But you cross it, and humanish will be a long time forgetting." She sensed Niall next to her, staring straight ahead, temper at the boil. *Sorry, Niall.* If a stronger worldskein made his job harder, it wasn't her problem. She was not of the Commonwealth anymore.

Wuntoi pushed a handful of braided fringe behind an ear ringed with gold studs. "And your solution to the Vynshà problem is?"

"They were his. Now they're mine." Jani held out her hands to the crowd. "Give them to me. Declare them Haárin, as a sign of your ascension. Declare them what you will. But give Tsecha's people to one who was also of Tsecha, and release them."

Silence fell, so profound that Jani could hear the breeze rustle the awning flaps. Then Scriabin cleared his throat. "That's fifteen million bornsect and over three million Haárin."

Jani shrugged. "He doesn't want them." She twitched a thumb at Wuntoi. "He would kill them. I am of Tsecha, as they are." She bared her teeth again. "I have died several times, and they are as dead. The dead leading the dead. It makes perfect sense."

Wuntoi regarded her with narrowed eyes. "They would need to leave this place and go to another."

Jani nodded. "And they will need places in which to live, and work to do and food to eat when they get to wherever they're going. The transit systems of two civilizations should be able to handle the load. We have experts to work out the logistics. We have builders and food experts. It will not be an instantaneous transition—it may take years. But it can be done."

Wuntoi cocked his head, as though considering. "You, as the dominant of a small enclave of most strange hybrids, are empowered to negotiate this agreement?"

"As dominant of Thalassa, I am acknowledged to be a Head of State by the Outer Circle colonies." She nodded toward Scriabin, who groaned softly. "If you doubt, propose such to Feyó, who will see her Outer Circle enclaves quintuple in size. Propose it to your suborns, who will eliminate Vynshà from their lives without blood. Propose it to Temple, and hear their screams—" That drew the equivalent of a nasty grin from Wuntoi. "—and if it serves, they will negotiate it, and come to the same conclusions, and you will have the diplomatic imprimatur you seek."

Wuntoi sat quietly. Then he looked up at Jani and bared his teeth. "To hear the screams of Temple would be a good thing, and truly." He stood. His shoulders held no curve.

Jani worked to her feet a little more slowly. Val's cardiopack had done *something*. The weight on her chest had lessened, and she felt tired rather than weak. "Humanish say that if a decision does not anger someone, it's the wrong decision."

"Do we really say that?" Niall managed to keep most of the sarcasm out of his voice.

"It is a good thing to say." Wuntoi seemed a different male than the one who had entered the enclosure a quarter hour before. His eyes had brightened. His voice sounded higher as the anger leached away. "I look forward to using it often, and truly." He nodded once to Jani, then walked out of the enclosure as the idomeni scrambled to their feet and parted for him once more.

Scriabin pressed a hand to the back of his neck. "Li Cao is going to have a stroke when we tell her this. She won't allow it."

"Then delay the final treaty signings, and make damn sure you win the next election." Jani patted his shoulder on the way out of the enclosure. "It's the best solution."

Scriabin followed after her. "It tips the population balance of the Outer Circle toward idomeni."

"If it's a good place, more humanish will come." Jani felt a looseness across her upper back, which was the only indication of how much it had ached previously. "What other decision could there be?" She started down the incline toward the double-length, where Val stood waiting.

"You know, I think I've figured it out."

Jani stopped and turned to find Niall standing at the top of the rise, lit 'stick in hand.

"On the first day of Creation, a Kilian cried out, 'It's dark in here—someone take care of it!' And then there was light." He doffed his lid and flipped it up in the air. "It's the only possible explanation!"

CHAPTER 34

Val's medical magic held. By the time Jani arrived at the embassy to see what diplomatic pitfalls and pushbacks awaited, it had once more donned its party finery. The mood seemed more subdued, however, as technical types in ill-fitting daysuits and uniforms bearing the white trouser stripes of the Sideline Service sat around tables with handhelds and trackboards and shook their heads in between trips to the open bar.

Mako met her at the opening to the garden, drink in hand. Whiskey, by the look of it, with no ice worth noting. "You realize you've set in motion a nightmare that will cause the logistics experts of two systems to awake screaming in the night for years to come?"

Jani shrugged. "It's good to spread the nightmares around."

"Hmm." Mako sipped his drink, then stared into his glass. "For someone who's just upended two governments and increased her own power and influence exponentially, you don't seem very happy."

Jani walked with him to an empty table near the stone wall. "It was his dream, this blending together. And he didn't live to see it."

Mako studied her for a time, then moved on to the sweeping tree branches that brushed to the ground. "I got to know ní Tsecha a little before he left Chicago. Niall always called him 'that wily old bird.'" He sat down and pondered his drink. "You reach a certain level in government, in the Service, you assume that . . . some might prefer if you did not exist. You don't dwell on it—you'd go mad if you did. It just crosses your mind occasionally that the day you're currently living might be your last."

Jani didn't say anything, even as the thought that she had earned membership in a very select club settled in her stomach to lie there and burn.

"He expected it, I think. The attempt, at least. No one could have written what he did, made the enemies he made, and not expected to have someone endeavor to extract the ultimate price." Mako rubbed the edge of the table with one thick finger. His hand was a battering ram, broad and brown and heavy-knuckled, the hand of a man who could handle any opponent face-to-face. Which was why he now concerned himself with the opponent that had been schooled in the use of sight mechs and long-ranges and explosives.

"He prepared as well as he could have, I think." Mako's voice grew tempered. "Feyó is sound. Not as much of a risk taker as she used to be, but she has managed to bring the conservatives to her side without losing the firebrands like Dathim and Meva, and that says something. There were those he influenced, the common idomeni, Haárin and bornsect both. The humans like Scriabin, who admired him." He looked out over the garden. "And then, in case all that failed, he had his second knife." He glanced up at Jani, then rose and headed for a table beneath the trees, where Cal Burkett had already opened the second bottle.

Jani sat in the chair Mako had vacated and watched the party. She had cleaned up with Val's aid, and changed into a dark blue wrapshirt and trousers that hid all her medical attachments and helped her blend in with the shadows. She gestured to a passing waiter and ordered iced water with bitter lemon. Sat back, and breathed, and closed her eyes.

"He told me, 'Meva, if anything happens to me, you must take her there.'"

Jani's eyes snapped open. Her heart skipped. "Dammit, Meva."

The female bared her teeth. She stood in front of the table, still dressed in her propitiator's overrobe, the object of stares from every part of the garden. "'You must take her to Shèrá,'" she continued as she sat across the table from Jani, "'because if anything ever happens to me, it will be from Shèrá.'" She picked up the tiny coffee service and poked through the sweetener packets, occasionally holding one up to the sun to examine it more closely. "'You must allow her to do that which she does, even if such maddens you. Even if such drives you to challenge her yourself.'" She set down the service with a clatter. "And I wished to, most certainly. When you accused Haárin of his death, I wanted to meet you at Guernsey and fight you in the middle of the concourse."

"I didn't accuse the Haárin . . ." Jani waved a hand, let it go, surrendered to the futility of trying to explain reality to those who preferred their altered truth. "I don't know how you talked Feyó into going along after she found out."

"I persuaded her."

"You bullied her. You're a bully, Meva."

"Pot. Kettle. Black." Meva bared her teeth. Sat back, hands folded in her lap, and watched the party, which gradually returned to its previous volume and activity levels once everyone adjusted to the propitiator in their midst.

Then the waiter arrived with Jani's bitter lemon. He set it down, then looked at Meva.

"That." She pointed to Jani's drink. "Galas thinks much of it," she added, as the young man headed back to the bar, aplomb itself but for the occasional backward glance.

Jani waited until he returned with Meva's drink. Waited longer, until the music and dancing started and she knew no one else could hear. "Dathim told me what you said to Tsecha about me." She breathed in until her chest ached. "You're right. I'm not a priest."

Meva nodded, eventually. Poked at the ice cubes with her straw. "This, I know. So did Tsecha, in the end. He saw that you did not study. He knew that you did not believe." She paused to sip. "But then he realized that which you were. You are the bringer of pain and change." She held out her glass to Jani. "Do that which you do. Leave the gods to me."

Jani hesitated. Then the token dropped, and she clinked her glass against Meva's, took a sip to seal the toast. "I think I saw him. After Cèel stabbed me. He was standing outside the circle. I heard him say, 'Nìa.' And he bared his teeth."

"He reminds you. His soul waits for release." The first hint of shadow crossed Meva's face, and she grew more subdued. "He asks you to do so."

"I thought you would do that."

"He would wish you to do so, I think."

"At Temple?" Jani shook her head. "Temple tried to push Wuntoi into slaughtering the Vynshà. It doesn't seem the right place." She paused, raked through all the Vynshà theology that she'd struggled to remember and now tumbled about her brain as though it had always been there. As though she had always known it. "Can I ask you . . . ?" She spread out a napkin and asked the waiter for a stylus, and talked while Meva listened. Until the music ramped up and the laughter and talking grew louder. Until Meva tucked the napkin into her overrobe, said that she needed to speak to those at Temple whom she trusted, and left.

Val came eventually, with John in tow, but the undercurrent of tension made conversation too painful to pursue. Lucien missed out due to the fact that this time he actually had pulled desk officer duty. No one mentioned Anais or regretted her absence.

As night fell, Jani pleaded fatigue and left, but instead of retiring to her suite, she departed the embassy and headed for the base. Stopped at the gate, asked if Colonel Pierce was on site, and received the surprising news that she had been cleared. That she was expected. That she would know where he was.

She found Niall sitting on a bench that had been set in a patch of lawn next to an office annex. The bench fell under the building's shadow and the lighting was poor. She would have walked past the spot if she hadn't seen the telltale pinpoint glow, stark as the reflection off a predator's eye.

"It actually does cool off at night." She sat near the end of the bench, an arm's length away. Close enough, but not too. "I remembered that it did, but then I wondered if it was just memory playing tricks." She quieted, let the silence settle. Her job wasn't to talk, but to sit, wait, listen. To be there.

"Haven't had time to think about this much over the past few days. Every time I turned around, you were getting yourself killed or pulling some diplomatic rabbit out of a hat. I suppose I should thank you for the distraction." Niall took a last pull on his 'stick, then rolled the gold-striped cylinder between his fingers. "It happened over there." He pointed to a place about twenty meters distant, the current resting place for a cluster of skimmer charge-stations. "Those stations weren't there, of course. Nothing was. Just a piece of open land in between the buildings." He sniffed. His face was in shadow, and maybe it was a good thing. "I wonder if anyone knows what happened there? Someone. One of the old-timers."

Jani looked toward the spot and imagined a night twenty years before. The darkness shattered by bombs and artillery. The shouts. The panic. And in the middle of it all, a twenty-one-year-old sergeant, sent to perform a very special task. "How do you feel?"

Niall laughed, a single, humorless jerk of his shoulders. "I really shouldn't bother to eat decent food until after we pull out of here." He leaned forward, elbows on knees, and continued to work the spent 'stick. "But the offices are open at all hours now, thanks to you. Always a bathroom handy. A can to kneel before."

Jani studied his profile, details muted by the half-light.

Sharp nose and line of jaw, set off by his brimmed lid. *He could take it off.* Yes, they were outdoors, but they were seated, and, technically at least, having a conversation. *But he won't do it.* He was an officer in the Commonwealth Service, with a tradition to uphold. Standards to maintain. An ideal to live up to.

"Go ahead and say it." Niall glanced at her, then faced front once more. "When you're this quiet for this long, I can just about hear the hum of machinery."

"That's the animandroid." Jani raised her left arm, then let it fall. Twitched her left leg. "Bad joke."

"You're allowed, gel." Niall sighed. "After the day you've had, you're allowed a lot."

Jani pondered for a time. Then she tapped him on the shoulder and pointed to his spent 'stick. "Got any extras?"

Niall stared. "Parini will bloody kill me."

"If it weren't for me, he wouldn't have anything to do around here but dance and pick up unsuspecting lieutenants." Jani held out her hand. "C'mon."

Niall scrabbled into his trouser pocket and pulled out his case. "When was the last time you smoked?"

"Years." Jani took a 'stick, crunched the tip, then paused to wipe a tiny fleck of the bulb material from her tongue. "I don't remember—can you swallow this stuff?"

"It's safe." Niall grinned as he pulled out one for himself and bit down. "Years ago, if the pieces were big enough, we'd have spitting contests." He shook his head. "I've said it before, gel. Just when I think you can't surprise me anymore."

"Drinking's a waste of time. I want to see if nicotine still has any effect."

"First Doc, then you." Niall paused to take a deep drag, then blew out a quartet of rings. "Gonna work on Meva next."

Jani eyed the 'stick warily, then took a drag. Her throat closed as the fragrant smoke flowed into her mouth, and she coughed. She bent double to take the pressure off her chest. Her eyes teared.

"Jesus wept—don't try to pull like me! I've been at it since the days o' me youth." Niall took the 'stick from her and tapped her between her shoulder blades until she quieted. "Baby puffs, until you work up to it."

"Thanks."

"What I'm here for."

Jani took back the 'stick and tried again. The merest sampling. "Taste's a little like the way *vrel* blossom smells." She dabbed her eyes with her sleeve, then stilled and watched the smoke stream upward until the night breeze took hold and scattered it. "If you had to do it again, now, how would you secure them?"

Niall sat back, one arm crossed over his stomach, the other straight, the 'stick dangling from his hand. "I'd have demanded more people. One guard per, and two to back them up in case friends decided to come to the rescue." His eyes narrowed as he considered the problem. "Armored skimvan right here near the building. None of this escorting through the base shit." Pause to inhale. "If I could coax a medico to come along, I'd just drug 'em and stack them in the van. Wouldn't even give them the chance to see one another, to get excited."

Jani nodded. "And if you had been put in that situation a year or two earlier?" She waited for him to speak, and knew it would be some time before he did. *Because he knows the answer.* "I think you'd have shot them without a second thought." She took another puff, and tasted the *vrel* blossom. "You were once a remorseless bastard, Niall Pierce, untempered by finer feeling or much of a moral sense. It wasn't that you lacked those things. They were there, and always had been. They were just . . . dormant. You lived a life in which you couldn't afford them, so you set them aside." She lowered her voice as a brace of file-laden clerks trotted past. "Then you met Mako, and somehow he instilled in you the notion that there was still a modicum of honor left to be mined from that calloused orphan heart. You learned that you could be part of something bigger than yourself,

and that realization hit you like a sockful of rocks. All those
sensibilities that you'd set aside awakened and roiled to the
surface."

Niall sat still, eyes fixed straight ahead. Breathing a little
quick, a little shallow. Might have been nicotine. Or memory.

Jani kept her voice level, soft. "The problem is, you need
tools to deal with bigger than yourself, and you hadn't acquired them yet. So, when the shit hit the fan, you fell back
on the bastard because that was still your default. It was the
man you still were, to some extent. But then, as time passed,
you changed. You became a better man, the man you wish
you had been twenty years before." Her throat tightened, and
she blamed the smoke. "One of the best I've ever known. But
I've told you that before." She watched a wad of paper skitter
down the walkway, coaxed by the breeze. "The bill's been
paid, Niall, with hard-earned coin. Give yourself a break."

For a time it seemed as though he hadn't heard. Then
came the voice, from twenty years away. "They keep me
posted, like old friends. I hear Ebben scream like she did
when she saw the others die and realized she was next. I
see the look on her face when I aimed the long-range at
her. I feel the pounding of my heart, the certainty that if I
let her get away, she'd flee to her friends, save herself by
giving Roshi and the rest of us away." He doffed his lid,
scratched his head, set it back on. "I relive it all as if it was
yesterday."

"And you likely always will." Jani pressed a hand to her
mended stomach. No pain, only pressure, as through someone had placed a foot on her diaphragm and pressed down.
"If you hadn't changed, you wouldn't see them. They'll always be there to remind you of how far you've come."

Niall stared straight ahead, a still image captured in a
moment of tension. Not a twitch, not even the flicker of an
eyelid, broke the stasis.

Then, after a few moments, movement, his nostrils nar-
rowing as he snorted. "You really believe that?" He stood,

straightening the line of his tunic with his free hand. "I've heard lines of bull from the psychs before, but I think you just won the prize." He edged away from her, one slow step after another, toward the charge-station array. "What's your default?"

Jani stood and walked after him, slowing every so often as her heart skipped. "There's a reason why we're friends."

"You? A remorseless bastard?" Niall glanced back at her, then shook his head. "You were born with the tools. If Ebben and the others had bolted on you, you'd never have—" He stopped in front of the charge-stations, reduced to shadowed shape by the darkness. "You never panicked in your life."

"How do you know?"

"Because you'd have told me. Sometime, during one of our bull sessions, you'd have dropped a hint." Niall touched the corner of one of the stations, then pulled back as though it burned. "What do you see, now that you're here? What do you remember?" His voice came soft, but there was an undercurrent. A plea for parity, for a weakness she could share.

Jani sniffed the Rauta Shèràa night air, tinged with dampness and city smells. Not baked. Not light. Not as clean as the desert. "It's like in the dreams. The openings to the Laumrau tents close like a self-sealing envelope, and the flaps make a ripping sound if you yank them apart too quickly. The tent material itself looks flimsy, like rotted silk, but it's stronger than it looks." She stared down at the 'stick in her hand, dose ring still indicating three-quarters full. Felt a tap on her arm, saw Niall's extended hand, and passed it off with a grateful nod. "When I reached the first tent, I tried shooting through it. But it was coated with barrier—don't ask me why I didn't assume it would be coated with barrier, I just didn't—and the charge dissipated across the surface." She moved her feet. Knew she stood on cement, yet felt sand instead. Shifting sand. "I panicked then. I knew whoever was inside had heard the shooter. That those in the surrounding tents heard it as well." Her heart tripped, and she blamed nicotine, the injury.

"I had resigned myself to death when I walked down the dune toward the encampment, but part of me wasn't ready to go. I grabbed the edge of the flap and yanked it back—" She tried to mime the motion until the grip of her incision stopped her. "—heard that ripping sound. A female sat at her altar table. She looked up when she heard me. Set down her fork. And just stared." Her hand came up, fingers closing around a nonexistent weapon. "She never moved, not even when she saw the shooter." She turned to Niall to find him watching her wide-eyed, 'stick stalled halfway to his mouth. "I know they heard me. They had to have—"

Niall let his arm drop. "What?"

"It was like fish in a barrel." Jani felt sweat bead on her temple and brushed it away. "Why didn't one of them try to stop me? There were twenty-six of them and one of me. They must have heard. They must have known what was going on. And rather than commit sacrilege by interrupting their sacrament, they remained in their tents, and let me slaughter them." She walked to the nearest charge station and leaned against it. "I wonder sometimes whether they wanted to die. Whether the enormity of their sins had borne down upon them, and they decided en masse that death was better than going on as they were."

"Suicide by homicide?" Niall paced a tight circle. "I think that's a stretch, but I'm human. We've a tradition of fighting to live." His voice had lightened now that they'd moved on to her nightmare. "I think they froze. They didn't expect a human to come into their camp and attack them, and when they heard it happening, they didn't take it for what it was." He snorted again. "Death by culture clash. The history pages are filled. I blame the bornsect mind-set. Damned lockstep thinking. If they'd had even one Dathim Naré in that encampment, you'd have been dead before you reached the first tent." He spun on his heel to face her and shook a finger under her nose. "Don't try to slap a coward label on yourself, Jani Kilian, because I won't let you. If just one of them had woken the hell up and realized what was happening, you wouldn't be standing here now questioning yourself. The potential for death was there." He shook his head in disgust. "Fish in a barrel, my ass."

Jani smiled. "That's our job, I guess. Prop up one another every so often. Shake some sense."

"You were here for me tonight. I'll be there for you tomorrow." Niall held his head high as he started again to pace, touching one of the stations each time he passed. Then he stopped and his shoulders sagged. "It won't ever go away?"

"I don't think so."

"Ah, well." Niall took a step closer. The light from a safety illumin fell across his face, revealing the greyness, the sheen of sweat. "Maybe it's worth it, if only to watch you try to smoke." He smiled. Walked to one of the charge-stations and leaned against it. "So what's next for the team? Release the old bird's soul at Temple? Allow him his rest?"

"In a few days." Jani leaned against another of the stations, savored the machine warmth. "Meva and I are planning something."

"Why does that phrase strike fear in my heart?" Niall looked around for a moment, then gestured to her. "Come on, gel. I'll walk you back. Some of us need our sleep."

CHAPTER 35

"They've been ferrying idomeni out there since the ceremony was announced early yesterday. Last estimates were upward of two million. Could be two and a half to three by the time we get out there. The logistics are staggering." Niall took a swallow of coffee, then smacked his lips. "You've been taking lessons from Shroud. This stuff really could wake the dead."

"Flattery will get you a refill." Val topped off Niall's mug, then hovered over Jani, carafe at the ready. "What's wrong with it?"

Jani set down her still full cup. Breakfast in the kitchen of Val's guesthouse had commenced a few minutes before, after hurried awakenings and conferencing with ministers and admirals general and quick showers. "Stomach's a little knotty." She jerked her chin at Niall. "He's trying to scare me."

"Don't get me hopes up, gel. It'll go to me head and there'll be no dealing with me." Niall moved from caffeine to sugar and carbohydrates, spreading a slice of toast with marmalade, then folding it over and dunking it in his coffee. "They've also set up displays in Temple and major squares. Other cities. Worldskeinwide transmission. We won't even talk about the Commonwealth networks."

"Good. *Don't*." Jani took a lemon wedge from a plate of garnishes and bit into it.

Val stifled a yawn, then sat next to Jani and eyed her with professional calculation gone a bit bleary around the edges. "You know how John and I feel about this?"

"I know." Jani took up her fork and picked over her food, forcing down some fried meat, some scrambled eggs. Protein seemed the best bet, given what her day held in store. "But Meva and I talked about it. Then she discussed it with some of the propitiators she knew at Temple, and they concluded that while there's no real precedent, it's theologically sound." She smashed an overcrisp rasher of bacon into bits, then set down her fork. "He and I talked about it once, for some reason I can't remember. If I ever went back, what could I do in order to . . . restore balance?" She held out her right hand and studied her redstone ring. The one Tsecha had given her when she graduated the Academy. The one that hadn't fit until she'd begun to hybridize and her fingers thinned.

"We could've delayed this, you know." Niall's verve ebbed, replaced by his more usual coiled spring wariness. "I could've taken you out there beforehand, let you see the place. Get a sense of it."

"It wouldn't have helped." Jani pushed away from the table and stood, her propitiator's robe falling around her knees, the red-slashed sleeves settling past her wrists. "I could visit it beforehand a hundred times, and it wouldn't help." She sniffed, smelled clear air and heat instead of coffee and toast, then looked down at Niall to find him studying her, eyes a little too shiny for comfort.

"We'd better—" He looked away, cleared his throat. "We've got a long ride ahead of us. We'd better leave." He picked up his brimmed lid from its resting place on the spare chair and put it on, squaring the angle as always by running his thumbs and forefingers along the edge of the brim. "I'll wait by the skimmer." He strode out the kitchen door without a backward glance, a rough-edged vision in tan and white.

"He does get emotional, our Niall. Especially where you're concerned." Val took a last swallow of coffee, then pushed back his chair and rose with obvious reluctance.

"I visited Knevçet Shèràa once. You were still in induced coma, and John and I weren't sure—" He inhaled shakily. "I wanted to see the place for myself. I'd heard rumors enough, and I wanted to see." As though in deference to the upcoming ceremony, he had donned a daysuit in dark cream, the jacket's lapels a fair match for an overrobe's shawl collar. "I couldn't get within ten kilometers of the place. The Vynshà had taken over that area, and they'd installed perimeter patrols. A gate with armed sentries."

"Tsecha wasn't sure when they razed the hospital. He didn't think it happened until after he'd been put under house arrest, but no one would tell him anything and he could never find the records of the destruction." Jani saw Tsecha in her mind's eye, overrobe billowing as he paced around her and ranted over Temple perfidy. "He always felt that they should have kept it open, as a reminder." She heard his voice in her head, the sibilant rise and fall, only to have it silenced when Val touched her arm.

"Let's go." He linked his arm with hers and walked with her into the morning.

"They'll kill you if you go out there, Captain. You know they will."

"They're at sacrament, Borgie. They don't even have any guards posted."

"What are you going to do?"

"Just go back inside. Wait until I return. Then we'll go from there."

"No need for you to get out." Niall steered the skimmer into the embassy drive. "We just need to join up with the ministerial cavalcade so that we all leave at the same time." He tapped the dashboard input, then studied the display. "Then it's on to the enclave—Feyó's skimmer is waiting just inside the gate. It will pull in behind and follow us to the destination, of course. *Protocol.*" He drawled the word as though it were a particularly foul descriptor.

"Knevçet Shèràa." Jani caught his gaze in the rearview. "You can say it, Niall. It's all right."

"I know that." Niall reddened, as he did whenever he was caught being delicate. He then disembarked to talk to Ulanova's driver, which left the vehicle unguarded.

Jani turned to Val. "Do you think—" She was interrupted by a rap on the window, and lowered it.

"Hello." Lucien looked in, stepping back a little as soon as he spotted Val.

Jani ignored Val's mutter. "You driving, as well?"

"Mako and Burkett. The cabin barrier will go up as soon as we set out, and I'll be left with my own thoughts for company." Lucien looked back toward the Service triple-length, near which the two men and various aides had already gathered. "I better go." He reached in and took hold of Jani's hand. "*Bonne chance.*" He brought it to his lips and kissed it hard, then trotted back to his post.

"Some of us have all the luck." Val sniffed. "I don't hold grudges. Please don't give it a second thought."

Jani surveyed the yard and spotted Scriabin standing by his own triple-length, talking to an aide. "I have some unfinished business to attend to." She felt Val's hand close over her own, a not so subtle attempt at restraint. "I'll just be a minute." She shook off his hold, pushing up the gullwing and exiting the skimmer.

Scriabin actually brightened when he saw Jani approach. "Good morning! I hope that you're—"

"A word, please." Jani ignored his proffered hand, saw the light in his eyes flicker.

"Zhenya?"

Jani and Scriabin both turned just as Anais Ulanova emerged from the passenger cabin of Scriabin's skimmer.

"We'll be leaving in a few minutes." She glared at Jani, but this time her hatred was tempered by uncertainty. Fear. A hint of panic. "There is something I wish to discuss with you on the way to the ceremony." She focused on her nephew, her voice ripe with conciliatory lilt. "It may take some time."

Scriabin studied his aunt for a few moments, then shook his head. "Oh, Ani." He pressed a hand to his forehead, then wiped it down his face. "What have you done now?" He looked past her to the center of the drive, and swore.

Jani followed Scriabin's glower. To her complete lack of surprise, she saw Lucien standing beside Mako's skimmer, watching them. Once again, hours of discussion whittled down to words left unspoken, to scant expressions. To Lucien's bland disregard as he met Ulanova's pleading eye, and the warm smile when he looked at Jani. To the way Ulanova's face paled as the realization hit home that her lover had betrayed her.

"I'll be a few minutes." Scriabin shot his cuffs. "I need to speak with ná Kièrshia now." No "Tyotya." No patient smile of Familial duty. Only the dead voice and cold eye of a man who had reached his limit.

Ulanova held out a hand to him. "Zhenya, I—"

"Get in the skimmer."

Ulanova flinched. Then she lowered her hand and, with a last sullen scowl at Jani, did as she was told.

Scriabin waited until an aide slammed the skimmer door closed. "I don't want to hear what you have to tell me, do I?" Weariness had replaced anger now, his normally powerful voice emerging weak. Defeated.

"I'll be brief." Jani led him to the small side yard, where the small fountain burbled just loudly enough. "The time wasn't right before to discuss this. It isn't any better now, but the way things are going, there may not be a good time for months." She picked up a handful of gravel from a hammered bowl and started flicking the stones one at a time into the water. "Anais sent Lucien to Elyas to kill me." She surprised herself with her casual tone. *Nothing to see here— move along. Happens every day.* "She convinced Mako that he and I were still close, that he'd make a useful . . . maybe 'spy' is too harsh a word. Maybe 'pair of eyes' will suffice." She flicked stones into the water with the beat of her words. *Plink—plink—plink—* "But the fact was, she felt Feyó more amenable and preferred the idea of having her in charge of

Thalassa. My dominance would garner her nothing. She knew I didn't trust her. Knew that if I had anything to say, she'd wind up on the sidelines."

Scriabin stood rigid, and stared at the stone wall in front of him. "If you heard this from Pascal—"

"He has this habit of telling me the truth." Jani tossed another pebble. *Plink.* "A choice between believing him or your *tyotya* is no choice at all." She recalled Mako's words. *You reach a certain level . . . you assume that some might prefer if you did not exist.*

"I don't—" Scriabin pulled a handkerchief from inside his sleeve and wiped his forehead. "I will do a little digging on my own, if you don't mind. Some things one must confirm for oneself, however much one trusts the messenger." He shook out the embroidered cloth, then folded it into a neat square. "I may . . . talk to Pascal, just to gather a few details." He glanced at Jani sidelong, his discomfort coating him like his sweat. "In any event, she won't . . . she won't bother you again."

"No. She won't." Jani tossed the last few pebbles into the water. "I should mention that Thalassa plans to nationalize John's share of Neoclona. It'll settle the question of ownership once and for all, and the income should help finance our expansion."

"I daresay." Scriabin paused to lick his lips. "I expect you would like assurance of my and Minister Ulanova's support for this, election win or not." He sighed heavily. He knew blackmail when he heard it, and who to thank for the privilege.

"I want the takeover to happen, and Chicago to stay out of the way." Jani brushed off her hands. "Financial support would be appreciated as well, as a show of good faith." *Because there's a GateWay to be considered, and millions of new colonists, and the security of one-quarter of your remaining Commonwealth.* A new Oligarch, eager to mend fences with disenfranchised Haárin. She didn't say any of that aloud, of course, because she knew she didn't have to. Scriabin was an old hand—he could do the math in his head.

"We should get going." Jani left him by the water and returned to her skimmer, where she found Niall waiting.

He pulled open her door. Offered her his hand for support. "Took a little break to stretch our legs and read someone the Riot Act, did we?"

"However did you guess?" Jani brushed off Val's questioning stare. "Let's go."

Her blood flowed down her arm, as warm as the wind, and she sopped it with strips of shop cloth that she'd worked into a braid. Then she tied the braid to a stake and drove the stake into the ground. According to an ancient Vynshà ritual, she had just taken her soul from her body and pinned it in place. Preserved it from whatever desperate act her now godless body intended to perform.

"I've never seen the streets this empty." Val stared out his window, shook his head. "Not even during the last bombing forays." He glanced at Jani. "I won't ask if you're nervous."

"It's not like I'm giving a speech." She tried to smile, but the effort made her face ache. "I'm numb." Her heart thudded as the entry to the Haárin enclave came into view and Feyó's skimmer appeared at the gate.

"What does he think of all this?" Val glanced toward the sky. "Wherever he is, in whatever form. What might he be thinking?"

"That it all ended up pretty much like he predicted it would." Jani watched one of Meva's suborns close the doors to a skimvan, and knew it contained the reliquary. "That he won."

Val lay his head back and stared through the curved window at the cloudless sky. "You could be right."

Jani turned to track the van as they passed it, as it floated out onto the road and slowly accelerated after them, like a shark chasing down its prey.

You won, inshah. She imagined a loud laugh, a loose-limbed walk and shining auric eyes.

* * *

Rauta Shèràa diminished as cities always did, from center to various sections and quarters to the outskirts, until it receded, shortened, faded into the horizon behind them. Thirty minutes passed, and the land rolled and roughened, stone in white and brown and coral pink dotted with grey-green scrub. An hour passed, and even that fell away, until all that remained were the outcroppings and the dunes and the high blue milky sky.

So where are the crowds? Jani was about to rib Niall that his sources had miscalculated by a factor of ten or more when they passed over a rocky ridge and into the shallow bowl that held the sands of light's weeping. She saw them then, seemingly as numerous as grains of sand, held back from the center of the bowl by low barriers and patrols of mixed humanish and idomeni security. A sea of faces—the true meaning of that hackneyed phrase was driven home with a hammer as in every direction she looked idomeni filled her view.

Then there were the skimmers, the vans and trucks and arrays and holocams.

"Oh my God." Val sat up straight, hand scrabbling along the seat to link with hers.

"Told you." Niall eyed her in his rearview as he halted the skimmer on the rim.

Jani nodded. Her mouth had gone as dry as the land surrounding them, her muscles clenched so tight that it hurt to move.

Niall exited the skimmer, setting his lid and straightening his tunic as he walked back to Jani's door and opened it. "Need a hand, gel?" he asked, and offered her his.

Jani gave Val's hand a last squeeze and let it go even as she reached out and took Niall's and held it fast. Stepped out onto desolation that had not changed over the course of twenty years, breathed the light, dry air that smelled the same, felt the heat that drilled her to the hybrid bone.

She looked off to her right, toward the site where the hospital had stood. Every block and tile had been knocked down and carted away years before, sunken into burial sites all over Shèrá, leaving only the telltale flatness that spoke of mechanical leveling and foundations and the incursion of civilization into a place not meant to contain it.

Jani imagined the outlines of walls, three stories high and devoid of windows, a flat roof. Remembered nightfall, that first chill in the air, and the warmth of her blood as it ran down her arm.

"Jan?" Niall leaned close. "You're wearing the bug. Anything goes wrong, just call."

"I'm all right." She let go of his hand, reached beneath her overrobe to the sheath on her belt. Slid out the short blade that Meva had sent her the previous day and started down the slope. Did her best to shut out the faces and the cams and the weighted silence, the faint whistle of wind and occasional cry of a bird the only discernable sounds. *How can so many bodies make so little noise?* No one spoke. Overrobes and sleeves fluttered, the only movement in the vast ring of mortality.

As she neared the bottom, she pressed the point of the blade to her right sleeve and slashed downward, the cloth renting with a sharp ripping sound, like the opening of a tent flap. She slowed, then stopped as she reached the foot of the slope. Off to the right, twenty or so meters distant, stood Meva, bracketed by Dathim and Feyó. Behind them, upon a small altar stone, rested the reliquary.

She started walking again. Four strides. A fifth. Then she stopped, raised her arm so the cloth tumbled back to the elbow, revealing her bare forearm. Drew the blade across her skin, then waved her arm in a sweeping arc, spraying her blood.

That first, wasted shot. The opening of the tent. Wide, staring eyes.

The second shot.

One—

Another tent. No wasted shot this time.

—two—

The next tent, and the next.

—three—four—

* * *

. . . another cut, another spray of blood. Another. Another. Too many times to track. Too many times.

—fifteen—sixteen—seventeen—
She tried to pray at first, impose order upon the random path she walked. Then realized that order had no place here.

One Thalassan day, her soul cloth vanished. She hunted for it, couldn't find it. Ran to Tsecha's house to tell him, only to find that he had taken it, or sent someone to take it. He had untied the knotting and shaken loose the braids. I have returned your soul to you, nìa, he told her.

And she returned theirs to them.
—twenty-four—twenty-five.
Twenty-six.

"That part's over." Niall's voice, in her ear.

"As much as it can ever be." Jani looked toward the network skimmers. "Hope they got it all."

"You're almost through it, gel. Just a few minutes more." Niall paused, cleared his throat. *"Give the old bird a nod from me when he goes."*

"What do we do now, Cap?"

"Place me under arrest, Sergeant Burgoyne. I've broken treaty law. You have to arrest me."

"No, you did it to save us—"

"If you don't arrest me, they'll think you were involved. Borgie—listen to me. You didn't know what I was planning— that's what you'll tell them because it's the truth. You didn't know, and when I told you what I had done, you did your duty and placed me under arrest."

"Captain—"

"I did what I had to. Now it's your turn."

Jani stood over the last place. The last. Her right arm had

numbed. She felt stiffness where blood had dried, the sting of the breeze across open wounds. But no pain. Not yet.

She sheathed the blade. Turned to the right and walked. Her head felt afloat, her knees wobbly. There was a hollow where her heart had been.

She fixed on Meva, who stood still as statuary, arms folded and hands tucked into the sleeves of her overrobe. As she drew closer, the female stepped to one side, allowing her a clear path to the reliquary.

Jani stopped before the altar. Lifted the reliquary lid. It seemed heavier than it had in Thalassa, hard-edged and unwieldy. She brought in her elbows and braced them against her sides for support, hefting the lid like an overladen tray and setting it down on the left side of the reliquary. As her hands slid along the edge, some roughness caught her finger, the one bearing the redstone ring. She felt the sliver slide in, the sting when she pushed the lid farther up the table and applied pressure to the wound. *Making sure I stay conscious, are you?* Her lip twitched as she fought the urge to grin. *Always the considerate one.*

She moved away from the lid and stood before the open reliquary. "Hello, old friend." She reached into the box and took hold of the scroll, clutching it hard with her left hand to compensate for the weakness in her right. "The place has been cleaned for you. Their souls have been healed." Her hands remained dry and steady, and she thanked her old teacher as she lifted the scroll and set it on the altar. "Follow them home," she said as she opened the cover, then turned each page. Felt something brush her cheek, and knew it was the breeze, but decided that for today she would imagine it as something else.

I understand more than you believe, nìa.
"Yes, nìRau. I think you did."

Jani braced her hands against the altar. "The stone is so nice and warm."

Meva moved in beside her and placed her hand against
the stone as well. "I find it cool." She touched Jani's right
hand, then took Jani's arm and led her up the incline. "You
feel most as yourself, ná Kièrshia?"

"I feel most as someone who's going to pass out if she
doesn't sit down soon." Jani fielded Meva's look of horror.
"Don't worry—I won't faint in front of the worldskein. I
will maintain my presence and my godly composure." She
breathed, felt her heart skip, saw golden flecks invade her
field of vision. "Stay away," she said to John as he started to
walk toward her. "Not until I get inside the skimmer." She
looked toward the crowds, who had not yet begun to disperse, and offered a slight hand wave to the nearest reporter,
who waved back. Slid into the skimmer as soon as Niall
flipped up the gullwing, then gripped the edge of her seat
as John and Val piled in after her and the weight imbalance
caused the vehicle to shudder and buck like a small boat in
a storm.

"When I watched you draw that blade down your sleeve
and make the first cut, I thought to myself, 'Hot damn, she
nicked her brachial artery. John and I will be running down
to get her in two, three minutes.'" Val pushed up her right
sleeve and swallowed hard. "I assume you're going to want
these to scar?"

"You assume correctly." Jani felt some remnant of tension leach away as Val and John eased her onto her back.
John then dragged a seat cushion out of its holder and tucked
it under her knees while Val attached a transfuser pack to the
crook of her right arm.

Niall immediately began the tricky exercise of maneuvering the triple-length through the dispersing crowds. "'Then
will he strip his sleeves and show his scars, and say, "These
wounds I had on Crispin's day." Old men forget: yet all shall
be forgot, but he'll remember with advantages what feats he
did that day.' Henry the Fifth again." He paused. Started to
speak, stopped, then tried again. "Is she all right?"

"She will be as soon as we get her blood volume back

up." Val grumbled under his breath. "Did you have to bleed quite this much?"

"She did what she had to." John pressed a scanner lead to her shirt just over her heart. "It was . . . the most starkly beautiful thing I have ever seen."

"Scared the hell out of me." Val adjusted the transfuser settings, then fell back onto the seat opposite. "Hundreds of thousands of idomeni, and none of them so much as whispering."

Jani closed her eyes. Felt the vehicle hum run along her spine. Drifted in and out of sleep. Dreamed of the reliquary. Dreamed she saw Tsecha, walking across the sand toward her, overrobe billowing behind him. Dreamed she heard John's voice, Niall's response.

Felt the skimmer slow, then stop, and realized that she wasn't dreaming at all.

"I'll only be a minute." John said as he placed his hand on her brow.

Jani opened her eyes just as he pushed up the gullwing and exited the skimmer. "Is this where I think it is?"

"Yeah." Val sat on the edge of his seat. Then he sighed, wiped his eyes, and followed his partner outside.

"Network vans are going to be coming through any minute. I told him he needed to make it fast." Niall sat back, pulled out his case. Soon the clove aroma drifted through the cabin. "Should've figured he'd want to see this place. It's his Knevçet Shèràa, after all."

Jani sat up. Moved her arms, her legs. *No stars in front of my eyes.* Walking might prove another matter entirely, but she wouldn't know until she tried.

"Can't sit still, can you?" Niall shook his head. "They might want to be alone, you know? They might just need some time."

Jani looked through the open door to the scene beyond. John pacing back and forth, Val standing off to one side, his hand over his mouth. No shrine on this site. No marker or fencing or designation of any kind.

"It was a turning point for me, too," Jani said as she disembarked. "I used to wonder what this place looked like." She walked carefully, slowing as the hollow sensation in her chest returned. "I thought about coming here once, when you and Val went to a meeting at the consulate." She came to a halt an arm's reach from John, who had stopped pacing and now stared down at the ground. "Eamon even left the place unlocked, probably hoping that I'd bolt. But I couldn't find a skimmer."

John didn't respond at first. Then he crouched, worked his hand into the sandy ground, gone from dune to semi-arid as they drew near Rauta Shèràa again. "Here." He let the ground trickle through his fingers, then made a sweeping motion with one arm. "Wreckage scattered for kilometers. Remains. We'd pick up some blackened bit the size of a finger and didn't know if we were looking at tissue or a charred piece of transport until we scanned it." He cleaned his hand on the leg of his trousers and slowly straightened. "Then we found—" He stopped. Swallowed. "We'd watched idomeni die for months. We weren't allowed to help. We weren't allowed to save . . . so many. I lost count. Then we found you, and decided—" He turned to look at her, eyes bright as the sun that blistered above them. "—and decided that we would save you, and that no one would stop us." He laughed. "Law of unintended consequences. If I knew then what I knew now . . . " He fixed on her for a long moment. " . . . I'd still do it. I wouldn't change—" He turned away. "My decision, to add to all the others that we made, and lived with, and paid for."

They stood in silence, each a prisoner of their own memories. Then Val stirred.

"We're getting the high sign." He jerked a thumb toward the skimmer, which Niall had converted into a holiday display of blinking warning lights. "The network vans are headed this way. We better get going."

Jani waited for John, then slipped her arm through his. They walked back to the skimmer side by side, at peace, at least for now. Got in and headed back to the city.

CHAPTER 36

" . . . and the first two thousand houses have been completed in phase one of the new western section." Dieter made a notation on his recording board. "That makes ten thousand in the past three months."

Jani nodded. Outside the library window a pair of seabirds swooped at one another, their squawks audible even through the filtering glass. *Are they fighting or mating?* She watched them circle one another, the tips of their wings seeming to touch. *Is there a difference?*

Then she sensed a ripple in the silence, and looked across the table to find her suborn eyeing her expectantly. "That's a lot."

"Yes, it is." Dieter set down the board, then tucked the stylus behind his ear. "A less preoccupied person might even be impressed."

Jani smiled. One thing she'd missed during her time away was Dieter's gentle chiding. *And now I've had a lifetime's worth in the past few months.* "I'm sorry. It's a marvelous achievement."

Dieter sighed, then started gathering up his files. "If you don't want the blow by blow details, just say so. I can save them for the monthly reports."

"When did we start doing monthly reports?"

"Last month, when the first funding arrived from Chicago to help cover phase two of the western expansion along with the far southern expansion near Meteora. Prime Minister Scriabin is an old Commerce hand. He likes reports with tables and charts and whatnot."

Jani tried to hand Dieter a file, but she had taken it out of order, and he frowned and set it aside. "Doesn't he trust us?"

"He simply wants an accounting." Dieter piled the first armful of documents onto the trundle that followed him everywhere like a loyal, overlarge dog. "He's entitled. He's a major underwriter of what is likely the largest resettlement project ever undertaken."

"The Commonwealth push into the colonies was bigger."

"You're going to argue now?" Dieter returned to the desk for a second armful. "The Vynshà migration involves fewer individuals, yes, but also a much shorter time frame." To the trundle, then back to the desk again. "And we're looking after things like infrastructure and such, which was more than Mother Commonwealth ever did for our great-great-however-many-grandfolk." The last armful. "This exodus will be handled properly."

By committee. With monthly reports. Jani sighed. "The teams are in place. We have departments now, instead of someone in a corner desk with a workstation and a good memory. All humming along."

Dieter stopped. Cocked his head. "What's wrong?"

"I don't know." Jani walked to the window and searched for the birds, but they'd moved on to another part of the sky. "Meteora? Didn't they have a corruption problem there?"

" . . . Yes." Dieter wedged the trundle between two chairs to keep it from drifting, then joined her at the window. "We haven't done much there yet. A team of engineers and architects traveled down last week to look over the proposed site for the first enclave." He slid the window aside and stepped out onto the balcony. "It's not as beautiful as Thalassa, in my opinion. Greyer. Greener, perhaps. Mountainous."

"It's cold." Jani pushed up the sleeves of her pullover and held out her arms to the summer sun. "I remember someone saying it's cold."

"That was me, sometime last month." Dieter stared at her scarred forearms and shook his head. "Sounded a bit like your homeworld. Acadia. Land of a Thousand Storms."

Acadia. She'd considered going home, for a little while. But while her parents would want to see her, she wasn't sure anyone else did. *Half Haárin. Cat eyes.* And those would be the kinder names. *Maybe later.* When she could tell Declan and Jamira Shah Kilian that she didn't care, and mean it. *Not now.*

Dieter waved a hand in front of her face. "Jani, are you—"

"Why is Meteora on the list of sites?" She opened her eyes wide and tried to look attentive.

"Governor Markos thought that the presence of some businesslike, physically intimidating Haárin might push out some of the more hardcore humanish criminal element. And some Oà expressed an interest in settling down there. Makes sense. It's more their climate."

"Oà?" Jani looked toward the once bare cliffs of Thalassa, now coated with houses like an overiced cake. "I didn't know—" She glanced at Dieter and shrugged. "Maybe I did."

Dieter contemplated her for a time, then shook his head. "Poor Captain Kilian. You'd have gone barking mad on a peacetime base. Or driven your commander likewise." He left her to return to his trundle. "Problems don't need to be life and death to be important. There is still much to be done here."

Jani remained on the balcony. Heard the library door close. Dragged a chair over to the railing, sat and propped up her feet. Because she was ná Kièrshia, Dominant of Thalassa, and had nothing to do until her next meeting.

* * *

"Sit down, Jani." Rudo Sikara ushered her into the office he kept in the business area of the Main House. "You are looking well." He looked dapper in charcoal grey, a red rose pinned to his lapel. "I met with Doctor Shroud yesterday, at the Karistos office. I told him I'd be seeing you." He sat at his polished bloodwood desk, bare but for a stylus stand and a trueleather blotter. "He sends his regards."

Jani nodded. She hadn't seen John since their return to Elyas. He had decamped immediately to oversee the expansion of the Thalassan medical facility in Karistos. When he did return to see patients, she spent the day in Karistos. She knew the ache would subside eventually, supplanted by a loss of trust on both sides that cut to the bone. "When next you see him, likewise."

Sikara nodded. Would have shuffled papers if there had been any on his desk to shuffle. "What did you wish to see me about?"

Jani leaned forward, elbows on desk, chin cradled in one hand. "Speaking as a longtime resident of Karistos, what can you tell me about Meteora?"

Sikara's beetle brows arched. "An unfortunate history. Rough sort of place. Smuggling, that sort of thing." He grinned, shifted in his seat. "I began my career there."

"Do tell." Jani took out a paper notebook and stylus, because she knew she would probably need to take notes, and in any case thought better with paper in her hand.

A few days later she stood at the walkway railing outside the library and inhaled the aromas of mid-afternoon sacrament.

"Veena made tandoori chicken." Dieter leaned beside her, his eyes on the mealtime bustle. "I would gladly crawl across the courtyard on broken glass for Veena's tandoori chicken."

Jani nodded. "It reminds me of my mother's."

Dieter stood quietly, fingering the cuff of his shirt. "When are you leaving for Meteora?"

Jani smiled. Did she really think her esteemed suborn wouldn't be able to figure it out? "Today." She watched the bustle in the courtyard below. Knew she'd miss it, even as she knew she needed to go. "Not for long. A few months, maybe. Change of scenery will do me good."

"The term is 'adrenaline addict.'" Dieter sniffed. "Who will I show my monthly updates to?"

"You can send them to me." Jani grabbed the railing and leaned back, enjoyed the sensation of a healed knife wound that no longer pulled or ached. "I'll initial them and send them back."

Dieter rolled his eyes. Quieted again. Started to speak, then hesitated. "Was it that bad?"

Jani considered her answer, because Dieter deserved a careful reply. "It's better now." The dreams had stopped, for the most part. Physically, she was as healthy as ever. Emotionally, she'd heal.

"It's different here now." Dieter's eyes glistened, until he blinked the shine away.

"It always will be." Jani's chest tightened, and she blamed the aftereffects of the wound that didn't bother her anymore. "And it's a good place. The best place. But Meva's propitiator now, and you're in your element with the organization. There's nothing left for me to do but sign off on others' work."

Dieter blew out a breath. "Best let Colonel Pierce know where you're going."

"I will." Jani stood still for a time, and took a last, long look. Then she patted Dieter on the shoulder and left him standing at the railing. Down a flight of stairs to her bedsit, the small room she had moved into when she left John. Opened her closet and grabbed her duffel from the top shelf, still heavy with stuff from the voyage to Rauta Shèràa. Coveralls. Boots. Small clothes. *Jani's Noah bag,* Lucien had once called it. *Two of everything in case of disaster.*

What have you been up to, Lucien? I haven't seen you since we got back. Probably toying with her as he had with

Val, declaring his interest, then holding back to see if she cared. *Eternal gamesman.* She checked the scanproof compartment beneath the duffel's fake bottom, which contained her scanpack and shooter. Tools. IDs in a number of names. Because she liked to keep in practice, and because you never knew.

She closed the room. Locked it, because she knew she would return. Took the stairs to the courtyard. Waved to Dieter on her way to the entry, and felt his stare serve as escort as she walked out the door.

The garage proved empty, for which she was grateful. She opted for an older, nondescript blue four-door because no one would miss it and it wouldn't attract attention. Popped the gullwing, tossed her bag onto the passenger seat, and inserted herself into the cabin. Pressed the charge-through, edged out of the parking slot, activated a music band—

—and stopped.

"OK." Jani pressed the charge-through again. The vehicle shuddered, moved forward a few meters, and stopped again.

"Way to make a break for it, Kilian." Jani popped the hood, then got out and examined the multicolored array of boards and battery casings. "Where the hell do you start?"

"Problem?"

Jani turned to the entry. Saw the rangy figure, backlit by outdoor brightness. Felt her heart stutter, and called it surprise. "What are you doing here?"

Lucien shrugged. "I haven't seen you since we got back." He wore civvies, white T-shirt and tan pull-ons. Trainers. "Just thought I'd, you know, stop by and see how things are going." He stepped up to the skimmer and pondered its innards. "What are you doing?"

Jani flipped up the top of a compartment cover, then closed it. "I'm trying to fix this thing."

"What's wrong with it?"

"It won't go."

A corner of Lucien's mouth twitched. "That narrows it down." He walked outside to his skimmer, a sleeker two-door the same coffee brown as his eyes. Opened the boot and drew out a large slingbag. "Would you like me to have a look?" Without waiting for an answer, he dropped the bag in front of the balky vehicle, crouched down and started rummaging. "I may have something here that can help." He drew out a scuffed grey oval about the size of a scanpack.

Jani caught a glimpse of the bag's contents before he closed the top. Other ovals. Squares and canisters. A lumpy polycloth roll tied with cord. "Are all those things what I think they are?"

"Just tools." Lucien placed the oval against the large flat-sided case that held the skimmer's brain. The device adhered. Hummed. Then dull blue light fluttered across the surface before settling down to a steady throb.

Lucien disconnected the oval and read the script that scrolled across the surface. "It's dumping your code. It's not that it doesn't recognize your permission to drive it, it's that it forgets. So you'll be able to reinitialize and start it, but as soon as you try to make a change that requires your code, like a Net setting or somesuch, it will have forgotten that you're allowed to drive it and shut down."

Jani shrugged. "So I won't try to reset anything."

"It's not that simple. You don't know the cause. Pinhole leak in the battery housing. Bad board." Lucien powered down the device and tossed it back into his bag. "The code-dumping is a symptom, not your main problem. Even if you don't touch anything, the skimmer could still stall out and leave you stranded between here and wherever you're going." He crouched down, concentrated on closing the bag. "Where are you going?"

Jani watched him fuss with the closures, drawing out the task, giving her plenty of silence to fill. "Just wanted to take a ride into Karistos."

"To see John?" Lucien stood, all perky helpfulness. "I can

take you." He nudged the bag out of the way with his foot, then started to push the malfunctioning skimmer back into its slot. Looked through the open gullwing into the cabin. "Don't forget your—" He eased the skimmer to a stop and stared at her.

I should've put it in the boot. Jani shoved her hands in her pockets and tried to avoid looking at him.

"You're leaving?" Lucien moved away from the vehicle and into her sightline, leaving her little choice. "Where are you going?"

I should lie. But she didn't want to. "Meteora. The site of our southern expansion." She walked to the skimmer, tried to open the passenger door—

"It dumped—"

"My code." Walked around to the driver's side and dragged out her duffel.

"For how long?" Lucien finished pushing the skimmer back into place, then shut the door.

"For as long as I need." Jani slung her bag over her shoulder and examined the other skimmers. "I'm surplus to requirements here. Everything's clicking along." She leaned against a charge-station. "I need to go someplace that isn't. Clicking along. Yevgeny likes reports with tables and charts and whatnot. I thought I could go in search of some whatnot."

"I can drive you there." Lucien hoisted his bag, then stood there looking like a star athlete in search of a gym. "I have time."

"You taking some leave?" Jani tried to remember the last time Lucien had more than a day's leave when she lived in Chicago, and found she couldn't. "For how long?"

"As long as I want." Lucien's voice went as dead as it had in the clinic garden. "It's been a busy few months. After Zhenya won the election, deals were made. Ani resigns her ministry in payback for trying to have you killed, shuts up and smiles and takes the ornamental position doled out by her nephew. Along the way, certain embarrassing issues get shoved under the rug." He waved. "Like me." He looked around the garage, brow furrowed, as though he couldn't wrap his mind around his predicament. "I was strongly advised to resign my commission. They didn't have to ask me twice." A shrug. "I'm out."

"You'll go back to Chicago?"

"I was also advised to avoid Chicago for the foreseeable future." Lucien laughed. "You always warned me that something like this would happen." He settled his gaze on her, and his smile faded. "Would you mind a little company?"

Jani pressed her hand to her stomach. Felt the thread of a scar just below her ribs, where Cèel had driven his knife. "It's not a glittery place. Not like Karistos. It sure as hell isn't Chicago."

"You'll be there." Lucien took a step toward her. Another. "Things never remain boring for long when you're around." The smile returned. "Which is why you need me. To get between you and all those people who would prefer that you didn't shake things up quite so much." He jerked his chin toward his vehicle. "And my skimmer goes, and I can cook, and I have many other uses, not all of which you're familiar with."

"Be still my heart." Jani looked at his skimmer and shook her head. "It's too nice. It'll attract attention."

Lucien walked up to her, took hold of her duffel and slipped it off her shoulder. "It's fast. In case you've forgotten, there have been moments in our past when fast came in handy." He carried the bag to his skimmer and tossed it into the boot, then followed with his. "Let's go. We can make it there in time for dinner." He slammed the lid closed, walked around to the passenger side, popped the gullwing and waited.

No. Jani watched him, as expectant as a groom at the altar. *Not again.* Even though he had his uses. Even though she could look at him forever. *Even though . . .* He didn't even love her. He admitted it. *And I don't love him.* But she and John had loved one another. *And look how that worked out.*

She stared at Lucien until she caught the flicker in his eyes, the realization that she just might say no. Then she took one step. Another. Walked to the passenger side, let him help her in, sat quietly as he closed the door and circled around to the driver's side.

"It's green there," Jani said as Lucien pulled down his gullwing and pressed the skimmer charge-through. "Green and mountainous and cool."

"That'll be good, for a change." Lucien steered around the garage and across the Main House yard, down the cliff road to the beach. Then the vehicle shuddered and they were out over the water, whitecaps lapping and seabirds swooping low.

Jani looked at the beach in her rearview and saw figures walking along the water's edge. Meva. Dathim. A few other Thalassans. She lowered her window, stuck her hand out and waved. Meva watched for a moment. Realized who it was and waved back, punching Dathim in the arm until he and the rest of the group started waving as well.

Jani kept waving as they grew smaller and smaller. Until they were bright specks in the distance. Until they were gone.